RUTHLESS LOVE

LAURA CARTER

B

Boldwood

First published in 2016 as *Vengeful Love*. This edition published in Great Britain in 2025 by Boldwood Books Ltd.

Cover Design by Colin Thomas

Cover Images: Colin Thomas

A CIP catalogue record for this book is available from the British Library.

Paperback ISBN 978-1-80600-076-0

Large Print ISBN 978-1-80600-077-7

Hardback ISBN 978-1-80600-075-3

Ebook ISBN 978-1-80600-078-4

Kindle ISBN 978-1-80600-079-1

Audio CD ISBN 978-1-80600-070-8

MP3 CD ISBN 978-1-80600-071-5

Digital audio download ISBN 978-1-80600-072-2

This book is printed on certified sustainable paper. Boldwood Books is dedicated to putting sustainability at the heart of our business. For more information please visit https://www.boldwoodbooks.com/about-us/sustainability/

Boldwood Books Ltd, 23 Bowerdean Street, London, SW6 3TN

www.boldwoodbooks.com

To all the dark romance BookTok girlies who've made Gregory and Scarlett relevant

1

Gusting wind pushes me through the revolving glass door into one of London's glossiest high-rise buildings and the home of Saunders, Taylor and Chamberlain LLP, my firm. Running a hand through my now-tatted, long, brown hair, I ride the lift to the tenth floor. Removing my black mac somewhat awkwardly whilst holding my laptop case and handbag, I step out onto the grey carpet of the glass and chrome lined corridor.

'Good morning, Scarlett.' I smile back at my new secretary as she flashes blinding white teeth and adjusts the tortoiseshell glasses on the end of her nose.

'Good morning, Margaret. It's horrid out there.'

'Would you like coffee?' she asks as I make my way along the corridor to my office.

'Please. You'd better get one for Jack too. We have a nine-thirty in his office.'

'I'll bring them through.'

I hang up my coat, dump my bags on my desk and set my laptop in its dock, lighting up my computer screen. 'Oh, and

Margaret,' I call, popping my head around the office door, 'thank you.'

I perch myself in my desk chair and wait for Outlook to load, casting my eyes around what's my humble abode for seventy hours a week, give or take. It's a small office but more than big enough for one. Most lawyers below partner level have to share but my previous roomie fell pregnant and decided to leave the unsociable hours behind her. So now I have my own space, with a modest, L-shape, wooden desk, walls lined with law texts and legislation, and a small coffee table where Cynthia's desk used to be.

My inbox loads ninety-seven emails from Sunday alone. *How dare I go a day without checking in?* I work through the backlog, shuffling the emails into various sub-inboxes and flagging them in order of priority. I have just enough time to read one or two urgent messages before my meeting with Jack. In anticipation of him being more grouchy than usual, I've worn my most professional trouser suit to work today. Jack is the kind of man a young woman can handle better in trousers. He's been on holiday for a fortnight and if the rumours are to be believed, his current wife has found out about his latest affair.

'Boys and their toys, lawyers and their secretaries,' I humour myself.

Here's the thing: being a lawyer in London isn't like being a lawyer in the United States, or at least the perception of lawyers perpetuated by shows like *Suits* and *L.A. Law*. In England, you study for four years and you train on the job for two, so there's less study time than in the US. Maybe that's why we aren't able to turn our hand to criminal law one minute and float a company on the Dow Jones the next. We specialise in one area and I chose to specialise in corporate mergers and acquisitions: M and A. Basically, my clients buy and sell companies and occasionally float them on stock exchange. Another difference is that we're paid a lot less than Manhattan's hotshot attorneys: enough to mingle with the middle classes, sure, but our pay per hour doesn't dazzle in the same way. What's not fiction is that we have to be turned out well: not quite so glamorous as on American television but dressed and blow-dried in a way that lets the client know he's paying over the odds for a *package*. Not only is he buying in to someone educated but also someone slick who knows how to get the job done – or at least looks like they do. Nevertheless, the sad truth is, the men I work with don't look like Harvey Specter or behave as gentlemanly as Mr Darcy in *Bridget Jones*. They look and act like Jack.

'Scarlett!' he yells from his adjacent office.

I jump, crashing my knee off the underside of my desk. *Cantankerous arse! It is only nine twenty-nine!* Picking up my laptop, I walk with purpose to his office. He joined the firm just over a year ago and took me under his discourteous wing immediately. At that stage, I was just under two years qualified. I'd have tried to move on from his hold by now but he put me forward early for a promotion to Senior Associate so, despite too often working through gritted teeth, I endure him.

'Good holiday, Jack?' I ask nonchalantly and instantly cringe.

He glares at me from the leather chair behind his desk.

Do I attempt to rectify the situation? I choose to sit.

'Where are we with the Portman deal?' he snaps, almost spitting through his whisky-and-nicotine-stained moustache.

'We pulled an all-nighter on Friday. I got both companies in the office. It got a little tense but we battled out the final points and signed in the early hours. I'll set to work on the condition precedents today. The money should transfer today too.'

'How much did they take in the end?' he asks, doing his best to hide the fact he's *actually* impressed with my work. Jack has been working on this deal almost since the day he arrived at the firm and each time he's tried to close it, the proverbial shit has hit the fan.

'Two hundred and sixty million on completion and with the earn out, it could rise to around three hundred.'

'Hmm.' He leans back in his chair, his belly pulling his shirt so tight that I can see flesh and grey stomach hairs escaping through one of the gaps.

'Project Amber?' he asks.

'We've completed our first round of due diligence and I intend to email our queries to the other side today.'

'You haven't done that yet?' Jack snaps.

No, Jack, I've been too busy picking up your emails and dealing with all the other shit you left me to manage.

'I'll get to it first thing,' I say meekly.

We go through each deal, eleven in total, in much the same stagnated manner. I'm grateful for the momentary distraction when Margaret delivers two coffees, a fleeting breather from what's otherwise an intense grilling.

'That's all,' Jack eventually says.

I practically run to his office door.

'Scarlett,' he calls as I reach for the handle. 'Your interest in my personal life is noted.'

He glares at me, his dark eyes wide, unreadable.

Shuddering, I step into the corridor and pull the door shut behind me.

Back at my desk, my email count has risen by eight. I hone in on the one from my best friend, who is incidentally also my colleague.

To: Heath, Scarlett
From: Darling, Amanda
Sent: Monday 6 Oct 2025 9.48
Subject: Old Coot

Why is he shouting at you today? He can't be sexually frustrated!

I smile to suppress a laugh.

To: Darling, Amanda
From: Heath, Scarlett
Sent: Monday 6 Oct 2025 10.16
Subject: Re: Old Coot

Shhhh, you can't say things like that on your work email! You know how it is, partner vs. associate, puppet master vs. puppet on a string. What he says goes!

To: Heath, Scarlett
From: Darling, Amanda
Sent: Monday 6 Oct 2025 10.18
Subject: Re: Old Coot

Don't worry, one day it will be us calling the shots! Post-weekend pick-me-up drink after work?

To: Darling, Amanda
From: Heath, Scarlett
Sent: Monday 6 Oct 2025 10.19
Subject: Re: Old Coot

On a Monday? Tut tut. Would love to but I really can't tonight, sorry. Maybe next week.

To: Heath, Scarlett
From: Darling, Amanda
Sent: Monday 6 Oct 2025 10.41
Subject: Re: Old Coot

Next week. I'll hold you to it!

I set to work on the long list of tasks that Jack and I discussed. Soon I'm immersed in my work and it takes my stomach rumbling to make me realise that lunchtime has come and gone.

'I've brought you a latte and a bun, Scarlett. You should eat something.'

Margaret has an uncanny ability to read my thoughts. She might be new to me but she's done this job for years now so she's used to looking after her fee earners and I'm thrilled her last one retired.

'You're a star!' I say, taking the food.

She rolls her eyes in a way that suggests my compliment is undeserved but I know she likes to hear my appreciation. I'm slowly getting used to having a secretary to myself. My previous was a share with Amanda but a perk of my promotion to Senior Associate is that I get my own. I suppose I have Jack to thank for that.

'Scarlett!'

My arms jerk midway between the desk and my mouth, spilling salad from my sandwich onto my keyboard.

Summoning my best faux smile, I step into his office, still clearing bread from my back teeth. 'Jack?'

The faintest smell of stale alcohol drifts past my nose. It's a little after half-past three but Jack would be sitting in near darkness if it wasn't for the cadmium green lamp illuminating the documents on his desk.

'We've got a new deal. A big one. I need you to clear the decks. Get Amanda and that boy, what's-his-name, you know the one, to take some work off you and give everything you can to what's-her-name,' he demands.

'Doug and Margaret.'

'What?' He jerks his head up from his desk to look at me. His eyes are fierce.

'Her name is Margaret,' I whisper.

Ignoring my remark, he gives me instructions to prepare for a meeting at eight-thirty tomorrow morning.

'And Scarlett.'

'Yes?'

'This is a big deal. You can't fuck it up.'

You can't fuck it up! You! I know how the game works and I know that there are years of this ahead of me but I'm still furious. The fact is, dwelling takes time and time is what I just don't have.

* * *

Margaret pops her head into my office before she leaves for the evening. 'Can I get you anything before I go?'

'Absolutely not. Go home, Margaret. Thank you for your help today; there was a lot to do.'

'It's my pleasure. Goodnight then. Don't let him keep you too late now, will you?'

'Never,' I say with a smile.

Switching on my lamp, I continue my preparations for

tomorrow, looking through the history of our potential new client – annual accounts, the nature of the company's goods and services, its key customers and suppliers, making sure that I'll be ready to answer any question they might ask.

Stiletto heels click the corridor floor, the volume increasing as they near my office, the overhead sensor lights reacting to the movement. From the sound alone, I know Amanda's strut. She appears at my desk looking as fabulous as ever in her tightest forest-green dress. She's tall and has the kind of curves women would kill for. Her red hair is bouncing as if she's just touched up her blow-dry in the ladies'.

'Sure you won't come for a drink? There's a group now.'

I really must get home. I promise I'll make it up to her next time and tell her to have a good night, then as soon as I hear Jack leave, I pack up my desk and take everything home that I'll need for the meeting tomorrow.

Cold air strikes me as I step into the night. It's close to freezing, the chill feeling more like winter than autumn. I button up my mac and fasten the buckle around the collar.

'Scarlett.' Jack's voice is hoarse. 'Can I drive you home?'

He drops the butt of his cigarette to the ground and stumps it out with the heel of his black, crocodile-skin shoe. He has the same prowling look in his eyes as earlier.

'I'm fine, thank you. I'm only a few stops on the Tube; it's quicker than driving.' I manage to force my lips to turn up. 'Plus, I'm out of your way.'

'I don't mind going out of my way for you, Scarlett,' he says. His voice is low and doesn't sound like him.

A shiver runs the length of my spine.

'Shall I meet you there in the morning?' I ask to change the subject.

He nods and uses his upper back to push away from the wall that's been propping him up. He crosses the road towards the car park and I finally breathe out.

My phone alarm begins with soft, calming music. As it grows louder, I fumble around, grabbing it from my bedside table. Just as the buzzer kicks in, I press *Dismiss*. Six-thirty.

I drag myself to the shower and clean up under the warm, soothing water. Just before I get out, I turn the water to freezing and put my face directly under the spray. Finally, my eyes feel fully open.

I dry my long hair into soft curls at the bottom and put on a small amount of eye make-up and blush. After tucking my blouse into my black pencil skirt, I put my patent heels in my handbag and slip on my flats.

It's a couple of degrees warmer outside today than it's been for the past week or so and I'm hot when I get off the Tube. The sun is seeping into my pale skin, making me regret my choice of charcoal silk beneath my mac and suit. The air is muggy and cars beep as I fight the traffic to cross the road with a handful of other suits, all rushing about their business. It's one of the things people either love or hate about London: the fast pace, the congestion, the smog that can't escape the high-rise build-ings. I love it.

Making a quick stop at a coffee chain, I drain a cool sparkling water and change into my heels before meeting Jack.

In response to my greeting, he grunts and offers me an ill-humoured nod as he haphazardly finishes dressing in the street, adjusting the knot of his red tie and tucking the tails of his shirt further into his trousers.

My quick assessment of Jack confirms that he's carrying nothing. This is going to be on me again. It's eight twenty-five and I have little time to brief him on my research, which means he'll expect me to dig him out of a hole when questions are asked. He smells of booze and cigarettes, a subtle stench that no longer surprises me. For a moment, I feel sorry for him; perhaps his wife leaving has hurt this time. My sympathy is fleeting.

We walk in relative silence to the company's office. I offer a few important details as to the internet and technology work of our potential new client but I'm not sure Jack absorbs much, if anything at all. We step through the glass revolving door and into the lobby where my heels are loud against the marble floor, a sound that's not lost despite the high ceilings of the atrium. A huge GJR Tower plaque sits on the wall to the side of the front desk. Scrolling through the list of twenty-eight floors, most of which are some variation of GJR companies, I see Eclectic Technologies listed on twenty-seven.

I'm hot and bothered by the time we reach our destination, the lift literally having stopped at every floor on the way up. My nerves build. *Do not fuck this up!*

'Mr Jones. Miss Heath.' A tall, aspirationally polished blonde woman steps towards us from behind her Eclectic Technologies reception desk. 'Mr Lawrence and Mr Williams will be with you very shortly. I'll take you through to the boardroom.'

Jack and I follow obligingly along the glass-paned corridor. Mahogany wood doors occasionally break the otherwise clear view of blue sky.

'Can I get you a drink while you wait?' the impeccable could-be model asks.

'Coffee. Black. Two sugars.' Jack's words are stern, his eyes assessing the long legs in front of him, their insane length accentuated by four-inch heels.

I suppress my desire to vomit in response to Jack's seedy demeanour. 'A cold water would be fantastic, please.'

I can't bear to make small talk, so I open my laptop and spread my printed research and handwritten notes around my place at the board table in silence. When I'm done, I distract myself with the view across London and the Thames rather than taking a seat.

'Ready for this, Heath?' Jack asks.

Irritation betrays my attempt to maintain a neutral tone, my increasing stress levels not assisting my ability to withstand his annoyingly casual attitude.

'To be honest, Jack, I would probably feel more comfortable if I knew more about this deal and what you were expecting of me today.'

His silence tells me I've startled him.

'Eclectic Technologies want to use us for a new acquisition,' he finally snaps. 'That's what you do, Scarlett, isn't it? Acquisitions?' He's angrier than reasonable or necessary.

I nod.

'I haven't told you anything because the deal is still highly confidential; I don't know everything. They'll expect us to sign a non-disclosure agreement before they tell us more.' He sits up and straightens the lapels of his blazer, suddenly businesslike, professional. Some of my tension fades. 'You just make sure you can flatter their egos and know their work. I'll seal the deal.'

'I can do that.'

'This is a big deal for us, Scarlett. You won't let me down, will you?'

He steps closer, leaning in as he speaks. My body responds, instinctively taking a step back. My discomfort only dissipates when the receptionist returns with our drinks.

'Won't be much longer,' she says, glancing up at Jack through her eyelashes.

Jack mutters something under his breath that I suspect I don't want to hear. *How do women find this man attractive?*

It isn't long before she's back, struggling to totter one foot in front of the other in her over-tight pencil skirt. 'Mr Jones, Miss Heath. This is Mr Lawrence and Mr Williams.'

Jack and I step towards the door. I shake their hands, consciously making my grip firm but not overbearing. Mr Lawrence has warm hands. His face is soft but his manner professional. He reminds me in some ways of my dad, although a slightly younger version. I imagine he has two personalities – Mr Lawrence the businessman and Mr Lawrence the teddy bear. Mr Williams smiles as he takes my hand but his fingers squeeze mine uncomfortably. He must be over six feet. His broad shoulders, sea-blue eyes and dirty-blond hair make him look like a surfer trapped in a grey-checkered suit.

Jack is right. The first thing we do is sign non-disclosure agreements. Once the formalities are complete, I breathe easier and the mood in the room seems to lighten. I'm excited, ready to get going and hear about the new deal. It must be big, the way they're dramatising the meeting.

'We must apologise,' Mr Lawrence begins. 'Our CEO is tied

up on a call at the moment. He's the driver behind deals of this size and he'll be the one to fill in the blanks for you.'

Oh. My excitement wanes.

'He'll join us if he can,' Mr Lawrence continues, as if reading my mind. 'In the meantime, he's delegated to us to decide whether you're the firm for the job.' He pauses for a sip of water. 'I know it's difficult to give quotes without much information but our main criteria is that we need to know we've got the best team. The rest we can negotiate.'

The room falls deathly silent and it becomes clear that Jack isn't going to pick this up. Taking a subtle breath, I rise from my seat and distribute a rushed capability statement I put together last night.

'Gentlemen, I can assure you that we *are* the right team for you,' I begin, with my most winning grin. 'If, or should I say *when*, you decide to go with us, Mr Jones and I will be your lead contacts.'

I turn from the table and move in front of the vast window, making myself appear much taller and confident than I feel inside: a trick I read in a book called *Climbing the Ladder*. Excitement starts to build in me again with the thrill of pitching.

'As you'll see from our capability statement, Mr Jones has a wealth of experience in the M and A market.' I somehow manage to summon a smile that says, *I'm so incredibly proud to work for this brilliant man*, and quickly glance back to Mr Lawrence and Mr Williams to avoid registering Jack's reaction. 'Mr Jones has worked on some remarkable deals and as a team, we have particular strength in the technology sector.' Words leave my mouth almost instantaneously with my thoughts as I work the room, maintaining enough eye contact to be sincere but not so much I appear arrogant or intimidating. Mr Lawrence and Mr Williams are responding well to my pitch.

They've relaxed a little. Mr Williams unbuttons his blazer and leans back in his leather chair.

The boardroom door opens, the same receptionist interrupting me. I want to scream, *What? I'm on a roll here!*

'Mr Ryans for you,' she says, stepping into the room and holding the door open wider to let the CEO enter. My torso constricts, pushing the air from my body.

My stomach flips and acrobats perform in my lower abdomen. Mr Ryans' navy suit lines his tall, broad but athletic body, resting perfectly on top of his crisp, white shirt and matching blue, silk tie. His dark hair shines in the sunlight that bursts through the office window. He's clean-shaven but I can't help imagining his face with a faint line of stubble – his off-duty look. He's younger than I could have possibly imagined. He can't be over thirty, yet the air around him oozes confidence and power.

His entrance silences the room. I'm vaguely aware that my lips are parted, my jaw dropped loose. His eyes fall on me, the centre of attention, illuminated in front of the window. They lure me in as if pulling on a rope tied tight around my waist. He pauses, probably to allow me to gain some composure. I'm suddenly extremely nervous again and my heart starts pounding in my chest.

Breathe, a voice in my head calls.

I take a deep breath and begin to return to my point of equilibrium. Mustering a polite smile, I step towards him, my legs weightless.

'You must be Miss Heath,' he says, very matter of fact.

My cheeks flush under the heat of his dark-brown irises, rich and intense like espresso, as he holds out his hand, staring into my eyes. I return his handshake and greet him professionally, hiding the fireworks exploding from every nerve ending in my body.

He turns his attention to Jack, greeting him in a voice decorated with just a hint of South African accent. The interruption gives me time to get back into the zone. *Do not fuck this up!*

I give a brief overview of my pitch so far, partly for the benefit of Mr Ryans, mostly to re-centre my thoughts. I continue where I left off but my nerves catch every time I glance at the CEO. I resolve to look anywhere other than at him but his gaze burns through me as he listens intently to what I have to say. He maintains a poker expression until the pitch concludes.

Jack gives my knee a subtle nip when I take my seat back at the table. I know he means to tell me I did a good job but I'm uncomfortable and unable to hide my flinch. I glance at Mr Ryans, who's looking at me without giving any indication of his thoughts. He leans back in his seat and folds his hands into one another, placing one index finger on his bottom lip.

As if taking a signal, Mr Williams glances from his CEO to me and then to Jack before he says, 'Miss Heath, Mr Jones, we'd like to work with you on this deal.'

Whoop! I mentally high-five myself. Outwardly, I nod at the three men on the other side of the table. It would be both a tad uncouth and massively uncool to *actually* pat myself on the back or do a little twerk.

'You've made a good decision, gentlemen,' Jack says assuredly.

The CEO shuffles and takes his phone from the inside pocket of his perfectly tailored jacket. 'Excuse me,' he says, inclining his head to the phone and exiting the room. 'Ryans,' he snaps into the receiver as the door closes behind him.

Mr Williams leans forwards, bracing his palms on the table.

'Mr Ryans has a lot to do today, some of which was unexpected, so we apologise. He'll brief you fully in relation to the deal at a later date.' I think I detect anxiety in his voice.

'It was a pleasure to meet you both,' Mr Lawrence adds as we rise from the table and politely shake hands. We make idle chit-chat as the four of us walk towards the lift. Stepping in, Jack and I turn to face the doors, my laptop and documents clutched to my chest. Just before the metal doors draw, Mr Williams calls to me, 'Good pitch, Miss Heath.' He flashes a smile I would've never expected, forcing me to beam back at him.

I'm on a high. I know I did well. I love my job.

'He's right,' says Jack, his voice a low rumble. The muscles in my body tighten in wary anticipation. 'You did well.'

My body relaxes when I realise he's not going to touch me or say anything more.

* * *

I'm in the mood for a celebratory drink when I get back to the office. I fire up my computer and email Amanda.

To: Darling, Amanda
From: Heath, Scarlett
Sent: Tuesday 7 Oct 2025 10.48
Subject: Rain check

How about that drink tonight?

To: Heath, Scarlett
From: Darling, Amanda
Sent: Tuesday 7 Oct 2025 10.48

Subject: Re: Rain check

6 p.m., on the button, no excuses.

Leaning back in my desk chair, I let my mind wander to Mr Ryans, perfect CEO. Those exquisite brown pools, his slicked hair begging to be pulled, his large, olive-skinned, manicured hands. It's been a long time since a man has touched me. In fact, I'm not sure I've ever been touched by a *man*. Boys, fumbling and stuttering, yes. But Mr Ryans looked like he'd know exactly how and where to touch a woman.

'Scarlett,' Margaret whispers as she steps into my office. 'Jack has a call, and he'd like you to join in his office.'

'Thank you. Do you know who it is?'

'A Mr Ryans, I believe.'

An electric pulse courses through my body just hearing his name. *Forget it!*

I pick up a notepad and head into Jack's office.

Jack places the call on mute on his screen so that Mr Ryans, and no doubt Mr Lawrence and Mr Williams, can't hear our exchange.

'Eclectic is ready to give us details of the acquisition,' Jack barks. 'They specifically requested that you were on the call. They must be looking to have it done on the cheap.'

His words are bitter and I know it's because of his targets. At Saunders, we have targets for everything: hours spent working on client matters, time spent in the office, the value of work billed to clients, the recovery rate of each invoice. If something can be expressed in numbers, Saunders will have a target for it. If I do the work for Eclectic, I get to put down my hours spent and I get to bill my time and every hour I work on the deal means an hour Jack loses towards his own figures. In truth, I don't care much about Jack's targets, or Jack for that matter, and I'm still reeling with delight from winning the pitch. I'm not sure anyone loves their job all day every day but the rush of closing a deal or winning a client more than makes up for the bad times.

Jack clicks unmute.

'Good afternoon, gentlemen,' I say.

'Good afternoon, Miss Heath,' Mr Lawrence calls. 'Lawrence, Williams and Ryans here.' His voice is matter of fact and professional without losing the soft tone he had when we met this morning. I imagine him sitting with his hands cupped and resting across his belly as he speaks.

'Miss Heath,' the others say simultaneously.

Mr Ryans begins to talk about Eclectic Technologies, mostly offering information I've already gathered from my research, but his enthusiasm is infectious, seemingly uncharacteristic of the taciturn and controlled man I witnessed this morning. His mood shifts when he begins to talk about Sea People International, the company he wishes to take over, and I have to wonder why he wants to buy a business he seems to resent. I remind myself that I know very little about Mr Ryans. Sea People runs a new social network site for travellers. The site is designed to make it easier for people to travel the world and stay in contact with friends and family. It gives them the opportunity to share experiences and has forums to provide tips to fellow travellers on the best places to visit in countries around the world. In all, it sounds like an interesting tool, if lacking a completely fresh take. I'm sure I would've used it if I'd ever ventured beyond Europe with my dad or on business trips to clients. I subconsciously make a note to ask Amanda if she's ever come across it when she's been travelling abroad.

'I want to buy it, take it to pieces and sell it to the highest bidder.' Mr Ryans' sharp words interrupt my thoughts.

'Well, subject to Jack's, erm, Mr Jones's thoughts...' I cautiously eye Jack, seeking permission to speak, but he seems happy for me to go ahead. 'I think much of the due diligence will need to be carried out on the intellectual property in the company. I'm assuming the social network site is the company's main venture?'

'It is,' Mr Williams adds.

'Okay, then we'll obviously review the incorporation and constitutional documents and pull together details of the intellectual property and any other assets. There'll be some questions it'll be easier to ask of the seller, such as—'

'Full due diligence won't be necessary.' Mr Ryans cuts me off again. 'Find out what you can and tell me what needs to be done from a legal point of view. There's a very pressing timescale on this.'

'I completely take that on board, Mr Ryans, but for the protection of you and Eclectic Technologies, I think—'

'Miss Heath, I'll have my people look into any matters that concern me. All I need you to do is deal with the logistics from a legal perspective. Understood?'

'She's got it,' Jack bites.

'Of course,' I say shyly, under attack from all angles. 'There'll be requirements on Sea People's part as the seller to make sure the sale is carried out legitimately. I'll pull together all the information I have access to and I'll start drafting documentation for Jack to review.'

There's silence on the line and I wonder what's happening in the Eclectic Technologies' boardroom.

'Thank you, Miss Heath,' Williams eventually says. The line goes silent again.

'Miss Heath?' Perhaps he thinks I could have left the room owing to their unnecessary and frankly rather rude time delay.

'Yes?' My voice has lost all conviction.

'We'd be grateful if you would carry out as much work as possible on this. Mr Jones, please supervise where necessary but for reason of... ah... costs, we would like Miss Heath to complete the majority of the work.'

'Of course,' Jack and I chorus in harmony.

'Miss Heath. Mr Jones.'

The line falls dead and I watch Jack, waiting for his back-lash, but it doesn't come and I guess he's thinking we'll take any crap they throw at us because the money is good. My working on the deal might not help his target-related bonus but as a partner, he'll still take a share of the profit.

I despondently trail back to my desk and slump into my chair. Something doesn't feel right. Mr Ryans seems to resent or even distrust the company he's looking to acquire, yet he isn't interested in due diligence. I shrug. Who am I to complain; I've just been handed potentially one of the biggest opportunities of my junior career.

My call app rings through my laptop and I lunge for my mouse to answer, not knowing how long I've been lost in thought.

'Miss Heath.'

I start to babble as quickly as I can. 'I'm terribly sorry for—' but true to form, Mr Controlling cuts me short.

'Miss Heath, I only called to...' he pauses and clears his throat, '...to ask that you forward all documentation to myself and Williams in the first instance.'

'Yes, of course. And, Mr Ryans, please forgive me for assuming our scope of work. I was following the usual protocol. I'm more than happy to indulge the sensitivity and intricacies of this deal and will be sure to do the best job possible for you and Eclectic Technologies.'

'I know that, Miss Heath. It was a pleasure to meet you this morning. I look forward to working with you.'

'I look forward to working with you too,' I say sincerely for some unfathomable reason. This devastatingly attractive man, whom I've known for less than twelve hours, has already shown me numerous sides to his personality. 'Oh, and Mr Ryans, please call me Scarlett.'

'Scarlett,' he repeats. His voice is baritone yet smooth, his mild South African accent intriguing and exotic. I let the sound of him saying my name replay in my mind.

To: Heath, Scarlett
From: Ryans, Gregory
Sent: Tuesday 7 Oct 2025 17.36
Subject: Future correspondence

Scarlett,

Thank you for your time today. I have discussed our call very briefly with Williams and Lawrence and we believe we may move forwards in a more productive and efficient manner if you collate the information you obtain and bring it in person to the office, in order for us to discuss it together.

Regards,

Gregory Ryans

CEO Eclectic Technologies

'*Gregory*. Gregory Ryans,' I whisper to myself.

To: Ryans, Gregory
From: Heath, Scarlett

Sent: Tuesday 7 Oct 2025 17.39
Subject: Re: Future Correspondence

Mr Ryans,

I am happy to progress the matter in the manner preferred by you and your board. I will be in touch as soon as possible with a suitable time, once I have collated sufficient information to make a meeting worth your while.

In the meantime, please do not hesitate to contact me should you have any queries.

Best regards,

Scarlett Heath

Senior Associate

Saunders, Taylor and Chamberlain LLP

'Time's up! Let's go!' Amanda yells into my office, swinging by one hand on the side of my doorframe.

I blush as if I've been caught red-handed doing something abhorrent but I've no idea why. I reluctantly shut down my computer but I could really use a drink. 'Give me two minutes. I need to make a quick call home.'

* * *

Amanda is nestled into a burgundy, leather booth when I return with a mojito for her and a 1930s cosmopolitan for me. She looks at home in the chic surroundings of the wine bar. As ever, her auburn hair is flawless, curled at the edges and resting just below her shoulders. Her cream, silk camisole looks effortlessly sexy as it flows over her curves and into the top of her ruffled skirt.

'Mojito time! Cheers,' she says, taking her cocktail from me and flashing her Hollywood smile. 'Nice!' she adds after taking her first gulp.

I laugh as she wipes her mouth with the back of her hand and slide into the booth beside her. 'Graceful. So, how was The Bod on Saturday?'

'His *name* was Joshua.'

I raise a suspicious brow. 'Was?'

Amanda's *love* life – I use the term loosely – is somewhat mercurial. She dates a lot and there's rarely a keeper. The last one, by Amanda's standards, was months ago and it never really got out of the blocks to start the race. Tom. A mummy's and money boy. A trust-fund baby. They made it to six dates and Amanda ate well and for free for five consecutive weekends but ultimately, she drew the line at picnics and polo and he drew the line at a club until the sun comes up.

'Was,' she confirms. 'He bought me a nice dinner and I thought I might actually like him.'

In response to my side-eye, she gives me a shoulder bump. 'Hey, I did!'

'So what happened?'

'Well, he said he'd go my way in a taxi. You know, to make sure I got home safe, but then he came on to me quite heavy in the cab and was a bit of a prick when I said I'd never put out on the first date. Soooo, I got the taxi driver to pull over outside of some amazing house and watched Joshua drive off. I waited until he was out of sight and jumped in another cab to take me to my flat.'

She pauses for a sip of Mojito and reflects on how little she has left in her glass.

'Can I get you ladies another drink?' a waitress asks as she passes our table, a tray held high in her hand.

Amanda lifts her empty glass onto the tray. 'Please.'

I glance at my watch. 'I really can't stay, Amanda; this will have to be the last.'

'Okay, last one,' she concedes. 'How did the big pitch go this morning?'

'Mmm,' I nod through my cosmopolitan. 'We got the work.'

'Excellent! Shame you'll have to spend more time under Jack, though.'

'Less of the "under Jack",' I say, only half in jest. 'Anyway, they've asked me to take the lead on the matter with Jack supervising. It's a really big deal, I think.'

'Wow, yeah it is; that's a great opportunity. Is it to save costs, do you think?'

'Hey!'

'I didn't mean it like that.' She giggles.

'Well, actually, yes. But like you say, it's a good opportunity and the CEO is a bit... interesting.'

'Interesting?' Amanda takes her turn to raise a brow.

'Okay, yes, he's extremely hot and must be filthy rich but that's not what I mean. He's kind of, I don't know, serious and sexy and polite and...' I shrug, genuinely unsure of how I feel about the billionaire CEO.

'Somebody likes somebody,' Amanda purrs.

'As if I do. I'd never go there. *We* can't ever go there. Clients are a strict no-go. Jack would throw me out on my arse.'

'Yeah, because you chose someone else over his ugly, wrinkling vileness.' She shudders for effect, the ultimate dramatic-arts prodigy.

'Amanda! He's my boss. Urgh, another year or so and maybe I won't have to work in his shadow. Anyway, no, Gregory, erm, Mr Ryans, is not interesting in a good way... I don't think.'

'Well, if he's a gorgeous bazillionaire and you're not interested, please send him my way. I'd gladly ruin my career for that!'

The waitress returns to take our empty glasses and Amanda settles the bill for the second round of drinks, tapping her smart watch against the contactless machine.

'Bear hug and smooches,' she demands, then plants a kiss on my cheek and squeezes me as tightly as she can before she heads in one direction for her bus north to Camden and I walk in another to catch the underground to West London.

3

My excitement builds as I ride the nine stops home on the Tube. I can't wait to see him. I can't wait to hear him say my name and watch his face light up as I read him chapters from his favourite book. In those brief moments, when he remembers, he's my same old comforting, sweet, gentle and polite Dad. He can still melt my heart with the twinkle in his eye that he reserves just for me.

The jerk of inertia as the Tube comes to a stop forces the couple who've been playing tonsil tennis beside me for twenty minutes to come up for air.

Two security men in padded, hi-vis jackets gawp as I burst from the Tube and bound up the steps from the platform to the street. I run along our road and halt in front of our townhouse to catch my breath before pushing through the wrought-iron gate and darting up the path to the porch. I fumble trying to place my key in the lock then throw my bag on the hall table as I practically jump inside.

'Hi, Sandy!'

'Hello, Sweets. How was your day?' she asks in her usual

singsong way, always sounding much older than her forty-two years.

'Busy but good. How's your day been? How's Dad?'

'He's doing well today,' she says, helping me out of my mac and hanging it on the hat stand in the vestibule. 'He sat in his chair for the best part of the morning. We even managed a game of cards.'

It's another fleeting and increasingly rare moment of good health and happiness. I know better than to be optimistic but Sandy still beams with pride, her smile reaching her brown cheeks, her warm eyes glowing.

'He's been asking for you,' she adds.

I can't prevent a goofy grin spreading from ear to ear as I kick my shoes off onto the polished, rosewood floor. 'He has?'

'He really has. Today's been the best I've seen him in weeks.' She's triumphant, as if an invisible barrier has been crossed.

'I can't wait to see him. Thank you so much for looking after him so I could have a drink tonight.'

'Don't be silly; you don't need to thank me. It's nice to hear you want to go out. You need to remember you're still *you* and you're still young.'

'I should say the same to you. Do you mind if I go straight up to see him?'

'Not at all. Should I heat your dinner and you can take it up with you?'

The irresistible scent of Sandy's jerk chicken suddenly fills the air around me and I realise I'm starving.

'You're my angel,' I say, planting a big kiss on her cheek, causing her to titter and fuss her tightly curled, black hair. 'I'll heat it myself. You put your feet up.'

I tap my foot on the farmhouse tiles that match the units in the kitchen, willing the microwave to flash my bowl of casserole quicker. Impatient, I open the door before the ping and take the semi-heated bowl upstairs with a freshly baked flatbread, still warm from the oven. Sandy's breads are to die for.

His television is playing, the blue light flickering under his bedroom door on the first-floor landing. Opening the door with my elbow, I tentatively step into the room.

Dad turns in his bed and gives me a dashing, warm smile. Despite his grey-white hair, he looks youthful, ardent and delighted to see me. This is what I've been waiting for all day. Neglecting my hunger, I set my supper on his bedside table, my need to hold him overwhelming.

He's still beaming at me as I reach down and wrap my arms around him. He holds me tightly as if he'll never let me go.

Don't cry; you'll frighten him.

I fight back the rivers building behind my eyes. I know my subconscious is right, so I unravel myself from his tight cocoon and sit into his bedside chair.

'Martha, I've missed you.'

The world begins to crumble around me, slowly, excruciatingly slowly; the syllables *Mar-tha* replay in my mind. My chest tightens and a lump forms in my throat.

'No, Dad,' I choke. 'I'm Scarlett.'

Confusion distorts his face. 'Where's my Martha?'

I bite down on my bottom lip to steady my wobbling chin as my eyes cloud.

It's not his fault, my subconscious reminds me.

But I can still be pissed! I yell back at it.

Taking a deep breath, I try to rationalise my thoughts, for me, for him. 'Mum left a long time ago, Dad. I'm Scarlett, your daughter.'

'No!' he yells. 'No. No. No.' He slaps his hands on the bed.

'Dad, please,' I croak. 'I'm your daughter. Martha was your wife. Martha was my mother.'

'I. Want. Martha!' he screams. His arms move from the bed to me, striking my chest and my face.

'Dad!' I plead, grabbing his hands, shocked that he no longer has the strength to fight me.

'Scarlett! Doctor Heath!'

My dad stills and looks at Sandy. He's coming back. He moves his gaze to me and I can no longer bear it. My shoulders shudder as uncontrollable sobbing takes over my body.

'Sandy,' my dad whispers.

'Yes, sir. Let's get you settled again, shall we?'

His face changes as his life story untangles in his defective mind. His features contort until he looks pained. He reaches towards me steadily, a little uncertain. My body, unquestioning, bends to meet him. His damp palm rests on my cheek and I dissolve into his touch.

'Dad,' I whisper.

'Scarlett,' he croaks.

* * *

I'm up and dressed early enough to make sure I can have breakfast with Sandy.

'Is he often like that with you?' I ask.

She flutters around the kitchen in her peach dress, a beige apron pulled tight at her curvaceous waist, her hair pinned back at the sides just behind her ears, the way she does when she's cooking. She avoids my eyes as she pours milk onto my cereal.

'I'm so sorry.' I will myself not to cry again but the restless night sleeping at my dad's bedside has left me tired and, if possible, more emotional than usual. I've never been a crier. It's as if all the tears I've never cried have erupted in the last couple of months as I've watched Dad's health deteriorate. Some days, most days, he's barely recognisable.

'Now stop that,' Sandy says, tenderly brushing an escaped tear from my cheek. 'Don't give up on him.' The whole thing is taking its toll on her too. The image of her standing in the doorway to my dad's room keeps coming back to me. Her eyes were red and swollen. She prepares Dad's pills and sets up his breakfast tray, intentionally keeping her back to me.

'He's getting worse quickly, isn't he, Sandy?'

She stops dead still at the breakfast bar, then continues to set out his tray.

'He still has his moments,' she says, turning to me and placing her warm hand on mine. 'He's a fighter, Scarlett.'

'Sandy! Did he do this to you?'

She pulls her arm from me quickly and wraps her other hand around the plump, marked, red skin of her wrist.

'He gets frustrated, that's all. It's nothing a tough woman like me can't handle!' She flashes me a big grin but her eyes are solemn.

'He's becoming too much for you.' My voice breaks. I know what the next step will be. 'Sandy, I really appreciate your help. I know Dad does too. He's just not the same any more, and you're not a nurse.' I take a shallow breath. 'You'll tell me when it's time, won't you?'

She returns her hand to mine. 'Doctor Heath is a good man. He's always been good to me and I'll help him for as long as I can. I love you both more than you could ever imagine.'

I manage to nod but my eyes are on fire.

4

I couldn't be more grateful for the latte Margaret has left on my desk. My eyes are drooping and my concentration is definitely lacking as my computer fires into life.

Amanda bobs into my office, taking off her outdoor coat and draping it over her arm. 'It was great to have a drink last night, like old times, except we managed to walk home.'

'There was only ever one of us who couldn't walk home.'

She winks. 'Anyways, I hope you passed my best to your pops.'

'I did. He said hi,' I lie.

'Such a sweetie. So, like I said, send the CEO's number my way.'

I scoff through my takeout cup as she strides confidently out of my room. My best friend can always cheer me up.

Confirmation lands that the Portman merger has gained clearance by the European competition law authorities. I shoot a quick email to Jack and almost as soon as it enters my sent items, he's yelling my name.

'Good work on Portman, nice to have that one tied up,' he says as I step into his office.

Oh.

'Just doing my job, Jack.' I give him a wry smile. 'Is there anything else?'

'No.' He waves a hand, signalling for me to leave.

Turning on my stiletto heel to exit, I feel his eyes burning into the back of my grey pencil dress.

'Scarlett.'

Though I cringe in response to his trying-to-be-smooth voice, I about-turn.

'I like that dress on you.'

Vomit rises to my throat. Another outfit Jack has successfully banished to the back of my closet.

Back at my desk, I open Outlook and calculate the days I think I'll have to wait for my next promotion, the promotion which will hopefully see me escape Jack's close scrutiny. If I do a good job, I could make legal director in two years. *Now there's an incentive.* Three hundred and sixty-five days, less twenty-eight days' annual leave, multiplied by two. Six hundred and seventy-four days, my calculator tells me.

My momentary contentedness disappears when it occurs to me that in less, much less, than six hundred and seventy-four days, I'm likely to be without my dad. *That's where playing around and not doing your work will get you.*

Shaking the thoughts away, I get started on my tasks for today and the rest of the week. Given the tight timings, I'll be working almost exclusively on the Eclectic Technologies deal.

'Margaret,' I call from my office to the secretaries' station.

She appears at my door, her voluminous, grey-blonde hair glued into place just above her shoulders by a can of hairspray, her freshly coated, pink lips turned up. Margaret is the kind of well-turned-out lady who'd never be seen in public without her lipstick. 'What can I get for you?'

'Have my reports come through from Companies House for the Eclectic deal?'

Companies House is the official registrar for companies incorporated in England and Wales. Reports from the registrar contain all sorts of key information about a company: its shareholders, directors, incorporation date – things like that.

'Just,' she says with an innocently smug smile, handing me the reports, already printed and ring-bound.

'What would I do without you?'

'Anything else?' she asks.

'Actually, you wouldn't mind getting me another latte, would you? With an extra shot?'

'Not in the slightest.' She rotates on her small kitten heel, the ends of her floral dress swaying beneath her tweed jacket, Anais-Anais filling the air as she moves.

The rich, indulgent scent of my extra-strong coffee fills the room and makes my mind fresher, sharper, whilst sifting through the Companies House reports. When I reach the details of Eclectic Technologies' directors, I slip off my shoes and roughly pin my hair into a crocodile clip then pull my legs up to cross them on my chair, settling in for the read.

First Director: Gregory James Ryans
Date of Birth: 09.10.1995
Date of Appointment: 01.07.2020
Associated Directorships: GJR Enterprises, Inc., GJR Europe Limited, Bio-energy Holdings Limited, Sound Telecommunications GmbH, Constant Sources Limited...

The list is endless.

I do the math and work out that Gregory is thirty in less than a week. *Only thirty! Not even two years older than me!* Surveying the shareholder details of the GJR companies, I confirm that he does, in fact, own those too. GJR Enterprises Inc. and GJR Europe Limited are owned exclusively by Gregory but he's the majority shareholder in most of the others. Casting my mind to the plaque in the entrance of GJR Tower, it's obvious now that the entire high-rise belongs to him. Outrageously handsome *and* accomplished. *What does a sexy bazillionaire CEO do to celebrate his thirtieth birthday?*

Shaking my head back to reality, my eyes move to the next section of the document: Mr Williams and Mr Lawrence.

Williams is older than Gregory, thirty-two, and seems to sit on the boards of almost all the same companies as Gregory. In fact, he isn't a director of any company that isn't at least partly owned *by* Gregory. He has shares in many of those companies too.

Lawrence is older, fifty-seven, which I'd estimated from his character creases and slightly drooping physique hidden beneath a paisley waistcoat. That and his thick but combed-over hair. Lawrence is a director on a few of the same boards as Gregory and a non-executive director on many of the others. Usually, that would mean he offers guidance to the Board as to how to run the company but doesn't have a right to vote on big decisions the way an executive director can. Unlike Williams, Lawrence is the sole shareholder of another company, Connektions Limited. I wonder whether Gregory knows this about one of his closest confidantes but as I delve into the ownership of Sea People International, Inc., the company Eclectic Technologies is taking over, I realise that Gregory must know. Sea People International, Inc. just happens to be majority owned by Connektions

Limited, meaning in effect it is majority-owned by
Lawrence.

As usual, the intricate links between the companies seem
more comprehendible when I sketch them in a diagram. As I
draw the tangled web of companies, directors and shareholders, the attachments become easier to follow but there's one
question playing on my mind: why wouldn't they have
mentioned that Eclectic Technologies is buying a company that
Lawrence partly owns?

I think about picking up the phone and asking the question,
but Gregory is a busy man and from what I've seen, I imagine
he's very much in control of what happens beneath him, under
him, in his companies. My thighs reflexively squeeze together
beneath the desk. Rubbing the temples of my hormone-
muddled head, I realise I'm probably beginning to overthink
Gregory himself, rather than the deal. I note the minority
owner of Sea People International Inc. as a Mr Pearson, then
resolve to ask my questions at our meeting and continue sifting
through my information about the companies, only occasionally having to blank out inappropriate and lascivious thoughts
about the CEO.

5

It doesn't take much for Amanda to persuade me that a Friday cocktail or two might not be a terrible idea. It's been a rough week and I'll rush straight home to Dad afterwards.

The bar is heaving with suits. Each group has spread itself out in a circle around a stack of handbags, briefcases and laptop carriers. Laughter and rowdy taunts are almost as loud as the music playing in the background. It's clear as I watch people stagger and gesture flamboyantly that some groups have been out for a boozy office lunch, which has tumbled through into the evening. The leather booths are full and the bar queue is three people deep. There's no way you could be alone with your thoughts in here and that's fine by me.

'What are you having, ladies?' a man asks from the second row of people fighting their way into the bar, the question almost certainly directed at Amanda.

'Thank you, I'll get my own,' I say.

It makes no real difference. The 'gentleman' is fixated on Amanda, who already has him wrapped around her finger like her auburn hair as she twists it, flashing her most flirtatious smile, her green, silk blouse making her skin dazzle.

'We'll take two cosmopolitans.'

Her wish is granted. We wait by a pillar close enough for me to watch the bartender make my cocktail and to witness it being carried to me un-tampered.

'Would you relax? We'll talk to him for five then he'll find a pretty blonde and leave us to enjoy our drinks,' Amanda says in her usual carefree way.

He doesn't leave us in five minutes. They never do. Amanda has a way of completely mesmerising men. In a bid to be polite, I talk to his friend, whose name is drowned out by the guitars of Oasis's 'Roll with It.' Feigning interest in his alleged mansion, complete with a ping-pong machine and full Sky package, is a struggle. When I ask his name for the third time after ten minutes of listening to his mindless dribble, he seems to take the hint and excuses himself to use the gents'.

Amanda glares at me over the shoulder of Mr Cosmopolitan but laughs when I raise my arms to my sides and shrug.

'Drink?' I shout in Amanda's direction, taking care not to appear to offer a drink to her suitor.

'Please. I'll come to the bar with you!'

And *that* is how she does it. Amanda slips out of Mr Cosmopolitan's arm around her waist and she'll never speak to him again.

'My round, since you got the last ones,' I joke.

As our number of cocktails increases, the number of suits in the bar decreases and there's space for us to hop on two bar stools at a table.

'These shoes are made for sitting under a desk,' I say, bending to rub my ankles.

'Tell me about it. Another?' Amanda asks, nodding towards my nearly empty cocktail glass.

'I'm not sure I can. Four on an empty stomach might be my limit. Do you want to get some food?'

'Can we have another if we eat?'

'Deal.' I tip my head back slightly to drain the last sip from my glass.

It happens in slow motion, one drop of reality at a time. Gregory shakes hands with the doorman first, then Williams does the same. Gregory looks as fiercely intense as he does at work but Williams looks comfortable and smiles, a rogue strand of sandy blond decorating his forehead.

'Shit!' I whisper, almost to myself but Amanda catches it.

'What?' She follows my gaze. 'Oh, shit indeed, he is N-I-C-E, nice!'

He is. His intensity adds to his mystery. He looks confident and self-assured, arrogant even, as he makes his way through the bar, his magnetism attracting looks from both men and women. The neat fit of his straight-cut, indigo jeans, soft blue jumper and navy blazer make him look effortlessly well-groomed and wealthy. His slick, dark hair is so perfectly, purposefully cool, I want to pull my fingers straight through it. An irrational need to have him pangs between my legs.

'We have to leave,' I demand.

'What? Why? The party's just getting started. Mr Every-Woman-Has-To-Try-This-Just-Once has just walked in.'

'Amanda, that's the bazillionaire CEO!' I say through my teeth, conscious that Gregory and Williams are walking in our general direction.

'Nooo! Really? I can see why you find him so, how did you put it? *Interesting.* I'd like to see what's under that jumper. Look at those shoulders. Swimmer. Must be.'

'Amanda. Stop it! I'm well on my way to drunk. I can't speak to him and I really can't see him like *that*, at all, ever, not when I've had a drink anyway,' I babble. Who am I kidding? I'd love to imagine him all over me.

'Wow, listen to you, you're a wreck. I can see why. I love a man who can wear red.'

'Red? Oh, you mean Williams. That's his sidekick. No, Gregory, erm, the CEO, is the other one.'

'Then I'm free to tantalise the tastebuds of the messy blond?' Amanda asks, her attempt at sultry disguised in a cock-tail-fuelled slur.

'Yes,' I say, relieved. 'No. No, you can't. They're clients. Both of them.'

'Even more reason for a little business networking, wouldn't you say?'

'No, let's go. We were going for food anyway. Let's leave before they see us.'

I pick up her bag and pass it to her but she's already off her stool and walking towards Williams.

'Amanda!' I snap but it's lost in the open space.

'Hi, I'm Amanda.' I hear in the distance.

Oh God.

I make a move to stand then sit back down. I reach for my handbag then leave it where it is. I don't want to look but my eyes defy me, lured like metal to his magnet. As if he felt my eyes burning into him, he's staring back at me with those devastatingly dark pools.

No getting out of it now.

As I walk towards the three of them, he never takes his eyes off me. I instantly regret my choice of slightly too-tight-fitting dress and probably too-high shoes this morning. I imagine he's scrutinising every inch of me that's out of place, whilst he looks immaculate. I'd feel no more exposed if I were naked in the crowded room. I wonder if he can see the tired, emotional wreck I am behind my cover of his legal advisor. I wonder if he can see how nervous he makes me. How nervous he's making me right now.

As I watching the protruding veins of his neck move with his swallow, I attempt to compose myself as I hold out my feebly trembling hand for him to shake. I manage a weak smile but no words leave my dry throat. He takes my hand as I watch his mouth greet me. His touch sends my irrational hormones into a frenzy.

'Miss Heath,' Williams interjects. A welcome distraction, an escape from the spell of Gregory Ryans, and a chance for the ache in my sex to dissipate.

'Mr Williams, it's a pleasure to see you. You've already met my friend, Amanda.'

'And colleague,' Amanda jumps in. 'I'm a lawyer too.'

Williams smiles politely whilst Amanda beams at him, flashing her best come-get-me pout and adjusting her body slightly, pushing her arse and tits further out. Without turning in his direction, I can feel that Gregory has not stopped staring at me.

Williams continues to indulge Amanda in flirtatious conversation and Amanda less than subtly shuffles until I'm presented with her back.

'So, what brings you here tonight, Mr Ryans? I mean, do you come here often? Not that you shouldn't, or should. It's up to you where you go,' I stutter as my cheeks flame.

He sniggers at me but returns the most delectable half-smile, half-smirk I've ever seen. The kind that travels straight to my vagina before taking me to dinner. He places his hands in his jean pockets and slightly flexes his hips towards me. Despite all the will in the world, I'm unable to stop my gaze from dropping to his crotch.

I rub the butt of my hand against my brow and search the floor. For something. Anything.

'Well, it was a pleasure to see you, gents,' I say, loud enough for Williams to hear over Amanda's chatter. 'I hope you have a nice evening; we'll leave you to enjoy yourselves.'

'Where are you going?' Williams asks. Seemingly, Amanda has already caught his attention.

'Yes, Scarlett, where are we going?' Amanda asks, engrossed in Williams' reaction.

'For food. We were just talking about food, remember?'

'So were we,' Williams jumps in, eyeing Gregory as he speaks. As is their way, they have an unspoken exchange.

'But you just got here,' Amanda says.

'We were only going to have one drink then go for food. Unless you have other plans, we could all eat together?' Williams suggests.

'Yes, and no, we don't,' Amanda replies, almost in a shrill with excitement. 'I'm starving.'

Now she's hungry?

I'm suddenly remarkably sober and Amanda is suddenly remarkably drunk, more on Williams than alcohol, I think. This has gone badly wrong. I can't possibly refuse to have dinner with a client. Likewise, I can't possibly have dinner with this *particular* client. How can I spend any longer in the company of Gregory Ryans without my raging libido combusting?

'Sure. That's a great idea. Erm, if that works for you too, Mr Ryans?' I will him to object and save me from myself.

'I'll go on the condition that you call me Gregory from now

on,' he says, leaning into me as he speaks, his big hands still resting in his jean pockets. 'On social occasions, at least.'

No, no, no to social occasions with the sexy as sin billionaire.

I nod in uncomfortable acquiescence. The shift of my head lands my gaze on that alluring crotch again.

'Settled then,' Williams declares.

Gregory takes the lead through the bar to leave. I'd bet he makes love the way he moves that fine, sculpted South African arse through the bar... with the grace of a gazelle and the command, pounce and salacious bite of a lion. He glances back over his shoulder and flashes that agonising half-smile once more.

Dear God.

The doorman dips his head as he opens the door. Gregory steps to one side and gestures for me to walk ahead of him. Almost immediately as we step on to the pavement, a black Mercedes pulls up to the kerb. The driver is a burly man in a black suit and white shirt. The veins of his hands bulge under his dark skin and his shaved head shows a few remnants of black hair amongst grey stubs. He looks good for his age but given I'd put money on him being ex-forces of some sort; he can't be under forty. He holds open the rear passenger door and Gregory steps to one side as I climb in, followed by Williams and Amanda, still giggling at each other. Gregory walks around the back of the car and takes a seat up front next to the driver.

'Where are we going?' Amanda asks excitedly. 'Nowhere expensive, I hope. My pops is already bailing me out this month.'

'Again?' I ask.

'I needed new work clothes,' she reasons. 'He's talking about stopping my monthly allowance.'

'You still get a monthly allowance?' Gregory and I ask in unison.

He shifts in his seat to look at me and smiles. It's an easy, soft, gentle smile. Uncommon, I'd bet, and undeniably attractive.

'I'm a single girl living in the city. A two bed in Camden doesn't come cheap. He can't cut me off.'

'We're interrupting your evening,' Williams says. 'The least we can do is pay for dinner.'

'Absolutely not!' I protest. 'Thank you for the offer but you're clients of ours. It would be our pleasure to buy you dinner.'

'This isn't a business meeting, Scarlett,' Amanda scolds me, then bats her eyelashes at Williams.

'Amanda—' I attempt.

'Ladies don't pay,' Gregory speaks, this time without turning in his seat. His voice is stern and although I feel entirely belittled, I know the discussion is over.

I fight my usual inclination to counterargue, but smoulder beneath my skin and resign to watch passersby through the window without saying another word for the rest of the journey. *Ladies don't pay.* It occurs to me that I've heard my dad use that turn of phrase before. The thought softens my prickly mood just enough to allow me to remember that I'm in the company of clients. If only Amanda could behave herself, just this once.

She's very much in her comfort zone, merrily chatting and flirting outrageously with Williams. Amanda's always on the prowl for a wealthy man who could allow her to be a lady of leisure. We had endless conversations at Cambridge about Amanda wanting that kind of life – lunching at fine establishments like The Beverley and having beauty treatments in the afternoon, like her mother. Amanda suffers from stereotypical OCS – Only Child Syndrome – but she has a good heart and I love her for having the conviction to be herself, to do what she wants to do and not what others expect of her. Reading my mind, she reaches for my hand, gently squeezing it in hers, and giving me a knowing smirk that amuses me enough to improve my mood 100 per cent.

The Mercedes slows to a stop outside Heron Tower, the glass structure looming over us so tall, it's impossible see the top, even craning my neck. I reach into my bag for my purse but Williams puts his hand over mine to stop me.

Gregory inclines his head in thanks to the driver. 'Jackson.'

Of course, he has a personal driver. Who doesn't?

Jackson opens my door first. Gregory's already waiting on the pavement. He offers his hand to help me out of the car. I hesitate but take it to be polite. The kiss of his palm drives a hot sensation all over my body, unsteadying me enough that I have to I put my spare hand on the first thing it touches for support. That first thing happens to be Jackson's shoulder, and he's mocking me with his eyes. I suspect he's seen Gregory's effect on women countless times. 'Sorry, Jackson. Thank you.'

'You're more than welcome, Miss Heath.' His voice is a deep, masculine rumble but there's humour in it, too.

I'm already walking away when it strikes me that he knows my name. I turn to ask him how but Gregory tugs slightly on my hand.

'After you,' he says, signalling for me to walk ahead of him onto the short, red carpet laid out to welcome guests.

'The fourth tallest building in London. Nice choice, Mr Ryans.'

His eyes narrow but there's a ghost of a smug smile creasing the sides of his perfectly plump mouth. I bite down on my bottom lip, trying to suppress my desire to taste him.

A concierge in black dinner trousers, a white jacket fastened with dazzling gold buttons and the shiniest black patent shoes I've ever seen, holds open the door.

Inside, we're received by a similarly dressed maître d'. 'Good evening,' he says to me. 'It is wonderful to see you again, Mr Ryans.'

The sound of my stilettos against the marble tiles echoes as we all follow him to the lift. Something about the whole situation makes me more mindful of my height in them, my body shape, and the rotation of my hips each time I plant my feet.

He greets Williams and Amanda in similar fashion and the mirror-panelled doors close. Catching a glimpse of my reflection, that confidence I felt momentarily dissolves into self-doubt.

'Your eyes look fierce in that colour,' Amanda whispers into my ear.

People have always commented on my green and hazel eyes, ever since I was a girl, but I'll never understand it. They're as ordinary as every other part of me.

The lift doors open onto another marble floor, leading to an equally fancy desk where we're met by an immaculately presented woman with a high-gloss, blonde French roll, wearing a tight, black skirt and white shirt that show her perfect curves. Her piercingly blue eyes are alive and wild as she studies Gregory. I half-expect her to lick her lips, growl and start humping his leg. Yet he never pays her more than a cursory glance.

'Good evening, Mr Ryans. Let me show you to your table,' she says, fluttering her eyelids one too many times, in my opinion.

'I bet she'd like to show Mr Ryans a lot more than that,' I mutter to myself, all the while smiling graciously at her delayed acknowledgement that Mr Ryans has guests.

Amanda tugs my shoulder, pulling my head back toward her as we walk in line to our table. 'Who *is* this man?' she whispers. 'I feel like I should have known him before I met him.'

A young male waiter is already standing to attention like a toy soldier next to our table.

'Wow, the view of the city is stunning from here,' I say, genuinely struck by the lights twinkling from each tower block and bridge of London. 'How high up are we?' I ask the waiter as he guides me towards the window seat on one side of the table.

'We're on the fortieth floor, Miss Heath. The highest restaurant in the city,' he replies proudly, placing a black napkin across my lap before doing the same for Amanda. Once again, I'm left wondering how a complete stranger knows my name.

'Would you like the usual to drink, Mr Ryans?' the waiter asks.

'Thank you, yes,' Gregory instructs.

The waiter immediately scuttles away.

'What's the usual?' I ask Gregory, who's taken the seat opposite mine.

He looks me in the eye and I study the flecks and enigma of his irises as he responds. I'm forced to look away to the view beneath us for fear he'll see right through my business façade to my racing heart. 'A bottle of Pol Roger 2002 to start, followed by a bottle of Penfolds Grange 1998.' His voice hosts an edge of superiority.

'Oh good, I was worried you'd try to impress us by diving straight in for Cristal.' I laugh sarcastically. 'You've certainly gone up in my estimations, Mr Ryans.'

The table sits in stunned silence. Clearly, people don't usually talk back to this billionaire.

He clears his throat and pauses, holding his closed fist to his mouth a second longer than necessary.

'You intrigue me, Miss Heath. I wonder how low I was in your estimations.'

His face is humourless, his strong, square jaw tight. I'm studying his masculine angles as I realise that I've been relegated back to 'Miss Heath.' I can't help but like the sound of it when it comes from him. I feel his words like hot breath on my clit, making my own hitch.

Him. He who is your client. Get a hold of yourself.

The silence at the table lasts for what seems like an age, broken only when our waiter pops the cork of the Pol Roger tableside. Gregory studies me intensely as the waiter pours four glasses of the champagne.

'Cheers,' Amanda says, thrusting her glass high.

I let the smooth effervescence cool my hot, dry throat.

'So, you know good wine, Scarlett.' Gregory's first words in what seems like an eternity are music to my ears. His manner is friendly, or as light as I've heard it at least. I realise he was teasing me, teaching me not to undermine him. I offer my best playful pout and he flashes me a mischievous grin. My internal organs perform acrobatics, from my chest right down to the lowest point of my abdomen. I hardly know this man and I can't comprehend the way he's making me feel.

'Her dad has an enormous wine cellar,' Amanda offers in a bid to rescue me. 'He and Scarlett used to holiday in chateaus in the South of France.'

'Used to?' Gregory asks.

'My dad,' I say, almost involuntarily. I check my watch and it's nine-fifteen.

'Sorry, Scarlett, I didn't mean to re—'

'No, please, it's fine, Amanda. Honestly. I just need to make a quick call, if you'll excuse me.'

Both Gregory and Williams rise from their seats when I hurriedly leave the table.

Sandy answers as I lean back against the stone sink in the ladies'. She tells me that Dad has had a good day and he's tucked up in bed. She intends to put her feet up with an eighties' movie and a peach melba pudding that she had delivered with the shopping today.

'I'm at dinner with a client and I'm not sure how long I'll be but I'll be as quick as I can,' I say, instantly feeling dishonest, despite telling the truth. 'If you need me, just call and I'll come straight back, I promise.'

'You have fun; we're fine here.'

'Okay, but call me, Sandy. Do you promise?'

'I promise, sweets, but we're fine.'

'Sandy?' I say before she hangs up the receiver. 'It's sort of a client. A client but not completely a work thing. I mean, it is more a work thing than not a work thing.'

She chuckles, her warm, homely giggle emanating from her stomach.

'You have fun,' she repeats, then hangs up. She really is an amazing woman. A life-saver for me these days.

Leaning forwards on my hands over the sink, I study myself in the mirror and ask myself what I'm doing. *Do not fuck this up!* My rational brain tells me Gregory is a client but it fights a losing battle every time I lay my eyes on him. I tip my head upside down, partly to shake sense into it and partly to inject some life into my day-old curls. I reapply my red lipstick and tell myself I'd reapply for anyone, not just a sinfully attractive CEO.

'Did I miss much?' I ask, retaking my seat at the table.

'Just Edward telling us tales of him and Gregory at their all-boys' school. Or so it should have been. Edward was Gregory's school 'buddy,' supposed to settle him into his new school, but he led him astray,' Amanda chirps and she laughs with Williams.

'You can't learn everything in a classroom,' Williams says.

My eyes flit to Gregory then quickly down to my glass of champagne and across the table to Williams. 'Do you prefer Edward?'

'I don't mind really, although I am more likely to respond to Williams. This old boy seems to forget that I go by any other name.'

'Less of the "old boy",' Gregory retorts.

I suddenly remember from my research that it's his thirtieth birthday today. I wonder if that's the only reason he's taken time off on a Friday evening or if this is a regular occurrence.

'Of course, happy birthday, Gregory,' I say, raising my glass into the middle of the table.

His eyes narrow on Williams.

'I didn't say a word,' Williams protests.

'You seem to know things about me, Miss Heath,' Gregory says as he clinks my glass with his. It's there again, smooth and slick, saying my name like he could be performing oral on me.

'More than you think but I still have a few questions.'

'Is that right? Please, indulge my curiosity,' he says as Williams and Amanda start up their own conversation in the background.

I look out to the view of the city and my office block, then back to Gregory. 'I don't like to mix business with pleasure,' I tell him truthfully.

'And which is this? Business or pleasure?'

Torture, I think. My cheeks flush under the intensity of his gaze. My mouth opens to speak but words fail me.

'What else gives you pleasure, Scarlett?' His voice is slightly hoarse, his irises dark, lids heavy.

There's another wave of wantonness between my legs. A tidal wave. And I'd hazard a guess that my sex just got very wet. I take a deep, endless breath and cross one leg over the other, trying to control the rush of blood that's pulsing in my clit and fuelling a need to be filled, completely consumed, by this man.

'Theatre.' I utter the first thing that comes to my head, barely audibly.

For a moment, if I didn't know better, I'd think the CEO had lost his composure.

He swallows deeply, his Adam's apple rising and falling against the taut skin of his throat. 'Do you have a favourite play?'

'*The Phantom of the Opera*: it's a classic. A new play has just come out and Judi Dench is taking the lead. I'd love to see her on stage but the tickets sold out within hours. Do you like the theatre?'

'Yes.'

I pause, waiting, wanting more.

'Yes?' I chuckle, the relief welcome. 'That's all you're giving me?'

'Yes.'

'You don't give much away, Mr Ryans.'

* * *

Our food is exquisite and we pass the time effortlessly, conversation flowing between the four of us. Gregory never looks entirely at ease but is always a gentleman. The wait staff fuss around him and at some point during our meal, every female in the room undresses him with her eyes. I'm guilty as charged.

'What do you say to a night cap, ladies?' Williams asks when our dessert plates have been cleared.

I check my watch. It's gone eleven. 'I'm sorry but I've got to get home; I hadn't intended to be out this late.' Gregory's brows furrow and I feel compelled to explain. 'My dad isn't well.'

He nods, his face stoic. 'I'm sorry to hear that. Jackson will take you both home.' It's a statement, not an offer.

When our waiter comes back to the table, Gregory shakes his hand and rises from the table.

'What about the bill?' I ask.

'Taken care of,' Gregory says, gesturing in the direction of the lift, telling me to walk on ahead of him. In the lift, I insist again on paying for half of the bill, or at the very least my own share, but Gregory won't engage in a discussion. I want to state my case but I know it would be querulous to continue an argument I'd never win.

Jackson asks Amanda and me where we'd like to be dropped. I protest that my West London home must be out of everybody's way but Gregory responds with silence and takes his seat in the front of the Mercedes with Jackson. I take my seat in the back, feeling the same sense of annoyance I felt on the way to the restaurant. *Who does this man think he is?*

We drop Amanda at her flat first, followed by Williams. I'm sure Gregory mustn't live as far from the city as I do but he refuses to entertain my suggestion that I'm dropped home last.

Sandy has left the porch light on for me but the rest of the house is in darkness when we pull up outside. I know it's my own fault but I'm sad that I won't get to speak to my dad today.

Jackson interrupts my self-pitiful thoughts by opening the car door.

Gregory is already out of the passenger side and watches me as I walk around the car towards him, leaning his tall, athletic body back against the Mercedes. I drink him in, everything about him, the alcohol fog in my mind rendering my inhibitions dangerously low. 'Thank you for a lovely evening,' I say, holding out my hand.

Gregory hesitates but silently accepts the gesture. His hold is gentle but there are undeniable sparks firing between us. I want to pull my hand away. I need to break the connection that's rendered me stupid in the face of this virile man. But he leans forwards before my limbs do as my head instructs. His musk of spiced aftershave, wine and masculinity envelopes me before his hot breath caresses my cheek. Then his soft, full lips press against the skin beneath my lobe. My eyes close as the sensation of his kiss travels to my breasts, hardening the expectant ends. My sex aches, widening, slick with lust.

I take a step back, swallowing my desire before peeling open my eyelids.

Summoning willpower from somewhere deep inside me, I force my weak legs to carry me to the house. With my key in the lock, I turn to find him still there, leaning lazily against the car, his hands resting in his jean pockets, fixed on me.

'Goodnight, Miss Heath,' he says, just loud enough to reach me through the cool, autumn darkness.

In the sanctity of my own home, I press my back against the closed door and slide down to my hunkers.

'Bloody hell!'

That's it. The one and only occasion. A completely unforgettable evening where I felt things that I've never felt before, yes. But a one-off, regardless. There's a line, I'm fully aware of it and I'll never cross it again.

But as the hot shower sprays onto my face, he won't leave my mind. *Damn him and his bloody hotness!* My fingers stroke my lips as I think of his. How I'd love to bite them, suck them, feel them against my skin. My mouth parts, filling with warm water, and I lean forwards, bracing my unsteady body with my hands on the tiles in front of me. I haven't imagined it. Those luring, lopsided smirks, the teasing glint in those otherworldly, brown gems and the fact that they spent most of the night watching me. My heart starts beating faster as I think about *that* pose, in the bar, and just now leaning back against the Mercedes, his hands in his pockets, his hips flexed seductively.

Maybe it was unintentional and maybe I *can't* ever cross the line again but to dissolve the dull throb in my sex isn't crossing the line. He'll never know. No one need ever know. And if I don't, I'm going to be walking around like a raging bag of oestrogen, desperate and denied.

I clean my teeth and dry my body, taking my time with my sensitive, erect nipples, and slip under the bedcovers in a short, silk nightdress. His face comes back to me without effort. His severe jawline, his dark features, those godforsaken, fucking delicious, hungry eyes. I lick two fingers then slide them under the covers to the source of rolling thunder. There was no need because I'm already drenched.

I gasp as my fingers slide across my clit. It's been so long since I've touched myself. It's rare. Completely unlike me. I picture him in his navy suit, the sharp suit from the first day I saw him. My fingers slip down to my entrance and glide back up my centre, dragging a moan from deep within me.

Closing my eyes, I see him taking off his suit jacket, standing tall at the bottom of the bed, looking down at me, insatiable. He kicks off his shoes and socks then smiles that excruciating half-smile as he unbuckles his belt. I move my free hand to my breast, circling in time with my fingers swirling around my clit. He slowly unbuttons his white shirt and lets it fall down his arms to the floor, revealing firm, lightly tanned abs and pecs.

My hips squirm, rising against my fingers, up and down. I groan as I imagine his hands move to the fastening of his trousers and I lick my lips as he draws down the zip. The steady rhythm of my fingers has my throbbing bundle of nerves building. He bends, taking down his trousers and tight boxers, then rises, proudly displaying his hard length.

'Gregory!' I whisper his name into the room as he crawls up the bed towards me.

Taking his weight on his toned arms, he hovers above me. As his cock thrusts inside me, my fingers push deep, the rhythm becoming hard and fast, lifting me to a delicious peak. I flip over to my front, my hips grinding against my hand in time to Gregory's driving into me.

'Fuck!'

I thump a hand against the pillow and bite down as my muscles tighten around my fingers. I thrust harder, faster, over and over, until I reach the brink and mumble my climax into the pillow, my insides in a frenzied spasm.

Oh God, that wasn't wrong. It was so incredibly right.

My breathing calms, my pulse relaxes and I turn onto my back, satisfied and feeling much more in control of the whole situation with Gregory Ryans. It's out of my system now. No more crossing the line.

An uncommonly bright autumn sun streams into my bedroom through a gap in the drawn curtains. The line of hot light across my face wakes me from the most pleasant dream, the details of which are amiss. For the first time in months, I feel content, happy even. I turn onto my back and lie in the sunlight, replaying the unexpected events of last night.

I must have been crazy to agree to go for dinner with Gregory and Williams. I wish I could blame Amanda, or Williams, or convince myself that I couldn't possibly refuse dinner with a client. But something else made me go. Perhaps intrigue, maybe hope. I've known Gregory for less than two weeks. I don't even know him, not really. I know a version of him. But what I do know is that no man, not Luke Davenport in the six months I was with him at university, not Josh Parker in the eleven months I was with him during my training contract, has ever made me feel the way I feel when I'm near Gregory. My mind knows that he's out of bounds but my body responds to him, the sight of him, the sound of him, his masculine scent. The thought of him alone fills me with yearning.

Is it possible he could feel anything like that for me? *Of course not.* A man like that, handsome, successful, rich, a beautiful woman on his arm every night. But he did flirt, I'm certain of it. There was a charge in the air, an energy around us. I felt it in his gaze. I felt it surge through my body. How could I have felt something so strong and him feel nothing at all?

I lie in the sun trying to rationalise my thoughts for some time and begin to think of my mum. When I got my first boyfriend at school, it was Sandy I told and begged to keep it secret. It was Sandy who slipped out to the shop to buy my first sanitary towel whilst I hid in the bathroom because I didn't want my dad to see that I'd changed. After my first kiss, it was Sandy I asked whether it's possible to give a bad kiss.

Sandy is a mother to me in so many ways but sometimes, times like these, I can't help wondering what it would be like to have my real mother here. Would she think and feel the same as I do? Would she tell me stories about how she felt when she met my dad?

Was it all a lie?

I hate her for leaving my dad, for leaving *us*, but I sometimes think about what it would be like if she was here. Maybe Dad would never have gotten sick. Maybe I'd always wear the right things and do my hair in the right way. I might be confident like Amanda and men like Gregory might be interested in me.

The smell of bacon drifts into my bedroom and I resolve to get up. Perhaps I'll discuss Gregory with Sandy later. That is, I *would* discuss Gregory if there was anything *to* discuss but there isn't.

Following the smell leads me across the landing into Dad's bedroom. Sandy's perched on the foot of his bed and they're laughing together. Leaning against the frame of the door, I watch them, enjoying listening to the incredibly sweet sound of happiness.

'What's going on here?' I ask jovially.

'Scarlett, Sandy was just telling me a joke,' Dad says, his shaking hands resting on the bacon sandwich in his lap.

'You know who I am?'

His brows furrow before turning to a smile, as if I've made a joke.

'Well, what would you like to do today?' I say, instantly cancelling any plans I could have had.

'Let's just sit in the garden together?' he offers. 'Whatever it is that's had me locked up in this bed must've been good. I still don't feel 100 per cent and Sandy tells me I've been here for a little while now.'

'Okay, great!' I beam, washing over his questioning tone.

Running back to my room, I throw on a pair of leggings and a shirt from my wardrobe, tie my hair roughly in a knot on top of my head and quickly clean my teeth.

'Ready!' I yell a few minutes later, bouncing to his bedside.

He chuckles. The sound magnificent.

When Dad is dressed, Sandy and I help him from his bed. He's gracious as we lift his upper body forwards, despite each vertebrae cracking through its own inertia. Only his eyes expose his true pain. He's become shockingly weak. His legs are skinny and frail and no longer meet in the middle when he stands upright. His trousers, once perfectly tailored, sag from his lower back. His arm feels so thin in mine that I'm afraid it will shatter if I hold on too tight. We walk with him to the stair-lift, each linking one of his arms in our own.

'Why is there a bandage on his arm?' I whisper to Sandy as we send him on his descent.

'He has a bed sore. I can't get it to heal because he forgets that he shouldn't put his weight on it.'

'Does he need medication?'

'The doctor came out during the week and gave me the dressings I've been using and some cream. He told me to persevere for now.'

'Oh,' is all I manage to utter.

I should've been here. I should've spoken to the doctor. Instead, work and gallivanting with some rich CEO were top of my priorities.

Sandy squeezes my hand tightly. We walk to the bottom of the stairs and help my dad stand. We struggle through the house and down the three small concrete steps into the garden. He apologises with each shuffle forwards.

The garden is bright, with sun shining on the yellow ash leaves on the trees and in piles on the ground. Birds are chirping and fluttering down to nibble nuts from the bird table Dad and I haphazardly handcrafted one spring day when I was nine or ten. We thought it would last a year or so at best but here it is, wood flaking from its roof and remnants of bottle-green paint scattered around its legs, but still standing strong.

My dad is more content than I've seen him for too long. He closes his eyes and leans his face to one side, pointing it in the direction of the sun. He sits on the wood bench that he claims to have rescued from a second-hand market shortly after buying our townhouse. He once told me, 'There's life left in it; all it needs is a good home.' He was right, as he always was.

'When I feel a little stronger, I think I'll trim those conifers,' he says nonchalantly, causing Sandy and me both to scrutinise the overgrown row of evergreens at the bottom of the garden.

'We could always arrange for someone to come in and cut them for us,' I suggest.

He looks at me, his face is taut, and I know what's coming, what comes every time. I've tried avoiding his questions and I've tried lying to him but he spent too long working in the medical field to be fooled. Each time his moment of realisation comes, it cuts through me in the way he would take a scalpel to his patients, slowly breaking my skin, drawing deeper as it moves.

'What's wrong with me?' he asks.

A deep breath fills my lungs but doesn't give me the strength I need. 'There's nothing wrong with you, Dad; you just forget sometimes, that's all.'

'I forget?' he asks.

The too-familiar sense of confusion lingers in his words. His scalpel slices deeper still, a laceration that will never heal.

'What do I forget? How often do I forget?'

No matter how many times we have this conversation, it never gets easier and I never get any better at dealing with it.

'Sometimes, you forget people.'

'Do I forget you?' he asks, his eyes glazing over, leaving him seeing the world through frosted panes.

'Yes.'

'What is it, Scarlett? What's wrong with me?' When my response doesn't come, he asks again, demanding an answer.

'You have Alzheimer's.' I say it quickly, swatting away the tears that escape from my eyes. I never used to cry.

As he absorbs my words, silent tears slip from his soft blue eyes. He grabs one of my hands from my lap and shuffles on the bench to face me.

'I'm sorry, my Scarlett. I'm so very sorry.'

'Stop it,' I say, taking his wet cheeks in my hands. 'It's okay, you're fine right now, you're here, let's enjoy our day.'

He closes his eyes and nods. 'You're a good girl. In case I

forget to tell you, thank you for being here with me. Today. Always. You mean everything to me, you always have and even if I forget to say it, you must remember that deep, deep in my heart and in the depths of my old, broken mind, I love you. I love you now, forever and always. I've loved you more than life itself since the first day I held you in my arms and I will never stop loving you, my beautiful girl.'

I throw my arms around his neck and we hold each other, rocking gently. His embrace familiar and warm.

'I love you too, Dad. Please never forget that.'

Sandy makes tea and later sandwiches and cakes, which we eat in the garden. Despite the air dropping cool, my dad is reluctant to go inside, preferring to place a blanket over his legs. We pass the afternoon easily, reminiscing about times we all remember. Dad watches Sandy and I play cards and attempts to join in when I let him see my hand. To my amazement, he remembers the rules of the card games we play, although he doesn't have the energy to play himself.

In the late afternoon, his blinks become longer and though he forces his eyes back open, they seem to weigh more each time he tries. I don't want him to sleep just as much as he wants to fight against it. We both know the world could be a very different place when he wakes.

Eventually, Sandy suggests that we move the card games into the bedroom where Dad can rest as he watches us play. The move upstairs is more difficult now, Dad's weary body feeling much heavier than it did this morning. I'm grateful to be here to help him get ready for bed but as he huffs and pants with each small effort, he avoids meeting my eye. I can tell that it hurts his pride to have me help. When it comes to changing his trousers and pants, I make an excuse to leave the room. He visibly relaxes and Sandy sets about helping him.

Once we've settled him into bed, he asks if I could just sit with him and talk. I wish we had longer; I wish he would never go to sleep and this day would never end. We talk for more than an hour, about life, my work and the kind of deals I do. He's surprised to hear that my training is complete.

'I'm so proud of you, Scarlett. You're a wonderful, clever young lady. I wish I could remember everything you tell me.'

'I never tire of telling you things, Dad. It doesn't matter that you forget them. They don't mean anything.'

'But they do. I know how hard you've worked to get where you are. And this,' he says, prodding his temple repeatedly with his index finger, 'can't have helped at all.'

'Stop that,' I say, pulling his hand away from his head. 'I get my work ethic from you.' I return his faint smile with my own and swallow the tears that lodge in my throat.

'You keep working hard,' he says. 'You deserve all the success in the world.'

He holds his next blink for seconds. His eyes are distant and sleepy when they reopen.

'Time to stop fighting and go to sleep,' I concede, kissing his forehead.

He lifts his arms to me, silently asking for a cuddle. I turn out the lamp on his bedside table and climb onto his bed, settling into his embrace, resting my head on his chest. His heartbeats come slower and his breathing calmer.

* * *

My head cracks off the floor after he pushes me from his bed, screaming for help.

'Dad!' I say, trying to control his arms as they swing for my face. 'It's me. It's me, Scarlett.'

'Help!' he screams. 'Help me, somebody!'

He swings for me again and this time, his fist lands on my temple before I can grab his arms. I fall to the floor again. Sandy bursts into the bedroom and restrains his arms but he keeps screaming and kicking his legs.

'I'm sorry! I'm sorry!' I cry.

'Call the doctor!' Sandy yells at me above my dad's cries for help.

'I'm sorry,' I say as I leave the room.

* * *

The doctor injects Dad's leg with a sedative. It shoots straight into his bloodstream, taking hold in seconds.

'My hands won't stop shaking,' I say to the doctor as he sits with Sandy and me in the lounge.

'You've had a shock,' he tells me. 'You should have a cup of tea with some sugar. If you can't settle later, I can give you something.'

I shake my head. 'I don't need anything. I'm so sorry. It was my fault. I fell asleep in his bed. It was stupid. Now look what I've done to him. Look what I made him do.'

'It is nobody's fault, Scarlett,' the doctor tells me. 'Your father is very, very sick. His rate of deterioration seems to be increasing.' He places a hand on my wrist and waits until he's certain he has my full attention. 'It will only get worse.'

My sobs become more violent and Sandy moves to the sofa next to me to hold me still.

The doctor places a prescription for sleeping pills on the coffee table. 'Just in case.'

He pulls up the footstool and sits down in front of Sandy

and me, his legs spread in his mustard cords. She grips me tighter. We both know what's coming.

'I think you need to consider alternative options for caring for your father,' he says to me. 'He's becoming too sick for just the two of you to take care of him here. He needs full-time support from people who can control him if necessary.'

'Give him shots, you mean,' Sandy snarls.

'If that's what's necessary, yes.'

'I can't,' I say. 'We can't.'

'Please, just think about it. I could suggest some very nice places where you could see him whenever you like. You could both visit and meet the staff first, make sure you like the place. Just think about it.'

Sandy shows the doctor to the door then makes us tea, which she carries into the lounge on a tray with yesterday's left-over cake. We talk and watch TV as Dad rests in his sedative-induced sleep, neither one of us discussing what happened, neither of us broaching the subject of a hospice. At least one of us knowing how much he would hate to be living like this.

7

The office is dark and eerily quiet when I arrive, the sound of each movement magnified by the empty space. On Friday evening, I received notification that I was granted access to a VDR – virtual data room – containing information and documents about Sea People International Inc. Now my emails tell me that hundreds of documents have been deposited in the VDR for me to review. For once, I'm grateful for the laborious task of sifting through a mountain of due diligence. Eclectic Technologies instructed me only to look at the absolute must-read documents but given the timeframe to complete this deal, that will still mean working flat out to prepare for a meeting with Gregory, Williams and Lawrence by midweek. I won't have time to torture myself with thoughts of hospices or the reality of how sick my dad is.

My ability to concentrate is almost non-existent and I try in vain to plough through the mass of documents. Throwing away the possibility of sleeping pills now seems like an idiotic move.

I rest my head on my hand and wince when I touch the cut

on my temple, bringing the memories of just how irresponsible and selfish I was flooding back.

By the time Margaret makes it into the office, I've barely made a dent in the goal I set myself for this morning.

'Scarlett! Hi!'

'Hi, Margaret, have you had a nice weekend?' I ask, unable to muster anything resembling chirpy in my voice.

'Yes, thank you. If you don't mind me asking, is everything okay? You don't look yourself.' It's probably safe to assume she's referring to my puffy eyes, resting on top of two big, black rings of tiredness and decorated with a deep, red cut.

'Just a big weekend.'

'Can I get you anything? Latte?'

'That would be great, thank you.'

Not even caffeine can improve the appearance of my tired eyes but it does at least give me enough of a kick to read the next few documents at an improved pace. The office starts to fill with stories of the weekend.

'Guess what?' Amanda yells as she bursts through my door, making me jump in my seat. 'Gosh, you don't look well. Are you okay?' she asks, lowering her decibel level to just above normal.

'Just tired.'

'Sooooo?'

'I can't guess,' I mutter. 'Please tell me.'

'Fine. Guess who has a date on Wednesday?'

I gasp. 'You?'

'Meeee. Guess who with?'

'I have no idea. Who?'

'Someone's in a grouch today,' she says in disgust. 'Only with Edward!'

'Edward. Edward who?'

'Edward Williams,' she sings again.

'Williams! What?' I realise too late to prevent myself that I'm snarling at her and up out of my seat. 'You can't, Amanda. I told you, he's a client. For God's sake, why can't you ever listen to anything I say?'

I'm annoyed and tired but most of all, surprising even to me, I'm jealous. I'm jealous that Amanda can get any man she likes just as easy as she can say hello. It doesn't matter how wealthy or attractive or smart they are, she can have them.

'You can't do this, Amanda, please. What if it goes wrong?'

'It won't,' she snaps. 'You could just try being happy for me instead of miserable and overly sensible. Jesus, Scarlett, you're such a goody-goody. What the hell's gotten into you today?'

I sit back into my chair with a sigh. 'Sorry, I'm just busy and this isn't really a conversation for the office.'

'Fine. Well, you would've known before now if you hadn't ignored my calls and texts all weekend,' she huffs like a petulant child and sits onto my windowsill, taking the weight off her Prada heels.

'Sorry, I hadn't realised. I just, I didn't look at my phone and...' Before I can stop them, tears are filling my eyes. 'I'm sorry, it's none of my business who you date. It's just been a long weekend.'

Amanda closes my office door then sits on the edge of my desk. 'Is your dad okay?'

I shake my head.

She leans down to my chair and hugs me until my shoulders stop chugging with each breath. Then she pulls away from me and strokes damp strands of hair from my cheeks.

'How did you get that?'

'It's nothing,' I say, pulling my face away from her and shielding my marked temple with my hand. 'This is ridiculous, I'm a mess, I'm sorry.'

'Stop apologising. You apologise far too much. Why don't you go home and be with your dad? Nothing here can be that urgent and if anyone argues, send them to me.' She throws her hands on her hips and purses her lips.

'No, I have too much to do. Plus, it's about the only place I can be to take my mind off it all. It might be the only thing I have left soon.'

Her soft smile is doused in heartbreaking sympathy.

'You know, if you need anything, anything at all.'

'I know.'

As the day goes on, I wake up and seem to be getting through my work at a much quicker rate. Thankfully, Jack's away for the day.

Margaret forces me to eat a hot meal before she heads home at five-thirty, leaving a bag of snacks on my desk. I lose myself in my work and remember how much I love it, how big the Eclectic Technologies deal could be for me.

To: Heath, Scarlett
From: Ryans, Gregory
Sent: Monday 13 Oct 2025 21.46
Subject: Meeting

Good evening Scarlett,

I hope you enjoyed the rest of your weekend. How are you progressing with your due diligence? When will you be in a position to set a time for our meeting to discuss your findings?

Regards,

Gregory Ryans

CEO Eclectic Technologies

I stare at the email, scrutinising every character, as if it's a crime scene and I'm an investigator searching for clues. The fact that I'm delighted to hear from Gregory adds to my terror that he might know just *how much* I enjoyed Friday. My fingertips move to my cheek, remembering the feel of his hot breath on my flesh. My tongue strokes my top lip and my back arches away from my chair as I recall the way he drove me to touch myself, the image of him naked, crawling over me, sating my hunger for him. *Christ!* Our relationship has to be strictly business. This deal means too much to the firm, to me. And more than anything, doing well at work means too much to my dad: that look in his eyes, his pride. Falling for Gregory is not something I can afford to do.

My first response is an email thanking him for dinner. I delete it. I shouldn't draw attention to our time outside work. My second response stays on the computer screen long enough for me to read it eighteen times. Then delete it.

More than an hour later, I reply.

To: Ryans, Gregory
From: Heath, Scarlett
Sent: Monday 13 Oct 2025 22.53
Subject: Re: Meeting

Gregory,

Thank you for your email. I hope to be in a position to have a meeting with the Board on Friday. Please let me know the most convenient time for you.

Best regards,

Scarlett Heath

Senior Associate

Saunders, Taylor and Chamberlain LLP

To: Heath, Scarlett
From: Ryans, Gregory
Sent: Monday 13 Oct 2025 23.07
Subject: Re: Meeting

Are you still at work?
> Gregory Ryans
> CEO Eclectic Technologies

To: Ryans, Gregory
From: Heath, Scarlett
Sent: Monday 13 Oct 2025 23.08
Subject: Re: Meeting

I should be in the office for the next hour or so, please feel
free to call if you have any queries.
> Scarlett Heath
> Senior Associate
> Saunders, Taylor and Chamberlain LLP

To: Heath, Scarlett
From: Ryans, Gregory
Sent: Monday 13 Oct 2025 23.10
Subject: Re: Meeting

I hope you are not working late on my account.
> Gregory Ryans
> CEO Eclectic Technologies

To: Ryans, Gregory
From: Heath, Scarlett
Sent: Monday 13 Oct 2025 23.11

Subject: Slave-Driving CEOs

With your tight schedule, Mr Ryans, you leave me very few alternatives.

Scarlett Heath

Senior Associate

Saunders, Taylor and Chamberlain LLP

I hit the *Send* icon before it dawns on me how outrageously flirtatious my email is. It doesn't even sound like me. It's confident and brash. I could kick myself.

To: Heath, Scarlett

From: Ryans, Gregory

Sent: Monday 13 Oct 2025 23.12

Subject: Re: Slave-Driving CEOs

In that case, the least I can do is have Jackson waiting for you outside to take you home when you finish.

Gregory Ryans

CEO Eclectic Technologies

To: Ryans, Gregory

From: Heath, Scarlett

Sent: Monday 13 Oct 2025 23.13

Subject: Re: Slave Driving CEOs

Gregory,

Please do not trouble Jackson but thank you for the offer.

Scarlett Heath

Senior Associate

Saunders, Taylor and Chamberlain LLP

To: Heath, Scarlett
From: Ryans, Gregory
Sent: Monday 13 Oct 2025 23.14
Subject: Re: Slave Driving CEOs

Jackson will be outside from midnight. Please see my
previous email.
   Gregory Ryans
   CEO Eclectic Technologies

When I step out of the office into the cool night air, Jackson
gets out of the Mercedes to greet me.

'Good evening, Miss Heath.'

'Call me Scarlett, please. I'm sorry to drag you out at this
time of night, Jackson; I didn't—'

'I work for Mr Ryans any time of day; it's no trouble.'

I smile with genuine gratitude. The thought of putting any
more time than necessary between my bed and me is less than
appealing. I sit into the back of the Mercedes and Jackson locks
me in. I lean my head back to rest against the leather seat and
inhale the lingering scent of Gregory. God, even that makes me
want him. My eyes close and his sexy half-smile fills my mind.

'Scarlett. Scarlett.' Jackson rocks my shoulders gently,
waking me up.

I thank Jackson and make my way to the house, rubbing my
dry eyes. Sandy's still up watching television in the lounge.

'What's wrong?' I ask instinctively, dreading the response.

'It's okay, don't panic. He's been very unsettled today but the
doctor called again and gave him something to help him sleep.'

With a sigh, I slump onto the sofa next to Sandy, who wraps

her arm around me. My heart rate returns to manageable as I lean into her shoulder.

'Are you okay?' I ask.

'Absolutely,' she whispers as she pulls me more tightly into her side. 'I know you don't want to talk about it, neither do I, but the doctor left some brochures today. Some of the places look very nice, like posh hotels.'

She leans towards the coffee table to retrieve the brochures and I slip out of her embrace, instantly missing the sweet smell of pastry on her wool cardigan.

'Can we talk about this tomorrow?'

Sandy nods.

I kiss her on the cheek and wish her goodnight then shuffle along the floor and up the stairs where I collapse onto my bed.

Flushing hot then shivering cold, I toss and turn all night.

8

It's a thoroughly miserable Friday morning. I fight with my umbrella in the wind and rain. The bottom of my knee-length dress is a darker shade of red than the rest when I eventually arrive into the muggy air of the Tube platform. The damp, grey mac that I thought was waterproof is clinging to my arms.

The signal on my phone drifts in and out as the Tube moves between over and under land but I have reception for long enough to find that my three o'clock meeting at Eclectic Technologies has been moved to ten this morning.

'Great! That's just great!' I say, unintentionally loud, thrusting it into my bag.

With the exception of the woman sitting opposite me, who rolls her eyes and tuts, no one else seems to notice my ill temper. The man sitting in the seat to my left still snores with his mouth wide open. The woman to my right is lost in her novel. The girl standing in the middle of the aisle continues to tap her foot and chew her gum in time to the sound bellowing out of her earmuff-sized headphones.

* * *

'Scarlett!' Jack yells before I even have a chance to swap my flats for the heels under my desk at the office.

Obligingly, I trudge in his direction.

'Hi! How was your trip?'

'How's the Eclectic deal coming?' he barks from behind his desk.

'Fine. I have a meeting with the board this morning so I'm heading straight back out. I have a few questions for them; could we discuss it when I'm back?'

Ignoring my question, he flicks his hand, motioning for me to leave his office.

His sleazy eyes burn into my back as I walk away and he makes a wet sapping noise with his mouth.

It's not long before Margaret tells me my transport is outside to take me to Eclectic Technologies' office. I have just enough time for a whistle-stop tour of Outlook and to gather my bundle of documents.

'My out-of-office reply is directed to you, Margaret. I'll be in a meeting for a couple of hours at least.'

'Understood.'

I ought to have known that my transport would be Jackson. When I step out of the office, he's already opening the back door of the Mercedes.

'Good morning, Miss Heath,' he says, showing his teeth as he smiles.

'It's Scarlett, please. And this is becoming a regular occurrence. Is he always this controlling?'

'That's what makes him good at what he does.' Jackson closes the door behind me and for the fifteen-minute journey, I quiz him. He's a sort of driver-cum-bodyguard, ex-forces.

Gregory frequently tries to give him the weekend off but it depends on his schedule and Jackson is always happy to work. A cleaner-cum-chef visits Gregory's apartment every day but she doesn't live in.

'Any other extravagances?'

'A few,' Jackson chuckles. 'When he gives himself time to enjoy them.'

Under the stress of my pitch on my first trip to GJR Tower, I've forgotten how impressive the office block is. I'm greeted at the entrance by a very merry receptionist in a grey suit and blue necktie. She passes me over to a concierge, who takes me up to the twenty-seventh floor. The lift opens to a sign stating this floor is the home of Eclectic Technologies, with a bolt of electric lightning flashing through the glowing, white words.

Another receptionist takes my coat and offers me a drink while I wait. She probably thinks I look like I could use some caffeine. She dials an extension and tells the person on the other end to let Mr Ryans know that his ten o'clock has arrived. On hearing his name, goose pimples form up my arms one by one like falling dominos. I quickly stomp on my thoughts and try to remember why I'm here.

I sense his presence before I see or hear him – the blood pumps harder in my veins, my temperature rises and a knot ties in my abdomen. When I glance up, he's watching me from the internal reception door. My neck heats under the intensity of his stare.

'Hi!' is all I manage.

'Hello, Scarlett.' He looks effortlessly cool in his tailored, charcoal suit and black tie, his thick hair slicked back and slightly to one side.

Dragging my eyes from him, I fumble around my seat, picking up papers and my bag. He holds the glass door open for me and I glance at the receptionist as I pass, giving her a polite smile but receiving a scowl in return. The short walk to the boardroom feels endless. We ask each other how we are. We're both well. I pass comment about the great British weather. Gregory apologises for moving our meeting forwards.

Williams is already seated at the sizeable oval table when we enter the room. 'I have to go,' he says into his phone. 'I'll pick you up at seven.'

'I hope that was Amanda,' I say. 'Sorry, that's completely inappropriate and absolutely not my business.'

I clumsily spill my documents onto the table then awkwardly pull my red dress straight.

'It's good to see you again, Scarlett,' Williams beams. His manner instantly putting me at ease, unlike his CEO.

A member of kitchen staff knocks and enters the room with three coffees, a pot for topping up and a plate of pastries that smell fantastic – butter, chocolate and sweet spices.

Williams takes a cinnamon swirl as soon as the plate lands on the table, then wipes his fingers on a serviette. 'And yes, it was Amanda.'

I nod, unsure of the most appropriate response. Unbundling my documents, setting up my laptop, and regaining my composure, I take control of the meeting and do what I know best, what my dad wants me to do and what I've worked hard to do. Settling in to my role as their legal advisor and pretending that Gregory is just another client, I start talking law.

Williams relays Lawrence's apology for not being able to make the meeting, which is annoying as a lot of my curiosity about the deal concerns his ownership of Connektions Limited and indirectly, Sea People International Inc. I decide to ask questions second and talk Gregory and Williams through my brief due diligence on Sea People first. Gregory pays less atten-tion than I think he ought to but Williams listens intently.

After the best part of an hour, I ask, 'Do you have any ques-tions so far?'

Gregory's usually focused eyes are distant. Distracted, as if he couldn't care less about the company he's taking over. Williams asks five or six questions, apparently more intrigued by the prospects of his investment. There's a silence after I answer the question and Williams and I both look to Gregory, expecting him to speak. He doesn't.

'Well,' Williams says eventually, 'it's eleven-thirty; why don't we take a quick break and I'll order more drinks?'

I have to admit Gregory's attitude towards the deal strikes me as peculiar and his lack of interest is clearly irking Williams. I excuse myself to the ladies' to give them some space.

They're standing side by side in front of the window when I return.

'I don't care.' Gregory sounds peeved himself now, his South African twang more prevalent than usual. Harsher even, more manly and sexy as hell.

Williams hangs his head then pats his friend on the shoulder and walks back to the table.

'Is everything all right?' I ask sheepishly.

Williams tucks in his seat. 'Absolutely. Where were we?'

Gregory lingers at the window. When he eventually joins us, his expression is unreadable. Uneasy. Angry. Something else entirely.

'Now it's time for you to do the talking and fill in some missing blanks for me,' I say cheerily.

Gregory's jaw clenches and his hands tense, nearly forming fists on top of the table. Angry, then.

'Of course, what do you need?' Williams says, his manner in complete contrast to the man beside him. The man whose conceited arrogance is really starting to piss me off, both because he's behaving like an ungrateful arse and because there's something completely, undeniably arousing about it.

'Let's start with the legals first. When I was reviewing the constitutional documents, I couldn't help but notice a whole web of connections between the companies that each of you and Mr Lawrence own. I presume you're aware of these connections?' I ask rhetorically, knowing that any potential conflict of interests *should* have been declared in directors' meetings. 'The one I'm most interested in is Mr Lawrence's ownership of Connektions Limited.'

Gregory visibly twitches in his seat.

'I assume you're aware that Connektions Limited is a majority shareholder of Sea People International Inc.?'

My question is directed to Gregory but Williams answers. 'Yes. We are aware of that.'

Irritation drives me to bite down on my gums.

What a supercilious prick he is! I'm pleased I had myself off over him because at least the CEO in my imagination was ruggedly handsome and attentive. At least he gave me *something*.

'I don't understand,' I say, failing to hide my frustration. 'Sea People International is very profitable. How could Mr Lawrence think it would be in his company's best interests to sell? I find that difficult to comprehend when the intention is for you to buy it and break it up.'

'The offer's too good to turn down,' Gregory says through gritted teeth. 'There are numerous reasons why a company would sell up. It might want to realise capital. It might want to throw in the towel.'

'But that isn't the case here,' I say, unable to stop my tone from rising to confrontational. 'It's Lawrence's money, in any event, and he obviously isn't looking to throw in the towel. And this other man, Mr Pearson, he owns 24 per cent of Sea People. Who is he and what does he think about the sale?'

Gregory rises from his chair abruptly, thrusting it back against the wall with a bang that echoes in the room and startles me into silence. He storms towards the window and jams his hands into his trouser pockets. His back is strong, his calves pushed back, his hips flexed forward. He exudes authority beyond his thirty years.

'The business is worth more as a going concern and everything I've told you in the last two hours shows you that, if you didn't know already. Forgetting Lawrence and Mr Pearson for a moment, it doesn't make commercial sense for you to pay more than the company's worth to buy it and sell it off in pieces. The assets are individually worth nothing by comparison to the trading company.'

Gregory faces me, the sinews of his neck taut. I want to leap for him and pull my fingers through his hair. I want to bite his angry lips and get lost in his touch.

'I instruct you to be my lawyer, not my business advisor. When I need help making commercial decisions from a girl who thinks she can question me because she once read corporate law, I'll let you know.'

'I'm not trying to—' I clear my throat and check my rising tone. 'I'm not trying to tell you how to run a business, Gregory, but something's off. You seem to resent this company yet you're desperate to take control of it. You know the maths doesn't add up. Basically, you want to throw money away. I don't know who Mr Pearson is but I can't see why Lawrence would want you to go through with this.' I take a deep breath and try to control my charged emotions. Somewhere in my head, the line between my job and legal sense is blurring with an irrational, personal need to protect this man and his wealth. 'You're right. I'm just your lawyer and if you tell me to make this deal happen, I guess I have to do that. But something doesn't feel right and I'd like to know what it is. I need to know this deal is above board.'

He takes a step towards me, everything about him purposeful, commanding.

'Why are you really doing this, Gregory?'

He's looking down on me, despite my high heels. 'My motivation isn't your concern.'

I try to stay focused, but when my words form, they're heavy, husky even. 'Why do I get the sense I could be putting my entire career on the line and you don't have the decency to tell me what for?'

He takes another step towards me and his eyes burn into mine. He's still but for the twitching muscle in his jaw. Seconds pass as we stand face to face, neither of us blinking.

'Excuse me, I need to make a call.' He strides out of the room, slamming the door behind him, leaving me feeling like he just left me alone in my bed, naked and vulnerable but wanting more.

Williams pulls his interlaced fingers through his tousled hair and audibly exhales. I daren't look at him for fear my face might betray my façade. I stand in the same spot, unmoving, completely dumbfounded.

'What just happened?'

Williams gestures for me to take a seat and tops up my coffee. 'He wouldn't let you do anything to jeopardise your job. Trust me, that's just about the last thing he'd want.'

I need to clear my head. Here I was worried that I could fall for a client and ruin my career by losing him. Now, I'm more concerned that very same client could ruin my career if I stick around. Yet every bone in my body is telling me to trust him.

Gregory returns as I bring my coffee to my lips and I halt, my cup mid-air, waiting for the next onslaught of his temper.

He drops his phone into his inside pocket and slowly resumes his position at the table, leaning back in his seat, crossing one foot over his opposite thigh and watching me through narrowed eyes.

'Scarlett, I wonder if you could help me with something tonight.' His relaxed tone takes me by surprise. The man is up and down like a bloody jack-in-the-box. 'I have to attend a charity gala. It's black tie, a bit of an extravagant affair, but there are some big business names that I have to be seen to speak with.' His expression suggests there are a million places he'd rather be going. 'Someone had to pull out at the last minute and we could use another female to balance the table numbers. It'd be a good opportunity for you to make some contacts, I think. Would you come along?'

'Oh. I – I actually have other plans,' I say sheepishly.

He cocks his head to one side. 'You do?'

'Yes, I, erm, I'm, I...' *Holy shit, Gregory Ryans in black tie.* As he seems to have the ability to do, he reduces my mind to a jumble of incoherent thoughts and my body into a sex-crazed frenzy of babbling nonsense. 'It does sound like a good, erm, opportunity. Thank you all the same, but—'

Damn my stunned synapses. I need to think up and articulate an excuse that will be easier than the truth: that it's hard enough to maintain barriers when he's being an absolute dick of a client but I'm defenceless against the thought of that body in a dinner suit. And, frankly, I don't want him to get his own way like he's so clearly used to doing.

Hell, who am I kidding, the thought of him having his way with me is what's got me wound as tight as a quartz watch.

'But?'

'Erm, I... I don't think I'd have time to finish up here and get ready.'

'I haven't told you what time it starts.'

I straighten my back. 'I'm sorry, Gregory, not this time. I could try to get a colleague to go with you, for the numbers, as you say. Maybe Amanda could go, I mean, since it's a business opportunity and all?'

He leans forwards as if we're the only people in the room.

'I want *you*.'

My lungs empty. I look straight up through my lashes to see his determined face questioning me. I'm frozen, unable to speak. Through my silence, I submit to his demand.

He looks at his Omega watch with a knowing glint in his eye. 'I'll have Jackson pick you up at seven.'

Fuck.

9

Frantic and sweaty thanks to running from the Tube, I bound up the stairs and straight into my dad's room. When I find him sleeping, I back out quietly but end up squealing as I step into Sandy.

'Let's move; you haven't got much time.' She drags me by the hand towards my bedroom.

'All right, Sandy, Jesus, you're going to pull my arm out of the socket.'

'Nonsense. Strip. You need to get in the shower.'

As I'm taking off my office attire, I notice a Harrods dress bag hanging on the front of my wardrobe, then a Louboutin shoebox resting by the bed. 'What's this?'

Sandy smiles. 'A lovely man dropped them for you earlier. Geoffrey Jackson he said his name is. Mr Ryans' driver, apparently. Quite a dish.'

I raise an eyebrow at the unusual sight of Sandy animated over a man. She uses the dress bag as a distraction, turning her back to me to pull down the zip and reveal an evening gown.

If it were possible, my jaw would quite literally hit the floor.

I stroke the tips of my fingers over the floor-length, crimson satin. The rim of the sweetheart neckline is encrusted with clear crystals. My heart sinks when I feel the bones in the tiny waist. *It'll never fit.* Sandy pulls open the shoebox to show me matching satin shoes, the buckle similarly crystal-encrusted. From another bag, she holds up ivory, elbow-length gloves.

I try on the gloves, holding out my hands and turning them in front of me. There's a small box beneath them and in it, what I suspect are real pearls – a beautiful, delicate necklace, a matching bracelet and drop earrings. With them, a note:

> *Because I know you're worried about timing, one less thing to think about.*

Timing really isn't my issue; that I'm falling helplessly for a client is a major problem. Regardless, I can't accept all this, not from a client, nor an extraordinarily sexy man.

'Lady, get in the shower; you need to get a move on.'

I look over the new bags and boxes. I don't have time to argue and he'll know it. Once again, the CEO is going to get his own way with me.

I decide I only have time to roughly curl and pin up my hair, which I do in a panic. I put on my make-up and look at the clock: seven-fifteen. I'm already late. Sandy helps me put the dress on over my head, being careful not to knock my hair or get make-up on the fabric.

'I'm going to return it tomorrow,' I tell her. Remarkably, the dress fits perfectly. 'How did he know?'

Sandy chuckles mischievously.

'Did he ask you?'

She shrugs. 'I got a call from Harrods.'

I can't begin to understand the logistics of that but from

what little I know of Gregory Ryans, nothing should surprise me.

Sandy helps me put on the jewellery and gloves. She holds my hand as I step into the Louboutins. The dress elegantly trails the floor by an inch at the back.

Sandy gasps as she turns me to face the floor-length mirror. I watch her reflection as she considers my hair then the dress and eventually meets my eye. It's a look I've seen before: when she watched my first school play, when she got me ready for my high-school prom.

'I can't believe he bought this for me,' I say, smoothing the sides of the dress against my hips.

'He obviously has very good taste.'

'We're not, you know—'

'Mmm-hmm,' she says, tittering again.

* * *

Jackson is waiting outside as promised and from their brief exchange, it's clear that Sandy's uncommon flirtation is reciprocated, a thought that makes me feel both happy and cringy all at once.

Jackson pulls up to the edge of the red carpet around seven forty-five. I'm suddenly nervous, my pulse rate higher than I would have thought humanly possible.

'He's in there,' I say as Jackson gives me his hand to step out of the Mercedes.

He smirks and I'm instantly embarrassed.

An extravagant gold and mahogany staircase descends from the hotel entrance into a large reception room. I stand at the top searching the crowd of dinner suits and dresses nibbling canapés and sipping champagne from waiters in black, buttoned waistcoats and black trousers or skirts. Lights glisten in the regal, crystal chandeliers. A female soloist sings soft soul music against her backing band.

I see him. A beacon in the crowd. His back is to me but the chill running the length of my spine tells me it's him. He turns. His eyes meet mine and I'm breathless. There's only him in the room. He moves his right hand to his chest and opens his mouth as if about to speak. My legs continue to move me down the staircase, my mind elsewhere. I blink and he's gone, as if he'd been a figment of my imagination. I'm almost at the bottom of the staircase, desperate to find him again, but I cast my focus down to watch my satin shoe as I take the last step.

When I look up, he's here, in his dinner suit and black bow tie, his dark hair slicked back.

'You're stunning,' he says, his hand still held to his chest.

My smile spreads across my entire face. 'Thank you for the dress.'

'God, you're welcome,' he whispers, bending to kiss me on the cheek.

His lips send fire through my veins. I close my eyes and liquefy under his touch, overwhelmed by his voice, his scent, *him*.

He leads me back to his group. Williams has brought Amanda and they appear in every way to be the perfect couple, his easy manner, her smiles, her royal-blue, sculpted dress and dazzling, auburn hair. She's barely an inch from his side as they laugh with the others.

'Scarlett, you already know Williams, Lawrence and, of course, Amanda. This is my mother, Lara,' Gregory says.

Lara grabs me with her champagne-free arm and kisses me on both cheeks. 'It's so nice to finally meet you, Scarlett,' she says, with a strong South African accent. 'How are you?'

'It's a pleasure to meet you, Lara,' I say, slightly startled by her overly friendly greeting and processing that word, *finally*. 'I'm very well, thank you.' I glance at Gregory, who seems to purposefully avoid my eyes.

Lawrence wraps an arm around Lara's waist. 'Shall we take our seats?'

'Okay, darling.' Lara floats away from us, her movements the epitome of elegance. Her long, demure, black dress trailing the floor as she leaves. Her brunette chignon exposing her neck and emphasising the length of her slim body.

The gents – Gregory, Lawrence, Williams and another business partner of Gregory's – take their seats at the table in unison after the ladies.

'Lawrence and your mum?' I whisper to Gregory as he takes his seat next to me.

He leans back as two waiters simultaneously place a napkin in his lap and a bread roll on his side plate. 'They've been together since I was ten.'

'Ten! What's next? Williams is your brother and your mum really owns Sea People International?'

Gregory glares at me then shakes his head. Lara thankfully interrupts as I mentally chastise myself for being too familiar and remind myself that I'm taking dinner with my client. Except, I've never sat next to a client and struggled to concentrate on my next move. I've never sat so close to a client and had to force my hands not to reach out and touch him. I've never had to squeeze my pulsing thighs shut beneath the dinner table because I'm thinking about how my client would feel inside me.

Lara leads the table in good-spirited conversation. It's catching. Between that and the wine flowing, I start to relax. Playful jibes pass across the table between the men, including Gregory. It's nice to see a small chink in his otherwise stoic armour.

'A toast,' Lara announces, holding up her glass. 'To having my favourite men at one table. You all look dashingly handsome. And to the gorgeous ladies: it's a pleasure to have you here. Scarlett, Amanda, welcome.'

We all stand to clink glasses.

'For the record, Williams is not my brother,' Gregory whispers to me. 'But he is my oldest friend. He was my first friend when we moved to England.'

Gregory catches his oldest friend's eye and subtly raises a glass to the air.

A waitress places a plate of foie gras, with the smallest amount of rocket salad and a slice of Melba toast, in front of me and my wine glass is topped up again.

'As for my mother, she designs bags,' he says, leaning into my ear. He pauses to sip his wine then continues, this time loud enough for his mother to hear. 'She's incredibly talented but she doesn't have a particularly business-savvy mind.'

Lara fakes a shocked gasp. 'You take that back, young man!'

He smiles. A true and shockingly handsome smile.

Another side to the CEO.

Amanda regales the table with tales of our time at university. I give her the playful warning eye but she knows which stories she can tell and where to draw the line. On more than one occasion, I find myself defending my uncoordinated dancing at formal dinners and unintentionally inappropriate comments to our professors.

What can I say, I liked the challenge.

'You should see her bust out the moves to "Mr Brightside".' Amanda tells everyone.

I almost splutter my wine, laughing as I remember the moves and Amanda sings the lyrics.

'Bruising your feet to The Killers is a right of passage,' I say.

When I'm composed, I notice Gregory watching me intently, a look that resonates in all my sensitive spots. I take a punt. It could be disastrous. It certainly is inappropriate. I lean into his ear and pause to inhale his deadly musk before I speak. 'Since we're sharing tonight, I want to put you straight on something. Today, you referred to me as a girl who once read a textbook. You were right about corporate law but you were wrong to call me a girl.'

I linger there, at his neck, both to shield my blushes and to question my motives. I'm there long enough to hear his subtle hitch of breath.

After pudding, an enormous cheese board is placed in the middle of the table. I press both hands to the bones of my dress and confirm that I really can't fit anything else beneath them. A waiter hands a decanter of port to Lawrence.

'Pass the port!' Lawrence announces. 'The decanter doesn't touch the table until it's empty.'

When the port reaches me, I fill my glass and take a sip. 'I really can't eat or drink anything else,' I whisper to Gregory. 'Perhaps get me a size up next time?'

'Next time?' he grins, raising one eyebrow.

I narrow my eyes on him. In response, he shuffles, straightens his trousers and leans back in his seat. His leg rests against mine, his heat searing through both our garments. I'm acutely aware of each curve of my body. Alcohol is making me confident... or stupid. I press back against him with my thigh and watch his seemingly impassive face. My arm moves before my mind can think to stop it, bringing my hand to rest on his thigh beneath the table. His lips part and he seems to pause momentarily before he puts his fingers gently on the nape of my neck and slowly traces my vertebrae down my back. My eyelids feel like steel as I melt into his touch.

'Gregory, would you treat your mum to a dance to her favourite song?' Lara asks.

We each snap our hands away from the other. He half-smiles at me, then stands, taking his mother's hand in his and leading her to the dance floor. Closing my eyes and inhale deeply.

Amanda whisks Williams away to dance to the Rat Pack tribute band, leaving Lawrence to ask me to partner. I, of course, oblige. I'm impressed by his slightly offbeat but nimble dancing. His pace is similar to my dad's. They both seemingly have one set tempo counting in their mind as they move, ignorant to the rhythm of the music. I fall relatively easily into Lawrence's mistimed steps and we move in stagnated circles.

'Is this awkward for you?' I ask.

'Why? Should it be?'

'Well, it's just that I'm your legal advisor and—'

'Scarlett, even an old fool like me can see that Gregory hasn't brought you here as a legal advisor.'

I pull away from him and twirl under his arm, my cheeks ablaze.

'So you're like a father to him?' I ask, returning my free hand to his left shoulder.

'As much as I can be. Gregory's a man. He's always been much older than his age. He had to grow up quickly.'

'Why's that?'

'I think that's his story to tell.' He pushes me away, turning under his arm again. 'He's a good man, Scarlett: the best. He'll move the earth for the people he loves.'

'Can I cut in?' Gregory says, standing to our side, his legs parted and strong, his shoulders broad, his hands folded behind his back. He's a man who demands attention.

Lawrence raises the back of my hand to his mouth Leo in *Titanic* style, then passes it to Gregory. His hand is big but his hold gentle when it wraps around mine. He runs his other hand from the bare flesh between my shoulder blades down to the small of my back and pulls me close to him. My legs are locked either side of his, my left thigh pressed up against his right. I stare at where our bodies connect and inhale a nervous breath. He gently lifts my chin with his index finger until I'm gazing into his hypnotic, brown pools. We stand like this until I realise that everyone in the room can probably read my thoughts and must know that, despite my better judgment, I've unequivocally fallen for this man.

His shoulders rise and fall with his breath, then he begins to turn us, slowly at first, growing faster with the music – Frank Sinatra's 'I've Got You Under My Skin.' He leads me into each step, never missing a beat. We turn faster and faster still, until the room is spinning and everything except his face is a blur. I'm flying and there's no one else in the space but the two of us. I submit to his hold, allowing him to move me. My head tips back as I laugh, genuinely happy. There's nowhere else I'd rather be than in his hench arms.

He slows us down with the rhythm of the music and pushes me away, twirling under his arm. As I return, he drops his foot in front of mine, bending me back towards the floor, the weight of my body resting in his arm at the small of my back. He leans his face towards mine, so close, I can feel his next breath on my lips. My body aches for his kiss. My lips part and my hips rise reflexively towards him, silently begging. He raises his head excruciatingly slowly, blowing caressing air up my neck, to my ear, and he whispers. 'I'm not going to kiss you.'

He pulls me back up to standing as the band switches to the next track. I can't tell whether my head is fuzzy from dancing, alcohol, or the ten thousand thoughts and emotions running in all directions through it. Taking my hand again, he begins to turn me, slower this time. 'I know you have your reservations,' he finally says.

'Yes,' I manage, fighting to remember what they are. 'You're a client, for a start and—'

'And?'

'And I can't help but wonder whether I can trust you. I just can't figure you out. You're up and down. Your family and friends tell me you're a great guy. Yet, I know you're hiding something from me and I don't like it.'

He turns us through the legato verse, his gaze penetrating me, challenging me. His Adam's apple moves under his skin and I force my eyes shut to stop myself from wanting to bite it.

'All you need to know is that I always get what I want.'

'And what is it that you want, Gregory Ryans?'

'You.'

He presses his thigh between my legs until I can feel my blood pounding in my clit, my entrance wet, craving him. I bite down hard on my lip. I can't let him take the upper hand.

'You're not going to let this go, are you?' he asks.

'I can let it go. I can forget about it. God, that would be so much easier right now. But I'm hoping you don't want me to.'

'How much do you need to know to just let go?'

'All of it. All of you.'

'I'm not the kind of man who exposes himself.'

'Then just tell me something. Tell me something true.'

There's a momentary flutter of panic in my chest, which I think is fear that he might not let me in, a feeling that makes no sense to me at all. Then he sighs. 'Like I said, Lawrence has been with my mother since I was ten. He moved us over here from South Africa and we've lived with him ever since. He met my mother when we were still living with my biological father.'

He swallows as he pushes me away to twirl but I'm not numb to his delay tactic.

'My father was a drunk, probably still is. The only thing he ever cared about was work, his businesses. He'd come home late, stinking of drink and he'd beat my mother. The first time I saw him do it I swore to myself that I'd make him pay.'

I feel his chest rise then fall with his exhale, pressing against mine, as he continues to turn us to the beat, but his attention's set over my shoulder, detached.

It's that small shift that brings realisation crashing into me, almost throwing me from my feet. I stop turning and release myself from his grip.

'That's it. That's the connection. Your father, he's... he's Sea People International, isn't he? Your father is Pearson.'

Gregory stands motionless, silently giving me his answer.

'You want to kill the company he made. That's what this is all about.'

He reaches a hand to my face but I recoil on impulse.

'It's unethical, Scarlett, I know that. But it isn't illegal. You aren't doing anything wrong. I wouldn't let you.'

'But Lawrence and Williams. They know. Lawrence has such a big stake in the company.'

Gregory sighs. 'Lawrence has known my father for a long time. They don't see each other, don't really know each other socially, but Lawrence keeps a stake in Sea People through Connektions. Keep your enemies close and all. As long as Lawrence holds that stake, he can keep tabs on Pearson.'

The room starts to spin. 'I – I need to leave.' I need to get my head straight.

I rush from the dance floor, grabbing my bag from our table, and seek out fresh air. 'Scarlett!' I hear him call after me as I run up the grand staircase.

Outside in the freezing dark night, he grabs my arm, turning me to face him.

'Scarlett,' he pants, 'if you don't want to work on the deal, tell me, but don't just leave.'

Emotion I can't explain balls in my throat as I stare at his pleading face. 'I get why you want to do it, Gregory, I do but I don't think I can be part of it.'

He drops his hands to his sides and looks at me through a wounded child's eyes.

'I need space to think,' I say, placing a hand over my mouth. 'I'm sorry.'

10

I was five years old the last day my mum kissed me goodbye at the school gates. It was overcast, I remember. The sun was fighting to peek through the clouds, the wind was blowing lightly, carrying with it the smell of fresh-cut grass past.

She rubbed her lipstick from my brow, then knelt in front of me, holding me at arm's length. She considered me, from my head to my toes, and made the kind of face that should be a smile but I thought it looked like a sad face, just upside down. If I'd known then, I would've taken in just how beautiful she was, her big, hazel-green eyes, her soft, flowing, brown hair. Her painted red lips and the dimples that formed beside them when she spoke.

'Go on, you don't want to be late,' she said.

She watched me as I ran with my bag to meet my friends. She was still watching when Mrs Tindale put her hand on my shoulder, encouraging me into school. When I waved at her, she blew me a kiss and mimed *I love you*, pointing to her eye, then her heart and, just before I walked through the door, at me.

It wasn't very often that my dad was able to pick me up from school with his shifts at hospital so I was bouncing with delight when I saw him waiting to collect me at four o'clock. He smiled but didn't seem happy to be there. I wondered what I'd done wrong and if I was in trouble.

I walked across the playground to meet him, replaying everything I'd done in the last day. I'd eaten all my dinner. I'd bathed when I was told. I'd cleaned my teeth. I was a little late getting dressed for school that morning because I wanted to watch the end of my cartoon and my mum did seem more vexed than usual. She'd tugged my hair into a tight ponytail and yanked the toggles on my coat to fasten them, but surely, she didn't tell my dad on me.

When I reached him at the school gates, he took my hand and said, 'Hello,' but he didn't speak whilst we walked to his car and he didn't speak for the entire journey home. I knew I must be in big trouble. When I got home, I realised why. My mum had packed up most of her wardrobe and gone away. She really was cross with me. *Stupid, stupid cartoons, why did I watch them?* It was the start of the weekend and my dad spent the next day at home even though he sometimes had to operate at the weekend if there were emergencies. I spent most of the day in my nursery playing. My dad did everything he needed to do for me. Everything my mum would normally do, like make my toast, comb my hair, help me get dressed. But he barely uttered a word to me as he did. I decided he must have been very cross with me for making my mum go away.

He had different women visiting the house all day. He made them tea in a pot and talked to them about me in the lounge. Sometimes, I popped my head out of the nursery to listen but if Dad caught me, I closed the door and ran back to my toys. One of the women, younger than the others, was called Sandy. I remember thinking she wore a pretty dress, that I liked how her bangles jingled, and she had sparkly, colourful eyelids. My dad brought her into my nursery to meet me.

She had the biggest smile I'd ever seen, and bright, white teeth shone between big lips.

'Hello, Scarlett, I'm Sandy,' she said.

'Hello. I'm Scarlett and I like your bracelets,' I said, turning a finger around one gold ring.

'Well thank you. I like your hair and your pretty bow clips.'

'How old are you?' I asked.

Dad suddenly had a tickle in his throat. He cleared it and said, 'Scarlett, you shouldn't ask a lady her age.'

'That's okay, Doctor Heath,' Sandy said. 'I'm nineteen, twenty next week.'

I smiled and offered her one of my dolls. She knew exactly what to do with my toys and played with me on the floor. I liked her a lot and I told my dad so that night. I asked if Sandy would be able to come to see me again. Dad said she might come to live with us. I was delighted.

After a day or so, my dad went back to work at the hospital and I started to wonder when my mum would come back. Dad didn't seem to want to talk about it so I asked Sandy. Sandy said my mum had gone away and it might be a while before I saw her again. I didn't understand why she'd gone away just because I took a long time to get dressed. I'd taken as long to get dressed other days and she'd never gone away.

I was so confused, I started to cry. Sandy hugged me and said I could stay home from school, 'Just for one day'. We made pancakes and ate them with crispy bacon and Sandy's special syrup. It was the best day off school I'd ever had. In fact, it was the only day off school I'd ever had.

That night, when my dad came home from work, he tucked

me into bed and read me a book. He read my favourite: *A Witch Got On At Paddington Station*. I was resting my eyes when he finished. He kissed my forehead and turned off my lamp then told me repeatedly, 'It isn't your fault.' I didn't understand what he was talking about but he sounded upset so I decided not to ask.

11

In the light of day, the new dress, shoes, bag and jewellery seem to have lost their lustre. As I pack them back into their covers and cases, resigned to returning them to Gregory, I replay that conversation and keep seeing the pained look on his face as he told me about his past.

His father owns Sea People International. This is a hostile takeover.

That's why he's paying over the odds for something he doesn't want. That's why Lawrence indirectly keeps control in Sea People. He's doing on paper what Gregory is doing in his mind: keeping watch over his nemesis.

Jack's words come back to me. *Do not fuck this up.* The opportunity I could have by keeping Eclectic Technologies and Gregory as a client is enormous. It's a career game changer.

I slump down onto the edge of my bed and cradle a pillow. But that's just not me. Gregory was right, a hostile takeover isn't illegal but he's doing it for all the wrong reasons. It's underhanded. He's plotting with Lawrence and Williams to take what his father most cherishes. I'm not that lawyer. I'm not that person.

My moral compass points in one direction and that isn't the direction of operating in the grey, blurring the lines of what's right and wrong in the eyes of the law.

Gregory wants revenge and I just don't think I'm the person to help him take it.

But I'm torn up over this man I've known for less than two weeks.

That look on his face is plaguing me.

I fall back on the bed and drop the pillow over my face, as if hiding from the world would make this all go away. I could make this disappear. I just tell him I won't act for Eclectic. Simple as that. I've seen corrupt lawyers. First, they dump time on a matter to be paid by a client. Next, they change documents without telling the other side. Then they're paying people off to get what they want. Acting for Gregory would be the first step down a slippery slope.

'But I want to help him,' I mumble into the pillow, crushing it harder to my face to stop the words.

With my only intention being to spend the day with my dad, I pull on my oldest and most stretched pair of jeans, and an equally comfortable, oversized knit jumper. I contemplate make-up but decide washing my face, cleaning my teeth and tying my hair in a rough knot will do.

After tapping on his bedroom door, I slip into Dad's room. He's still sleeping but I take a seat in a wicker chair by his bed and watch him. Sleep is the only time I can guarantee he's at peace, not hating his life stuck in this bedroom with the demon in his mind stealing him from his old life.

I watch the rise and fall of his chest and the intermittent flickering of his eyelids as he dreams. He used to do everything for me. I can't imagine growing up with a parent who hated his own flesh and blood so much, he'd let his little boy see his mother being beaten. The two people who are supposed to love him and cherish him beyond all reason, fighting, destroying his life. Making him grow into a man whose past follows him like a dark shadow and dictates the kind of person he wants to be years later.

The thought of any man raising a hand to a woman disgusts me. Holding my knees to my chest, I lean my head on the side of the chair, somewhere between awake and asleep, that window of irrational thought. The dangerous place where nightmares are a reality.

I envisage myself in my dad's hospital as a child, in his office, standing on a pink, plastic stool in my dungarees and light-up, pink shoes, trying to reach his desk. He's young and healthy. A stethoscope hangs over the shoulders of his white coat. His skin is golden and his hair still has traces of dark brown interspersed with grey strands.

Years away from the pale, aged man sleeping in front of me. I'm handing him bandages which he's packing into an already full storage cupboard, when a male nurse dressed head to toe in pastel green bursts into the room and yells that there's an emergency. I follow my dad as he runs down the blue and white corridor.

I remember the day as if it were yesterday, except now we're in an operating theatre and this isn't my true memory at all.

A woman who's been badly beaten lies on an operating table, bleeding heavily, utterly helpless. Tubes rest into the creases of her mouth, pulling it wide and open. Her purple eyes are swollen shut.

Dad shouts orders into the commotion but the room falls silent. As I dream the hospital drama unfolding, a noise builds in my ear until it's loud enough for me to recognise as soft sobs. In the corner of the theatre, a little boy sits on the floor, his knees pulled into his body, his head tucked under his hands. 'Mummy, please be okay, Mummy,' he sniffs, with a hint of South African twang.

The boy has blood on his shirt. He looks up at me through deep, brown irises, the same irises that pleaded with me as I left the charity gala last night. Tears stream down the boy's beautiful, young face.

'Please don't let her die,' he cries.

My lungs jump to action with a thick, jagged breath and my chest aches so bad, I raise my hand to it. Looking at my dad, still sleeping despite my panic, I know that he'd do everything he could to help the little boy.

* * *

When I eventually leave my dad and head downstairs, Sandy has made my favourite: pancakes with maple syrup and crispy bacon. She sets a plate with four pancakes in front of me on the breakfast bar.

'There's plenty more if you want.' She smiles, pouring me a large cup of coffee.

'Amazing,' I grunt through a large, graceless bite. That I hardly slept last night has left my stomach raging, acidic with hunger.

'Aren't you eating?' I ask as she busies herself around the kitchen in a blue blouse and a black, A-line skirt that I bought her for Christmas last year. Not an outfit she'd usually wear in the house.

'I've already eaten; I've been up for a while.'

'Couldn't sleep?'

She shakes her head, scrubbing bacon fat from the grill pan in the steaming water of the ceramic white sink.

'How was your evening?' she asks. 'You know, I wasn't sure if you'd be back here last night.'

'Sandy!' I blush. 'If I didn't come back, it would've been for fear of catching Jackson humping your leg.'

She tuts and puts a marigold-gloved hand on her hip.

'I saw you two flirting,' I tell her.

'You have a very vivid imagination.'

'Mmm-hmm, and I suppose I'm also imagining seeing you dressed in a skirt and blouse to scrub the dishes?'

'I thought I'd pop out today, that's all.'

'With Jackson?'

'No, not with Geoffrey Jackson. My goodness.' She wafts a hand as if she's annoyed but the sides of her cheeks betray her smile as she turns back to the sink. 'Anyway, I asked about *your* night.'

The sick, churning feeling comes back to my stomach and I push away the remainder of my pancakes.

'Actually, it didn't end well. Gregory and I sort of had a fight. Well, a disagreement.'

'Does that mean you're, you know, together?' she asks, turning from the sink, drying her hands on a towel.

'Oh, erm, no, no, we're not together.' And we aren't, so why is this whole thing driving me to the brink of sanity? 'Gregory's a client. Maybe not even that any more.'

'I've not known your other clients buy you designer dresses and jewels.'

The problem is, I don't know whether he bought those for the woman he danced with, the woman whose skin he caressed and pressed his warm lips against or his lawyer. The lawyer he needed to bribe into a dodgy deal.

'Sandy, can I ask you something?'

'Always.' She pulls up a stool and sits opposite me, her hands wrapped around a hot cup of tea.

'What would you do if someone asked you to do something that you knew wouldn't really be right but for their sake, you wanted to do it and doing it somehow felt like the right thing to do?'

She regards me with a frown, assessing a person she's unsure of, a person she doesn't know. Or perhaps my own subconscious just thinks that.

'Well, I would think that if you wanted to do that maybe *wrong* thing for that person, that person must mean a lot to you. Having said that, if you mean as much to that person as he, or they, do to you, perhaps they shouldn't have asked you to do something that wasn't really right in the first place?'

'Okay, and supposing they said that, or implied that, you had the option not to do the *thing*, but you really wanted to help them?'

'Scarlett, what's this about?'

'I can't really say.'

'This is what you and Gregory argued over?'

I nod.

'Scarlett, I know you and I know how you've been brought up. I know the person you are and whatever this thing is, I know you'll make the right decision. Just remember that you haven't known this Gregory chap for long. It's a tough time at the moment, with your dad, and I understand Gregory is wealthy and—'

'It's not about that, Sandy, I promise. He's more than that, much more, I think.' The words seem for the first time to be real when I say them aloud. 'I want to help him, I really do, more than anything, but I know it's wrong. I can't explain why I want to help him so much. It doesn't make sense. It probably doesn't even matter after last night.'

Sandy suppresses a smile behind her cup.

'Did you really say "chap"?' I tease, changing the subject.

'What's wrong with "chap"?'

'Nothing, nothing at all, it's very *happening*.'

She clips me playfully with a tea towel. 'Be quiet, you. It's hard to be happening in your forties.'

'I can see that.' I laugh.

Sandy hangs the tea towel onto the rail of the range oven door then walks behind me and places one hand on my shoulder. 'I'm sure you'll make the right decision. I'm going to see if your dad is ready for breakfast.'

I think about everything my dad has ever done for me and all the things the little boy from my dream didn't have. His childhood blackened undeservedly. It hurts me that my mother left and didn't want me. I can't imagine how awful it must've been for Gregory to see the things he saw.

If you mean as much to that person as they do to you, perhaps they shouldn't have asked you to do something that wasn't really right in the first place. He didn't. He owned the truth and gave me the opportunity to walk away from the deal.

Maybe he does care for me.

12

It's Monday and time to deal with the hangover from Friday night. I pull up an email from Gregory and dial his number. It's before nine in the morning and I wonder if he'll be in the office. My heart is beating so fast, I feel my blood pulsing in my head. Not helped by the incredibly annoying hold music. The weight of my decision draws my hands to my temples, as I wonder for the last time whether I'm about to do the right thing.

His face appears on my screen. 'Scarlett.'

'Hi.'

'I didn't know if I'd hear from you again.'

I've turned myself inside and out for two days and now the moment is here.

'I need to return my dress.'

His exhale is louder than he probably intends it be through my headphones. 'It's yours; keep it. No one else would do it justice. Is that the reason you called?' There's disappointment written all over his face: the confirmation I needed. I won't be another person who lets him down.

'No. I – I wanted to let you know that I'll finish my markup of the Sale and Purchase Agreement and send the latest version to you before lunch. If you're free, we can walk through the changes this afternoon.'

'You're going to stick with us?'

'No. I'm going to stick with *you*.'

After a silence he says, 'Thank you, Scarlett.'

Even through the computer, I know he's looking directly at me, I feel it. I could listen to my name slip from his tongue a thousand times a day and never tire of it. But that's not the deal I made with myself and after this transaction closes, he won't be saying my name again.

* * *

The usual receptionist snarls at me and flashes a toothy grin to Jack then leads us, Jack first, keenly following her perfectly formed arse, to the Eclectic boardroom. Before I have a chance to say hello to Lawrence and Williams, who are already sitting at the table, a hand grabs the bare flesh of my wrist. The sensation ignites my skin, telling me instantly who it is. My body reacts before my mind. I stagger back against the glass pane of the empty office adjacent to the boardroom. Everything I felt on Friday night as he held my body to his and moved us around the dance floor is still there, as I stare at his lips.

'I just want to say thank you.'

His face is close to mine, closer than it ought to be. My mind feels dizzy with his proximity and I think I could break even my own rules. But...

'Gregory, you should know that I'm here as your lawyer. *Only* your lawyer. What Pearson did... no child should have to see that. But after this deal, I think you should find another lawyer.'

I press my fingertips to his dark-blue blazer and keep my gaze down, too afraid to look up and be hypnotised.

He holds open the boardroom door for me. As we step inside, Williams gives Gregory a questioning look, which is no match for the *what was that about?* glare I receive from Jack. Gregory takes a seat next to me as we walk through the key provisions of the Sale and Purchase Agreement. Our eyes meet on numerous occasions and he seems more engaged with the deal than the last time I saw him. It's a good thing. He's my client and this is a corporate transaction. Yet I can't help feeling bereft.

After an hour or so, a loud snort, followed by Lawrence jerking himself awake in his chair, makes us all turn towards him. He wipes his mouth and looks at the saliva on the back of his hand like someone else must have put it there.

'Nice one, old man!' Williams laughs, patting Lawrence's belly.

'Terribly sorry, Scarlett,' Lawrence says to me. He sits up to attention in his chair and feigns excessive interest. 'Carry on, it's excellent.'

I will myself not to react but the stress of the last few days gets the better of me. My laughter bursts from me like helium from a popped balloon. It's loud and childlike and feels amazing. I place the tips of my fingers in front of my mouth but the laughter keeps coming. I stop when I hear Gregory laughing with me, a soft but baritone sound. Williams joins, followed by Lawrence and, with the exception of Jack, who seems to have missed the joke, we laugh until my ribs ache.

Gregory shuffles in his chair, regaining composure. He straightens his trousers and spreads his knees apart. I inhale sharply when his knee touches mine and glance in his direction, hopelessly wishing it were intentional. His expression gives nothing away. I should break our contact but my limbs don't move. With my knee pressed lightly against his, I continue to trawl through the provisions of the Sale and Purchase Agreement.

* * *

Lawrence calls a break a little after six-thirty and I excuse myself to the ladies'.

Jack's standing outside, staring at me, when I open the door back into the hallway. I assess the corridor. We're alone.

'Jack! You gave me a shock.'

He continues to glare but says nothing. The sound of the lift crossing between floors is the only noise. I make a move to step around him but he blocks me with his arm, forcing me to back into the cold, metal wall. The sensor ceiling lights to our right go out. He's been waiting for me for at least five minutes, long enough for the sensors to detect a lack of movement.

'Excuse me,' I say, lightly pushing at his chest, trying to move along the wall. He slams his left hand on the wall close to my head, blocking my path.

'Running off to your boyfriend?' His voice is hoarse. His breath is hot and stinks of tobacco.

'Jack, please, you know he's not my boyfriend. He's a client, that's all.'

'You know what the problem is, Scarlett? You lead everyone on. You make men think that you're desperate to spread your legs.'

He moves his mouth so close to mine, I can taste his breath.

I turn my head away from him. The lights next to us flash on. Gregory appears. Tall. Broad. Still. Protective and intimidating all at once. Jack drops his arm from the wall, opening my escape route. I want to run to Gregory. Instead, I nod in gratitude as I walk past him. He doesn't acknowledge me. He doesn't even move. His eyes are locked on Jack.

I pause before re-entering the boardroom, waiting for my hands to stop trembling. It must be five minutes before Gregory returns, maybe longer. He examines me from afar and I hang my head, shamed and embarrassed. Gregory lies that Jack was feeling unwell so had to leave. Williams looks confused but asks no questions. Not knowing what else to do, I go back to working through the Sale and Purchase Agreement. From the corner of my eye, I see Gregory take off his silver-grey tie, undo the top button of his white shirt, then rest back against his leather chair. I briefly glance in his direction and see red, swollen knuckles on his clenched fist. My distraction causes me to pause, giving Gregory time to check his watch and call time on our meeting.

'Jackson will take you home.'

* * *

Gregory's hands rest on the frame of the back door to the Mercedes. I look from his red knuckles to his eyes and wonder just how many sides to this man there are.

'Thank you.'

He watches me. His face constricts. Then he closes the door before having an agitated conversation with Jackson. Gregory shakes his head then rubs his knuckles. Jackson gets into the car and we drive away, leaving Gregory watching from the street. I turn to look at him through the back window as he grows smaller and eventually disappears.

'Are you okay?' Jackson asks, addressing me through the rear-view mirror.

I nod. That's all I can do.

* * *

As I walk the corridor to my office with Amanda, who's discussing her date last night with Williams through a bite of breakfast bagel, a man from General Office wheels a stack of boxes labelled *Jack Jones* past us and in the direction of the exit.

'Whoa, whoa, whoa!' I place a hand against the tower of boxes until the man stops. 'Margaret?' I call towards the secretaries' station. 'Margaret, where are these boxes going?'

'You haven't heard?' she says, toddling towards me. 'Jack resigned from the partnership last night. Well, rumour has it he was pushed.' She taps her index finger to one side of her nose.

'What?'

The image of Gregory's angry, swollen fist comes crashing to my mind and I stomp to my office. Livid, I call him.

'Ryans.' It sounds like he's answering on the move.

'Tell me this is nothing to do with yesterday.'

'Pleasure to hear from you, Scarlett. It would be more pleasant if I knew what you're talking about.'

'You know *exactly* what I'm talking about. Jack Jones. You've had him fired, haven't you? Christ, how hard did you hit him?'

'He's a sick fuck, Scarlett, and I won't have him anywhere near you. He's going to get what's coming to him.'

My head jerks in shock at his venom first but the adrenalin coursing through my body has nothing to do with that.

'He didn't touch me, Gregory.'

'I'm not taking any chances with your safety and that's the end of it.'

'I'm not your responsibility.'

There's silence on the line and so many emotions are

mixing in my head, my body doesn't know which to react to first. Part of me really wants to be his responsibility. And the logical part of me remembers that I'm just his lawyer and that's all I'm ever going to be. 'I can't do this without him, Gregory. I'm not qualified enough or good enough to finish this deal alone.'

'You are good enough, Scarlett. I trust you and that's not something I say lightly, believe me.'

With that, he hangs up, leaving me to wallow in my own panic.

So now I have two days to complete the Sale and Purchase Agreement and all the ancillary documents for the takeover. The hostile takeover. Alone.

My client thinks he can trust me but I can't even trust myself. Thursday can't come soon enough. I'll go right back to ordinary Scarlett Heath and I'll forget all about this man who's sent my entire world spinning on a new orbit.

13

My palms are hot and damp as I lay out the completion documents for signature. I have thirty minutes before everyone arrives at Saunders to finalise the deal. Long enough for me to consider and get nervous about how the meeting will go.

It's the first chance I've really had in the last few days to just stop and let my mind absorb what's happening.

I'm about to do something unethical for the first time in my life. But as I lay pens beside each set of documents, I know that it isn't just going through with the deal that's got me on edge. I'm going to come face to face with the reason I feel compelled to go through with it. I'm going to meet Gregory's father, and I can't stand the thought that Gregory is going to be stuck in this room with the man who destroyed his childhood. He protected me with Jack, and it seemed absurd to me that he'd go to those lengths for a woman he hardly knows. Yet I'm standing here now trying to think of any way I can protect him, shield him from his past.

The digital phone in the middle of the conference table

beeps, dragging me from my trance. A receptionist announces Williams and Lawrence have arrived.

My foot is bouncing as I unfold my arms to look at my watch for the third time in less than a minute.

Williams pours himself a glass of water and does the same for Lawrence, who's red in the cheeks and perspiring. A reaction I don't think is the result of him rushing to get here on time. He knows that the man who beat a woman, the man who ruined the life of his partner and stepson and forced them from their home, will be looking him in the eye in just minutes.

Williams's usual easy manner is gone as we stand in the meeting room, waiting. We don't move to sit and we don't speak. Williams intermittently checks the time on his phone. Lawrence stares out of the window at the darkening sky. Tension coats the room like gloss, making us sticky and hot. I pull at each of my nails in turn and roughly rub my hand across the flesh of my throat.

My phone vibrates on the table, making us all jump.

To: Heath, Scarlett
From: Ryans, Gregory
Sent: Thursday 23 Oct 2025 14.58
Subject: Completion

I'm running late but I will be there. Get everything ready to go, I'll be there to sign.
  Gregory Ryans
  CEO Eclectic Technologies

'That's it? That's all he can say?' Clearing my throat, I face the room. 'Gregory's running late; he said we should go on without him and he'll be here to sign as soon as he can.'

There's a knock on the meeting-room door. The three of us shift our attention to the sound.

'I have Mr Pearson and his lawyers for you,' the receptionist announces.

My breaths come shallow and fast and the receptionist makes way for two lawyers. Then my jaw drops as I stare at the six-feet-tall monster stepping into the room. His body shape and the way he holds himself are not dissimilar to Gregory. He has dark features, too, but it's clear Gregory gets his looks from Lara. Pearson flashes me the sort of seedy smile that I'd love to wipe straight off his face.

My fists clench at my sides and I don't return the hands offered to me by Pearson's lawyers because all I can do is glare at Pearson and try not to hurl myself across the room and scratch out his eyes. My body is rocked by profound anger – heart thrumming, fingers trembling. I don't want Gregory to come here. I don't want him to be anywhere near this man.

Pearson speaks with a strong South African accent, holding out a hand. 'Stephen Lawrence, it's been a long time.'

Lawrence doesn't move to accept the hand but he does nod in response. He seems to have composed himself a little now. More than I can say for myself. Williams rolls his jaw and introduces himself with a clipped manner.

Bile rises in my throat as I watch the monster's two suit-clad lawyers explain the documents to him. My mind flashes to the image of the little boy from my dad's hospital and I close my eyes to make him disappear.

I take a seat, my focus held intently on the tabletop, and my hands shakily move the documents from one side of the table to the other for Williams to sign. He eyes me briefly. I know I can't give the game away.

As Williams signs the final document, there's another soft rap on the door.

'I have Mr Ryans for you.'

I swallow sick as it reaches my throat. My fingertips rise to meet my mouth. I want to run towards him and stop him from coming into this room. Chills trace my spine, making the hairs on my neck stand up. My head throbs as my heart pounds. I close my eyes and when I open them again, he's there, in the doorway, a man, a grown-up, taller than Pearson, stronger.

There's noise in the room but my ears hear nothing as I watch Gregory step inside, glaring at his biological father.

'Gregory, you need to sign here,' I manage as I shuffle the documents towards him.

He begins to sign. The Sale and Purchase Agreement is first. I can feel sweat beads forming at my temples.

He pauses after signing the final document and looks up to the devil on the opposite side of the table.

Time stops.

Pearson's face contorts as he realises he's staring into the eyes of his son.

Gregory grins, a sick, sadistic grin, baring his teeth to his father. 'Time to tear it apart.'

Pearson is out of his seat, sending the chair crashing to the ground. Water glasses shatter and documents fly as he launches himself across the table.

'Fucker! You fucker!'

He grabs Gregory's tie, pulling his neck towards him. I can see and feel the rage build in Gregory. His entire body tenses as he clenches his fist and pulls his right arm backwards. Acting on instinct, I wrap both my hands around Gregory's fist as Pearson is pulled back by his lawyers.

'You're better than him,' I say, staring into Gregory's eyes. 'Don't let yourself be like him. Don't let him win.'

The fire in Gregory dissipates.

'Ja, controlled by a woman, huh?' Pearson yells. 'A bitch's boy again, ja? Don't worry, bru, I know exactly how to treat a woman.' He throws his head back on a sardonic laugh.

Gregory pulls from my grasp and dives towards his father; this time, it takes Williams and Lawrence to restrain him.

Pearson's lawyers drag him from the room.

'You'll regret this, boy! And so will your bitch!' he spits as he fights against them, his face red, his words menacing. 'Ja, ja!' Gregory yells, tearing himself away from Williams and Lawrence.

I realise I've been holding my breath. My shaking hands are now rocking my entire body. I fumble around the table and floor, trying to collect the scattered documents into a pile but dropping them. Gregory bends down with me to pick them up from the floor. I close my eyes to stop tears from running out, reaching up a hand to steady myself on a chair as I rest on my hunkers.

Then Gregory's warm palm is on my face. 'Are you okay?'

My lip wobbles as I nod unconvincingly. He strokes my cheek and I lean into the heat of his touch. The warmth of his soft skin making everything feel better.

'I'm fine. Really.'

'We'll be outside,' Williams says sheepishly. 'Thank you for your help, Scarlett. I know what it took for you to do this.'

I nod, my mind drawing a blank on the most appropriate thing to say.

'Thank you, Scarlett,' Lawrence says, stroking my arm as he passes me.

'You should go too, Gregory.'

He looks at me, hurt I think, as if I'm pushing him away.

'I need to tidy all this up now.'

'Have dinner with me tonight.'

I recoil, wanting so much to say yes, but surprised by his request and knowing that I can't. This is the deal. I wanted to help him. I needed to protect him. But it's done. He lives in a different world to me. One that I'm not sure I can be part of.

'Gregory, I told you I was done after this.'

He takes my face in both hands. I close my eyes, anticipating the touch of his lips to mine, but it doesn't come.

'It's a completion dinner, Scarlett. A thank you for closing the transaction, just the same as every other deal and every other client, that's all. Jackson will pick you up from home at eight.'

I eventually open my eyes as the door clicks shut behind him, my body cold from the loss of contact.

14

It's done. I've taken the steps necessary to finalise the deal. Gregory Ryans is about to become the proud owner of a company he hates and his own father's demise.

Now I'm standing in the window of my office, watching people going about their business on the streets below. It's approaching rush hour. If I'm going to dinner, I have to leave soon.

Am I going to dinner?

I fold my arms across my chest. I think it would be best if I didn't. If I walked away.

It wouldn't help to see him again. This is cleaner. 'But...' I practically exhale the word.

I should really go, see Lawrence, Williams and, yes, Gregory, because they *are* clients. Even if they don't come back to me, the legal world is small, we should part ways on good terms.

Then there's Jack. Gregory wiped out my boss and had some part to play in his resignation from the partnership. I want to know what that is.

I move to my desk and slump into my chair as Margaret calls goodnight.

And why does he feel the need to protect me?

And what was that, in the room, before he left? Was he going to kiss me?

Flopping forwards, I drop my head in my arms on my desk. I can't remember ever being so confused.

He's had more than one chance to kiss me and he hasn't. I'm not delusional. He's chosen not to kiss me.

Do I even *want* him to kiss me?

In the few times I've met him, he's lost his temper with me – and just as quickly turned on the charm. He's punched my boss. He's tried to fight Pearson – for good reasons. He's taken something, immorally, underhandedly – although I understand why.

'Damn it, even now I'm defending him.' Closure is what I need.

Glancing at my watch, I quickly shut down my computer and start packing up my tote.

I'm going to put an end to this.

As I head out to the street, I decide to treat myself to a cab instead of the Tube. After the last few days, I deserve a cab.

My phone starts to ring as I slip into the back of the car and relay my address to the driver.

'Sandy, hang on a second.' I clip in my seat belt as the driver pulls out into traffic. 'Sorry, I'm back.'

'Scarlett,' she sobs. 'It's your dad.'

A feeling of terror slithers around my torso and constricts my chest. 'Sandy, what's wrong? What's happened?'

* * *

In less than half an hour, I'm running from the cab, throwing notes at the driver, hurtling into Accident and Emergency.

'I'm looking for my dad, Doctor Phillip Heath,' I say frantically to the girl at reception. I watch, my feet bouncing, my temperature rising, as she types details into her keyboard. 'Please hurry,' I beg.

'Scarlett!'

I turn to Sandy and grab her tightly, pulling her in to me. 'How is he?'

'They won't let me see him because I'm not family,' she says, clearly distressed, her eyes red, wet and swollen.

'What! Excuse me,' I snarl at the receptionist, 'this lady is more *family* than anyone else I know.'

'Sorry but the policy is immediate family only.'

I have to think quickly. 'She's my stepmother. She's lived with my dad for more than twenty years. They're common-law husband and wife.'

The receptionist pouts as her eyes run from Sandy's head to her toes. 'She didn't tell me that. He's in room seven. Go down the corridor, all the way to the end, turn right, go through the double doors and it's about halfway down on the left-hand side. You can both go.'

Thanking her, I take Sandy's hand and we march towards room seven at such a pace, Sandy is forced to remove her burnt-orange, wool coat.

Sandy bursts into tears as soon as she sees the frail man lying before her, bruises already showing on his body. I'm numb, unable to move from the spot where I'm standing. He's propped up on one pillow, his head wrapped in a thick bandage, blood seeping at his temple. He's dressed only in tubes beneath the sheets and his clothes, which have been torn from his body, are piled on the plastic chair at his bedside.

Intravenous drips are strapped into the back of each hand. Tubes pumping oxygen into his tiny, helpless body are wrapped around his head and nestled into his nose, artificially inflating his lungs. His eyes are red and black, swollen shut. A machine beeps, frightening me out of my trance and I step towards him, saying his name. There's no response. The hairs on the back of my neck stand up and goose pimples form on my arms. The shell lying in the bed, the shell wired up to these machines, is not Dad.

A doctor dressed entirely in green enters the tiny prison of a room with a clipboard. His grey hair is in stark contrast to his black skin. 'You must be…?'

'Scarlett, his daughter.'

His large hand is ice cold as it shakes mine.

'This is Sandy, my stepmother.'

'I'm Doctor Jefferson,' he says, turning to shake Sandy's hand.

'How bad is it?' My words are shaky.

'Your father has sustained some superficial wounds and broken his right arm. We can clean the wounds and x-ray the arm but we needed to stabilise him first. When he fell down the stairs, he suffered serious injuries to his head.'

'I think he must have hit it on the stair lift.' Sandy sniffs. 'There was blood.' She shakes her head and retrieves a tissue from inside her jumper sleeve.

The doctor nods as if Sandy has offered the next piece of a jigsaw puzzle and it fits. 'The impact fractured his skull. It caused severe swelling and haemorrhaging.'

An intangible weight forces the air out of my lungs and my hand moves to my open mouth.

'Will he be okay?' Sandy asks through a tissue.

The doctor flashes a look of sympathy to Sandy then speaks

to me like a professional, stoically. 'Scarlett, it's possible that your father may never regain consciousness. We have machines breathing for him. We're keeping him alive to give him a chance to recover.'

'Why do I get the feeling there's a but?'

'Your father's health was already poor. The chances of him recovering are reduced because of that.'

Sandy steps between the doctor and me. 'I don't understand. He will recover?'

The doctor sighs, in the way medics sigh in movies for dramatic effect right before they tell the relatives that their loved one is dead. 'If he does wake up, he will have irreparable brain damage. How bad that will be is a guess at this stage.'

Sandy sobs hysterically into her tissue.

I don't know whether I thank the doctor but he leaves the room. I slip my fingers into my dad's cold, lifeless palm.

He would hate to live like this. Even if he wakes up and goes back to his old life, the life he had just hours ago, I know he hates living that way. But he still has good days. They might be few and far between but they exist. For so long as he has coherent days, days when he looks at me like my dad and I can see and feel how much he loves me, I'm not ready to let him go.

There's an unbearable, mounting pressure in my brow and behind my eyes but I don't cry.

He'll recover. He's my dad.

* * *

Dad is moved to a side room on a ward and registered as an inpatient. I wonder if he'll ever become an outpatient. Sandy and I watch him in his vegetative state whilst auxiliary nurses bring us endless cups of tea – the good old English cure for anything – and give us each a plate with four cheddar triangle sandwiches and half a bag of ready salted crisps.

'The only other spare meals we have are dysphagic but you're welcome to try if you like?' Valarie, the evening nurse, asks.

'Thanks all the same but cheese sandwiches are great,' I say.

Valarie chuckles. 'I thought you might say that.'

The food reminds me where I'm supposed to be.

The completion dinner.

I slip out of the room and I'm grateful for the fresh, crisp air in the hospital car park. I find Gregory's number on my phone and dial, staring up to the dark sky, trying to keep it together.

'Scarlett.'

It's crazy but something in his voice, the sound of my name, brings everything that's happened crashing down on me.

'Scarlett? Are you there? Is everything okay?'

I sniff back the first sign of tears and pinch the bridge of my nose between my finger and thumb. 'Gregory, I'm sorry but I can't make it to dinner.'

'Scarlett, what's wrong?' His tone shifts to rigid concern.

'I, ah, it's my dad. He…' I breathe out slowly and wipe a tear from my cheek. 'My dad has Alzheimer's. He, ah, he fell down the stairs and…' A sob unwittingly breaks from my throat. 'I don't think… He's, he's brain damaged. I don't know if he's going to wake up. I'm sorry. I shouldn't be crying to you. I've got to go. I'm sorry about dinner.'

* * *

I send Sandy to the café on the ground floor of the hospital for a break. It's getting late and we're both exhausted but as long as the nurses keep turning a blind eye to us being here, we won't leave him.

I sit with my dad, having a one-way conversation for almost an hour. There's no change. Once or twice, I imagine him responding to my voice, answering my questions, but if it weren't for his chest subtly rising and falling, he'd be still. The machines that keep him alive beep and whisper in rhythm. A score of death. That's the brutal reality. Dad, the man he was, has been slowly dying. But this can't be the end.

My body goes stiff with both realisation and disgust. Part of me, tiny though it is, is relieved that his suffering might be drawing to an end.

His skin is increasingly pale, almost translucent under the fluorescent lights when we eventually leave. Sandy and I walk out of the main entrance linked together. She carries a plastic bag containing my dad's torn clothes in one hand and holds the lapels of her coat closed at her chest with the other.

'Scarlett, I'm sorry.'

She stares at her shoes as tears drip to the ground at her feet. She looks young and vulnerable. Her coat hangs loose at her waist; the toll of the last few months has led to her weight gradually decreasing. I wish there was an upper limit of tears that one person could shed in a day.

'I left him,' she cries. 'He couldn't feed himself so I tried to help him. He got angry and—'

Throwing my arms around her, pulling her head onto my shoulder, I rest my chin on her soft, black curls. 'It's okay.'

'He spat his soup at me then started screaming that he was hungry. I just – I needed a break. I went out for a walk around the block. I shouldn't have left him for so long.'

'Shh.'

Her sobs become uncontrollable, taking over her entire

body. 'When I got back... it was too late. He was at the bottom of the stairs. I thought, I thought—'

'Hey, enough!' I say sternly, pulling back and holding her shoulders, forcing her to look at me. 'This is not your fault, Sandy. You're not his nurse. I should've never let you take on so much responsibility. It's me who should be apologising.'

'Scarlett.' The voice is one I recognise. Deep, male, wary. 'Can I take you home?'

'Jackson. How did you know we were here?' I say, brushing tears from my cheeks.

'We worked it out. Mr Ryans insisted that you have a lift home whenever you need it.'

I don't have the energy to refuse and let Jackson lead Sandy into the back of the Mercedes. He gently wraps one arm around her shoulder and takes the burden off her legs by tucking her other arm in his. She's still sniffling when she sits onto the back seat. Jackson pulls her seat belt across her and fastens it into the holster, then he turns to offer me a hand.

'I'm okay, thank you,' I say, genuinely touched by his compassion for Sandy.

When I climb into the car, I fold Sandy's cold hand in mine.

Jackson's phone rings and he draws up the black glass divider between the front and back of the Mercedes as he punches the button for the speakerphone.

'Greg, I've got them.'

'Good. What about the other thing? Did you find anything on Jack Jones?'

I sit forwards to listen but the partition reaches the roof and I can't hear a word. I'm too weary to deal with work and Jack Jones right now. I rest my chin on Sandy's head and close my eyes.

* * *

Jackson wakes us and helps Sandy out of the car. Carrying my dad's torn clothes, Sandy's handbag and the documents from my meeting at Eclectic – which feels like more than just a few hours ago – he walks alongside Sandy as I lead us to the house.

'I think I'm going to make a cup of tea,' Sandy says. 'Geoffrey, would you like tea?'

'That would be lovely.'

I hang my coat on the stand by the door then stare at the bloodstains – on the chair lift at the bottom of the stairs, on the wood floor, sprayed on the wall. 'I'm going to clean this up.'

'Would you like me to do that?' Jackson asks.

'No. Thank you. You've already done enough.'

As Sandy and Jackson head to the kitchen, I make my way upstairs, my eyes taking in each drop of blood. I follow them into my dad's dark and empty bedroom. I flick on the light and my eyes are immediately drawn to the soup bowl cast into the middle of the floor, red sauce spilled across the carpet. Dad's small lamp has also fallen to the floor by the bedside table, the bulb shattered. The bedside table is out of place from its normal position parallel to the bed. A water glass rests on its side in the crevasse between the table and the wall.

I take a step back, absorbing the scene. The duvet is in a messed bundle, as if it's been flung from one side of the bed to the other. I wonder if that's what has knocked Dad's favourite picture out of place at the opposite side of his bed. It's a framed photograph of Dad, Sandy and me on Brighton Pier, each of us holding candy floss. It's always positioned where he can see it, a perfect angle, just so. Now it faces away from his bed.

I rest my back against the wall and slide to the floor, taking in everything that's wrong with this tableau, rubbing my hands up and down my suddenly ice-cold arms.

'Are you okay?'

'Jesus! Jackson, you scared me.'

He steps into the room and turns his head almost in sequence around the same evidence I just witnessed.

'He struggled,' Jackson says matter of factly.

'He was weak,' I tell him, rising to stand by his side, my arms folded across my chest.

Jackson continues to stare at the bed. 'How weak?'

I shrug. 'Very weak. Struggled to feed himself, clean himself, walk even.' As I say the words, my brows scrunch and the subtle shift in the air makes me think Jackson is having the exact same thoughts as me. 'In theory, he'd have struggled to throw his bowl or even cast his duvet to the other side of the bed.'

Jackson drags his fingers along his jaw but doesn't speak.

'And if he couldn't do those things, I'm standing here wondering how he could've made it to the stairs alone.' My head starts to pound and a heavy shiver moves through my bones. Sandy said she was outside. I drop my head into my hands and rub my fingers roughly into my eye sockets. Of course she was. This is insane. He obviously *did* struggle to get out of bed; that's why everything is such a mess.

15

I'm nestled into the corner of the sofa under the lounge lamp, my knees curled up in my leggings to make a table for my sheets of case law, when my dad walks through the front door. I hear him place his keys on the side table and drop his bag by the hat stand, then make his way to the lounge.

'Hello, darling. You're still up.'

'Reading case law for Torts,' I say, holding up the documents on my lap. 'Sandy left your supper in the oven.'

'Is she in bed?'

'Yes. She fell asleep watching a movie.'

'Just us then.'

Dad turns a crystal glass from the bar table the right way up and pours himself a glass of his single malt Scotch from a decanter.

'Would you like one?' he asks.

'I'm okay, thanks.'

'It's nice coming home to see you in the holidays. I miss you in term time.' He takes a seat on the sofa next to me. He leaves his coat and scrubs at work but I can still smell the hospital corridors in his beige cords and caramel jumper. 'Torts, eh? Negligence.'

'Mmm-hmm, not my favourite. I'm reading a clinical negligence case just now, actually.'

'Duty of care, professional skill?'

'Yep.'

He takes a small sip of his Scotch and sighs heavily.

'Are you okay, Dad?'

'Yes, sweet pea, I'm just tired. It's been a long shift.'

I put my case law on the coffee table and lean into him, resting my head on his shoulder. 'You've got sad eyes, not tired eyes. You've come straight in and poured yourself a neat Scotch, and even though the house smells of Sandy's pastry, you haven't even gone to look at the pie in the oven.'

He wraps an arm around my shoulder and kisses my brow. 'Do you remember Mr Harrington, Gareth Harrington?'

Of course I remember. One of the few patients my dad has ever referred to by first name. Gareth Harrington has been in Dad's care for almost a year and a half. He was diagnosed with an aggressive brain tumour that was wrapped around his spinal cord. He was told he had six months to live.

'The man that no one else would agree to operate on,' I say.

Gareth has two young daughters and a wife. When Dad looked at the scans, he knew all he could offer would be time, but he told the family that he would try, if that was what they wanted. They begged him to operate.

'Yes, that's him. He's back in hospital now.'

'He's sick again?'

'I guess he was never better. Not really. It was never possible to remove the whole tumour, but it's grown back and there's nothing more I can do.'

'Is he palliative?'

'I'm afraid so. He might have a week.'

'I'm sorry to hear that. I know you like him and his family.'

Dad rests his chin on my head. 'He's stuck in a bed. He can't hold a conversation and today, the nurses couldn't get him onto a commode so they're taking his food away in the morning.' With a gulp, he drains the remainder of his Scotch and rests the empty glass on his knee. 'Sometimes, I wish we were like dogs. The way it all ends for dogs, it's humane. When it's the end and the dog is ill, we don't pretend. We do what's fair. We recognise that they're in pain, that they have no quality of life, that they don't want to be around any more and we make a decision to cuddle them whilst we put them to sleep and send them to a better world, a world where they won't hurt.'

I turn my head and kiss his shoulder. 'What you did for Mr Harrington was humane, Dad. You gave him a gift that no one else was willing to give him. You gave him time. Time to play with his daughters, time to say goodbye properly.'

'I wish I could help him now, Scarlett.'

The next day, Dad came home from work. Gareth had died in his bed, peaceful, with his family around him.

16

The hospital is even grimmer than last night, if that's possible. The grey, overcast sky shadows the corridors. Sandy and I are amongst the first visitors and if it weren't for the occasional laughter of the nurses at their station, my dad's ward would be deathly quiet.

'Hi, Dad,' I whisper, kissing his scalp.

The deposits in his catheter bag are dark and there's a yellow cast to his skin that I haven't seen before. I've called in a working-from-home day, but I have no desire to look at work. Sandy and I nestle into two seats on either side of my dad's bed. We sit and we watch him. We take it in turns to make a coffee trip or a toilet trip, never leaving him alone. We exchange pleasantries with the nurses as they pass through to check on their patient. One nurse tells us the doctor will be doing his rounds in the early afternoon and he intends to discuss Dad's condition with us.

Amanda turns up on her lunch hour with two big bags of goodies: sandwiches, muffins, chocolate bars, pastries. A nurse brings in a third chair and Amanda tells ridiculous stories that seem to keep the three of us laughing continuously for an hour. She tells Sandy about her new casual relationship with Williams as if Sandy is her best friend. I cringe, hoping my dad can't hear. 'Anyway, you've had your head in files all week but don't think I've forgotten that you never told me what happened after the charity gala,' she says through a bite of brownie. 'It didn't go unnoticed that you and Gregory left together right after that steamy dance. They didn't even say goodbye, you know, Sandy.'

Sandy raises a brow above the walnut whip that's half in and half out of her mouth. She and Amanda share a cheeky giggle.

'Gregory didn't come back?' I ask.

Amanda shakes her head as she munches down on a double chocolate chip cookie.

I have to fight from closing my eyes and rolling my head back, remembering *that* dance and the press of his lips against the skin of my neck in the hollow by my collarbone.

'I honestly can't tell you where he went but we didn't leave together. We had a row and I left. I thought he would've carried on with the party.'

'You had a row? But you looked so into each other. He couldn't get enough of you. At one point, Sandy, I thought he was going to take her right there on the table in front of everyone.'

'Bloody hell, Amanda!' I exclaim.

Sandy laughs heartily through the last bite of her walnut whip.

'Oh come on, Scarlett, we're not three years old,' Amanda says, rolling her eyes and wiping chocolate remnants from the side of her mouth.

'Still, you can't say things like that. What if my dad can hear you? Pass me some of those goodies.'

Amanda throws a cookie from her side of the bed to mine.

'So, you had a fight, what about?' Amanda probes.

I want to tell her but I can't. I can't betray Gregory and I can't tell her that I willingly closed that deal, knowing what I know.

'Something and nothing.'

I walk Amanda out to her car after lunch, turning on my phone for the first time today. As I'm waving her off, I listen to my voicemails, ignoring all but one.

'Scarlett, I didn't get a chance to say how sorry I am about your dad. I can only imagine how you're feeling and I'd like to help in any way I can. I thought, if you'd let me, I could take you out tonight. Make up for last night and take your mind off things. I'd like to do this, Scarlett. Please.'

What would you make of Gregory Ryans, Dad?

I knew or hoped somewhere inside me that Gregory wasn't offering the usual completion meeting last night. The norm would be all clients, Lawrence, Williams *and* Gregory, going for dinner. Toasting the latest addition to their empire. I think part of me wanted him to be offering dinner alone, just the two of us, and the other part of me wouldn't dare to think it. He's insanely attractive and wealthy; he could have any woman he wants. Sure, that's part of it. The other part is that, I knew last night and I know now, if I'm alone in a room with that man, client or not, I won't be able to resist the effect he has on me.

My reasons for saying yes last night still stand. I have questions to ask him.

And, God, I want to go and see that face, drown in that scent, be close to the heat of his body again.

'Just go,' Sandy snaps when I'm back at my dad's bedside, my legs crossed beneath me in the chair.

I stop twisting my bottom lip in my fingers. 'No.' I sound much more emphatic than I feel.

'You heard Doctor Jefferson; there's no chance he's going to wake up today. There's no sign of improvement.'

'Which is just another reason why I shouldn't go. How can I go out for dinner when my dad is half—' I stop myself short of admitting that final word.

'We've got to leave here sometime, Scarlett, and what else are you going to do except mope around the house?'

'I'm not going.'

'If your dad thought you weren't living your life because of him, he'd be so cross with you.'

'Sandy, I... It's not just that.'

'It'll take your mind off all of this. It's just dinner.'

The thought that dinner could lead to me feeling his touch, feeling his lips against my skin again, makes me crave everything about him. I know it would mean more to me than *just* dinner.

Sandy reaches a hand to my shoulder. 'Trust your instincts.'

17

Jackson pulls up before I've even finished my hair. Half the curls are pinned loosely to the back of my head, the other half still hang impatiently around my shoulders. As I pin frantically, I consider the two dresses hanging on my wardrobe, both black, one tight fitting to the knee with a high neck and open back, the other with tiny straps and a loose gather at the chest, also with a drooping open back.

At least five minutes pass as I hurriedly finish my updo. Hearing the doorbell ring adds to the butterflies in my chest and the anxiety churning low in my abdomen.

Sandy opens the door and boisterously jokes with Jackson downstairs. By the time I've added the finishing touch to my make-up – poppy-red Clarins lipstick – and spritzed myself in Flower Bomb, another five minutes have passed. I take a pair of black tights from my drawer and sit on my bed but before they reach my knees, I pull them off and swap them for stockings. I opt for the thin-strap dress and slip my feet into an uncomfortable pair of black, calf-leather Jimmy Choos: possibly the most extravagant purchase of my life.

'I'm so sorry, Jackson,' I say, interrupting the surprisingly flirtatious conversation taking place in the hallway.

Both Jackson and Sandy turn sharply, as if they've been caught in the act. Sandy hands me my tailored, black winter coat and tells me to have fun as I pull the waist belt tight. I give her a cursory *what-was-that*? look before leaving the house.

'I doubt Gregory will be thrilled with my timekeeping,' I say to Jackson as he holds open the door to the empty back seat.

'Somehow, I think you'll be forgiven,' Jackson says, buckling himself in.

'Where are we going?' I ask.

Jackson shrugs and chuckles. Something, or rather someone, seems to have put him in a peculiarly jovial mood.

Just before seven-thirty, we roll to a stop alongside a red carpet. My eyes trace gold railings from the pavement up to the theatre entrance. There, on the top step, Gregory is waiting, legs parted, shoulders back, hands tucked into the trouser pockets of his dinner suit, separating the tails of his jacket from the fastened button at the waist.

Jackson winks as he opens the door and gives me a hand out of the Mercedes.

I can't take my eyes off Gregory. Everything else in the world disappears as I get lost in this perfect man.

He walks down the steps and kisses my cheek. His lips linger against my skin. The sensation exactly as I've replayed countless times in my head. I lean into his kiss, wishing I could feel his mouth on mine. When I open my eyes, he's gazing right back at me. I've never wanted anything more in my life.

'You're beautiful,' he whispers.

My insides defy the concept of gravity.

He traces one finger down the side of my face to my chin, never dropping his gaze from mine. I try to swallow my insatiable need to touch what lies beneath his suit, to have his naked body take over mine the way I've imagined. He gives me a half, knowing smile. I'm defenceless against my own desire.

'Some completion meeting when we're the only two people here, Mr Ryans.'

'I thought you wouldn't mind if we celebrate closing the deal alone tonight.'

'Presumptuous,' I tease, raising a brow.

'Indeed,' he says, his half-smile still arrogantly toying with me. Delicious. 'Come on, you kept me waiting; the show's about the start.'

I shake my head and ask myself as much as him, 'Why can't I seem to say no to you?'

'I'm not the kind of man who takes no for an answer. Especially not from you.'

But it's not true. When I've refused him, he has accepted it. It just hasn't stopped him from asking again.

He steps to one side, gesturing for me to move into the theatre, and rests his hand at the bottom of my back. A small move that makes me internally scream at all the sensitive sites in my body to *back the hell down*.

'What are we going to see?'

'The new Dame Judi Dench play.'

There's a distinct air of cocky self-satisfaction about him but I'm too delighted to care. This is the escape I need.

An attendant leads us into the box Gregory has reserved. A bottle of Dom Perignon with two glasses and a selection of canapés are waiting for us on a low, dark wood table between two velvet chairs. I manage to catch a glimpse of the flavours written on small white place cards before the lights turn down.

The band strikes up and there's rapturous applause when Dame Judi Dench, followed by Jude Law, enters the stage for the opening scene. My grin is so big, I feel like Julia Roberts. Gregory watches me as I clap loudly from the edge of my seat.

Leaning in to his ear, I whisper, 'This is amazing, thank you so much.'

He snaps his head round to face me, his lips almost brushing against mine, his minty breath drifting into my mouth. My stomach leaps. I want him to do this. He lifts my chin with his index finger and my lips open wider, my tongue braced, ready for his taste. Something about the dark room full of people increases my need for the forbidden touch. His thumb trails my lips, then he audibly swallows any desire he might have had and hands me a glass of champagne. He clinks my glass with his and turns to the stage, leaving me feeling utterly confused, disoriented and desperate.

Have I imagined everything?

* * *

'I can't believe you remembered,' I say as the applause for the end of the first act dies down.

'I think I remember everything you say to me and the exact manner in which you say it. Some of it I wish I didn't remember.'

'Why?'

He turns in his seat and leans forwards across his parted knees towards me. 'Because your body's reactions to me tell me one thing but your words tell me something else. It's... perplexing.'

I almost laugh at the thought that he can't see right through me. He crosses one leg over the other and leans back in his seat, clasping his hands and raising his index fingers to his lips, studying me in an almost mocking fashion.

Those fingers. Those lips.

The walls of my sex clench and I'm both grateful for and pissed off by the attendant who steps between us to top up our champagne and take away our empty plates. I cross my legs, locking my thighs tightly, wishing I could read his mind.

We sit in this standoff, for my part charged and bewildered, until the attendant returns with replenished canapés.

'So that we're clear, I'm thinking that I'm hungry, so I'm going to take a canapé.' I reach for a strawberry, dipping it in the ramekin of melted dark chocolate. He watches me as I sit back and re-cross my legs. I don't know what's coming down the river but my chips are in. I run my tongue slowly up the side of the strawberry, swirling around the tip, savouring the chocolate sauce, and revel in the subtle loosening of his jaw and the darkening of his irises.

I wrap my lips around the head of the berry and slide my teeth through the moist flesh. Before the second half reaches my lips, he leans forwards, clasping his hand around mine. He sees my chips. Then he raises me, placing his mouth over the berry and closing his mouth around my fingertips. I watch as he slides his lips to the end of my fingers, sucking the tips, turning his tongue the way he might lick my clit.

I fold.

The lights dim for the start of act two. Gregory once again flashes a knowing smirk and turns towards the stage.

My body is left pulsing in places I didn't think it could pulse in public.

* * *

Jackson is waiting outside for us at the end of the show. Gregory walks around the car as he usually does and Jackson opens the door to the back seat for me.

'How was the show?' Jackson asks.

'The first act was fantastic,' I say.

'And the second?'

'I've no idea.'

I sit into the back seat, startled to find Gregory next to me. We drive to the restaurant in silence. I want to speak but I can only think of pointless small talk. His body is too close to mine. Those lips are next to me and all I can think of is what I'd like them to be doing, where I'd like them to be. The tension in the car is unbearable. Arriving at the restaurant is a relief.

We're greeted by a short man with an Italian accent who I assume is the restaurant manager from his black suit and sparkling gold badge that reads *Amerigo*. 'Good evening, Mr Ryans, how wonderful it is to see you. I have reserved our finest table for you and your guest this evening.'

Amerigo bobs from one foot to the other as he leads us to our table, like his hips are tired from working until after ten already.

As is seemingly customary, Amerigo is overly familiar with Gregory, full of chatter and smiles. He places us in a booth, closed off from the sight of other guests but with a fantastic view of the city.

'Do you ever go to restaurants on ground level?' I whisper to Gregory.

He grins smugly as he lifts his hands to allow Amerigo to place a napkin across his lap.

'Would you like water, Mr Ryans?'

'Please.'

'And your wine?'

Gregory considers me as he rubs his index finger and thumb along the line of his chin. 'The lady will pick the wine.'

Amerigo initially looks completely stunned but quickly recovers and hands me an open wine list. I accept the menu, playfully scowling at Gregory.

'We'll take two glasses of Dom Perignon brut while we look over the menu, please. I'll choose wine for dinner once we've made our food choices.'

Amerigo nods and leaves us alone in the booth. The tension from the theatre instantly returns. It's a relief to see Gregory remove his jacket and tie and open the top two buttons of his shirt. My eyes lock onto the few fine hairs exposed on Gregory's chest. I want more.

The sommelier brings two glasses of Dom Perignon. I'm vaguely aware that he's making comments about the wine maker and the vintage. I take the opportunity to coax my eyes away from Gregory and inhale deeply, trying to push oxygen to my clouded mind.

'Have you decided?' Amerigo asks, holding a white pad of paper and a small pen. When he arrived at the table is anyone's guess.

'I. Oh. I haven't.' I clear my throat but it brings no more cohesion to my words.

'Actually, Scarlett,' Gregory interjects, 'I know what's good here. Perhaps I could choose for us?'

I nod and take a sip of the cool, effervescent champagne. I don't hear the exchange between Gregory and Amerigo.

When Amerigo leaves, we're alone again. Closing my eyes, I take another sip of bubbles. Desire wells in my throat. I'm out of control. Every logical thought I've had about why I shouldn't want him has escaped me. I have to have him.

My glass is gently tugged from my lips and guided to the

table. I open my eyes to find Gregory's face unbearably close to mine, our thighs touching under the table. He sighs and the scent of his breath, cool and fresh, pervades my senses.

'I'm going to kiss you,' he whispers.

My entire body tenses and my breath abandons my lungs.

His palm holds my cheek. His thumb traces the line of my jaw, resting at my chin, and my body yearns for him. He lifts my head to face him and leans closer to me, like he did in the theatre, like he did at Saunders, like he did at the gala. I don't think I'll survive another withdrawal.

'Please.'

His eyes dart to mine, impeding the beating of my heart.

Finally, his lips are on mine. His kiss is soft, gentle and teasing. He nips my lower lip in his and I squirm closer to him, my hips tilt towards him as I groan into his mouth. It's everything I imagined and more, so much more.

His full lips cover mine and my tongue brushes his front teeth, receiving a moan from him that resonates right where I want him. My fingers grab his hair at the nape of his neck and his kiss intensifies. It's rough, carnal and exactly how I need it. With a firm hand on my lower back, he pulls my body towards him, my leg crossing his beneath the table, my back bowing towards him. I finally breathe, a heavy, hot pant as our tongues entwine.

A waiter feigns a cough at the tableside. 'Your starters.'

Instantly shifting away from him and pressing my back into the booth, I'm hot, blushing and wired like a compressed spring, ready to explode. I smile meekly at the waiter as he places a deconstructed sushi plate in front of me. Sashimi salmon, crisp rice, soy jelly cubes and wasabi globules. It looks fantastic. Another waiter places a similar plate in front of Gregory.

The sommelier immediately replaces the waiters at our table and discusses our bottle of wine. *Did I pick that or did he?* Once again, the sommelier's efforts are entirely wasted on my fuzzy mind.

I've never craved sex, never ached with the need to have a man inside me. Until now.

Staring at the reflection of the restaurant in the floor-to-ceiling window, I wonder if the other guests could see *that* kiss. I wonder if they think Gregory Ryans is mine. The restaurant is busy, each table full of finely dressed diners in twos, fours and sixes. Everyone looks happy, conversations flow, animated hand gestures dance and laughing heads are thrown back but no words are decipherable. Candlelight flickers in the window and wait staff float between tables carrying white plates of various sizes, wine buckets, champagne and bread rolls. Soft jazz notes play in the background, well suited to the dimmed, purple lighting and cloths, I think. I look to my already empty starter plate, then at Gregory's. We've both eaten like we were Oliver Twist and there was definitely no opportunity for more. We laugh at the already empty plates. It's a short release, pent up. Once our dishes are taken, Gregory removes his cufflinks and rolls up his sleeves two turns. They move further up his smooth, tanned skin as he reaches for his glass and I notice three small imperfections on this otherwise aesthetically flawless man. With a troubled expression, he watches me across the rim of his wine glass.

'They're cigarette burns,' he says.

'Sorry, I didn't mean to stare. Did he do this to you?'

Gregory doesn't respond but the tightening of his jaw tells me the answer.

'Have you ever really hated anyone, Scarlett? I mean hated someone so much that the thought of what you could do to them scares you because no matter how bad it might be, you just don't care?'

'I thought I did.'

'You thought you did?'

I feel my brows furrow. It's something I've never admitted before but Gregory seems to have an ability to draw out sides of me that I didn't know were buried. 'My mother left my dad when I was a child. The first time I realised she wasn't coming back, I wanted to, I don't know, hurt her maybe, the way she hurt Dad.'

'And you don't feel like that any more?'

I shake my head. 'I've grown up, moved on, and I guess she's become a smaller part of my life. I still feel angry when I think of my dad alone. He should have someone. He shouldn't be going through this illness by himself.'

'He's got you.'

'He has. He has me and he has Sandy but it can't be the same for him. He hasn't really been with anyone since my mother, that I know of. I think everyone deserves to love and be loved in return, don't you?'

He stares at me but doesn't respond. It's the kind of look I want to box and keep forever.

'You know, Scarlett, I would have understood if you hadn't wanted to come here tonight. For many reasons. Your dad being one.'

'I thought about not coming but I'm glad I did. Since I've been with you, I've forgotten everything else for a while. I like that you can take me out of my head, if only temporarily.'

'That's a feeling I understand.'

A waiter places a main course of steamed fish dressed with scallops and langoustine in front of us. Gregory glances from his plate to me and back to his plate.

'It smells delicious,' I say.

'It does,' he says without picking up his knife and fork.

'Aren't you hungry?' I ask.

'Starving.'

Everything south of my waistline pulses in response to him. I can see him consider moving closer to me but he hesitates, looking questioningly at my untouched plate of food. I inch it away from me with the tips of my fingers.

'I've lost my appetite for food,' I whisper.

Amerigo is at our table in seconds.

'Charge my account,' Gregory says.

* * *

Jackson is waiting outside but doesn't step out of the car.

'How does he always know what you're doing?' I croak through my dry throat.

Gregory smiles, a delectable half-curl of his lips. He reaches to open the door to the back of the Mercedes and I press my hand over his, keeping the door closed.

'Look,' I say, pointing to the clear, starlit sky. 'It's so rare there's a night like this in the city.'

'It's really something,' he says.

His eyes fall from the stars to meet mine and he gently turns me, pressing my back against the side of the car. He tucks a loose tendril back behind my ear. I absorb every line and curve of his face as it moves toward me. His lips meet mine with a full embrace. It's like a blackout. All I can think and breathe is Gregory.

'You're amazing,' he whispers.

'Kiss me again.'

My soul ignites with the second touch of his lips. His mouth moves roughly against mine until my body is begging him to take me. My rise to him and I can feel his hard length against my stomach, the final confirmation I need that the attraction is not just mine.

'I think we ought to step inside the car,' he says.

'Why? Has something come up?' I cheekily bite my bottom lip.

He smirks – a break from wearing his impenetrable super-power – as he opens the car door and ushers me inside.

The privacy screen is up, shielding us from Jackson, or him from our furious kiss, but when we hear his voice over the speaker, Gregory pulls his fingers away from the lace garter of my stockings.

'Ah, where would you like me to go?'

Gregory looks to me for confirmation then tells Jackson to take us to his place.

'Naturally, you live in the Shard,' I joke as the Mercedes drives into the underground car park of one of the tallest build-ings in the world. Jackson holds open the door for me and tells Gregory he's going to check on things in the basement – guy code for, *I know exactly what your intentions are and I'll leave you to it.*

Gregory nods, then takes my hand and leads me into the lift vestibule.

When the lift doors eventually open, we step inside, where Gregory types a code then presses the button for floor sixty-four. I run my hand from his shoulder blade to the small of his back and down to his thickset thigh. He turns, pushing me up against the lift wall and attacks me with his kiss. I return the ferocity, showing him everything I've felt and suppressed since that first pitch in his boardroom. The looks, the touches, the sense of something in the air when we're together that awakens a passion deep in my core. His hips flex into mine and he pulls my body into him.

It's game over, Scarlett Heath.

I let go of my lines, my black-and-white world, and I savour the feel of our bodies welding together.

The lift announces we've reached our destination: the sky.

Dim mood lighting automatically turns on when Gregory opens the large, white double doors into the enormous main room. It's a bachelor pad, no mistaking. There's a lingering scent of hardwood floor polish and leather interiors. The brilliant-white walls contrast the black, leather furniture and the hanging art is abstract, emotionless. The lounge is a huge open space with a breakfast bar and kitchen to one end, two doors to adjoining rooms at the other and a spiral staircase in the middle, close to the door where I'm standing. One black, marble sculpture of a naked torso rests on a tall, coliseum-style podium, a feature piece almost central in the room.

The night's stars are visible through the wall of windows that runs the periphery of the apartment, giving a panoramic view of the lights of London's bridges and skyscrapers, a burnt-orange dot-to-dot over the city.

'It feels like stepping into a dream,' I say, walking to the vast glass panes, towering above the bustling city. 'You really do love the high life.'

The rising hairs on my skin tell me he's moved closer to me. I turn to him, primal lust whirring inside me.

'It makes me feel closer to God,' he says with a smirk.

'Makes you feel closer to God or makes you feel like you *are* God? It's an important distinction.'

His smirk dissipates and he's staring at me, deadly serious. 'Why's that?'

'Because you don't look like you're having very holy thoughts right now.'

'Are you?'

'I'm having the most ungodly thoughts I've ever had in my life.'

I turn back to the window to shield my blushes. He steps behind me, so close that I can feel his heated breath on my neck. He takes my bag from my hand and casts it onto the sofa. His firm pecs press against my back and he kisses the skin behind my ear, down to the hollow between my collarbones.

'Tell me.'

I lean into his chest, reaching my arms back, dragging my fingers through his hair.

'Tell me what you want, Scarlett.'

He trails kisses, one after another, down my neckline to the top of my back. I watch his faint reflection in the glass, following his every move.

'I want you.' Admitting it aloud sends heat exactly where I want him to be.

He traces a finger down the length of my spine and follows it with his lips.

I whimper under his touch. I wanted him to take me out of my head. He's doing it.

He pushes the thin straps of my dress over my arms, the material falling to the floor, pooling at my feet. His hands and arms are warm against my bare waist, exposed in only a stocking ensemble and heels.

'Where do you want me, baby?'

I reach behind me, digging my nails into his thighs.

Holding my chin in his hand, he forces me to look at our reflection. 'Show me where you want me.'

I move my hand over his on my stomach and slide it south

until his fingers cup me over my lace thong, all the while watching the erotic sight of two strangers in the window. It feels bold, brazen, another moment that's far outside my comfort zone. Yet, I groan as he firms his hold, pressing my swollen lips against my clit, sending thrills through my core.

With his hands on my shoulders, he turns me to him, Gregory Ryans, in his fine tailoring with his stunning intensity. The way his hungry eyes take in each curve of my body makes me feel more woman than I've ever felt. More confident. My fingers trace the line of his jaw and I press my chest against him, feeling the delicious chafe of his shirt against my stiff nipples. Our lips crash against each other fiercely and I swallow the vibrations of his moan when his tongue meets mine.

We match each other stroke for stroke, lapping, sucking and biting frantically. My need to have him throbs between my legs. The touch of his warm, wet mouth on my neck has me throwing my head back, baring my skin to him, wanting more. He cups my naked breasts in his hands as his tongue moves across my collarbone and I gasp as he tweaks the hard tips between his finger and thumb. Then he moves his mouth over the sensitive skin, sucking hard before pulling the end through his teeth on an animalistic growl. The wicked sensation of pain and delicious pleasure makes my back arch, my breaths heavy.

'You like that.'

I run my tongue across my thirsty lips. 'It's news to me, too.'

My hands grope his toned chest. Impatient to see what's beneath his clothes and feel his skin on mine, I push his blazer to the floor. Looking down to where the fabric of his trousers is pulled tight across his bulging package, I loosen his belt then the button of his trousers with trembling fingers. My boldness rises with every move and sound of satisfaction I drag from him.

Unfastening his shirt, I trail slow kisses from his chest to his navel, finding the strength to maintain control. I push the smooth cotton back and down his arms, taking a moment to appreciate his sublime, lean torso, his toned muscles beneath olive skin, the trail of hair leading to exactly where I want to go.

Every one of my senses is in overdrive. This can't be real. This apartment. This man. He wants *me* and in this moment, I think there's no price I wouldn't pay to have him. Nothing I wouldn't give.

He traces my collarbone with his lips, his tongue sweetly licking my charged skin as he kicks off his shoes. A breathy moan leaves his chest as I slip my hand inside his trousers, cupping his solidness over his tight boxers. The sight of him, looking at me through lust-filled, hooded eyes drives the muscles inside my sex crazy. Keeping my eyes on his, I bend to my knees, taking his trousers down with me, and remove his socks. His chest rises with a heavy breath and he leans his head back. I take his boxers in my teeth and slowly lift them from his hips, praying I can pull off this move. Relieved, surprised and turned on beyond belief when his hard cock is exposed.

It matches his body – long, wide. I have no idea whether I'll be able to accept it but anticipation has me licking my lips. His index finger lifts my chin so I'm looking into his seductive browns. Following my gaze, I stand, rubbing my pelvis against his shaft as I rise. The tip of his length grazes my clit, driving me to a place beyond desperation.

My head is spinning and the only thing that's clear to me is how much I need him to fill me.

'Like what you see?' His words are deep, sultry.

'Fuck me, Gregory.'

In a swift change of pace, he pushes me back against the window and pins my wrists above my head with one hand.

With the entire city beneath us, he kisses me passionately, pressing his body against mine, growling as his hips circle against my pelvis. My legs part to allow his erection between them. With his free hand, he feels his way through my labia, his movement smooth against the slick flesh, and teases my taut knot with the head of his cock. Then he holds my face with a hand on my neck and takes my mouth, his tongue swirling around mine with the same purposeful, controlled rhythm of his gyrating hips.

Everything that attracted me to him – power, danger, control – I want to unravel. I want to be the woman who takes a wrecking ball to his shield. Cliché doesn't make it any less true.

Unlike in every other part of my life, I want to lose myself. I want to relent control to him. 'Now, please.'

He traces his fingertips down my body, every nerve ending tingling in their wake, and cups my sex, stroking his fingers through my centre, driving the air from my lungs. He stares deep into my eyes as he moves his fingers to his mouth and sucks my wetness from them the way he took the juice of my strawberry just hours ago.

My hips rise at the sight of him indulging in my taste. I'm close to orgasm just watching him.

'You taste so fucking good, Scarlett.'

My eyes close and I swallow, trying to suppress the burning need. Then two fingers thrust inside me and as my breaths come thick and fast, his thumb moves over my clit, lifting me to the brink.

'You're drenched.'

I open my eyes, watching him through the haze of ferocious hunger. 'I want you inside me.'

I've never uttered those words or been so direct about my intent in my life.

I've never known Gregory, or anyone like him.

He withdraws his fingers and crashes his lips against me. 'I need to get something.'

He pushes back from me, leaving me craving more. I'm too desperate. Too close to the edge. Grabbing his forearm, I pull him to me. 'I can't wait. I'm clean and on birth control.'

It's reckless. It's not like me. But I have to have him now.

'Fuck.' He growls into my mouth, grinding his pelvis against me. 'Do you know what a fucking turn on it is to know I'm going to feel you around me with nothing between us?'

I push my fingers into his hair and pull, yanking him to my mouth, my tongue attacking his. 'Now.'

He lifts my leg to his waist. 'I'm clean, too, but not on birth control.'

I smirk but my amusement is short lived. With one hard, punishing drive, he crashes into me, reaching the end of me with a strike of decadent pain. I throw my head back on a cry of satisfaction as he consumes me, mind and body, transcending euphoria.

'Jesus, Scarlett, you're so tight.' He holds us still. 'Give yourself a chance to adjust.' His words are a croak, betraying his outward control.

I look down to see where he's entered me, the sight so erotic, my muscles clamp down on his erection, held on the precipice.

Leaning forwards, my teeth find his chest. Then he begins to move, withdrawing slowly, stroking the hidden spot that no other man has ever found. He crashes forwards, the shock driving me wild, my panting breaths drawing my world to a blur. As he pulls out and pounds back into me, his breaths come hot and heavy against my neck.

'Fuck, Scarlett. You're so beautiful.'

I wrap my tongue around his and groan into his mouth as the next blow comes. He lifts my leg higher on his waist, the angle pulling him against the most sensitive part of my wall. My hips rise to meet each thrust and my back bows, every muscle in my body tensing.

'Gregory, I'm going to come.'

He bites my neck. 'I know baby, I can feel you.' His words and relentless rhythm build me to climax. His solid cock swells inside me, then I can feel him starting to pulse as my muscles spasm around him.

'Gregory!'

He withdraws and smashes into me again. 'Let go, baby. Give it up for me.'

My world spirals out of control as my orgasm takes over my body. As my head crashes back against the window, I call out his name and feel him release, pouring himself into me on a round of expletives. My hips rock of their own volition, squeezing everything from him, exhausting me.

'I didn't know it could be like that,' I mumble into his shoulder.

I might have fought it but now I've had him. I've broken all my rules and there'll be no going back from Gregory Ryans.

He lowers my leg to the ground and rests his chin against my temple. I pull his body into mine and kiss his neck, tasting the salt of his sweat as our breathing calms. He turns his head and places his lips on mine, then runs his fingers down the side of my body, leaving goose pimples in their wake.

'That was worth the wait,' I tell him.

'I'm not even close to done with you yet, Scarlett.'

He withdraws his length, stroking my sensitive skin as he exits. That small act keeping me high, making me want more. In one smooth move, he grips my arse cheeks, my legs hooking onto his svelte hips, and carries me through the lounge. I tug his hair and work my lips down his temple as he takes us upstairs and into his bedroom.

Dim blue floor lights illuminate the room. As he places me down, the leather sleigh bed rests against my calves and he nudges my shoulder until I fall back onto the luxurious sheets. I writhe against the smooth satin until he bends my legs and slides me back up the bed, removing my heels one at a time, then taking his time to roll down my stockings. His fingers trail unhurriedly down to my navel.

I want to tell him to stop, to let me clean, but the sight of him crawling between my legs, his strong body hovering over me, the continued excitement of his cock, drive my salacious thoughts. My body is ready for him again.

His tongue is caressing my clit before I can say stop. My breaths are sporadic and take me to a light-headed state of sheer, indulgent gratification. My body stiffens. My chest rises. My hips move in time with his tongue.

I throw my hands above my head and grip the frame of the bed as impending pleasure takes control of my body.

I want him inside me.

Like he's tuned into me, his fingers slip through the evidence of our first round and stroke the most responsive part of my wall. I sweat under the pressure of his touch and the feel of his tongue; he keeps going until screams escape me.

'Show me how much you want it, baby.'

Another orgasm attacks each of my senses, overpowering me.

I open my eyes to see him kneeling over me, deliciously self-assured. Locking my legs around his waist, I roll us until he's lying on his back. I straddle him and watch him, captivated by the change in his face as I lean one hand back and run a finger from the bottom of his sack to the tip of his hard-on. I grab him in my hand and move my hips in time with the movement of my fist.

'I want to come inside you again,' he groans.

His hands grip my hips tight and raise me so I can slide down on top of him. My head falls back as I delight in the feel of him against my tender insides. He growls when I start to move around him and his fingers dig further into my flesh.

Circling, rising and pushing back down on to him, I build us both, relishing in the power of giving this to him.

His body stiffens.

He reaches up, grabbing my breasts and flicking his thumbs over their hard ends. It's too much.

I fall forwards and kiss his lips, tasting myself on him.

He rolls me onto my back and thrusts harder, faster, until I think I might faint. Then he slams one hand onto the bedframe and with one last thrust, his rhythm falters and finally it's my turn to see him come undone.

18

I'm alone, cocooned in white bed sheets. A hot streak of winter sun peeks from behind the bedroom blind, illuminating the white walls. I'm intensely aware of my body, my breasts and the moist sensation between my legs. My lips are soft to touch but feel plump and delicate. It's as if last night woke me for the first time in my life.

He made me forget everything. All the bad stuff. The complications, who I am, my lines and my rules.

What he did to me... I've never felt that way. Physically. Emotionally. Touch, smell, sound, taste. He took over them all and I willingly relented.

Smiling to myself, I search the room for my clothes, expecting them to be scattered across the floor. I find my dress folded, along with my jewellery, on a sleek, black, velour chaise longue in the corner of the room. The stiletto heels that bore witness to all last night's events are neatly paired on the floor.

The smell of fresh coffee permeates the room and mumbling voices come from somewhere in the apartment. I hold my dress across my body in front of the floor-length mirror, so obviously the morning after the night before. Amanda would call this the walk of shame. No matter who's down there, I can't really walk out in my LBD and heels. Scanning the room, I realise how little I took in last night. There's no wardrobe, no real practical furniture other than the enormous sleigh bed and the seductive chaise longue. A bachelor room. I throw away the thought of how many other women have probably had the pleasure.

Gregory's shirt from last night hangs invitingly on the end of the chaise longue. There's no getting away from it; whoever's out there is going to know exactly what we did last night. Mostly, I'm mortified, but there's a part of me that wants to shout from the rooftops that Gregory Ryans, *the* Gregory Ryans, the insanely sexy CEO, made love to me. No, fucked me, twice.

I button up the shirt I was so keen to unbutton last night, hang my head upside down to shake the bedhead from my hair, tap my cheeks in the mirror and quietly open the door. Tiptoeing along the hallway and down the stairs, I hold the tail ends of the shirt closed to preserve what little dignity I have left.

Gregory and Jackson are deep in conversation at the breakfast bar. They both sip fresh orange in sweat pants and gym tops. It's the first time I've seen Gregory look casual and he's still truly captivating.

Jackson leans forwards on the kitchen breakfast bar looking more serious than I care for anyone to be this morning.

'Are you certain it was foul play?' Gregory asks, receiving a shrug from Jackson.

'I can't be certain. His body will be so battered, it'll be hard to tell.'

I stand upright, putting my hand on the wall to steady my legs.

'But like you said, the struggle could have been him trying to get out of the room.'

'It could've been but I want to bring in extra security in case this thing isn't over.'

'Fine. Bring them in. Make sure my mother has twenty-four seven.'

'What about you?' Jackson asks.

'I'll be fine; just make sure Lara's protected.'

'Greg, if he had anything to do with it, it's not about the girl, it's about you.'

'Jackson,' Gregory interjects, 'go and enjoy your weekend. You live here. How much harm can I really come to?'

Jackson nods in agreement then stands at attention, feigning a cough when he notices me.

'Are you talking about my dad?'

Gregory turns from his stool, his stoic mask replaced with a rabbit-in-headlights expression.

'Well?'

'No.'

'Bullshit! Tell me what you were talking about.'

'Scarlett, Jackson was concerned by your reaction the other night, that's all. It got him thinking about security.'

'You mean the state of my dad's room?'

Jackson steps from behind the breakfast bar. 'You didn't seem to think he could get to the stairs himself, Scarlett. If he couldn't then someone—'

'Jackson!' Gregory barks. 'Enough. It's ridiculous. You're scaring her, for Christ's sake. Unnecessarily. You've put two and two together as usual and come up with a fucking detective plot.'

Jackson shakes his head but backs down.

'So I shouldn't worry?'

Gregory rests one elbow on the counter and drops his hand to his thigh. 'No. You shouldn't worry.' He pats his leg. Eyes wild, salacious. 'Get here,' he says in a way that makes me want to submit to his every demand.

My sore muscles react, bringing back memories of every luscious stroke and caress of last night. I force myself to remember that we're not alone.

'Morning,' is all I can manage to say.

'Good morning, Miss Heath,' he returns with that enchanting part curl of his lips.

Jackson subtly exits, leaving the two of us alone in the kitchen.

'I like this on you,' he says, tugging each side of his shirt collar, pulling me between his legs.

He strokes his fingertips down my cheek. His touch delectable. His smooth, orange-flavoured lips press against mine and my body intuitively leans into his.

'Mmm, I like your juice,' I say, tracing the inside of his top lip with the tip of my tongue until he groans.

He flashes a boyish grin and gives me one final peck on the lips. He holds me between his thighs by the small of my back, my hands resting on his shoulders.

'Gregory, is Jackson serious about my dad?'

'No, baby. He has an overactive imagination. Years in the forces will do that to a man, apparently.'

He drops his head to the bare flesh of my chest and his hands roam to my arse cheeks.

'I like when you call me baby.'

He pulls the lapel of his shirt to one side and digs his teeth into the round of my breast. 'And I like calling you baby.'

This is weird. Yesterday, he was my client. Ex-client. Now,

I'm happily pushing my female bits against his male bits and he's sucking on my breast.

He slaps a palm against the bare globe of my arse and I squeal at the oddly erotic sting. 'Now, what would you like for breakfast?'

I look around the worktops but only see coffee and a fruit bowl.

Shrugging, I say, 'Coffee will be fine.'

He chuckles and shuffles me so I replace him on the stool. Opening his large, American-style fridge, he asks 'Pancakes? Bacon? Eggs? I'll call my chef.'

'Oh. Please don't.'

'I'm joking, Scarlett, I can cook... Well, a little. Amy does most of my cooking but she doesn't work a weekend unless I ask.'

'Amy?'

'Cleaner. Cook. All round domestic angel. How do smoked salmon bagels sound? I can use a toaster,' he grins.

Smiling, I pour a filter coffee and sit back on his warm stool to get a front-row view of him moving around the kitchen. 'Have you been working out?'

'Running, then sparring with Jackson.'

'I wondered where that body came from. Where do you spar?'

'In the gym.'

'Yes, thank you, I guessed that much. Where's the gym?'

He points to a white door at the back of the lounge.

'Naturally, you have a gym in your apartment.'

He pops the two halves of a bagel from the toaster and turns them onto a plate. 'Cream cheese?'

'Please.'

'This is good,' I say after chomping through my first bite of bagel in seconds.

'I can see that.'

'So, Jackson lives here?'

'He does.'

'Hmm, okay.'

Gregory laughs. An unexpected sound from the usually serious CEO. 'There're five bedrooms and Jackson's is furthest away from mine.'

'Oh. I didn't realise it was so big.'

He glances to his crotch. 'Why thank you.'

'The apartment, fiend.' Images of his toned body lowering down onto me fill my mind. 'I just don't know where my head was last night.'

He stalks towards me and I pause midway through taking a bite of bagel. He pushes my legs apart and stands between them, then rubs his thumb across the side of my mouth and sucks cream cheese from the tip. A sight that parts my lips, upstairs and down.

'Are you free today?' he asks.

I swallow, giving myself a second to recover, and make him wait for my response, rotating my hand in the air.

'Am I free? Yes and no.'

'Ah, we're back to cryptic Scarlett.'

I scowl light-heartedly. 'I was planning on seeing my dad.'

'Of course, I'm sorry, I didn't think.'

'No, please, there's no need to be sorry. I'll go this morning and maybe we could do something this afternoon? You see, I had this big deal on at work which was taking up my weekends but that ended yesterday so I guess I have some time on my hands.'

'I wonder if your client could find you any more work to do.'

'He'd better not.' *Certainly not of the same fucked-up kind as the last deal.*

'What if I came to the hospital with you?' he asks sheepishly.

'Oh, Gregory, it's not that I wouldn't like you to meet my dad but I, well, I don't think he would want you to meet him like this. He's not, well, he's not—' Suddenly, the image of my weak, dying dad is in my mind and I can feel the black feeling of guilt creeping from my fingertips and toes, riding up my limbs. While he was at the hospital last night, I was—

Gregory's warm hand on my leg stops the black poison and when I look up at his face, it starts to retract.

'Actually, I was planning on going to the hospital sometime soon anyway. I visit the children's ward every now and then, a few times a year. Don't look at me like that. It's a self-satisfying deed; it actually makes me feel good to play computer games and Mr Potato Head. Anyway, I haven't been for a while, so maybe I could go there while you visit your dad and then we can do something together?'

Words have escaped me. If I was the type of woman to have a checklist, I think I could by now have mentally ticked each and every box and handed Gregory a piece of paper marked with an A+ and a smiley face.

I move my plate to the sink. 'I'm going to need some clothes.'

'I quite like what you're wearing.'

'Hmm, that's a shame. I was just about to take it off.' I bite my lower lip as I make my way to the stairs. Gregory runs towards me before I can blink. I yelp as he throws me into a fireman's lift over his shoulder and runs me back upstairs to the bedroom.

19

How quickly delirious happiness can fade into complete, utter helpless sadness.

I reluctantly let go of Gregory's hand at the overhead blue-and-white sign pointing west to Paediatrics. He kisses my cheek then I continue alone to visit my dad.

I whisper, 'How's he doing today?' as if I might wake him from a light sleep.

Sandy shrugs and offers with no conviction, 'I think he has a little more colour in his cheeks.'

With a nod, I take a seat in the chair beside her.

'Well?' she asks, nudging me with her elbow.

'Well, what?'

'Well, how was your night?'

There's no hiding my bright-red cheeks and beaming smile so I confess, 'It was perfect.'

She chuckles, no doubt reading the details of last night, and maybe this morning, from the look on my face.

'Your dress looks pretty,' I say, acknowledging the effort

she's made in her lilac, wrap-over dress and small-heeled, nude shoes.

'Pfft,' she replies, rolling her eyes and wafting a hand in the air.

She offers me a chocolate from a packet in her bag and for a while, we eat the caramel-filled chocolate in silence, listening to the sound of my dad's beeping machines. The stench of reheated food that makes visitors feel hollow.

On reflection, my intentions for last night got a little, or a lot, lost. I don't know when closure turned to going to bed with my billionaire client but now the last thing I want is for that door to close. Nor did I ask him about Jack Jones. I think my questions about Jack fled my mind the second I saw Gregory standing outside the theatre. Or maybe when he sucked strawberry from my fingers, or when his tongue turned my clit to a quivering mess.

'Did Jackson drop you off at the hospital?' Sandy enquires in her best impression of nonchalant, breaking my mouthwatering daydream.

'No, actually, Gregory drove. Why do you ask?'

In spite of my teasing, she keeps her gaze firm on Dad's bed.

'Oh, Scarlett, really, I'm just trying to make conversation,' she snaps, still refusing to make eye contact with me.

'Sure,' I purr, taking another Rolo from the packet on her lap.

Sandy slips out to the ladies' and I stand, watching my dad sleep. 'Come on, Dad, wake up for me. I know you can get through this.'

I lift my hand to my lips, being careful not to tug on his intravenous drip. I follow his bruises and marks from his hand, up his arm. Glancing at the doorway to make sure Sandy isn't headed back, I move my dad's sheet and look at his black and blue ribs, his frail, purple chest. Then I check his back, as far as I can see without disturbing him and the machines keeping him alive. I check his neck.

This is ridiculous.

He's bruised because he fell down the stairs. But there was enough doubt in my mind to look.

Stop overthinking.

'Sandy!' I jump when she comes back into the room and I hurry to place my dad's sheets back around him, as though I've been tucking him in.

Two hours, eleven games of hangman, three games of noughts and crosses and no change from Dad pass before Doctor Jefferson makes his rounds. His obvious procrastination as he reads my dad's charts is further confirmation that things aren't looking up.

'Please, can you just tell us,' I say impatiently.

He hangs the clipboard back onto the end of Dad's metal bedframe, puts his Biro back into the top pocket of his white coat and folds his arms across his chest.

'I'm afraid your father's condition hasn't improved as we'd hoped. His brain function isn't improving as the swelling reduces.'

'Can't you wake him up?' Sandy pleads.

'It's really about whether he's strong enough to come 'round. You must understand he suffered a heavy trauma.'

'There's a chance he won't recover.' I don't know whether I'm telling Sandy, asking the doctor to confirm what I already know, or re-telling myself the truth of the situation.

'But he might?' Sandy almost begs.

Doctor Jefferson is visibly uncomfortable and rocks from one foot to the other, pushing his hands into the pockets of his white coat. 'It would be sensible to prepare yourself for the worst. There's still time but we need to see an improvement. Doctor Heath's body is weak and unresponsive but we'll keep trying, waiting. I'm not suggesting you give up hope but you need to be realistic.'

Biting down on my gums, I see Sandy in my peripheral vision sink into her seat. 'If it would help, I can arrange for someone to come and see you. We have an excellent counselling service here. Some people find it helpful.'

Sandy shakes her head, staring at her boss, her friend.

'We're fine,' I say. *He'll come through, I know it. It's not his time.*

It's there again, a small but repugnant sense of relief overshadowed by an overwhelming sense of hatred. For myself and everything bad in this world that happens to good people like my dad.

When the doctor leaves, I tell Sandy she really must get away from the hospital and do something for herself.

'Where would I go?' she asks.

'Anywhere, Sandy. Go shopping, take a bath, bake, go to the cinema. I just don't think it's healthy for you to be here all day, every day. I want to be here too but Dad isn't waking up.'

Moving to his bed, I stroke Dad's cheek then place the most gentle of kisses on his warm forehead. 'I love you. I always will and I'll see you tomorrow.'

Sandy and I walk the long corridor away from him arm in arm.

'Let's just grab Gregory and we'll give you a lift to wherever you want to go. He's visiting the children's ward.'

Sandy follows whilst grumbling about putting us out. Like one lift is worth more than the twenty-odd years she's spent running around after me.

Before we even see the children, the laughter and screams of delight are infectious. Three nurses dressed in navy, two-piece uniforms chuckle and shake their heads as they watch the activities of the general ward unfold. My feet move more quickly as my interest is piqued. Just before I turn the corner to see what's causing the commotion, the almighty roar of a man's voice vibrates in my ears. I glance at the three nurses; the tallest of the three, the most sensible looking, who wears her hair in a French chignon, says through her laughter, 'Every time... every time we tell him not to get them too excited but does he listen?'

Turning the corner into the ward, Gregory comes into view, towering over a group of deliriously happy children. He's wearing the fluffy, ginger head of a lion, his hands curled into stiff paws and held up to the sides of his mane.

Laughter unwittingly bellows from the depths of me. A beautiful little girl of maybe five or six with the largest, most dazzling blue eyes I've ever seen, slowly raises a frail finger from where she stands in front of Gregory and points over his shoulder in the direction of Sandy and me. As the lion slowly turns, lowering his hands one at a time, to see Sandy and me, our laughter becomes uncontrollable. Sandy leans on me for support.

Tears of sheer joy stream down my face as I hold my aching ribs in place.

'Sandy, Scarlett, come and meet my friends,' Gregory says.

He waves us over and relieves himself of the lion head, then whispers something to the little girl with sparkling eyes who nods exuberantly and flashes Gregory a toothy grin.

'Thiiiiis is Isabella,' he says, his voice straining slightly as he lifts her onto his knee.

'Hi,' I say, reaching out my hand to take hers, mesmerised by the innocence of her smile.

Gregory moves Isabella's hand up and down and left and

right as we try to make our hands meet for a shake. It makes Isabella chuckle, the most delightful sound.

'Isabella is one of my faaavourite reasons to visit the hospital,' Gregory declares, receiving a hug from the girl in return.

'I have cancer,' Isabella tells me in the same way she might tell me what she ate for her last meal or what time she got up in the morning.

I notice for the first time the dark clouds beneath her beautiful eyes. Her head is bald and her body under her rainbow-covered hospital gown is pale and boney.

I swallow the enormous lump of reality that has formed in my throat. 'I'm very sorry to hear that, Isabella.'

'It's okay, Gregory says it means I get to have more fun than lots of people because I get to play with my friends every day,' she says, very matter of fact.

'Well, I guess that's true.'

'Scarlett?' she sings. 'Are you Gregory's girlfriend?'

'Oh, I, erm, well—'

I cower under the weight of the enormous question from this little girl who's less than half my height.

'I don't mind if you are,' she continues. 'He can just have two girlfriends.'

I chuckle. 'Can he indeed?'

Gregory pulls his arm tighter around Isabella's waist and offers her the most adorable smile. He looks me in the eye, tying my insides into knots then takes my hand and presses the base to his lips. 'I'd like two girlfriends.'

* * *

'Why do you keep looking at me like that?' Gregory asks as we drive away from Borough Market.

Through my smirk, I ask as innocently as possible, 'Looking at you like what?'

Glancing in my direction before checking his blind spot to change lanes, he raises one brow to me.

'Okay, okay, it's just, I would never have expected a man who drives a car like this...' I gesture towards the magnificently complex dashboard and immaculate, black, leather interior. 'What kind of car is this anyway?'

'A Maserati GranTurismo.'

'Right. I wouldn't expect a man who drives a Maserati Gran Turismo, who smells divine, dresses like he just stepped off the front page of *Forbes* and who's frankly more arrogant and aggressive than a wild cat at work, to be so... so...' I shake my head, struggling to articulate how I feel, '...wonderful and caring.'

'You don't know me as well as you might like to think, Scarlett.'

I want to know him. Everything there is to know. Though something tells me Gregory doesn't share easily.

'Those kids did nothing to deserve the hand they've been dealt in life. They're just kids: pure, innocent. They've been born into a certain life, scarred by disease. I like to see that they can still laugh. I want to help them remember the good things they have, the reason they fight to stay alive.' His words are sombre, betraying his confident exterior. *What are you hiding beneath your skin, Mr Ryans?* 'Children shouldn't have to deal with what's dark in the world.'

'Are we still talking about the children in the hospital?' I ask warily.

He swallows, his features set and distant. Then he leans back in his seat, one arm working the steering wheel, the other moving to rest on my thigh.

'If my money and time can help make those children laugh and feel like someone cares, even a little bit, that makes me feel – it gives me a reason. A purpose. Like I said, my going there to visit isn't a selfless act.'

It seems completely selfless to me but his face is forlorn as he focuses on the road ahead. I stroke his hand then entwine my fingers in his, receiving a squeeze in return. On some level, I understand. When my mother left me, I asked myself why I was even born. That my dad needs me gives me purpose. And there's still an element of me, despite my acceptance of my mother having left now, that works so hard because helping others achieve their goals gives me worth too. Gregory's past runs deeper than that, darker than that, I'm certain of it. But I think I can empathise on some level. I grip his hand tightly. I'm starting to think I have a new, gorgeous, accomplished and utterly spellbinding reason to be alive.

'I look like I just stepped off the front page of a magazine, huh?' he teases.

Looking to the heavens, I ignore his question. 'Where're we going?'

He shrugs – *touché*. There's the ghost of a smile around his lips. I feel the warm embrace of contented silence.

Buildings fade into trees, clutching to retain their last leaves. The sound of congestion and the burn of red traffic lights are displaced by the soft whisper of tyres on open country roads. The scenery whizzes past my window so fast that it reflects the dream I feel like I'm starring in, the kind of dream that you know, even in your subconscious, is too fantastic to be real.

Gregory brings the car to a stop, encouraging my eyes to open. *Oh I didn't!*

'You look cute when you sleep,' he teases. The very words I did not want to hear.

I fumble to check my clothes are in place, quickly doing a drool swipe of my mouth and chin just in case. 'I'm so sorry; it's the motion.'

'You must have needed it.' He's smirking as he leans his head back onto his headrest.

'No need to be so cocky.'

Searching our surroundings, I look for anything to help me legitimately change the subject. I have no idea where we are. The sky is clear; the day looks fresh. It takes time for the unfamiliar sight of fruitless vines in perfectly parallel rows to sink into my mind. A smile takes over my opened mouth as I turn in my seat to an ivy-covered archway and hanging from it, a sign engraved with the words, *Chapel Down*.

'Chapel Down?'

Gregory is now wearing an even more self-satisfied grin than before, a grin that makes him enigmatic, beautiful and irritating to me all at once.

'You've brought me to an English vineyard in one of the few months you are guaranteed to find vines with no grapes.'

I'm deadpan as I watch Gregory's mouth open and close like a fish, silently gulping water. No one pushes back with him.

'I'm joking! This is wonderful, thank you. I've wanted to visit for ages; I've just never found the time to do it.'

Gregory's staggered look turns to a soft smile.

'My dad would love this,' I find myself saying. 'Are we going in?'

'Yes. I thought we might stay the night and have dinner, if you'd like to?'

Anticipation and longing instantly course through me. Leaning towards him, my nails dig into his denim-covered thigh. My lips part so close to his mouth, I can feel his breath, smell his sweetly spiced, natural scent. His eyes squeeze tightly shut and his hand clasps mine, holding me still as he takes a deep, controlled breath.

He whispers dryly, 'Not here.' Then presses his lips to my temple in an act that feels more intimate than being in bed with him last night.

But I'm fuelled by lust.

I move my hand higher, brazenly cupping his growing crotch. His eyes are still nipped shut. I press my fingers harder against him and moan appreciatively at his clear arousal.

'Fuck it!' He pulls my face to his, his tongue breaking into my mouth. Taking his signal, I unfasten his trousers and move my hand down his hard shaft, absorbing his groans. I work his length, turning my thumb around his tip but I want more; I want to taste him.

I pull back, questioning him with a lick of my lips, wondering whether I can really be so forward, but I have a primal need to take him. He gives me the pass I need with a single look and I lean forwards, circling his tip with my tongue, swallowing the bead that's already formed.

He takes a sharp inhale of breath as I wrap my mouth around him and slide down until he's touching the back of my throat. My eyes fire open and I gag, I hope subtly.

'Take a second,' he breathes, his words husky.

I do as he says, mentally preparing myself for the next movement, then I draw down his length again, opening my throat.

'Jesus, Scarlett!'

With confidence I never knew I had, I continue to slide up and down his shaft, twirling my tongue around the bulging head, savouring the taste of him.

'Your mouth is fucking magic.'

I cup his sack in my hand and work him there, continuing to suck. He moves his hips, pushing into me as he groans.

'Fuck, I'm nearly there.'

Grabbing my hair, he holds me still as he fucks my mouth and I'm focused on only him, the pleasure he's feeling.

His body stiffens, his balls lift and his cock swells.

I wrap a hand around his base and pump as he pushes into my mouth, my own body charged by the knowledge that I can bring this extraordinary man to his knees.

I feel him pulse and his fingers yank at my hair. 'Scarlett, I'm going to come.'

I hear his warning but I don't stop. I want this. I want him. I want him to lose control for me, forget whatever it is that keeps him so tightly wound.

Warm liquid bursts into my mouth and I swallow everything he gives to me.

20

The crisp, evening air fills my nose and makes me realise just how fuzzy my post-wine-tasting head feels. Four reds, three whites and five sparkling tasters will do that to you. Gregory pulls my cream scarf higher up my chin and wraps my autumn coat tighter around me like I'm something he has to protect. He adjusts his perfectly tailored, navy trench coat, fastening the buttons to the top of his neck. The combination of wine and the knowledge of how his body feels entwined with mine makes my head fog even more with a need to be wrapped up in him again.

'So, you never answered my question.' The white air around his words is doused in the fragrance of sparkling wine.

'What question?'

'Would you like to stay over tonight?'

Before my impulses scream, *YES!!!* I remember one problem. 'My clothes. I don't have any.'

'Hmm, well, I happen to think you look very good in my clothes, or better yet, no clothes.'

His boldness gives me an idea of my own. 'If you want to take off my clothes, you'll have to catch me first.'

I dash into the nearest row of vines. He follows, chasing me in a parallel row. He's faster than me but the grapeless branches between us stop him from catching me. Cold air strikes my chest, wind lifts the tails of my coat and pulls my hair back from my face. The chase is exhilarating. Knowing I'll eventually be captured in his arms is even better.

He's already at the end of my row when I try a dummy dart, first stepping towards him then quickly turning to run in the opposite direction. He leans full stretch, his strong hand grabbing for my waist, turning me towards him. My right foot slips in wet soil and my left leg struggles to keep me up, kicking helplessly. I try to shuffle my right foot, my arms ride a bike in the air, a high-pitched squeal escapes my lips before I thud to the earth with Gregory falling quickly after me, squelching in the mud.

'I definitely need a change of clothes now,' I manage through delirious laughter.

'That makes two of us.'

Gregory shuffles until his waist is hovering above mine, the weight of his body resting on his forearms and between my legs. He kisses me, softly at first, then tugs my lower lip between his teeth and intensifies his assault. 'I'm going to make an executive decision, Miss Heath: we're staying.'

'That's why you earn the big bucks, CEO.'

* * *

The receptionist frowns as she considers our mud-stained and sodden clothes but is quick to sign us in when she checks her computer and realises Mr Ryans has made a reservation in the Penthouse Suite.

'Presumptuous,' I say as the concierge leads us to our room.

'Or informed.'

The Penthouse Suite is draped in heavy, gold-trimmed, red curtains that match almost exactly the regal carpet. An antique bar table is decorated with a crystal decanter and glasses. Through an open door, I see a four-poster bed dressed in what I can only assume is the finest of Egyptian cotton.

The concierge leaves Gregory's leather weekend bag and a large Harrods carrier next to the dressing table. I can't wait for him to leave. Gregory is calm and gracious as ever. He tips the concierge then closes the door behind him and turns to meet my lascivious gaze.

'Get here.'

His demand is too hot to resist. I'm in his arms, my legs wrapped tightly around his waist. He kisses me furiously – my lips, my neck. We move against one wall, the pressure on my back pushing my raging body against his. We bang off another wall, messy, clumsy, then he lifts me onto the dressing table. I pull off my own scarf and coat, then his.

With a change of pace, he unzips my knee-high boots, creeping the zip a centimetre at a time. I push my fingers into the rim of his jeans and pull him towards me, grinding against him, the harsh material of my chinos pressing my silk thong against my labia. The pressure makes my legs shift wider and he rolls himself against me, holding me to him with a hand gripping my arse.

Frantic, I undo his button and zip then force his jeans to his thighs. His cock is already so hard, it tents his tight, black boxers. I grasp it with my full palm, thriving on his responsive groan.

He pulls me forwards by my belt and briskly unfastens me. In one fast, rugged move, he pulls off my pants and bottoms. I'm exposed. My legs spread and wanting. The feel of air between my legs is enough to make me palpitate.

A low rumble leaves his chest as his palm cups my sex. 'This is mine.'

I nod vigorously, delirious with the sight of him, rock solid and too desperate to take off his clothes completely.

He yanks my hair and his lips meet mine with force. I grab his arse, digging in my nails, then force down his boxers.

'Say it.'

I stare at his angry erection. At this moment, I'll say anything he wants. 'It's yours.'

With his right arm, he lifts me onto him, burying his cock deep inside me. We both groan and he waits, somehow restraining himself, giving me time to adjust.

'Gregory, please!'

'Please what?'

I lose myself. Lust and desperation take over. All modicum of strength and inhibition disappears. 'I need you. I need you, please.'

His moan is close to a growl as he takes my lip between his teeth. He lifts me, sliding out of my centre, then lowers me down, meeting me with a punishing drive of his cock. We thrust, matching each other blow for blow, ravishing each other's lips, tongues swirling, hands grabbing, squeezing. I dig my nails into his back and thrust until I'm groaning with sheer pleasure. He pulls harder on my hair and pushes deeper into me. I press my breasts against his chest and bite down on his neck. My breathing is erratic and deep, so deep, my head begins to fuzz. I groan again louder and push faster, bouncing on him as he takes my weight.

Like a volcano, my internal muscles rumble to the brink of eruption.

'I'm there, Gregory.'

'Together, baby.'

He pounds into me again and bites, hard, on the plump flesh of my breast. I roll my hips against him as he drives into me, unable to get enough of him, my fingers clutching his shoulders as my body screams for release.

'Christ, Scarlett.'

My nails pierce the skin of his arse as every muscle in my body spasms and I explode around him.

He pulls me into his chest, resting his chin on my head as we pant, our damp bodies moving against each other.

'Let's clean you up,' he whispers into my neck.

'Sleepy,' I mutter.

'I'll take care of you.'

He skilfully removes the last remnants of our clothing as he carries me to the walk-in monsoon shower with my legs wrapped tightly around his waist and my arms gripping his neck. He turns on the shower with one hand, not letting me go, and holds us under the warm spray, kissing my neck.

'Can you stand so I can wash your hair?'

I nod, already dreading the loss of contact. He places me down and turns me away from him as he massages shampoo into my scalp, placing kisses on my shoulders intermittently.

'Rinse,' he says, encouraging me to step under the water. I do as I'm bid then he repeats the process with conditioner. Next comes the shower gel, which he works into a lather over my torso, down my arms then down my legs, life finally coming back into my limbs as he moves his hands in circles around my thighs.

I turn and rub my hands over his shoulders as he bends. He

trails kisses up my stomach as he rises. 'You're back,' he says on a sublime half-smile.

'As are you.' My eyes fall to his hardening crotch.

He raises a brow, asking for permission, then moves a strong hand under my hair to my neck and pulls me into him. I get lost in his kiss. His hand covers my still-smouldering sex and he dips two skilful fingers inside me. I'm not fully down from my last orgasm and I build almost immediately. I don't need to open my eyes to know he'll be pleased with himself.

He turns me away from him and pulls my hips toward him, guiding my arms to the wall in front of me. He strokes his fingers across my clit and back inside me.

'Perfect,' he hums.

Spreading my legs wider with his feet, he guides himself to my entrance then holds his position, his hips teasing me.

On one thrust, he's deep inside me and I lose myself to pleasure I never knew existed just days ago. He pauses. 'Are you okay?'

I nod my head, unable to speak as he drives into me, one hand pinning my hips, the other massaging my knot. He thrusts again, this time more controlled, finding his rhythm, still reaching the same inspired angle. 'Fuck, Scarlett, now you've given me this, I don't think I can ever let it go.' Another gruelling blow.

I know his words are the product of lust but they lift me, together with the intensity of each attack, until I'm ready to tip.

'Not yet, Scarlett. Together.'

'I can't, it's coming.'

He powers forwards again, brutally. It's painful but a kind of exquisite pain I've never felt. The kind I want to keep coming again and again. Another drive takes me to my limit and I detonate as he fills me.

* * *

I feel soft fingertips drawing circles on my clean, naked body as I rest on top of the super king bed.

'Room service is here; wake up,' Gregory whispers.

'Strawberries and champagne. Is this the part where I run to the bathroom to floss and you accuse me of taking drugs?'

His brows furrow.

'You have seen *Pretty Woman*?'

'Oh, right. Yes, I think I have.'

'You *think* you've seen *Pretty Woman*? It sounds like somebody needs educating. Do you ever have a movie night? Make your own popcorn, binge on chocolate?'

'You might have to show me,' he says, passing me a champagne flute and strawberry as he sits back on the bed, his toned torso displayed by his waist-high, white towel.

Picking up the telephone, he dials 0 and requests popcorn, chocolates and ice cream and asks that someone arrange for *Pretty Woman* in the Penthouse Suite. 'Now seems as good a time as any,' he says simply, as if none of life's materialities are trouble to him.

With our picnic laid out on the bed and *Pretty Woman* playing on the oversized television, I nestle into his chest, turning the few fine hairs in my fingers. The last two days have felt just like a movie to me. An exhilarating dream of everything I never knew I was looking for in reality. My very own Richard Gere.

At some point during the night, it becomes apparent to me that I missed the end of *Pretty Woman* and Gregory has tucked me into the covers, still snuggled into his chest. His heavy arm weighs down on me, pulling me closer to him and his fingers gently stroke my hair.

21

The Harrods bag Gregory brought to the hotel contained skinny, indigo jeans and a Ralph Lauren striped shirt that he had sent to the hospital yesterday to bring with us. After a tussle about me paying him back, which he of course won, I had to admit to being grateful for clean lingerie.

'I love those boots,' Gregory says through a cheeky grin as I zip them to the knee. 'Can I make you mine again today?'

'You have no idea how much I wish I could say yes but I want to see my dad.'

'Of course you do. Later maybe?'

'You're not sick of me yet?' I laugh but it's quickly stifled by his serious face. 'I'll give you a call when I'm done at the hospital.'

We drive back towards London, talking easily. In fact, everything is so comfortable between us, it's almost surreal. Gregory has an opinion on just about everything: business, law, the world. But it's not annoying or self-righteous; it's informed and intelligent. There's a warmth in my chest as I watch the way he moves and speaks.

That feeling disappears when we pull up to the entrance of the hospital. Something feels off: wrong, not safe or right. An eerie sensation makes me shiver and the hairs prick up on my arms. I'm watching the sky turn dark and the world grow small around me from outside my own body. I don't remember whether or how I say goodbye to Gregory as I leave the car and float to the hospital entrance.

A sudden jerk against my shoulder throws me back into the reality of my body, a jerk so hard from a hooded man that I turn to watch him walk out through automatic doors. His head is down, his face angled towards the floor, his hands stuffed into the pockets of his navy jumper. He never looks back or ventures to offer an apology. I shake my head to find sense and tell my legs to keep moving towards the lifts despite the increasing weakness they feel. The lift clicks past each floor, stopping to allow people on and off until we finally arrive at my dad's ward.

'Scarlett.' Elexis, the nurse, has come to know me by name. Her voice is unusually leaden, her effervescent personality vanished. 'We've been trying to call you.'

My chest tightens. 'What? What is it?'

Doctor Jefferson steps towards me from behind the nurses' station. 'Let's go to the relatives' room.'

'Tell me, please,' I beg, unable to hide the panic in my voice.

The doctor moves to touch my arm but I snap it out of his reach.

'Let me see my dad. I want to see my dad!'

'Scarlett,' Elexis pleads, 'I think you should go with the doctor first.'

'No,' I cry, tears falling from my face, saliva bursting into my words. 'Let me see him! Let me see him.' Elexis glances to another nurse, who steps out of Dad's room, removing her nitrile gloves and placing them on a trolley of plastic bottles. The nurse nods to Elexis and I run to my dad.

My legs give way beneath me at the sight of his grey, lifeless body laid out in fresh sheets. His eyes are closed and his arms rest perfectly still at either side of his body. His hair has been combed in a way Sandy and I would never comb it, and seems darker than it did just yesterday. His face is peaceful and for the first time since I can remember, there are no signs of pain. He looks like my old dad, the one who's been lost for too long. The machines are gone, and the wet lip swaps have been removed from the side table. The clouds in the sky have dispersed to allow a small ray of sun to beam through the window and across his cheek.

Wiping my face, I walk hesitantly to his side and take his cold hand in mine.

'How long?'

'About an hour,' Elexis says, placing a hand on my shoulder.

'Does Sandy know?'

'No, I'm sorry, Scarlett, we couldn't call her. If you like, with your permission, I can call her now for you.'

'No, thank you. I'll do it.'

She nods and turns to leave the room.

'Wait. Was he alone?'

She sighs, which I take to mean yes. 'Scarlett, you really need to speak to the doctor.'

'Please tell me how it happened.'

She sighs again. 'I found him.'

'Found him?' I ask, turning to face her.

'It was time. I've been in this job many years and you can tell, by their breathing, their colouring. I knew it was almost time. I left the room to call you but I couldn't reach you.'

A small sob escapes me.

'When I came back to him, his machine... his oxygen, had... well, I don't know, maybe come loose. He was gone.'

'What are you saying, Elexis?'

'I – I... it could have happened I guess if his body jumped at the last minute, like a reflex, I'm not sure.'

'Did his machine coming loose kill him?' I probe.

'It would be hard to say which came first, Scarlett. Like I said, his body was failing him; he was going. I just wanted to give you the full picture because there might have to be an inquest. I hope not, because it was natural in my opinion, but that's what Doctor Jefferson will explain to you.'

Confused, I thank her and ask to be left alone. As she's leaving the room, I hear commotion in the corridor: the sound of someone running. Suddenly, Gregory is at the entrance to the room, sweating and panting. Seeing my dad's lifeless body, he pulls his hands through his hair then drops one hand to cover his mouth.

'Christ. Fuck. Scarlett.'

Something is very wrong. Dad was frail, yes, but just yesterday, just hours ago, he was still fighting.

'W-what are you doing here?' I ask warily, unsure if I want to know the answer. 'Gregory!' I shout at his blank expression. The colour drains from his flushed cheeks and his desperate breaths stop. 'Gregory!'

He opens his mouth to speak but nothing comes out. His face twists and his eyes darken with something – anger or pain, maybe. He bites his knuckle and pulls his free hand through his hair again. This usually composed man is undone.

'Gregory, you're scaring me.'

'Scarlett,' he croaks, moving closer to me.

I take a step back, pressing my legs against Dad's bed.

Gregory reaches his hands towards my face but drops them when I flinch.

'There was a note,' he says, his voice more certain.

'What kind of note?'

'At the apartment. Jackson left me a voicemail but – but I didn't get it until I dropped you off and checked my messages.'

Jackson. The man who thought my dad had been pushed down the stairs. The one who'd seen – who'd shared – the seed of doubt I'd refused to let grow.

'What did the note say? What did the note say, Gregory?'

I don't need an answer. I know what it said. Jackson was right. I was right. Pearson was seeking revenge. Gregory's father has killed mine.

Realisation comes crashing to me. My hands rise to cover my face. 'It was him. All along. Jackson knew. It was him. Pearson was at my house but he found my dad instead of me. He put my dad in here. He put him here and the sick fuck came back to finish what he started.'

'Scarlett, baby.' He steps towards me and I lash out, smacking his hands away.

'I'm not your fucking baby! I'll never be your baby. This is—'

I stop myself short of telling him that this is all his fault. I don't know why but even now, I can't say those words.

'Why?' I cry. 'Why me? Why my dad? Why us?'

Gregory takes a deep breath and pulls his body to stand straight. He looks to the lifeless body on the bed and back to me before saying, almost inaudibly, 'Because of me.'

The words impale me. The words I was expecting but didn't want to hear strike my body like lasers, burning deep beneath the surface.

Pearson killed the person I love most in the world.

Murdered him to avenge that deal. Gregory's deal. The one I helped him close.

I killed my own dad.

Cramps tear through my stomach, causing me to fold forwards then drop to my knees. I open my mouth to scream through the agony but no noise materialises. Pain courses through me, a pain so bad, I think my head might split into two halves. Gregory steps towards me but I manage to raise one hand to tell him to stop.

'Get out!' I whisper through clenched tenth.

'Scarlett, please,' Gregory begs, taking another step towards me.

Finally, I find my voice and scream, 'Get out!'

As if hearing my cries, Sandy is at the door.

'Jackson told me,' she says to Gregory before running to be next to me on the floor. 'Breathe, darling, I'm here,' she says softly into my ear, then kisses my brow.

'He's gone,' I sob into her chest. 'It wasn't time. He wasn't ready. He's gone.'

What I don't say is, *He was murdered.*

22

I know I've been in my room for two days because it's been light and dark and light and now it's an hour into darkness again. For two days, questions have thrashed around the vortex of my mind and I've been unable to find an answer amongst the disarray. In no order, thoughts, concepts, subtle movements and noises are being absorbed but not processed. I've begun to notice some things for the first time: small, insignificant things. Like the seal of my white, Georgian sash bedroom window allows air to seep inside and gently blow the curtains. The door between the kitchen and hallway squeaks as it opens and closes, loud enough to be heard upstairs. Scotch appears to grow lighter in colour as the volume in your glass diminishes.

I hear voices sometimes, coming and going, saying nothing of consequence. Generally, people are sorry, sorry for our loss and the tragedy of Alzheimer's. They never apologise for hiding from my dad as his illness got worse and they never acknowledge that it was not Alzheimer's in the end but me, his only child, who killed him.

The day it happened, the day he was murdered, I kicked

and punched but Jackson still brought Sandy and me home. I'm vaguely aware that he carried me into the house and onto the sofa where Sandy covered me with a blanket and gave me neat Scotch to drink. The first mouthful burned through my insides, along my veins, exactly as I deserved. The second burned less, the third and fourth less again.

I woke on the sofa during the night and poured another whisky, which I carried with me to my dad's bedroom. It was different: cold and desolate. I'd intended to sleep in his bed, to cover myself in his sheets and sleep with his familiar, loving smell. But that smell was gone, replaced with the smell of stale urine. Medicinal products filled his room and displaced all that used to be safe and homely. I wondered then whether I was happy, not for myself but for my dad, or rather, relieved, relieved that he'd suffer no more, that he could sit on his cloud and play chess with old friends in good health. Perhaps he could even help people, put his skills to work.

Then I retched. I retched with hatred of myself and my disgusting thoughts because I knew that in no world could I justify what I brought upon my dad. After that, not even the Scotch could take away the agony I felt. That agony stayed with me as I left Dad's room and entered my own. It stays with me now, burning like fire. My eyes sting constantly, the skin on my lips is broken and to speak feels like shards of glass ripping the flesh of my throat.

I loathe myself. I detest Gregory and his father and the fact that either of them ever came into my life. I can't get hold of which of us I hate more and I fear for how I'll feel when my anger finds its rightful home. I fear that the vicious circle of darkness hasn't ended. That for me, it's only just begun.

* * *

I think somewhere, deep inside me, I knew she'd come, so Lara's voice offering sympathy to Sandy at the front door is no surprise. Their voices are quiet but it's clear that Sandy, Jackson and Lara are taking turns to speak. I hear the kettle being filled then placed on its holster and I imagine they're sitting around the breakfast bar, Lara in a long, black coat, elbow-length, black gloves and a veil across her face. Jackson in his black suit and tie, wearing a black homburg and carrying spare silk handkerchiefs in his pocket.

Sandy taps on my bedroom door before stepping inside. For some reason, I feel compelled to change from my leggings and hooded jumper before I see Lara. Fleetingly, I wonder what Gregory would think of my dowdy clothes, my pale skin and the black rings beneath my eyes.

I change into chinos and a cream blouse but, reaching to release my hair from the messy knot on top of my head, I realise my arms are devoid of energy and the desire to cover my shame in make-up no longer exists. I want the world to see what I've done.

The light in the hallway is much brighter than the dim lamp in my bedroom, forcing me to squint. Anxiety or nervousness builds as I descend the staircase and I clutch the banister to steady my weak legs. The house feels different: detached and unfamiliar. The curtains seem old and the gold frames around the hanging pictures have lost their shine. Each step moves me forwards in slow motion, like a scene that's been time-stretched in a movie for dramatic effect.

She can't see you like this. You can't let her see what they've done to you.

With each inward breath, my back straightens, my shoulders move back. Suddenly, vicious anger takes over my body until I'm biting down on gums and the taste of iron seeps into my spit.

A low, careful voice says, 'Scarlett. I wasn't sure you'd see me.' Lara hangs her head.

'Do you think I have good reason to refuse?'

I acknowledge Jackson's presence and note his position on a stool close to Sandy. Perhaps for her sake more than my own, I thank him for bringing me home from the hospital. He only nods.

'Let's go to the lounge,' I say, already walking in the direction, my back to Lara.

I was wrong about her clothes. She's immaculate but understated in tapered, black trousers and flat shoes. She hasn't removed her three-quarter-length, black, wool coat and zebra-print scarf. That she truly didn't expect to see me, that I have enough control to send her away, makes me feel stronger.

Pouring myself a neat Scotch from Dad's decanter, I finally look at her face.

'Why are you here, Lara?'

She sighs, squeezing her eyes shut. 'I realise I have no right to ask anything of you, Scarlett. I know what that beast has done and I wish I could undo it. But I can't, so I also know that I can tell you how sorry I am about your father as many times as I like and whilst it might make me feel better, you either won't believe me or won't care. But please know this: Gregory's a good man. He's not like his father. There's nothing of that hateful man in my son. I'm here to tell you how sorry I am but also to beg you not to blame my son for his past.'

Unwillingly, my body whispers loud enough for her to hear, 'I would believe you.' I think part of me knows Gregory couldn't have stopped this and I do know that little boy in my mind is not to blame. The other part of me hates everything that's happened and everyone I've met since that pitch in Gregory's boardroom. The knife already buried in my gut twists. A searing pain threatening to tear me apart.

Lara exhales, long, slowly, purposefully, as if she's been holding her breath. Her bright-red lips are pursed.

I walk to the fire that Sandy has lit and rest my hand on the old, wooden mantelpiece to give myself a chance to remember that I can't feel sorry for this woman. I drain the Scotch in my glass, pinching my eyes shut to feel the burn.

'Scarlett, I want to tell you a story. Can I tell you a story?'

I'm terrified of what she might tell me. I don't know whether I can take any more of this family and their convoluted web. I say nothing and continue to stare into the orange flames.

'Imagine you're five years old.'

I close my eyes but don't see a five-year-old version of myself; I see the little boy from my dad's operating theatre.

'You're five years old. Your mum has cuddled you to sleep in your bed because you can't sleep alone. You're terrified of the dark, you jump whenever you hear a bang or a creek in the house, you shake when you hear the sound of your own father's voice. Your mum has tucked you into bed in the knowledge that in an hour, maybe two, your father will be home. You both hate it when he's drunk but he's drunk so often that you only pray he's drunk enough to pass out when he comes home. Even when he's that drunk, you'll probably wake and most likely wet the bed at the sound of his keys fumbling for the door lock. Your mum will be back to change your bed and cuddle you to sleep again.'

I open my eyes and watch the roaring fire. Taking my glass back to the bar table to top it up, I pour Lara a drink too, which she sips elegantly without looking up. I retake my position by the fire.

'Your mum is still watching you from the chair in your room when his car pulls into the driveway. From the way the tyres squeal, you both know it's one of his worse days. You open one eye to check that your mum is still in the room with you, then pretend to be asleep. You both listen as your father bounces from the door to the wall and throws his keys onto the side table in the hall. Your mum leaves your room and pulls your door closed. She's trying to shield you from him but you know what he'll do to her and you know that it'll be bad; you've seen it before.'

Lara pauses and I listen as she swallows down another sip of Scotch in the quiet of the room. I want to tell her to stop. I want to tell her that she doesn't have to do this but I need to know what happens to the boy.

'He yells up the stairs for your mum and you listen to her steps as she goes to him in the hope he'll stay downstairs and leave you alone. The next thing you hear is him shouting at her. "Get me a drink, slut."

'"Fucking bitch." He pushes her against the living-room wall and the banging and screaming starts. That's when you leave your room. Trembling, you creep down the stairs in your wet pyjamas. Through the banister, you see him slap her as she slumps on the floor. You start to cry but he won't hear you over the yelling. You shout, "Stop!" You beg him to leave your mum alone but that only makes him angrier. Terrified, you walk to the door of the lounge and he laughs at you, he calls you "puff boy" and "pissy pants". Then he snarls, "Stop what?" and grabs your mother by the hair, dragging her across the lounge floor.

'He pulls her onto her knees by the coffee table then smiles at you before he starts banging, banging, banging her head on the corner of the table. Blood streams from her head and her eyes start to roll back. "Me!" you shout. "Do it to me instead!"

When he doesn't listen, you run to where he's standing and with full force, you punch yourself in the face to show him what he could do to you instead.'

I glance back at Lara and watch her shaking hand raise her glass to her lips. I quickly turn away, I can't watch as she relives this. Gregory tried to protect her. He saw all this and he was willing to hurt himself to protect his mother. That little boy. I hold a hand to my chest to stop my heart from shattering.

'You have his attention. He lets your mum's body fall to the floor. She tries to reach out her hand towards you but she's too frail. She tries and tries but she can't. Your father beats his fist in his palm and you take a step backwards. He does it again and you stumble to the ground. He puts his foot on your head, pinning you to the floor, and starts to fumble in his pockets. You stare into your mum's eyes as she lies desperate on the floor and she's begging you not to do any more. Tears fill your eyes and your cheeks burn with anger. "She's a whore," he snarls. "She's a whore and you're stupid. My stupid fucking boy!" He pulls out a cigarette from his inside pocket and sticks it between his lips. In your anger, you struggle, kicking your legs. You manage to knock him off balance and he staggers back against the wall but he's irate now. You get to your knees and try to crawl to your mum but he kicks you, striking you in the chest, knocking the wind from your lungs. Then he kicks you again in the head and you're on the floor. You can't breathe. He picks up the cigarette he dropped and pulls out his lighter. You curl into a foetal position as he stomps on your head again. He lights the cigarette and laughs, a fierce, deep, cackling laugh, as he takes two puffs. Then he puts his hand around your throat and pulls you to your knees. You think he'll stump his cigarette on you but instead, he hands you the cigarette. "Do it," he says. You shake your head slowly from side to side as tears stream

down your face but he tightens his grip on your throat. "Do it!"
he snarls. You take the cigarette in your hand. "Do it or I'll kill
the bitch," he screams. You look at your mum, who's trying with
all her strength to get to her feet but she can't. "I'll kill her," he
screams. You take the cigarette and stub it once, twice, three
times on your own arm. You don't scream; you look him in the
eye each time as the cigarette singes your skin. He laughs when
he releases his grip on your throat like it was a game. Then he
staggers out of the room and you're left, five years old, burned,
soiled and broken, to look after your beaten and bleeding
mother.' Lara sniffs and wipes her face with one hand, finishing
her Scotch with the other.

'Gregory hates his father, *hates* him, and I do too.'

I want to say I hate Pearson and I hate Gregory too but no
words leave my mouth. I stare at the cement between the bricks
on the fireplace.

'He can't stand the thought that you're hurting because of
him.'

I continue to stare at the cement until it starts to infiltrate
me, crushing my ribcage, the weight excruciating against my
heart.

'You probably think he deserves to hurt and I don't blame
you but I do want you to know that the last thing he would ever
want to do is cause you pain. He's my little boy, Scarlett. My
brave, five-year-old, little boy and I wouldn't be here if it wasn't
for him.'

'A life for a life,' I whisper.

I hear Lara place her glass on the bar table and leave the
room. Within seconds, Sandy closes the front door behind Lara
and Jackson.

'Are you okay?' Sandy asks in her soft, comforting way.

I wipe silent tears from my cheeks then move to the sofa,

not knowing or understanding how I should answer that question. Sandy takes the almost-empty whisky glass from my hand and places it on the bar table without offering me more. She comes to sit beside me so that her hip is touching mine. 'Jackson told me everything.'

Pulling my knees into my chest, I wonder whether Jackson has always known about Gregory's past and whether he's betrayed Gregory's confidence in telling Sandy the truth but I'm grateful that she finally knows what I've done.

I ask the question I've been trying to answer for myself. 'Do you hate me?'

'Hate you? Of course not! This is not your fault.'

I shake my head.

'It's nobody's fault but one very sick man.'

'Sandy, I knew what Gregory was doing. I knew the whole thing and I still helped them do it.'

She places one hand on my knee. 'You weren't to know anything like this would happen, Scarlett. You did what you did for the right reasons.'

Whether it's her words or the comfort of her hand on my knee, my eyes fill again.

Silence hovers in the room: a manifestation of a thousand unspoken words. The grandfather clock in the hallway chimes quarter to then on the hour and ticks perfectly in between.

Sandy eventually pierces the air. 'I can understand why Gregory would want to hurt that vile man. Which child wouldn't want revenge against a man who tried to kill someone so dear to them, someone who's the centre of their entire world?'

I turn to see her arms folded across her chest. Her expression steely. It's a look I don't ever remember seeing on Sandy.

'Doctor Heath should never have been caught up in all of

this but... but I will say this once and once only: there were times in that hospital that I wanted to end it for him.'

One violent sob escapes me and I admit, 'Me too.'

Sandy kisses me on the cheek and wraps an arm around me, pulling me into her chest. 'Scarlett, I'm angry, incredibly angry, but I've only ever seen you smile with one other man the way you smile when you're around Gregory.'

I push back from her chest. 'You're not defending him?'

'No. I'm not. I don't give two hoots about *him*. I just want you to make sure your anger is in the right place, that's all, for your own sake.'

I stare blankly, trying but unable to organise the multitude of thoughts and emotions locked inside my throbbing head.

Which child wouldn't want revenge against a man who tried to kill someone so dear to them?

'Shall we bake?' she asks.

'Pardon?'

'Let's bake something. Together, like old times.'

Bemused, I let out a short, snotty, tearful laugh.

We sing to the radio and blend cake mixture into the early hours of the morning. Sandy lets me scrape the last of the mixture from the bowl and she licks the wooden spoon.

It's two o'clock by the time we sit down to eat our cream cakes with milky hot chocolate.

23

GREGORY

The last thing I needed was the man I'd trust with my life, the only man I'd trust with my life, going behind my back.

The door to the apartment opens, pushing the remnants of a crystal brandy glass across the hardwood floor. The floor lights break the darkness of the lounge.

'Greg?' Jackson shouts, panicked.

Then he sees me, sitting in the black, leather chair where I've been since I left the office, the remaining half decanter of brandy on the glass-top table next to me.

'Are you hurt?' he asks, assessing the broken glass at his feet and the hole I've punched in the plastered wall.

I turn to face the city and take a swig of liquor. 'I told you not to take her.'

Jackson takes a brandy glass from the kitchen, fills it and takes a seat on the sofa. He leans forwards, resting his elbows on his knees, and drinks.

'You going to fire me for the second time in three days?'

'I ought to.'

'Lara asked me to take her to Scarlett.'

'And I told you not to.'

He sighs and rubs a hand across his face. 'We're both trying to help you.'

'I don't pay you to make my fucking decisions for me.'

'No, but you do pay me to watch your blindside.'

'Scarlett isn't my blindside, Jackson; she's all I can fucking think about.'

It's true. I don't know when it happened but every time I close my eyes, I see her perfect face, those captivating, green eyes with the lightest tinge of brown. Exquisite. The way two cute half-moons crease at the sides of her beautiful, soft lips when she smiles. The innocence of that perfect fucking giggle, so alluring, it could come close to infiltrating my iron heart. And in contract to it all her razor-sharp mind. Her quiet strength. Her levelness.

'That's exactly why she's your blindside.'

I put down my glass and pull both hands through my hair, walking to the window to look down over the city.

'How was she?'

'A mess.'

'I've really fucked up.' I'll never see the way her lean body moves again. Her immaculate, naked flesh, like silk to touch. The scent of her perfume like nothing I've smelled on anyone before: dumfounding. The way she questions herself, not knowing just how devastating those curves are when she's moving over me. The way she literally questions me about everything else.

'You didn't know he'd go after her, Greg.'

'I've put her in danger. She'll never see me again and I don't fucking blame her.'

Jackson moves to stand beside me and takes a swig of

brandy, looking straight ahead at the bruising night. 'Does it matter?'

'What kind of question is that?'

'A legitimate one.'

I push my hands into my trouser pockets and watch Jackson's faint reflection in the glass pane.

'Is she just another one? Do you want her because you can't buy her? Or do you care about her? If she's just another notch on the bed post, Greg, then be fair to her and let her go. She's been through enough.'

'And what if she's not? What if she's different?'

'Then you've got to do what you seem incapable of doing. You've got to let her in.'

I thump the window with the side of my fist and let it rest there above my head.

'You have to stop letting the past dictate your life.'

I don't know how.

Jackson refills his own glass then tops up mine. 'Let's end this. Let's end it for good. My way this time.'

I move back to my seat and gulp half the brandy in my glass. 'Find him.'

24

With my phone strapped to my arm and ear buds in, I run in the morning light for miles, my breath forming clouds around me, my fingers glowing red under the cold bite of the air. The music shields me from passersby who might want to say, *Good morning,* or, *Condolences*, keeps me concentrating on making sure my feet touch the ground without tripping and prevents my mind from wandering into the shadows. I run until sweat pours out of me and I have nothing left to give.

Dereck Marshall – Dereck Death, as Sandy calls him – arrives at eleven. It's such a peculiar choice of vocation, a funeral director. At what age does a person wake up one morning and think, *I know what I'm going to do with my life; I've found my true calling: I'm going to be a funeral director*? This is what I'm thinking about as Dereck Death shuffles his glasses on the end of his nose, then pulls out a leather-bound picture book. The snow-white album looks ironically like a wedding album, only, rather than signifying a new life, Dereck Death's album represents the end of a story, the finale to the play of life. He begins some rhetoric about the importance of an eloquent close to one's time on earth as he flicks the pages from high-gloss, white coffins to a soft, rosewood option, then from black, marble, heart-shaped headstones to grey, angular alternatives.

Perhaps because of the way my dad used to deal with death – professional, detached – I find it easy to be emotionally disconnected from the process of choosing flowers and deciding whether my dad would like a gold or silver plaque on top of his coffin. The minute detail of how he'll be buried bears no relation to my dad: his life, the man he was or still is in my memory. We agree to hold a wake at a hotel close to the church where the service will take place but even as I work through the details, I know I won't attend. I have no desire to listen to those who were absent in Dad's time of need regale a room with stories of how close they were and the good times they shared. They can brag amongst themselves.

After he places his leather book back into his zip-up bag and straightens the legs of his trousers, Dereck Death makes his own way towards the door.

'I've had confirmation now of the postmortem results. Natural causes, so I see no reason why we won't be able to work to Friday,' he says.

I know the truth.

'Scarlett. Scarlett. Dereck is leaving,' Sandy says.

'Hmm? Sorry, ah, yes, thank you,' I say, shaking Dereck's hand.

'Are you okay?' Sandy asks when the door is closed.

'Yes, of course. Fine. Are you okay?'

She nods once.

'Would you mind if I go into the office today?'

'Oh, Scarlett, I know you feel better but I don't think you're ready for that.'

'That's just it. I feel better today because you took my mind off things last night and I've been for a run, made breakfast and spoken to Dereck Death and it all means I can stop thinking about *it*. I don't have time to go over the details of what happened in my head when I'm doing things. I can't miss him and I can't wonder what would've happened if I'd never taken that deal. You could come with me, if you like. We can call into my office briefly then maybe go for coffee, get out of this house?'

She shakes her head. 'Just don't do too much.'

'I won't, I promise.'

In my mind, I think the process of getting the Tube to work will be so incredibly normal, it'll be easy to forget that everything has fundamentally changed. I take a seat and watch as a man sits opposite me and opens his broadsheet newspaper, spreading it wide so that the boy next to him is forced to lean to one side. Two girls with northern accents get on a few stops later, pouting and holding their mass of shopping bags from high-street stores. Things are normal. The problem is, things are so normal, I can't stand it. I want to scream to these people, *How can you be normal when my dad is dead? Do you hear me? Dad is dead!* I once read somewhere that if a person thinks of having a clear mind, they can eventually manifest it. Over and over in my head, I repeat the words, *Clear mind, clear mind.* My mind is not clear. Turning up the volume on my music, I close my eyes and focus on the lyrics.

At the next stop, the Tube jerks, rocking my body to one side. People alight and are replaced by others. A man with a sausage dog on a tan, leather lead. A businesswoman wearing a navy, checkered suit, holding a briefcase and smelling of sweet, exotic flowers. Then I see her: a middle-aged woman in knee-high, brown boots and a wrap-over, floral dress beneath her winter coat. She turns at the doors to face the platform and her bouncing, red curls fall from her back around her shoulder. She bends to pick up a small, Garfield cartoon suitcase on wheels. Then, standing by her side and clutching her coat with two hands, I see that familiar little boy from my dreams. The Tube jolts and is moving again. The boy stares at me, afraid, asking for my help.

At the next stop, I get off and walk the rest of the way to the office under the cover of grey clouds and threatening sky, which makes it too muggy for the scarf around my neck. The streets are quiet compared to rush hour but the sounds of fast-paced heels tapping the pavement as they make their way to an important engagement and smart-suited men chatting into phones with animated, flailing arms are still present. There's always the quiet, studious man or woman wandering with their head in a book or a newspaper, inevitably bumped by an impatient passerby in a hurry to get to their next meeting or to the front of the coffee shop queue for their next caffeine fix.

Paul, the homeless guy who usually keeps a daytime plot outside my office block with his blue sleeping bag, smiles at me as I drop two pound coins into his white cardboard cup. 'Thanks, Scarlett.'

I'd usually make conversation but today, I'm just not in the mood.

A receptionist in the atrium greets me as I push through the glass doors of the building; she waves me on towards the lifts. Staring in the lift mirror at the bags under my eyes, I ask myself why I'm doing this.

Whispers in the secretarial area begin as soon as I step out of the lift. Margaret almost covers herself in coffee as she splutters the sloshing liquid from her Best Grandma mug.

'Scarlett! I didn't expect to see you so soon.'

What she really means is, *Don't you care at all about your father?*

'I've got a lot to do,' I say, biting down on the inside of my cheeks.

Everything in my office looks as it did just days ago yet it's changed somehow. As my computer beeps into life, Margaret finally plucks up enough courage to ask if I'd like a coffee. Almost reluctantly, she asks how I am. 'I'm sorry for your loss,' she says quickly but not as quick as the move she makes to leave the office to get me a latte.

Amanda appears at my office door.

'Hey you,' she says, her arms already around me, pulling me up from my chair. 'How're you doing?'

She doesn't ask why I'm in the office; she's just Amanda, perching herself on the end of my desk.

'Much better for seeing you,' I confess. 'Talk to me about anything except my dad, please.'

Her straight face breaks into a pursed-lip smile. 'Okay. Just let me say, you know where I am and you know I want you to ask for my help if you need it. Whether it's an ice cream and movie companion, a work bitch to dump stuff on or a shoulder to cry on, okay?'

'Okay.' I give her a short, uncomfortable laugh. 'What's been happening? Did you have a good weekend?'

'It was – oh, have you heard about Jack?' she says excitedly, jumping from the edge of my desk and sending her amber curls bouncing from her shoulders.

Insects crawl over the tiny hairs on my skin beneath my black, fitted dress, causing me to shudder. 'What about him?'

'One sec.' She runs from my office then returns at lightning pace, holding a tabloid newspaper open to page seven.

'All right, all right, I'm not blind,' I say, grabbing the paper from her to read.

LOCAL MAN CHARGED WITH SEXUAL ASSAULT

A local man by the name of Jack Arthur Jones was arrested and charged last night after voluntarily confessing to police the names of three female victims he has sexually assaulted. A lawyer for Jack Jones has informed the press that his client will not be requesting bail and a trial date will be announced in the coming weeks...

'Can you believe it?' Amanda squeals. 'I always thought there was something seedy about him. He never tried anything with you, did he?'

I shake my head and pass the paper back to Amanda.

'I wonder why he would just hand himself in like that,' she says, throwing the folded newspaper into the bin at the side of my desk.

'Guilt, maybe.' I shrug, feigning nonchalance, but already wondering what part Gregory played in this.

'A man like that? I doubt it. And three women? I hope he rots in jail.'

I see Gregory's red knuckles in my mind and hear his words, *He's going to get what's coming to him.* Chills strike my neck and shoulders. I'm grateful for the interruption of Margaret's tiptoeing kitten heels.

'One latte,' she smiles, handing me the warm, cardboard cup. 'Scarlett, I, well, I—'

'It's okay, Margaret, I'm okay. Thank you.'

Her relief is audible.

'Oh, Mr Wallace called earlier and asked me to let him

know when you were next in the office. He said not to rush you, just when you're in. Would you like me to tell him you're here today or should I put him off for you?'

Neil Wallace is the head of the corporate division and my ultimate boss. A lanky, wealthy-looking man, well spoken. He made his name in his early thirties on two or three enormous deals and now, only in his forties, he earns seven figures a year. He's one of those charismatic men who can charm a client until they want to polish his shoes whilst writing the firm a hefty cheque. I glance from my watch to the stack of documents on my desk. The stack marked *Eclectic Technologies* that I've been trying to ignore since I arrived.

'Tell him I'll see him whenever he's ready please, Margaret.'

'Will do.' The hem of her blue, tweed skirt twirls as she turns to leave the room.

'Speaking of the billionaire,' Amanda croons as she picks the top Eclectic Technologies document from the dreaded pile, 'how are you guys? Is it super saucy?'

Her mischievous wink is usually impossible to resist, but today, it doesn't lighten my mood.

'It fizzled out,' I say, taking the document back from a theatrically huffed Amanda and returning it to the pile.

'He's free now, Scarlett,' Margaret interjects.

An invitation to Neil Wallace's office is, I imagine, like an invitation to visit the king: an incredible honour but scary as hell. I would've chosen a different dress if I'd known. I'm not sure which other dress but I'm sure I would've chosen a different one.

What will I say to him? How should I say hello?

I've only spoken to Neil on a handful of occasions, mostly because he's trawling the globe a lot of the time, trying to tap into the emerging markets. When he *is* in the office, his door is *not* 'always open,' so to speak, although I have to wonder whether that's just a phrase used by people taking up a new position to mask the truth. What they're really thinking is, *Hi new team, I'm scared shitless that I'm not actually the right man for the job so I'm going to say something truly cliché that I read in a* How to be a Leader *book that I downloaded for free from Amazon, in the hope I can get you onside.* Perhaps one day, I'll enter the higher echelons and find out for myself.

How do I even knock on his door? I think before gently tapping three times.

'Neil, you asked to see me.'

'Scarlett. Come in, come in.' He rises from behind his light, oak desk and walks the excessive span of his office towards the door to greet me.

The office is as bright as the weather will allow, with daylight flowing through the floor-to-ceiling glass panes.

'Sit down, please.' He indicates for me to take a seat on the opposite side of his desk. 'Now, before we talk about anything else, how are you? I'm terribly sorry to hear about your father.'

'Thank you. He was ill for a long time but it's still a shock.' I hold my blink longer than intended.

The office door opens and the kitchen staff wheel in a trolley containing a pot of coffee, a pot of tea and four bite-sized cakes.

'It's not just a view you get then?' I ask, changing the subject.

'Thank you, Ashley, we can pour ourselves,' Neil says with a pleasant smile.

Taking a cup and placing a piece of lemon drizzle cake on the side of his saucer, he tells me to help myself.

If perceptions could be more wrong. I take a piece of chocolate sponge and a cup of tea.

'Now, why have I invited you here?' he says once he's chewed the last crumbs of his sponge.

He shuffles in his chair so that he's leaning back slightly and takes the foot of one leg across the knee of his other.

'Well, I've been watching your results for some time in any event but this recent transaction...' he casts an eye over a piece of paper on his desk, '...Eclectic Technologies. We've had superb feedback from the client and the figures speak for themselves. In fact, they've thrown you over your targets for the year and I'm fully aware of the circumstances of that deal... that you essentially carried the entire transaction yourself.'

'Erm, thank you,' I mutter from behind my fingers, which are held a little in front of my mouth to disguise any possible rogue chocolate crumbs.

'No, thank *you*. As you've been off for a couple of days, and arguably should still be off, by the way, you probably don't know that Stephen Lawrence has been in touch about potential future work. And there's plenty of it.'

My stomach sinks, in part from the thought of another convoluted deal but mostly from the thought that Gregory would rather delegate to Lawrence than speak to me himself.

'They've specifically asked that you're the point of contact for all deals from Eclectic Technologies and any of the GJR group's companies.'

'Wow. Great. That's, that's really great,' I say, faking excitement.

'Now for the good news.'

'There's more?'

'Well, you don't think it would be appropriate for us to have just a senior associate in that position, do you?'

'Hmm, well, I hadn't thought about it but I guess you're

right. I'll speak to them and tell them that I can't be the lead contact. Who would you like me to—'

'Scarlett.' He laughs, resting his palms on his desk. 'I'm offering you a promotion, to legal director.'

I stand from my seat, causing it to rock backwards. 'You're what? Why?'

He smiles casually, genuinely. 'So you'll take it?'

'Take it? Of course. Thank you.'

My hands wiggle uncomfortably by my side, unsure whether to shake his hand or go in for a hug. I decide to sit down, doing neither. But those seconds give me time to register the situation. I lost Dad for a promotion. I can feel tears knocking on the back door to my eyes and I know I need to leave.

'Excellent! Do you want to discuss the finer details now or would you rather get the paperwork first and take it all in?'

I wonder whether he's noticed the chemical change in my body, the way dogs can sense whether their owner's happy or sad.

Nodding, the lump in my throat subsides just enough to let me explain that I'd rather read the paperwork first but that I'm grateful for the opportunity.

'It's all rather overwhelming, isn't it?'

'You've no idea,' I say, shaking his hand. I can't get out of there fast enough.

'Sooo, what did he want?' Amanda sings, her words reaching my office before her bouncing body.

'Erm, he wanted to offer me directorship,' I offer sheepishly.

'What? Amazing! Crazy! That's fantastic news, Scarlett; you really deserve it.' She throws her arms around my neck.

'Do I?' I whisper.

She pushes me away from her body, her hands resting on

my shoulders. 'Of course you do. You work harder than anyone else in here.'

'I just – I just don't know if one deal means I really deserve it.'

Amanda shakes my shoulders. 'This isn't about *one* deal. This is about you working solid for years. You're always the last person in here on a night and, rather distastefully,' she adds with a forced regal accent, stiff upper lip and all, 'you're the first to refuse a cocktail in the name of work.'

'I hope you're right.'

'I am. Now, let's celebrate. Lunch somewhere nice? Your treat because you're about to earn a lot more money than I do,' she says with a wink.

'I'd love to but I actually need to tie off some pieces for a deal.' I glare at the pile of Eclectic Technologies documents that I've been trying to avoid.

'See, that's exactly what I'm talking about.' She looks to the ceiling. 'Okay, well, what are your plans for the rest of the week?'

'I haven't got that far yet.'

'Would you like my opinion? I'll give it to you anyway. You should go home and put your feet up. Pamper yourself, do something with Sandy.'

'You know what...' I sigh. 'I think you're right.'

'I am,' she states with her hands on her hips in jest. Then, softening, she tells me, 'I'll see you on Friday. If you need or want me before then, just call and I'll be there in a flash.'

'Okay.'

I hug my best friend.

* * *

The smell of fresh polish permeates the air when the elevator doors open on to the high-gloss floor. The usual immaculately presented receptionists are in position beneath the gleaming Eclectic Technologies plaque. Artificial lighting reflects in the windows, illuminating the space. One man in a navy suit and red tie sits on the sofas, perusing the *Financial Times* and intermittently glancing at the flat-screen television playing *BBC News*.

'Good afternoon, welcome to Eclectic Technologies,' says Juliette, according to her gold name badge.

'Good afternoon, I'm Scarlett Heath. I'm here to see Mr Ryans and, if they're available, Mr Williams and Mr Lawrence too.'

'Do you have an appointment?' she chimes as she taps on her keyboard.

No, and part of me hopes you're going to tell me he isn't in the office then I can leave these documents with you and be on my way.

'No, I don't, but it'll only take five minutes.'

'Ooh, let me see... it looks like they're all in a meeting together until—'

'I can wait.'

'Oh,' she says in a way that makes me think her blue, silk necktie is choking her. 'Well—'

The sound of his voice constricts my torso. I stare with wide eyes along the corridor as he draws closer, unable to move. *I can't do this!* Sweat forms on my palms beneath the pile of documents I'm gripping tightly.

'This has been a productive afternoon, Mr Cheung,' he's saying.

I contemplate running, hiding, dropping to the ground, but it is too late. He sees me. He stops dead in his tracks, his eyes locked on mine, his conversation suspended. All rational thought has escaped me. Blue suit. Crisp, white shirt. Hair neatly combed.

Williams coughs, breaking the near silence of the room. 'Mr Cheung, allow me to introduce you to Scarlett Heath.'

'Hello, Mr Cheung,' I say, my professional alter ego kicking in. 'I'm a legal advisor to Eclectic Technologies.'

He takes my hand in a limp shake. 'It is a pleasure to meet you.'

I muster all the charm I can. 'The pleasure's all mine.'

'They have a lawyer involved already. Should I worry?'

I laugh, a fake hearty laugh. The kind I reserve for business networking. 'Only if you're doing something you shouldn't be, Mr Cheung.'

'Quick! Hide the documents!' he shouts theatrically to three others in his group.

The men laugh, except Gregory, who remains taciturn.

'Let me show you out, Mr Cheung,' Williams eventually says.

'Yes, yes, we shall be going. We'll see you tomorrow.'

Williams leads the four men to the elevators, leaving Gregory, Lawrence and me in silence. Gregory and Lawrence both watch me, waiting. *Compose yourself, Scarlett.*

'I need you to sign some documents in wet ink, all three of you,' I say, glancing over my shoulder to acknowledge Williams. 'Do you have five minutes? It won't take more than that.'

Gregory grips his chin between his index finger and thumb and then pulls his right hand back through his hair, all the while staring at me like I have ten heads.

'Yes, we have time,' Lawrence says.

He starts to walk and I follow him back down the corridor they emerged from just minutes ago. As we turn the corner, out of the view of reception and preying eyes, Lawrence clears his throat. 'I'm very sorry about your father, Scarlett.'

Neither he nor I expect a response and I don't offer one. Instead, I keep my focus on the documents in my hands.

'Just in here,' Lawrence says, gesturing for me to walk ahead of him into the boardroom.

The light flickers to life as we're joined by Gregory and Williams. Lawrence and Williams walk to the far end of the rectangular room and Gregory stands next to me at the head of the oval table. I allow myself a split-second glance at him and instantly chastise myself for meeting his eye.

'I have three documents,' I say to the room. 'I need you all to sign a copy of this one.'

I push the document to the end of the table for Lawrence and Williams to sign.

'These two are just for you,' I say to Gregory, refusing to move my attention from a particular grain in the wooden table.

Gregory makes no movement to sign anything. I can feel his gaze burning into me and strings being pulled taut in the depth of my abdomen. *Please, just sign.*

'Do you need a pen?' I ask, eventually turning to face him, holding a pen out for him to take.

My heart rate doubles. I can feel moisture forming on my palms and sickness rising in my throat. Those lips I've kissed. That brooding frown. *Stick with it, Scarlett; you can do this.*

I shake the pen twice, encouraging him to take it.

Eventually, he grabs it, his fingertips grazing mine.

He bends towards the table, leaning on his left hand. I watch the movement of his shoulder beneath his blazer as the nib of the pen almost reaches the paper, before he stops. Sighing, he turns to me.

'Is this really how you want things to be?'

How I want things to be? Yes, Gregory, I wanted to meet you and get sucked into some dark, twisted game, then fall madly in love with you so there was no hope in hell of me ever walking away. Then I wanted to find out that me being in love with you would lead to my dad's murder and that I'd be forced to hate you when all I want to do is jump into your arms and feel the touch of your lips on mine.

Holy shit.

I'm in love with him.

'Is that supposed to be a joke?' I snap, glaring back at him, adrenalin rushing to my head.

He holds his position for an excruciatingly long second or two, neither of us willing to blink. Then with the speed and determination of a raging bull, he signs his name on all three documents. Finished, he throws the pen down and makes to leave the room. Gripping the door handle so tight that the whites of his knuckles show, he pauses. I hold my breath, expectant. But then he leaves, slamming the door behind him. As I stare after him, the image of his cigarette-burned wrist consumes my mind.

I don't want to hurt him. He's breaking my heart and I still can't stand the thought that I might be just another person in his life causing him pain.

Williams walks to my end of the large table, sliding signed documents towards me.

'I'm sorry about your father, Scarlett. We all are. What happened was unfair and should never have happened.'

I open my mouth, then close it without making a sound.

Williams shakes his head. 'It wasn't his fault and no matter how much you hate him or *think* you hate him, you can't make him loathe himself any more than he already does.'

'Wasn't his fault? He's the reason everything happened. He

got me involved in this whole fucked-up mess. *Everything* is his fault!'

Williams appears uncommonly severe. 'You know, Scarlett, you were only supposed to be his lawyer. You played a part in changing that.'

'You're all so quick to jump to his defence, aren't you?' I snarl.

Williams sighs. 'Everything he does lately is about you. He would never, *could* never, have imagined this would happen.'

'Ah, I get it, the promotion was his doing? Well, I guess when you play sick games, it makes a lot of sense to have someone on your side. To take the hit for you when it all goes wrong, doesn't it?'

He shakes his head again and I can't help but think how I would like to slap his face repeatedly until it's red raw and stinging like my raging eyes. Like his friend, he places his hand on the handle of the door and turns to me before he leaves. 'How many people do you know just hand themselves in to the police for a life sentence?'

I knew it. 'Jack.'

He leaves with Lawrence following quickly behind, placing a comforting hand on my shoulder as he passes me.

I stand alone in the empty room until the sensory light turns out.

25

'Hi Sandy,' I mutter as I walk into the house. 'How's your day been?'

'I'm in here,' she calls from the kitchen.

The smell of sweet biscuits is delicious and the scent leads me to Sandy.

'Oh my word, what have you been up to?' I ask, scanning the results of hours of baking spread across the granite worktops.

'I just thought I'd bake something nice for dinner but I had spare pastry, so I made some tarts for pudding too. Hmm, then I decided to make some ginger biscuits and a cheesecake.' She giggles, washing a large, plastic bowl in the sink.

'And these?' I ask, pointing to a stack of whoopee pies.

'I have no excuse for those.'

She balances the bowl on top of a mound of draining dishes then rubs her hands down the sides of her flour-dusted apron.

'Right, what would you like first?'

I wrap my arm around her waist and rest my temple onto hers. 'You can always cheer me up, Sandy.'

'Rough afternoon?'

'You could say that. Okay, I'd like to start with a nice big fat wedge of this delicious-looking cheesecake, please.'

'Tea?' she sings.

'Absolutely. I'll put the kettle on.'

* * *

Unsurprisingly, the lethal combination of sugar, caffeine and the day's events kills my ability to sleep. Rain pounds my bedroom window and wind gently rocks my curtains forwards and backwards. Images flash through my mind like storyboards, mapping my life with my dad, how I met Gregory, the bloodstains on the staircase, how Dad died, Lara's visit to my house, the story she told me about Gregory's past. Thoughts of the future and unanswered questions – what will I do with the house, will I continue to live with Sandy, will I accept my promotion – intermittently break my trips through the past.

A thunderous rap of the front door knocker startles me, echoing through the house. I bolt upright in my bed. I wait for a few seconds then the rapping comes again, longer and louder, once, twice, three times. There's a sound like Sandy's flicking the switch of her bedroom light, followed by soft footsteps and the creak of her door. Slipping into my silk kimono, I poke my head out to the landing.

Sandy holds a finger to her lip, where she's standing at the head of the staircase. 'Shh.'

'I'll come with you,' I whisper.

We tiptoe down the staircase together, startling each time the floorboards creak. We reach the front door in darkness and the door knocker thuds again, making us cling to each other.

Sandy picks up two golf umbrellas and hands one to me.

'What on earth am I supposed to do with this?'

'It's all I could think of.'

We each take one side, peering through the door curtain.

'Gregory,' I say, jumping back from the window.

Sandy looks at me in anticipation then undoes the dead lock.

'Wait!' I whisper. 'I don't want to see him.'

'But Scarlett, he's getting soaked through out there.'

'No, I don't want to. Please send him away. Tell him I'm not here or something, anything. I don't want to see him.' I scurry behind the wall into the lounge, close enough that I'll be able to hear his voice.

His soft South African twang asks where I am and Sandy tells him I'm not home.

'Is she okay?'

There's silence and I wonder what's happening, then Gregory shouts, 'Scarlett, please.'

There's a genuine pleading in his voice that makes me want to go to him, to soothe him and tell him that everything will be fine.

'Scarlett!'

'She doesn't want to see you, I'm sorry.'

There's silence again and I listen to drops of rain hitting the ground. Leaning back against the lounge wall, I close my eyes, thinking of the last time he wore that outfit. *Chapel Down.* I bite my cheeks but it doesn't prevent tears forming in my eyes, welling, waiting to fall.

'He's gone,' Sandy says.

I nod but can't speak.

'Come on, it's after three and the vicar is coming today; let's go to bed.'

I nod and take the hand Sandy offers me.

* * *

'Scarlett,' Sandy whispers through my opening bedroom door. 'Sorry to wake you but the vicar will be here in an hour.'

'What time is it?' I mumble with my face squashed into my pillow.

'Eleven-thirty.'

'Oh my God! I'm up, I'm up!' I say, not moving at all.

'Okay, I'll pop a pot of tea on. Would you like some food? Pancakes, maybe?' she says too temptingly, forcing me to sit and smile in response. 'Oh, and Scarlett,' she says, stepping back into my room from the landing, 'mind your use of the Lord's name for the next few hours, won't you?'

Reverend Griffiths arrives in smart, black trousers, a black shirt, a white dog collar and a tweed blazer. A remarkably ordinary outfit. His grey hair is thinning but still covers his head and his bright-blue eyes look pure and honest beneath his large, round-rimmed glasses. It almost seems silly how long it took for me to eventually settle on a blue dress and navy cardigan. Sandy has made an extra special effort to look angelic too. Her hair is tightly curled and pinned back. Tiny kitten heels have replaced her slippers and she wears a pretty, pastel-green, wrap dress with a white, Victorian collar.

We exchange pleasantries and sit to take tea in the lounge. The reverend sits in my dad's striped, high-back chair, which irritates me more than it ought to. Sandy takes the lead with conversation, being more familiar than I am with how to address a man of his stature. Watching them smile and converse politely, they look like nice, good people. I feel increasingly like an imposter. Clinging to my cup and saucer for support, I walk to the bay window and stare out to the low, end-of-October sun.

'It would be helpful if you could tell me about how Doctor Heath passed on,' Reverend Griffiths says.

Sandy reacts with wide, startled eyes.

'It's nice to be able to put the congregation at ease, if possible. To say Doctor Heath passed peacefully in his sleep, for example.'

I want to tell him, to confess everything to the reverend and pray for his forgiveness, for my dad's forgiveness. The words play out in my mind. *He was ill, yes. He was dying, yes. But it wasn't his time. He was murdered. I brought it upon him and he was alone. He was alone because I left him alone whilst I played Gregory's fucked-up games and drank wine.*

'Doctor Heath had been sick for a long time, Reverend. Alzheimer's disease, he had. Oh but he still had his moments; he could still make us smile,' Sandy sings. 'He was peaceful enough when he died. He was the most peaceful I'd seen him for months.'

'No!' I yell, banging my cup down onto my saucer. 'No, Reverend, he was not peaceful; he was alone! He was in hospital because I wasn't here to look after him and he died alone because I didn't stay with him. I should've been there. I could've stopped it.'

'That is not true!' Sandy snaps. She walks halfway across the space between us and gestures for me to sit. I can't meet her eye but do as instructed and take a seat on the sofa next to her.

The reverend shuffles in his chair to place one hand on my knee and says, 'I can see you're angry, Scarlett, but remember this: if your father knew you loved him, he would have died a happy man.'

I wish I could hear truth in his words because if I could, my dad would've died the most loved and happy man I've ever known.

'Tell me, what was he like?'

'The best,' I say honestly. 'He brought me up. He did the best job he could and it was more than good enough.'

Smiling as memories of our life in this very space flash through my mind, I stand and walk to the centre of the room beneath the sparkling, crystal chandelier.

'Do you remember how he taught us to dance, Sandy?'

'Oh, yes, he twirled me around so fast, I could hardly breathe.'

'He lifted me onto his feet and turned me and turned me until my head was in a spin. I had to hug into his stomach to stop me from falling but I kept telling him, "Faster!" We spun, faster, faster...'

'And you spun until he fell back onto the sofa still holding you in his arms,' Sandy adds.

'He was the best.'

'Oh dear me,' Sandy says through a laugh. She tries to speak but ends up hugging her ribs, almost folded in half as she chuckles from the pit of her stomach. 'Do... you... rem... remem... remember when he... when he taught us how to do a sack race.'

I laugh too. It's short but genuine.

'It was for my sports day at school,' I tell the reverend. 'I was nervous about being picked to represent the red team in the sack race. I had no idea how to do it. In the past, I'd always been picked to do the relay or the egg-and-spoon race.'

'Ooooooh,' Sandy calls, wafting one hand to cool her face in an attempt to cease her laughter. 'Go on! Go on!'

'Sandy told my dad how nervous I was and when he came home from work, he'd brought with him two large, yellow clinical waste sacks. They were obviously plastic,' I add for the reverend's benefit. 'After dinner, we all went outside to the garden and Dad marked out a track for us to jump. "Right, get in your sack," he said. Sandy helped me shuffle to the start line. "Ready, steady, go!" she said. Dad took two flawless jumps forward in his clinical waste sack. "See how easy it is!" he said. It did look easy, so I took two jumps forwards. Dad hopped twice again and I followed. "Keep going! Keep goooooiiiiiiing!"'

'And splat!' Sandy adds. 'His bag slipped on some cat poop and he went flying.'

'He tried to save himself by kicking his legs but he was kicking against the plastic and the cat poo had spread by then.'

'Next thing we heard was, "Whoaaaa!"' Sandy says. 'He realised it wasn't quite as easy as he thought after that but the next day, when I stood at the start line and looked over at my dad watching me, all I could do was giggle. It turned into one of the most fun things I ever did at school.'

'Jolly good story!' Reverend Griffiths says with a clap. 'Excellent! Would you be happy for me to use your stories tomorrow?'

Tomorrow. It strikes like a lightning bolt.

'That would be nice,' Sandy says.

We stand at the door and wave to Reverend Griffiths as he drives away from the house.

'Do you know what occurred to me today, Sandy?'

'What's that?'

'You're the only family I've got.'

26

I watch myself in my floor-length mirror, slowly stepping into black heels then pulling tight the waist belt on my black mac over my suit. I move my loose curls back over my shoulders.

'Ready?' Sandy asks beneath her black net veil as I walk down the stairs.

'As I'll ever be.'

The door knocker is tapped and Sandy steps towards the door, her heels clipping once, twice on the floor.

'Good morning,' she says, motioning for the greying man to step into the house.

As he crosses the threshold in his striped trousers and black morning jacket, the undertaker removes his top hat and dips his head.

'I'm Richard,' he says in a broad Cockney accent, stepping into the hall.

'I'm Scarlett and this is Sandy.'

His hand is covered in a thick, black, leather glove protecting him from the frost in the air.

'D'earse is ready. D'ya 'ave flowers ya'd like me to take?'

I motion to the large arrangement of blue, orange and white flowers to be placed on top of Dad's coffin.

'And this one's from me,' Sandy says, handing him a small, delicate posy of winter flowers she's made herself.

'It's beautiful, Sandy,' I say.

Resting a hand on her shoulder, we both watch Richard leave the house. My body stiffens at the first sight of my dad. His perfectly polished coffin gleams through the shaded windows of the hearse. Sandy's body convulses beneath my hand then she begins to cry. I take a deep breath and hand her the cotton tissue I tucked into the pocket of my mac.

I stand in front of her, my body shielding her from the view. 'Come on, Sandy, let's be strong for him.'

She nods and wipes her nose with the tissue. Pulling the door shut behind us, we slowly make our way to the black limousine parked behind the hearse. When we're inside, the undertaker signals and both cars crawl behind him as he walks the first hundred metres away from the house. At the first T-junction, he climbs into the front of the hearse and the cars pick up some speed as we head towards the church.

I've never noticed before now the reaction that seeing a funeral car procession evokes. It seems obvious that a hearse carrying a coffin held in place by one thin, metal prong is limited in speed but why would a person ever put their mind to the speed of a hearse if it's never affected their life? I was one of those people: the unaffected. Dad is the first person I've seen die. It occurs to me that the shitbag who revs his Volvo V40 alongside the hearse in a desperate urge to overtake us when the traffic lights flick to green is probably also one of the unaffected. I could slap his bum-fluff covered, New York Yankees cap wearing face.

We move forwards through the lights. An elderly man

pauses in the street, takes off his flat cap and, holding it in front of him with two hands, he dips his head to my dad. This turns Sandy's whimpers to a sob. Pulling her towards me, I rest my chin against her brow and she blows her nose into my handkerchief.

Reverend Griffiths meets us at the church entrance and motions for Sandy and me to walk behind the coffin. I squeeze Sandy's hand as she weeps quietly into a handkerchief. Reverend Griffiths leads us into the church and down the aisle. Dad is set down centrally, on display for the mourners to see. I'm pleased to reach the front of the church and turn my back to the staring eyes.

'I am the resurrection and the life. He who believes in me will live, even though he dies,' Reverend Griffiths recites from John 11:25, just as he said he would.

Sandy wraps her arm tightly in mine as we take a seat in the front pew. I stare blankly as Reverend Griffiths continues the service and all of the way through the first hymn. I'm considering the words of John: *he who believes in me will live.* My dad believed, so somewhere, somehow he's looking down on us and watching as sniffles and tears fill the church. He'll still be watching tonight, tomorrow and the next day, watching every move I make.

What would you do, Dad? What do you want me to do?

Anger builds like a weight in my body. I want revenge.

The reverend talks about my dad and relays the stories Sandy and I shared with him. I try to listen to distract me from my rage.

At the end of the service, Reverend Griffiths asks God to care for my dad. I hope that God does a better job than I did. The reverend explains that only close friends and family are invited to the committal but that all other guests can make

their way to the wake. Some make their excuses and leave
directly from the church; others kiss and hug me before I'm
able to climb back into the sanctity of the limousine with
Sandy and drive to the committal grounds.

'I'm not going to the wake, Sandy. The cars can take us
home or we can drop you at the wake first. I'm sorry, I just can't
sit in a room with those people.'

She nods, neither agreeing nor disagreeing with my
approach but understanding.

At the first set of traffic lights, a lorry driver leans forwards
in his seat when his vehicle brakes to a standstill parallel to the
limousine. He leans as far forwards as he can to see into our
cars. Sandy flaps a hand angrily to tell him to look elsewhere
then breaks into another round of tears.

Small, light, infrequent raindrops begin to fall on the tinted
windows. I hold up my hand as I step out of the car beneath the
dark sky and rub a drop of rain between my finger and thumb,
then put on my black, leather gloves. Our driver offers me an
umbrella.

'Let Sandy have it,' I say, motioning to the back of the car
where the driver offers a hand to Sandy.

Reverend Griffiths leads the way to my dad's plot, followed
by four men bearing the coffin. An ominous-looking hole
awaits, a mound of dirt resting to one side of the plot. I take
note that Dad will rest between Martha and Roger Haines to
his right, eighty-two and seventy-nine years old, respectively,
and Patricia Whelehan, sixty-six, to his left.

Sandy stands to my side, to the left of the reverend, who's
positioned himself at the head of the coffin. As my dad is being
lowered, I briefly search the small gathering of people who've
come to see the committal and offer Amanda a soft, grateful

smile. The rain is suddenly heavy and loud as it bounces off the polished wood.

'We now commit his body to the ground. Earth to earth, ashes to ashes, dust to dust. In the sure and certain hope of the resurrection to eternal life.'

And that's it. That's my dad's goodbye.

'Scarlett,' the reverend says, placing a hand onto my elbow, encouraging me forwards.

He opens a small casket filled with soil. I take a handful and step forwards to throw it over the gold plaque displaying my dad's name, followed by the white rose I've been holding since we arrived.

People begin to disappear into the grey background, their faces with silent, moving mouths step closer to mine, some kissing my cheeks. More than once, I feel the faces touch my sodden, padded shoulder or my gloved hands. They walk away, hidden beneath their large, black umbrellas. Some run, their grey coats blending into the decaying headstones that cover the ground of the cemetery.

The rain suddenly stops in just the spot I'm standing. I turn my gloved hand in front of me. There are no fresh drops of water. The smell of dampness and loneliness is smothering. I'm vaguely aware of an arm around my shoulder, encouraging me to take my eyes from my dad. My thick, brown hair is stuck to the sides of my face. My once buoyant curls are drowned. My suit clings to my trembling body beneath my soaked, black mac.

The arm around my shoulder tugs but I can't take my eyes from the coffin, despite desperately blinking through dripping eyelashes. Dad would scarcely recognise his little girl – who she's become and the corrupt web in which she's gotten herself entangled.

The hand tightens on my shoulder and becomes strong enough to turn the weight of my heavy body, dragging my heels from the saturated ground. The groundkeepers move in to cover the coffin and the white rose. This is it: all his years of goodness, caring and strength, buried deep beneath sand and dirt. He deserves more than this. For every time he picked me up when I'd fallen, for every time his thumb swept tears from my face, he deserves more than this.

'Let's get you to your car,' says Reverend Griffiths.

I raise my head, my mind returning to real time. His words resonate as the world, a new world, comes into focus. Amanda is leading Sandy back to the limousine. I feel the sharp, cold air blow across my cheek. Thick, charcoal clouds drift slowly through the grey sky.

Reverend Griffiths speaks again. I shake my head, forcing it to register the sound, ordering my eyes to focus on him, but they're drawn to movement behind him.

The black Mercedes rolls to a stop in the distance at the edge of the cemetery.

It's him. The reason all this came to be and the very person I want to hold me and tell me everything's going to be okay.

I burst from the grip of the reverend and with all the strength left in my broken body, I surge towards Gregory as he steps out of the car. I reach him, punching frantically at his body and striking my palms against his face. Tears stream down my cheeks and uncontrollable sobs burst from the depths of me. He does nothing to stop me. He absorbs each impact like he deserves it, as if he wants to feel the pain.

'I hate you. I hate everything you've brought on us. I hate that deal.'

My energy is drained. I have nothing left.

'And I hate myself for not really hating you at all.'

Before my legs give way under the weight of my body, he wraps his arms around me. He pulls me into his chest and lowers me to the sodden grass in his lap. I feel the touch of his lips on my head and the gentle tug of his body rocking me. He warms my cold, wet body as we sit. The rain pounds again, washing away my gushing tears. My world fades to black, the shade of my soul.

'I've got her; grab the door,' Gregory says.

He lifts me into the back of the Mercedes and rests my head on his lap. I open my eyes wearily to see Jackson glance at me in the rear-view mirror before he pulls us away from the cemetery.

'Drop us off then get some food, something warm; she needs to eat,' Gregory says quietly.

'Sandy,' I croak.

'She's fine, angel; she's with Amanda.'

The cold from my wet clothes seeps into my bones and my body starts to shiver uncontrollably. My teeth chatter and my breathing becomes audible. Gregory lifts me from his lap and pulls me into his chest, stroking my hair with his warm hand. His soft lips press against my scalp and like a baby, I drift to the fringe of lucidity, exhausted.

* * *

Jackson wakes me when he opens the back door.

'Do you want me to carry her?'

I recognise the underground car park of the Shard.

'I can walk.'

In truth, my legs are weak and my body is still trembling from the cold. My head is so confused, I don't know what I am or what I should be feeling but I know there's nowhere else in the world I'd rather be than with Gregory.

The elevator pings as it arrives at the basement. Gregory gestures for me to step in ahead of him. I watch my feet as we rise in silence, neither of us knowing where to go from here. I'm exhausted. My dad is dead and I have no idea how to talk to the man I love. This all started because of one sick bastard. And he's out there.

Gregory opens the door to his apartment with a hand on the small of my back, guiding me to the lounge.

'Take this off,' he says, undoing the belt around my mac and pulling it from my shoulders. I'm even colder without it.

'I'll run you a bath.'

I walk to the window and look out over the city. Gregory was born into a life he didn't deserve, that no child deserves. And his demon is down there somewhere, hiding. Weaving between buildings. Most likely out of his mind with a toxic combination of alcohol and the thrill of my dad's kill.

'Here,' Gregory says handing me a crystal glass with a small amount of brandy in the bottom.

He wraps a wool blanket around my shoulders and I sit down onto the sofa, pulling my knees into my freezing-cold chest. The glass shakes in my hand as I shudder, part from cold, part from seething hatred.

'I want to kill him,' I whisper.

'Pardon?'

'I. Want. To. Kill. Him.' The words leave my mouth through gritted teeth.

Gregory takes a seat on the sofa beside me, his legs wide, his elbows resting on his knees.

'Don't let it take over you, Scarlett. He's not worth it.'

He takes the brandy from my hands, then leads me to the

bathroom. The freestanding bath is deep and full of bubbles. The lights are dim and Gregory has lit candles around the room.

I cast my eyes from the bath to him.

'I'll leave you to it. I'm sorry but this is the best I can do for now.' He pats the blue hooded jumper he's placed on the heated chrome towel rail.

'Thank you.'

I watch him leave the room, his white shirt still tucked into his trousers, despite the events of the last few hours. *He should be working.*

Sinking into the bubbles, the hot water stings my skin at first then settles to soothe me. I close my eyes and see Gregory, pulling his own hair in the lounge. Dipping my head beneath the water, I stare up to the dark ceiling, candles flickering in my vision.

'He'll never be free,' I whisper to myself.

I realise that the hate, the anger I feel now, Gregory has felt all his life. The little boy I keep seeing felt like this instead of having a childhood. What he said about the children in the hospital – how they should be shielded from the darkness of the world – it all makes sense now. I want to end it for him. I want revenge for my dad and an end to Gregory's pain.

The hooded jumper only just preserves my modesty. Gregory watches me as I walk from the bathroom, towel drying my hair, to the kitchen island where he's perched on a stool, now wearing jeans and a fitted, black tee.

'You showered,' I say, acknowledging his wet hair and fresh scent.

He continues to watch me, his head moving with me as I walk towards him.

He clears his throat. 'Jackson brought food. You should eat something.'

Standing from his stool, he lifts the lids from the various dishes he's set out on the island.

'Salmon. Chicken. Pasta.'

I run my hand down the length of his spine and press myself against his side. 'Kiss me.'

Gregory turns, his back against the bench, and pulls my waist into his. He runs his fingers tenderly down the side of my face and exhales, long and slow, a slight shudder in his breath. Then his lips are on mine, his hands holding my cheeks. I let my mouth linger on his, enjoying the sensation. His tongue parts my lips and touches mine. I bite his lower lip and he groans, pulling my hips into his hard crotch. My legs part instinctively. Breathing softly onto his neck, I lift the bottom of his T-shirt, exposing his chest.

'We don't have to do this,' he whispers.

'I want to. I want to forget.'

'Are you sure?'

'Help me forget.'

I kiss his pecs and pull his tee roughly over his head.

He grabs my bare arse cheeks and I grind against him. His groan reverberates in my mouth, taking my last ounce of conservatism. I roughly undo the button of his jeans and he pulls the hooded jumper over my head, uncovering my naked body.

'I've missed you,' he whispers.

I don't let myself think of anything: not why we've been apart, not how I've felt in that time, and not how I truly feel about him. I yank him towards me and kiss him fiercely. He lifts me and shifts us so that I'm sitting on the island. I wrap my legs around him, pulling him into me, feeling his length beneath his jeans. He strokes his hand through my wet hair and I kiss him harder. I can't stand it any more. I want him. I need him.

He leans me back to lie on the island and slips off his jeans. I feel bereft in the brief seconds it takes for him to climb on top of me. Supporting his entire weight with one strong arm and tracing the contours of my body with his other, he places his lips on mine and pushes his hand between my legs, first cupping me then moving his fingers inside. I groan with desperation.

'God, Scarlett, what are you doing to me?'

My eyes widen. *Exactly what you're doing to me, I hope.*

My hips rise towards him and I dig my nails into his back. He resists me at first then in his own time, he lowers himself. He's inside me. My breathing deepens with each thrust of his body, my muscles clamping down on his stiff shaft. My impulse to push back against him increases and I feel myself move slowly to a heady euphoria, a place I've longed for, where there's no one and nothing else.

He drives and rotates simultaneously, stiffening further. He's almost ready. Squeezing my legs tighter around his waist, I push my hips up until he's so deep, he reaches the end of me. I'm lost in him. Out of my own head. All his.

Another gorgeous grind and his name leaves me as we climax together.

He collapses onto my chest and it's my turn to stroke his hair as his body trembles.

'I'm sorry,' he says when we eventually dress. 'I didn't mean to—'

I pull his chin to look at me and gently kiss him. 'Now, salmon gets my vote,' I say.

'Salmon it is,' he says, unsmiling.

We eat dinner on the sofa, probably the most informal

we've been together, and it's remarkably comfortable. Gregory dims the lights low enough that we can see the stars in the sky and occasional red flashes of aeroplane lights flying by, going in and out of Heathrow and London City airports. He pulls the glass coffee table closer and plants his bare feet on top of it, then wraps an arm around me and pulls me into his side. I don't want to ruin the moment, I could stay in this moment forever, but I have questions he needs to answer.

'I need to ask you some things.'

He sips his wine. 'Okay.'

'Let's start with the note. You said there was a note and that's how you knew to come to the hospital.'

He takes a deep breath, bracing himself, then moves towards the window, his hands resting in his jeans' pockets, his bare back tense.

'Do you remember the first time you stayed here?'

A half-smile rises on my lips. He glances over his shoulder but his face is serious. My smile fades.

'That night, during the night, someone tried to tamper with the apartment alarm.' He glances back at me but I don't react. 'It's not the first time someone's tried something. Money and power can attract a lot of animosity. Jackson checked the stair-wells, lifts, ground floor and there was nothing. The concierge hadn't noticed anyone coming into or out of the building. Then he checked the basement.'

Gregory turns to face me, shaking his head. 'I honestly had no idea, Scarlett.' Turning back to face the outside world, he continues, 'There was pen or paint – I never saw it – on the window screen of the Mercedes. It said... it said, "Accidents Happen".'

I swallow a lump in my throat. 'He meant my dad.'

'We didn't know for sure. God, I should've realised that he

knew who you were and got Jackson to step up security right after we closed the deal. He used to be in the forces, then the police, and has a lot of friends still there or ex-cops who do similar work to him. So, the next day, he put two men on my mother. Williams wasn't interested, said he could handle himself, although I think he's wanted the opportunity to come face to face with my dad since we were boys. And you, well, I just... I didn't plan to let you out of my sight anyway and with Jackson here, I didn't think anyone else was necessary.'

'That's what you were talking about when I interrupted that morning.' *And that's why you wanted to take me away.*

'Yes. Fuck, I could kick myself.'

I rise from the sofa and stand by his side, looking out at the bright city lights again. 'What about the note?'

'He went a step further when we were at Chapel Down. He must have walked straight into the building. I don't know why or how... Part of me wonders if he wanted me to find out and stop him but...'

'The note, Gregory, tell me!' I snap.

'He posted a note under the door of the apartment. It said, "Tell your girlfriend to stay strong".'

My hand reflexively covers my mouth and I swallow bile.

'Jackson picked it up. He was on his way to see Sandy; that's how they ended up at the hospital together,' he says, turning to look at me. 'He tried to call me but I didn't pick up his message until I was outside the hospital.'

Anger stirs within me. 'You should have told me.'

'I didn't think it would—'

'No. You should have told me.'

'I'm sorry, Scarlett. You'll never know how sorry I am. I wish I could take it back. All of it. Even if it meant I had to live my life never having met you and never having felt— I wish I could go back to the boardroom and not be desp—'

'Shh,' I say, placing one finger over his lips. 'I'm not sorry that I met you.'

I don't know at what stage my feelings changed; I don't remember thinking it wasn't his fault. But I believe it.

'Gregory, don't you think it's time the police were involved?'

He regards me with troubled browns. 'The police can't be involved.'

'Because you don't think there's any real evidence.'

'No, Scarlett. Because when Jackson and I find him, we won't be staying on the right side of the law.'

His statement should shock me. I've never been on the *wrong* side of the law. But the first thing I feel is vengeance. Pearson deserves to pay for what he did.

'That's enough for tonight,' I whisper.

He nods and looks back out across the city.

I rest my hand into his. 'Let's go to bed.'

He considers me from beneath a furrowed brow.

'It's okay.'

I shuffle in the bed to nestle my head into his firm chest and he wraps a strong, warm arm around my shoulders.

I close my eyes and finally drift into a deep, settled sleep.

27

I've been watching him for some time, watching the rise and fall of his chest as he sleeps. He's perfect. His angular jaw and straight nose are a peculiar contrast against his soft, red lips. His dark features – brows, eyes and hair – are fiercely attractive. Everything about him embodies masculinity. I run a finger along the line of his collarbone and lean in to place my lips on his neck.

'You're awake,' he mumbles.

'Yes.'

He opens one eye to look at me and that familiar, soul-melting half-smile draws on his lips.

'Are you watching me?'

'Yes. You were drooling,' I lie.

He quickly wipes his face with the back of his hand, forcing me to chuckle.

'I love that sound.'

His expression turns playfully stern and he lunges for me in the bed. I squeal when he pulls me onto his chest, his arms wrapping tightly around my back, forcing me to surrender.

Then he stills, reading me, lost in me like he might get lost in a book.

'You have no idea, do you?' He tucks my loose hair behind my ear and presses his mouth to mine, slow, still, unmoving. 'You're a witch, Scarlett Heath, and I'm completely under your spell.'

Then I kiss him. Fully, passionately. He rolls me onto my back and lies between my legs, the soft, plump skin of his lips owning mine. I feel whole under the weight of his body. He nudges his hips forward lazily and he grows against me. I want to surrender to him. I want him to control my body totally, utterly, completely.

He teases my top lip with a stroke of his tongue and circles his hips against my stomach.

'You're not the only one under a spell, Mr Ryans.' *I am 100 per cent besotted with this man.*

He makes sure I'm ready – I am. I most certainly am. Without warning, he thrusts his length into me. A welcome hit. But the look in his eyes tells me he's not going to fuck me; he's going to make love to me.

* * *

Showered and dressed in yesterday's clothes, I smile at the sight of Gregory sitting at the breakfast bar, remembering the events of last night, and this morning.

'Have I told you how unbelievably sexy you look in a suit?' he says, watching me walk down the stairs and into the kitchen.

'Hmm, if you plan on keeping me around today, I'm going to need to pick up some clothes from home.'

'If that's what I have to do to keep you, deal.'

I smile. 'Why don't I make us some pancakes? Sandy makes the best pancakes. I can't promise to make pancakes like hers but how hard can it be?'

'Erm, sure?'

A door bangs somewhere in the apartment, or duplex, or house, or whatever Gregory's oversized city pad is most appropriately called.

'Is Jackson here?'

'Most likely. He has an almost self-contained flat up there,' he says, pointing generally in the direction of upstairs and east. 'I haven't really shown you around properly, have I?'

'Always been in a rush to do other things,' I say, grinning at my wit as I crack eggs into a glass bowl.

Gregory's amusement decorates his voice. 'Well, if I'd shown you around, you'd realise Jackson doesn't need to come through the lounge. There's a staircase to the side of the front door that goes straight up to his room. A sort of guest wing. It's like he doesn't live here most times which is good; we spend a lot of time together as it is and I like the space. I'm not always the most sociable of people.'

'You don't say.'

He scowls. 'Plus, he knows you're here.'

I smirk over my shoulder. 'And all that implies.'

He winks. I could orgasm on the spot.

I fumble in the fridge to distract myself from desire. 'Why did you ever employ Jackson?'

'I needed a driver. Getting from A to B can be tricky in the city sometimes so it's convenient and it means I can work, take calls, answer emails if I need to, whilst we're en route. Then there were a few other things: incidents. Like I've said, having money can piss a lot of people off.'

'So he's a bodyguard.'

'I don't really see it like that. He's a driver, a personal trainer and to an extent, yes, something *like* a bodyguard. He watches my blindside.'

I trickle olive oil into a frying pan and turn on the induction hob. The oil heats almost instantly and sizzles when I pour in the wet pancake mix.

'I'm not sure how these are going to fit with your personal training regime.'

'I can make an exception.'

A burst of female laughter comes from the adjoining door on the mezzanine level. I turn my head toward the sound.

'I take it Jackson isn't alone?'

'Doesn't sound like it?'

'Why do you look so confused?'

'I've never known Jackson have anyone here.'

'And he's worked for you how long?'

'Four years.'

'Wow, four years. I'd bet he didn't last very long.' I smirk. 'Does it bother you that he has someone here?'

Gregory scratches his nose, then glances towards the staircase. 'I'm not sure. No?'

I slide the first two pancakes on to a plate and pour another two circles in the frying pan. As I search the cupboards for syrup, Gregory's phone rings.

'I'll be back for the masterpiece; I need to take this,' he says, holding up his phone. 'Ryans,' he snaps, bounding up the stairs to his home office.

The female laughter comes again as I happily continue creating breakfast.

'Would it offend you if I said I'm surprised they smell good?' Gregory asks on return.

I grin like a child, genuinely thrilled with my efforts. 'Work?' I ask, taking a seat on a stool next to him and drizzling syrup on my plate.

'These are amazing. And yes, I might have some work coming your way actually: a new deal.'

'Oh, Gregory, I—'

'Sorry, that was thoughtless. You don't have to do it. I didn't think. For the record, it's completely above board, usual business. I wouldn't have asked you to do anything that—'

'It's not that. I know you wouldn't get me messed up in anything like that again.' I stab my pancake with my fork. 'I know that because I have far too much control over your balls these days.'

We both laugh, although Gregory's is nervous. 'I'm the one with the control, angel. C.E.O. Don't forget that.'

As arrogant as they are, his words completely turn me on.

'I was going to say that I need to have a think about conflicts of interest and sort out some compliance issues within the firm, that's all.'

'Understood.'

'Which reminds me, I want to know about Jack. And don't fob me off, Ryans.'

The door to the staircase opens and Jackson comes into the kitchen, saving Gregory from a discussion he seemingly does *not* want to have.

'Ah, morning.'

'Morning,' Gregory says over his cup of coffee.

Jackson scratches his chin then puts one hand in the pocket of his eighties-style, straight-leg jeans.

'Jackson.' I try my best to hide my amusement behind my coffee cup.

'Ah, I just want to check that it's still okay for me to take off today. I don't want to leave you in the lurch and I'll have my phone all day so if you need me, anything at all, and if it's anything about, you know—'

'It's okay. She knows it all,' Gregory says. 'Yes, take off. I'm going to take Scarlett out to the farm. We'll be fine there.'

I've got no idea what 'the farm' is but Jackson seems content with the response. He nods then runs back up the stairs. 'Good to go,' I hear him say.

I get back to my pancake. Placing the forkful of food into my mouth, I'm distracted by movement on the stairs. I try not to look but intrigue gets the better of me.

Gregory coughs into his coffee, spraying some remains of his mouthful back into the cup.

Swallowing my pancake with a gulp, I jump off the barstool.

'Sandy!'

Sandy freezes in the middle of the open lounge. Jackson rests a hand on her back to encourage her forwards.

'Sandy!'

Gregory walks to Sandy and says good morning, shaking her hand. He offers them both breakfast and coffee. Sandy smiles and responds to Gregory but watches me, motionless.

'Sandy!'

She bites her finger, then shrugging her shoulders, says, 'Morning!'

Jackson and Gregory look back and forth between themselves, Sandy and me.

'Sandy!'

I hadn't realised my jaw was hanging loose between each round of 'Sandy!' but Gregory puts a finger onto my bottom jaw and pushes it closed.

'Well, we'll let you get on,' Sandy says, nudging Jackson towards the entrance door.

'Sand—'

'Shh,' Gregory whispers as he lifts my hand to cover my mouth.

28

'Can we make a detour to my house for clothes?' I ask as we pull out of the Shard.

'Ahh, she's back in the land of the living.'

I glare at Gregory as he looks right then left behind the wheel of the black Aston Martin DB9. He's wearing a weather-appropriate black wool coat and scarf, and I could do with similar.

'I guess it's quite funny,' I concede. 'Thinking about it, it's really funny. The look on her face was priceless.'

'The look on _your_ face was better.'

I scoff. 'It's strange, I've always thought of Sandy as a kind of mother figure but without realising, she's become a friend. She always seemed much older than me when I was a child and, well, when she was looking after me and putting pigtails in my hair, but she isn't old at all.'

'I think the older you get, the more age becomes just a number, don't you?'

'I guess you're right. Sometimes, she looks out for me and

others, we're in role reversal. I'm glad she's having a chance to do things she's missed out on.'

That thought reminds me of my dad and I have to force his ill face from my mind.

My street is grey and forlorn when we pull onto it. The red post-box seems a deeper shade than I'd left it and the leafless trees look tarnished by death. I sense Gregory's concern but continue looking straight ahead as he rolls the car to a stop outside the townhouse. I stare at the porch and the Saturday edition of *The Times* that Dad will never read, wasting on the welcome mat.

'Do you want me to come in?'

I shake my head. 'I won't be long.'

I look around the street nervously, feeling like an intruder as I walk through the wrought-iron gate and up the pathway to the house. Cold penetrates from the metal handle and the door creaks as I push it open, a sound I've not noticed before. The hallway is empty, lifeless. I take two steps into the house and jump when the floor squeaks under my feet. I dash up the staircase, slamming my bedroom door shut behind me, leaning my back against the door until I catch my breath. Fear consumes me, a fear of something irrational and intangible.

I rub the balls of my hands into my sockets, trying to convince myself that if I can close my eyes, I can't be scared. Taking a deep breath, I open my eyelids and start to undress. I pull on some jeans and a shirt and pass a belt through the loops as fast as I can. After throwing my suit into my wash basket, combing my hair and cleaning my teeth, I spritz myself with perfume. Pulling on my black, knee-high boots, the pair Gregory likes, then grabbing my black, wool coat and crimson scarf, I leave the house as quickly as I can.

I'm breathless when I sit back into the passenger seat of the

DB9. Sinking into the warmth of the heated seat, I try to calm my breathing.

'Are you okay?' Gregory asks, placing a hand on my thigh.

'It doesn't feel right any more.'

'The house?'

'It's cold and miserable.'

He runs a hand down my hair. His mouth parts and closes silently, his eyes betraying his anxiety. He wants to say something but doesn't know how. His palm moves to my cheek, my body responding by leaning into his anchor.

'Why don't you come and stay with me this week? I don't want you to stay here alone.'

'Stay? With you? At the Shard?'

He takes his hand away, moving his gaze to the front window. 'Yes.'

'Well, I—'

'It's only a week, Scarlett; I'm not asking you to marry me,' he almost snarls.

Unsure which of us is wounded more, I twist my lip between my finger and thumb. A week of Gregory and a week away from this house whilst I figure out what to do with it.

'Okay.'

'Okay?'

'Okay.'

He pulls his key out of the ignition. 'Let's get your stuff then.'

'Okay.'

'Okay.'

* * *

He's looking at an old photograph of my dad and me hanging on the wall in the hallway when I finally arrive at the top of the staircase.

'That was my eighth birthday. Dad threw me a party in Richmond Park. It was a teddy bears' picnic,' I say with an enormous smile. 'He invited all the kids from my class. Sandy made far too much picnic food, as ever, and the best birthday cake. She made a giant bear wearing dungarees. I loved dungarees. I was also going through a phase of being obsessed with teddy bears and the idea that all my toys came to life at night when I was sleeping.'

Gregory looks at me, amused I think, and gives me his stunning half-smile.

'I read *A Toy's Palace* a lot during my phase.'

'Let me help you,' he says, climbing the stairs to take my suitcase and shoulder bag. 'I'll be outside.'

I look around the house one more time. 'Goodbye, Dad.'

After lugging my last three bags onto the porch, I pull the door shut behind me.

'Flip, Scarlett, these cars aren't made for their boot space,' Gregory says, getting back out of the car to help me.

Raising my arms at my sides, I look down to my luggage. With a sigh and a shake of his head, he picks up all three bags as if they're stuffed with air.

'And I thought you were scared about staying for a week. You've got enough stuff for year.'

'Scared for you,' I say with a purposeful mischievous glint in my eye.

I follow him to the car where he's forced to put the final bag on the *almost* back seat. Buildings disappear, the road opens up and the clouds begin to part as we drive into the evergreen of the country with Elton John's 'I Guess That's Why They Call It The Blues,' playing through the speakers.

'So you're taking me to a farm?'

'Yes.'

'Like a farm with animals? Or like a country retreat?'

'Like my house in the country that used to be a farm.'

'You have a house in the country?'

'Yes.'

'Why? You live and work in the city.'

'That's exactly why. The press don't seem to know about it and—'

'The press?'

'Once your name is published in *The Times*'s Rich List, your life becomes public property.'

'*The Times*'s Rich List? So if I Google you—'

'Don't do that,' he snaps. 'The press prints all kinds of rubbish and I'd rather you make up your own mind.'

I already have.

'You see the problem is, Mr Ryans, when you tell a person not to do something, generally, they have a greater desire to do that exact thing.'

He continues to focus on the road ahead but his jaw rolls stiffly.

We turn left at a roundabout then right onto what's little more than a dirt track. The Aston Martin bounces as it flies across loose stones and uneven road. The daylight dims as we drive through a small forest with pine trees flanking us on either side. Then the light increases again and the trees disappear so that I can see the farm. I gawp in Gregory's direction but he pretends not to notice.

The farm is really more of an estate. The red-brick building with white, Georgian windows continues to grow as we drive closer. The long, old barn has been extended into an L shape and the old farmhouse stands tall at one end so the whole thing looks like an angular horseshoe. The uneven surface beneath the car has been replaced by soft gravel. We drive up to a circular, stone fountain in the middle of the horseshoe. I close my open mouth with the back of my hand as Gregory walks around the back of the DB9 to open the passenger door for me.

Perfectly spherical trees mark the start of the path to the house. I turn at the sound of the DB9 being driven away from the fountain by an elderly, grey-haired man and see a younger, slim, mousey-blond man carrying our bags behind us. We continue up the pathway passing stylised trees: noughts and crosses, a figure of eight, love hearts. At the end of the path, an archway made from one unbroken tree decorates the porch entrance.

'Wow, these are amazing!' I say almost inwardly. 'I take it you have a gardener?'

'As much as I'd like to say they're my handy work, yes, I do have a gardener, though an old friend actually did the trees. He's a sculptor. He dabbles in quite a lot of techniques and materials. These are essentially made from one tree. It's a process called—'

'Grafting. I've heard of it. Two different species grown together to make one purposely designed tree.'

'Exactly. This one,' Gregory says, resting onto the tree that looks like a noughts and crosses board, 'is based on a piece called *Needle and Thread* by Axel Erlandson. He created an entire place called *The Tree Circus* in California and displayed his work there.'

I nod, running a hand over the marvel. 'My dad had a book about him. I remember looking through it as a child. Your friend is really fantastic.'

'He has an exhibition right now at The Saatchi Gallery. Maybe we could go.'

'I'd like that.'

He opens the door into the vestibule and two dogs bark wildly until they realise it's Gregory walking into the house. He bends to stroke them as they spin and wag their tails excitedly.

'They're gorgeous,' I say, bending to knee height to stroke the liver-and-white-spotted dog. 'I didn't have you down as a dog man.'

'Well, they live here and they're supposed to be guard dogs, aren't you?' he says, ruffling the head of the almost entirely liver-coloured dog. 'They're pointers; they come on shoots and hunts.'

'You hunt?'

'In season, yes.'

'Do you ride horses?'

'For the hunts, yes. The shoots are on foot.'

Lord Sexy Bazillionaire CEO Ryans.

The young man carrying our bags is Kian. Gregory makes introductions then instructs Kian to take the rest of the day off.

'Yes, sir,' Kian quickly agrees.

'That goes for John and Marian too,' Gregory adds.

'Yes, sir.'

Gregory shakes Kian's hand. Despite his subtlety, I catch a glimpse of notes sliding from Gregory's hand into Kian's.

'Come on, I want to show you the other reason I have this house.' There's a mischievous glint in his eye that's a rare but beautiful show of his age.

He presses a remote control and the doors to the triple garage rise from the ground. Gregory grins as we wait. Soon, the doors are high enough for me to understand why. The garage opens to expose six motorbikes – big, immaculate and shiny.

He strides to a clothes rail of leathers on the side wall of the garage. He moves one hanger then another and pulls out a third. He holds it up and looks beyond it to me.

'This should get over your clothes.'

'What? Me? No way! I've never been on a motorbike in my life.'

'Okay, yeah, sure. You don't want to do anything dangerous. I guess you're not that girl.'

He turns his back to me and places the female leathers back on the clothes rail.

'Give those to me,' I say, snatching the leathers. I watch from the corner of my eye as Gregory strips down to his tight-fitting Armani boxers and white T-shirt then pulls the leather bottoms up over his sculpted thighs. Shaking salacious thoughts from my head, I quickly pull my leather bottoms over my jeans, then tie my hair into a loose ponytail.

Gregory is an absolutely indulgent sight to behold, seated on a shiny, electric-blue-trimmed Harley Davidson, his helmet under his arm. Heat traverses my body thinking about peeling him out of those intoxicating leathers.

'Will I do?' I ask.

He doesn't respond but his eyes remain fixed on me, feral and hungry.

'Get here,' he says with his sexy South African twang.

He places a helmet on my head and tells me to sit on the back of the bike. Throwing my right leg across the seat, I shuffle closer to his back until I can feel him snuggly between my legs, pushing back against my sex. My bud pulses when he moves his right hand behind him and pulls my leg tighter around his waist. I roll my breasts against his back. He exhales slowly as he puts on his helmet and kickstarts the bike. The rumbling vibrations and the sex god between my legs reduce my mind to a fevered muddle of hormones.

I squeal as I feel the initial inertia, then we're on the dirt track and driving back through the small forest.

On the open road, Gregory picks up speed. I bend with him as he corners with the road; the combination of speed and the sensation of my legs wrapped around him is exhilarating and doing nothing to clear my mind of filthy thoughts. We drive until there's nothing but green land and sheep, until we're the only two people in sight. I wrap my arms tighter around him and he starts to slow the bike so I can hear his voice.

'Do you want to stop?'

'Yes,' I say breathlessly.

He pulls us over next to a large, leafless tree and kills the engine. I dismount and walk onto the grass to see the view but Gregory's hand grabs mine and pulls me back against the trunk of the tree. Excitement shimmers through every part of me. I've thought about this for the last thirty minutes; I'm desperate for him to strip me down and fuck me.

He moves my right hand above my head and presses his leathers against mine. When my eyes tell him how much I want him, he kisses me, hard. He opens his leather bottoms then slowly pulls down the zip of mine. I undo the button of my jeans and let him pull both down to my thighs. I can't believe I'm doing this but my need for him tramples any sensible thoughts I might have.

I push my hands inside his boxers and rub his hard length. I'm not the only one whose mind has been wandering. He bites his lower lip and closes his eyes. His hand slips under my hair, gripping my neck and drawing my head into his. I wrap my tongue around his, licking, tasting, absorbing him.

'These leathers.' I swallow his heavy, gruff words.

He wets two fingers in his mouth then moves them to my soaked sex, stroking my centre before sliding through my wetness into my entrance. He swallows my groan and rolls a thumb across my swollen clit, driving me wild.

'Always ready for me.'

He lifts me from my feet and pushes me back against the tree. I call out his name as he brings me down on his hard cock. His growl fills my mouth as he draws slowly out and thrusts back into me, filling me.

'Harder!' My words are riddled with insatiable lust.

'Fuck, Scarlett, you always surprise me.' He lifts me and crashes me down onto him repeatedly as sweat beads form on his brow. I can feel myself building to an enormous climax.

He crashes me down again, somewhere between pain and pleasure – exactly what I asked for – and I feel myself rise to my peak. 'Again! Gregory, again!'

'Fuck!' His bark is carnal, his eyes crazed, lost in need. He lifts me and thrusts then drops me down again, his sack slapping against my skin.

This isn't love making, it's hot, hard, frantic fucking. On another punishing blow, my climax tears me apart. My orgasm lasts an age, my muscles greedily squeezing his cock as he works me down with delicious, controlled turns of his hips. I didn't feel his release but he's still throbbing inside me when I finally come to and my muscles begin to relax.

On our way back, rain starts to spit and the temperature falls to a little above freezing. Shivers have taken over my body by the time we park the Harley back in its space in the garage. Gregory takes my hands in his and blows hot air between them.

'That was unbelievable, thank you,' I say.

He brings my hands to his lips and presses his warm skin against mine. 'The ride?' he asks mischievously.

'Both rides,' I say, pushing his shoulder away from me.

* * *

I bathe in a ceramic, white tub with floor taps set in the middle of a marble-tiled room with original wooden beams drawing lines overhead. As I lie in flickering candlelight, jasmine-scented bubbles cover my body to my neck, shielding me from the cold of the dark night. The sound of Billie Myers's 'Kiss the Rain' drifts up the staircase, I suspect from the lounge.

I dry my body and slip into a black, silk, floor-length night-gown. Unleashed from a gold slide, my hair falls across one shoulder.

Candles and a roaring log fire light the lounge. Gregory is pouring two glasses of red wine on the rustic, oak coffee table where he's laid a selection of hors d'oeuvres. He's washed and changed into a different pair of dark jeans, hair still wet. The candlelight shows the toned contours of his bare chest. He's spread a thick fur throw in front of the fire.

He stills when the wood floor creaks under my feet and watches me as I make my way towards him, where he runs a hand down my neck, over my silk gown to the small of my back. He kisses me once and lets his lips linger on mine.

With a glass of wine, I rest down onto the fur throw.

'I'm sorry in advance but, well, you made it so appealing to me, I googled you.'

At first, I think he looks annoyed, then joins me and lies back, resting his elbow onto the throw and his head in his hand. He pulls two olives and an anchovy from a cocktail stick with his teeth.

'Despite the fact I asked you not to?'

'Temptation got the better of me.'

'Well, I guess that makes us even,' he says.

'How so?'

'I *googled* you a long time ago, Scarlett. Rather, my security team did. I needed them to do a little due diligence before I let you work for me.'

I scowl in jest then sip my drink.

'So you dated Elise Alonso?' I ask, trying to mask my feeling of utter inadequacy.

He sighs, then rests back with his hands interlaced behind his head, his chest exposed and inviting. 'We dated two or maybe three times, that's all. The press blew that up into something it never was.'

'She's beautiful.'

'She's a supermodel; that's her job,' Gregory says, almost irritated.

'I guess. There was a picture of you with Princess Clara, too, and at the Cannes Film Festival no less.'

'Get here,' he says, encouraging me to lean back on one arm, a mirror of him.

He runs a firm palm along the silk covering my thigh, then slides it across my hip and continues his long, smooth stroke up my abdomen, through my cleavage. My eyes close as my body submits to his touch. He gently sucks my neck then nips my lobe. 'I've never met a woman who's beautiful and intelligent and makes me forget everything and everyone else in the world. I have this insane, insatiable need whenever I'm around you and when I'm not, I just want to hear your voice, to see your face.'

My lungs are paralysed and I allow myself to wonder, hope, that he might have fallen as hard and fast as I have. I place my

mouth over his and try to tell him in a kiss just how bad I've
fallen for this incredibly attractive, filthy-rich unicorn.

'I'd really like to go to the Cannes Film Festival,' I say when
we open our eyes, both breathless.

He chuckles. 'Anyone can get an invite to the Cannes Film
Festival.'

'Oh, really, Mr Big Shot?'

'Well, anyone who's anyone.'

'You're such an arse,' I joke, playfully flicking a hand at his
chest. 'This is incredibly surreal.'

'Because I've been to the Cannes Film Festival?'

'No, silly. Just, being here, with you. It's... bizarre. One
minute, you're being snapped by paparazzi and the next, you're
lying on the floor of an old, converted barn with... *me* of all
people. Little old me.'

'I know where I'd rather be,' he says, pulling me onto his
chest.

I rest my head on his pec and watch the orange flames burn
in the open fire.

'I can't remember the last time I had nothing to worry
about. The last time I thought, I don't need to rush home.'

'You must miss him,' Gregory says.

'I do. Enormously. But...'

He nods but doesn't speak as he tucks my hair behind my
ear. Why is it this man can penetrate all my walls with no effort
at all?

'I hate myself for evening thinking it, but... I'm pleased his
suffering is over. I haven't admitted that aloud to anyone. I
wasn't ready to lose him and it wasn't his time to go. I can't
stand the thought of how terrified he must've been in those last
moments. I'll never forgive Pearson for what he did. I wish I'd
been there at the last minute to hold his hand and tell him

everything will be okay, better even, where he was going. But I think Dad was tired, sick of being ill and being dependent. I miss him, I miss him so much, but more... more my dad from before. Before he got sick. That's how I want to remember him and that's how he would want to be remembered.'

Gregory presses his lips against my scalp. 'I'm sorry, Scarlett. I'm sorry that your dad ever got sick, that I didn't get to meet him and ask his permission to date you. More than anything, you'll never know how much I hate myself for the way it ended and how I wish I could go back and stop it. I didn't protect you. I should have and I'll never forgive myself. This will end, Scarlett, and it'll end the way Pearson deserves. I swear to you.'

The flames become blurred in the mist of my eyes. I wrap my arm around Gregory's waist and hug tightly into his warm skin. I wonder where Pearson is right now and *how* this is going to end.

'Will you be honest with me if I ask you something?' I say after a long, contemplative silence on both our parts.

'Yes.'

'Did you make my firm promote me?'

'No. I told them how good you are, which is the truth, and what a great job you did for me. I told them I'd stay with the firm on the proviso that you were the lead contact but I didn't ask them to promote you. I actually found out about it because Amanda messaged Williams.'

A half-smile curls onto one side of my mouth but quickly subsides.

Procrastinating by rolling a finger around his chest, I finally mount the courage to ask my next question. The question that's been bugging me and remained unanswered for too long. 'What about Jack?'

Gregory shakes his head and sits up, knocking me from his chest. 'Jack fucking Jones.' He pulls two hands through his hair and I know I've ruined the evening. He stands, hands me my wine glass and takes a gulp from his own, then leans over the fire, one hand against the wooden mantel.

'That son of a bitch. He deserves everything he gets and more. I can't stand the thought of what he could have, what he *wanted* to do to you.'

'But he didn't,' I whisper into his back as I rub my hands down his biceps.

'If he'd touched you. If he'd even—'

'Shh,' I say, turning him to face me.

'People shouldn't cross me, Scarlett. And now, they really shouldn't cross you, either. He's lucky things ended the way they did.'

My body shivers despite the blazing heat of the fire. Gregory makes me feel safe, but he's dangerous. 'Tell me.'

His muscles are rigid under my palms.

'Jackson had the security team look into Jack. They threw up a load of old cases which had started to be investigated but been dropped, most because the victims were unwilling to testify or there wasn't enough evidence.'

'Jack? I just. I can't believe it. I mean, he's, he... Jack? I mean, I knew. He could have—'

'Jackson was irate when he found out but I think he was worried about telling me, worried about what I would do. He left it a day and asked his friends to get the details of the victims. Then he told me. I wanted to rip his fucking head off. Men like Jack deserve to go to hell. But Jackson kept telling me, and I suppose behind the anger, I knew that I couldn't deal with it the way I wanted to. We couldn't trust—'

'Me. You thought if you hurt him, I'd know and you couldn't trust me.'

'It's not the way it sounds. I'm in the public eye enough as it is. We have to be careful.'

I try to put this all together. The way Gregory lives and deals. His morally grey, sometimes outright black world. But his reasons are... right.

I lift my palm to his cheek. 'You can trust me.'

His face contorts and his eyes shift, soften, like that little boy. He shakes his head. 'Jackson said there had to be another way. He went to see some of the girls, told them about you, us, but they wouldn't testify.'

'I can't believe Jack could do that, that any human being could do that. There were so many times, so many nights when we were working together. I just thought... I don't know what I thought; I didn't think. I guess it's hard to believe.'

Gregory takes my hands in his. I'm instantly protected. 'We didn't have a choice in the end. The only way was to make him confess, so that's what we did.'

He lifts my hands to his lips. I watch as he moves. His usually perfect hair falls forwards, a strand covering his eyes as he gazes at me.

'What did you do to him?'

'No more than he deserved. Men like that make me sick. Fucking dregs of society. They deserve a fucking bullet between their legs. I'd never have let him go free once I knew. That's the choice we gave him. Live in prison or die.'

'Shit, Gregory, that's—'

'He'd have been dead if he ever laid a finger on you again. He got off lightly.'

'Kiss me,' I whisper because I don't know what else to say or how I feel about his confession.

He does. He kisses me slowly, in a way that liquefies me in his arms. He runs a hand up my right thigh, lifting my gown, then winds my legs around his waist. He lays me back onto the floor and runs a finger from my hip, across my stomach and up to my chest. The feel of his touch through the silk is smooth, elegant, not like the man he just described. I struggle to reconcile the two versions of him: dark, ferocious, tender and safe. But I've fallen for both.

I push up to place my knees either side of his hips and slowly pull my dress over my head…

After he's made me see colours I've never seen before, I lie on his chest in front of the fire. As he kisses my brow, I swirl my index finger around the few hairs on his pecs.

'What was it like growing up in South Africa? I mean South Africa the country, you know, not home life.'

'Dark. Dangerous. There was a lot of crime and, though I was born right after apartheid ended, there was still a lot of entrenched racism and animosity.'

'I can't imagine a place like that.'

'But South Africa is one of the most beautiful places I've seen too. The coast is ethereal: high cliff drops, white sand, crashing waves, penguins. The land is lush, the deepest greens. And the animals, they're proper: lions, elephants, rhinos.'

As he speaks, I visualise the green pastures with zebras grazing and lions bathing in afternoon sun. It's as if I'm there, walking on the plains. Then the sky grows darker. I pass a cheetah devouring its blood-doused prey. I continue to walk south past two grey-brown hyenas with matted fur, scowling through a menacing laugh. The open plains turn to cliff tops: rocky, lifeless.

The cry of a child startles me. I peer over the cliff's edge and see the familiar young boy in shorts, a shirt and braces. He sobs, his knees tucked tight into his chest, perched on the edge of a rock. A grey-haired man approaches from my left. I recognise him. He takes the boy's hand and makes him stand. The boy stops crying and smiles at the man. My dad.

Dad smiles back, ruffles his hair then leads him down to the beach from the rock. I dart my head right to where I hear heavy breathing, almost snarl like. Pearson. He sneaks from rock to rock, moving closer to my dad and the boy. I know he wants to kill them. I try to move but my legs are rooted to the ground. I try to scream, to alert my dad, but nothing comes out. Pearson moves from behind the last rock standing between them and pulls a gun from the back of his stained, stonewashed jeans. I try again to scream, I try with all my might but it's not until Pearson has his gun to my dad's head that I'm able to make a noise.

Eventually, I scream, 'Dad! Dad!' and Pearson turns his gun on me.

I wake abruptly, panicking and hot. I'm alone in front of the rescinding fire. Gregory is in his jeans and on his phone, his back to me.

'Don't leave their side,' he's saying. 'I don't care, Mother. For once, would you do as I ask?'

He turns to see me awake.

'Ja. All right, then. We'll see you for lunch tomorrow.' He ends the call. Looks at the phone in his hand then places it on an oak sideboard. Without looking up, he says, 'Scarlett, move in with me.'

'What was that about?'

He fixes me with a stare – not one that's full of honeymoon and new-home vibes. 'Nothing.'

'Gregory, why would I move in with you if I can't trust you to be honest with me?'

He pauses for a second, then pulls a hand through his hair.

'That was my mother,' he finally says. 'After what happened to your dad, I asked Jackson to bring in some extra guys. He's brought in two to stay with her and Lawrence.'

'You're worried he'll come after Lara?'

'Yes.'

'And that's why you want me to move in with you,' I mumble. 'You think he'll come for me. Again.'

He sighs. 'It's possible, yes.'

Tears form in my eyes. I nod, roll back my shoulders and straighten the sides of my nightdress as if it were a suit and I was about to walk into a meeting at work.

'Okay then.'

'No, Scarlett,' Gregory says as he moves swiftly across the room towards me. 'Yes, I want to protect you but I want to have you around because... because I don't know how to let you go. I don't know what you do to me or how. My life is a certain way, structured and controlled, grey. But you, with your sarcasm and wit, your insightfulness and hot-headedness, you make things... different. Fascinating.' He steps close to me and brushes my cheek with his fingertips. 'I've got no idea what someone like you would want with me but somehow, for some reason, here you are, and I never want you to leave me because I'm worried you'll realise what I am and you won't come back. I'm not ready to lose you, Scarlett. You make me feel... alive.'

'Really?' I whisper.

He lets out a short laugh and shakes his head.

'Are you making fun of me, Mr Ryans?'

He wraps his arms around me and pulls me into his tight embrace. I close my eyes and absorb his scent.

'For the record, I'm not going anywhere, Gregory. I'm not

afraid of who you are or who you might be whenever you decide to let me in.'

He kisses my brow and pulls me tighter into his chest.

'About moving in, though,' I say, leaning back to look at him. 'It's not that I don't want to be with you but I have a lot of stuff to sort out at the moment, with the house and Sandy. I mean, if I'm not living in the house, it doesn't make sense for me to keep it. I could at least rent it out. Then there's Sandy: it's her home as well and at least in theory, she still works there.'

I break from his arms as I ponder the situation. 'I've been so wrapped up with everything else that I haven't thought enough about Sandy. She's lived with me nearly all my life, always been there, and now... I can't afford to keep her and I don't have enough work to keep her busy. If I leave, she'll have to go too. Oh my God, what will Sandy do?'

29

'Come on, let's go.' I flick the *Sunday Times* Gregory is reading cross-legged.

'Go where?'

'Let's take the dogs and go for a walk; it's a gorgeous morning and we've got hours before we go to your mum's for lunch.'

He folds his newspaper at an almost comically lazy pace and places it on the coffee table.

'It's freezing but I'm impressed with how quickly you got ready, for a woman, so let's do it.'

'Are you a closet misogynist, Ryans?'

'I thought that would rattle you.'

He disappears and returns as I'm buttoning my coat high up my neck at the rear entrance to the farm.

'You were right; it is freezing!'

'Of course I was right. I'm always right and it would pay you to remember that fact. Here, put these on,' he says, handing me shiny, black, Hunter wellies.

Glowering, I take the wellies from him and pull them over my denim trousers. 'Whose are these?'

'Spares or Marian's, maybe.'

Gregory's also wearing a pair of wellies over his jeans and has buttoned his fitted Barbour coat to his neck. He really can look splendid in anything.

'There's a country boy in there just crying to get out,' I say.

He flashes his sexy half-smile then puts two fingers in his mouth and whistles: an ear-piercing sound. Both dogs come running straight to him.

'What are they called?'

'This one's Hugo,' he says, patting the liver and white dog. 'This one's Betsy.'

'You're joking? Hugo and Betsy?'

'No joke.'

'For dogs?'

He shrugs and strides out into the field, illuminated by the low winter sun, the green grass sparkling with dew. The dogs run to be the first to collect a stick he throws far out in front of us. For a moment, a fleeting, unrealistic moment I could kick myself for, I wonder what it would be like to live here. Our country retreat. Me. Gregory. Our dogs. We could set up an office with two desks and spend days working from home, having indulgent, hot sex between calls and emails. We'd drink an aperitif by the fire before dinner and eat at the large, oak dining table by candlelight, our chairs pulled close together at one end of the table, so close, we're almost touching.

Shaking my brain back to reality, banishing my wishful thinking, I remind myself that I'm probably just Miss This Month for Gregory and next month, he'll be back to dating royals and Victoria's Secret models. I run to catch up with him and walk by his side. He reaches down and slips his strong, warm hand into mine.

I can enjoy it while it lasts.

'Tell me, Gregory Ryans, how does one come to have all of this by the age of thirty?'

'Greed, pride, arrogance.'

'For the record, I don't consider ambition to be any of those, although you can certainly be arrogant.'

He laughs: a short, tense sound.

'Really, I've always wanted to be my own boss and control my own future. I get a kick out of deals, seeing the worth of a company grow, discovering an innovative product and getting it into a market. There aren't many jobs where you get to do all of that and do it *mostly* the way you want to.'

'I know what you mean. The close. For me, closing a deal is such an adrenalin rush. I don't love my job all day every day but closing is what I live for.'

'Until a few weeks ago, my job was the reason I got up in the morning. It was my purpose. And then this whirlwind lawyer burst into my office with her stiletto heels and tight-fitting dresses.'

'You mean it wasn't my razor-sharp mind?'

He stops and turns me to face him, then lifts my chin with his index finger and kisses me. When he withdraws, his expression changes; his brows furrow.

'You should know that there're times when I can't be around, Scarlett. I want to be fair to you. I travel overseas and sometimes, there's just a lot going on and taking up my time. And I'm not... I'm not like other men. I don't do emotional.'

Panic booms under my ribs. A siren.

'I just want you to know up front because I don't want you to get stuck in something you're not happy with.'

My torso relaxes on an exhale.

'Well, that makes two of us. I know how the city works and I know what it takes to stay at the top of your game. As long as you respect me and trust me, I can cope with not seeing you every day.' We can work on the emotional stuff, whilst ever this lasts.

He bites the tip of my nose, then slips his hand back into mine as we continue walking.

'So, how did it all start? I know you have a degree from LSE, then what?'

He looks at me, bemused.

'Oh, Gregory, come on, legal research, due diligence. I told you I know more about you than you think.'

'I have a degree in Economics from LSE but it started before then. I'm not sure when but I used to idolise Lawrence. I hadn't known a good man, a role model, until Lawrence. I used to watch him working in his office from home and making calls on one of those old, clunky mobile phones. Do you remember those? With aerials? As I got older, I started offering to help and Lawrence would give me things to do: sums, basic things. When I got older still, he'd ask me what I thought of deals and ideas he was working on. By the time I went to LSE, I had an idea for a product.' He laughs and shakes his head. 'It was a sports bag alarm. A device to put in your sports bag while you were playing tennis, rugby, rowing or whatever. If anyone tampered with your bag while you were playing, the alarm would sound.'

'Hmm, did it take off?'

'I'd say it bombed but it never really took part in the race. That was the start of everything for me. I told Lawrence about my idea and in hindsight, he never really thought it was a flyer but when Easter break came around in my first year at LSE, Lawrence agreed to take me on a business trip to China. He did his thing: met clients, networked and tried to strike deals. In the evenings, he made me put on a suit and go with him but during the day, I visited factories and markets and learned a bit about manufacturing. That's when I realised that I wasn't a creator and the money was in being the middle man.'

Hugo and Betsy run towards us. I take a stick from Hugo's mouth and throw it as far as I can. A few steps later, Gregory picks it up and throws it properly.

'Then what happened?'

'Well, then I came home, took exams and soon, it was summer break. Williams graduated that year and had nothing lined up so I told him to come out to China with me. He explored during the day but I did the same thing again: went to factories and markets and introduced Williams to some of the men I'd met with Lawrence. One of them told me about these LED lights, said they'd be the future. I agreed to visit his factory the next day and that was my first product. I agreed to take a shipload on a sale or return basis and try to sell it into the UK. When I got home, I lined up some big wholesalers who supplied big retailers and slowly but surely, the lights took off. The business still exists. I place people there when they start working for me. It's a relatively small business so I figure if they can't do a good job there, they're no good at all.'

'Where does Williams come into it?'

'I still had two years left at LSE and I knew I needed a fall-back. Plus I was too competitive to back out without kicking the arse of every guy on that course.'

'I hadn't noticed that competitive streak,' I say sarcastically, receiving a glare in return. 'So Williams ran the business for you?'

'It was always my business, I called the shots and Williams ran all decisions by me. He's more numbers than commercial, but he managed the business day to day during term time. Within a few months, we made enough money to pay him well so he stayed.'

'Then you branched out?'

'Mmm, by the time I graduated, we had five or six high-value products and we were selling into all major wholesalers in the country. A year after graduating, we were selling into America, Australia and Europe. Then we diversified, acquired some additional companies, set up some sub-divisions and here we are.'

'You make it sound easy.'

'It definitely wasn't easy but it was fun, still is, but the bigger you get, the greater the impact of your decisions. The stakes are higher.'

A pheasant flaps its way from a bush in the distance and the dogs shoot off after it.

'Hugo! Betsy!' I shout.

Gregory bends forwards on a chuckle. 'Scarlett, they're not really called Hugo and Betsy.'

'You're an arse.' I laugh, nudging into his arm. 'Aren't you going to get them?'

'Buster! Bramble!' Gregory growls.

The dogs stop the pursuit and immediately turn back towards Gregory.

'Good boy. Good girl,' he says, giving each a treat. The dogs sit, waiting for their master's next instruction. Gregory flicks a hand forwards and both dogs sprint out in front of us.

'Even your dogs are intimidated by you.'

'They know what's good for them. And you, Scarlett Heath, how did you come to be a yuppie in one of the best law firms in the city?'

I shrug. 'There's really not an exciting story.'

'Tell me anyway.'

I drop my hands into my coat pockets and stroke the bobbled wool lining.

'I went to Cambridge. Girton College. I read Law. In my second year, Saunders approached me and I accepted their offer of a training contract.'

'They approached you? Isn't that unheard of?'

I shrug again. 'Depends on the circumstances, I guess.'

'You were top of your class, weren't you?'

I nod once and feel my cheeks flush. 'After I graduated, I had to study legal practice for a year. Saunders runs a course specific to the firm so I had to do that. Then I trained for two years and whilst I was training, Saunders paid for me to study for a Master of Laws.'

'And you got a distinction in that too.'

I glance at him. My brow scrunched.

'Due diligence, Miss Heath. Believe it or not, I didn't take you on for your looks.'

'I can well believe that.'

He shakes his head. 'Did you always want to be a lawyer?'

'I wanted to be a lot of things, exciting things, but definitely not a lawyer.'

'So how? Why?'

'Your perception of what constitutes excitement changes as you get older.' I laugh. 'Probably when I was making a decision about my college courses, I had a realisation that I wouldn't be a ballet dancer, or an astronaut or whatever else I'd considered. When I thought about it, I mean seriously considered career paths, I didn't think much further than being a doctor like...' I pause and unwittingly glance up to Gregory.

'Like your dad.'

I nod once and watch my wellies as I step forwards. 'My

dad kept telling me I was only to be a doctor if that's what I really wanted to be. He told me that I should study sciences but also study something I enjoyed. I remember thinking it was a strange thing to say because I hadn't thought about whether I enjoyed studying or which subjects I enjoyed; I just saw everything as a challenge, a competition that I had to win. I don't know when that happened to me. Anyway, I decided I enjoyed English as much as anything and I was good at it so I studied Biology, Chemistry, Maths and English.'

'So when did you change your mind?'

'When a good friend of my dad's got sick. He worked all his life to help others with medicine and care, then when he needed help, there was nothing that could be done. It's not like I don't think doctors do an amazing job but I just sort of fell out with the idea of medicine.'

'I get that.'

'Falling out with medicine opened my eyes again, I think. I realised I really did like English, writing and creating something. So it came to university time and my English teacher suggested some career paths. Law was one of them and I thought to myself, well, that's not the worst idea I've ever heard.'

He laughs. 'That's not the worst idea I've ever heard?'

I shrug and laugh too. 'I love it now, though – the law, I mean. I like the order of it, the logic and rationality, and I still like creating something, using and manipulating language.'

'And kicking arse?'

'That's the best bit.' I glance at my watch and reluctantly tell Gregory, 'We should head back if I'm going to be ready in time for lunch.'

He whistles through two fingers and the dogs bound

towards us. He takes a stick from Buster and throws it in the direction of the farm.

'You really studied for a masters whilst you were working?'

'Yup.'

'You're a glutton for punishment.'

In more ways than one, Mr Emotionally Detached.

In more ways than one.

30

We pull off the gravel path in the DB9 and I pull down the passenger mirror to apply a pink blush lipstick. I ran out of time to blow-dry my hair after Gregory joined me in the shower. Consequently, I've ended up styling my wet hair in two tight French plaits brought together at the nape of my neck.

'You look pretty,' Gregory says, considering my cobalt, high-neck dress.

'Thank you, but I feel like I look like I ran out of time to get dressed after having sex in the shower.'

'Maybe that's why I like how you look.'

I watch his hand moving across the steering wheel, the diamond bezel of his Rolex – one of multiple extortionate watches – gleaming. There's something strangely erotic about that hand.

'Who will be at lunch?'

'My mother and Lawrence. Charles and Camilla, their friends. Wi—'

'Charles and Camilla?' I giggle.

'Is that *really* funny to you?'

I giggle some more. 'It sounds like we're having lunch with the king and queen.'

His steely eyes stay on the road ahead but there's a cute crease at the side of his mouth. 'I don't understand what's funny about that.'

'Your self-importance really knows no bounds.'

He guffaws so loudly, I'm left rolling my eyes but smirking out of my window.

'Williams will probably be there too. He usually turns up regardless of whether he's invited. He can't resist my mother's honey-glazed ham.'

'Your mum cooks?' I ask, returning to real time.

'Well, the honey-glazed ham she pays for.' He laughs. 'There's someone else going you might like to see.'

I ponder the very small list of people we both know. 'Who?'

'Jackson. And he's bringing Sandy.'

'Sandy?' Of course, *Jackson and Sandy*. I still can't get my head around that. 'Does Jackson usually go?'

'He'd usually be there in one capacity or another. Driver, security. But my mother invited him to dine, and to bring Sandy today.'

'Is that strange?'

He shrugs.

Does it matter? Everything in life has been strange since I met this man.

We travel out of the countryside and back towards civilization, the evergreen trees replaced by tarmac and streetlamps.

'Are you and Jackson friends?'

'It would be unfortunate if we weren't. I spend more time with Jackson than anyone else I know. We go most places together, he lives with me, we work out together. He's definitely not just an employee, if that's what you mean.'

'Kind of like Sandy and me. It's quite cute actually, Jackson and Sandy, isn't it?'

He scoffs and raises his shoulders again. 'I guess.'

'What's he like? Objectively. Will he be around a lot to see her, if things get serious? What about their living arrangements – I mean, where would they live? With you? Will you give him more time off so he can take her out on dates?'

'Scarlett, I—'

'Do you think they'll have kids? Maybe they're too old now, would you say?'

'Scarlett,' he says, slightly louder than normal. 'I really have no idea. It's all new; I doubt even *they* know the answers to your million questions yet.'

I scowl at him then watch the cars in the middle lane of the motorway as we fly by. My nerves build as we pull off the main road and drive closer to Lara's house. The last time Lara saw me, she was begging me to forgive her son. I was cold and uncompromising.

'Gregory,' I say meekly, 'do you know your mum came to see me? It was after my dad died. Before... before you came that night in the rain.' The memory of Gregory's face flashes painfully in my mind. 'You should know that I was sharp with her.'

Gregory's jaw tenses. I wish I could read his thoughts.

'Whatever happened between you is private. Unless, she didn't upset you, did she?'

'Oh, it's not that, I just don't want today to be awkward.'

'Scarlett, my mother invited you,' he says, resting his hand on mine.

'She told me some stuff. About you... About Pearson.'

He takes his hand away and concentrates on the road. He

swallows subtly but the sinews in his neck tense. He's not ready and I won't push him.

The road becomes increasingly lined with conifer trees and flanked by grass. Gregory pauses the car at tall, black, iron gates and waits until a voice comes through a speaker on the white wall.

'Where are we?' I whisper, so the intercom voice can't hear me.

'Cobham. Surrey.'

He picks up speed as we drive another hundred metres or so along a tarmac pathway. The trees come to an abrupt, perfectly straight, trimmed end, exposing an enormous, white mansion, three triangular peaks and floor-to-roof windows marking the front of Lara and Lawrence's home. Gregory rolls the DB9 around to one side of the house and stops in front of a four-door garage. An inordinate amount of land is accessed at the back of the house by twenty or so steps leading down from a large veranda. A pool house extends from the side of the house furthest away from us. On the lawn, maybe fifty metres from the house, men are working to construct what looks like a grand pavilion.

'It's for the party,' Lara says, having appeared from the front of the house.

'Party?' I ask Gregory as Lara approaches.

'Hi, handsome,' Lara says, kissing her son on both cheeks. 'Go on, get inside.'

I know immediately she wants to be alone with me. Gregory does as instructed and walks to the front of the house but not without casting one last look over his shoulder to me.

Lara stands in front of me, putting us face to face. The last thing I want is conflict. Doubt begins to ask me why I agreed to come.

'How're you holding up?' she asks me softly.

She's not pissed at me? It takes a moment for that to hit home.

'I'm okay, thank you.'

She places one hand on my shoulder. 'I don't know why or how or what convinced you and I don't ever need to know but for his sake, I'm pleased you changed your mind.'

I study her face, trying to understand the *mens rea*, the motive, the hidden meaning, but there's nothing to uncover. We both wait in anticipation of me finding the right words to say but they don't come. Eventually, she rubs her hand briskly up and down my shoulder and that's the end of the matter.

'Come on, you must be freezing,' she says, turning on her patent heel, her wide-legged trousers swinging to expose their full width. She offers me a flexed arm that's sheathed in a silk blouse.

'What's the party in aid of?' I ask, linking my arm through hers.

'That son of mine hasn't told you yet? I throw a bonfire night party every year. A hideously extravagant thing but I love it. You have to come.'

A housemaid opens the large, white, double front door for us and I smile at her as I step inside.

'If nothing else, it's an excuse for a new dress,' Lara adds as she scuttles along the high-polish, wood floor and dips into a room to the right of the hallway.

'She's a whirlwind,' the housemaid says. 'I'll show you along. This way.'

'Do you live here?' I ask of the slim, mousey-blonde whom I'd I guess is about my age.

'We all do.'

'All do?'

'Me, Mack who works the garden and Tony, the chef. You'll enjoy his food. His honey-glazed ham is the best.'

'That's not the first time I've heard that today,' I admit. 'I'm Scarlett, by the way.'

'Oh, I know.' She glances at me without breaking pace. 'I'm Miranda. It's this one.'

She motions to the open door and walks back down the corridor when I step inside. The first thing I notice is the regal crystal chandeliers hanging over the sea-green, suede sofas and two large, leather chairs, one brown, one burgundy, in that 1920's, stately-home library kind of style. The second thing I notice is the touch of Gregory's hand on the small of my back.

'Scarlett, I'd like you to meet Charles and Camilla.' Surprisingly less regal than he sounds, a very ordinary man with a wealthy, rotund stomach shakes my hand, a short woman with a precisely styled bob and more diamonds on her fingers than in a De Beers window next to him.

'It's a pleasure to meet you,' I tell them.

'Camilla designed all the interiors here, Scarlett,' Lara calls from the sofa.

'Wow, they really are beautiful. You have such a talent.'

'Thank you. It's easy to decorate a beautiful home,' Camilla says.

Charles takes a seat in the leather reading chair, picking his half-full glass of champagne from a side table and crossing one tweed leg over the other. Lara pats the space beside her on the sofa and Camilla fusses with the gold chain belt, pulling her blouse neatly onto her pleated trousers.

As I wave to Lawrence at the far side of the lounge, a familiar form stands from the sofa opposite to Lara and looks nervously around the other faces in the room before shuffling towards me.

'Sandy.' I throw my arms around her.

Across her shoulder, Jackson rises, still dressed as if he's on duty in his black suit, white shirt and black tie. He nods towards me in his usual way then he, Gregory and Lara leave the room. 'How are you?'

'Fair to middling, as your dad would say. Lots of change: some bad, some good.'

'I know what you mean. Have you been staying at home?'

Startled, she opens her mouth to speak then closes it again. Her cheeks flush to a beetroot shade.

'I didn't mean, you know, I'm just worried that you're in the house on your own. I went back yesterday to get some things and it was... different.'

Sandy's cheeks return to a shade of normal. 'I couldn't face it. Actually, I stayed here last night.'

'Here? This house? Why?'

'Something to do with Gregory's work, I think.'

'Gregory's work?'

'Champagne, Scarlett?' Miranda interrupts, holding a full single flute on her black tray.

I remember waking by the fire to hear Gregory vexed on the phone to his mother.

'Thank you. Erm, could you tell me where the ladies' room is?'

'I'll take you.'

'I'll be right back,' I say to Sandy as she holds out a hand to take my champagne.

'You can just point it out to me,' I say quietly as I follow Miranda out of the room.

'It's no trouble,' she sings, much too conspicuous for my liking.

We walk further down the long hallway. I hear Lara's voice

coming from a room opposite a grand staircase that veers off both left and right at the top.

'Just here,' Miranda says, directing me to a door under the stairs.

'Thanks.'

I tuck inside the bathroom and draw the door closed, watching Miranda walk away. When I'm sure the coast is clear, I tiptoe across the wood floor, back in search of the muffled voices, until I come across a billiard room with the door ajar. I can just make out Gregory's navy chinos and grey, wool jumper pacing back and forth.

'Show me,' he snaps.

Squinting through one eye, I see Gregory accept a small box, which he opens, examining the contents.

'You're sure this is yours?' he asks.

'For God's sake, Gregory, I know my own wedding ring. The last time I saw the pig, I threw the damn thing at him.'

'How did he get to the house, Jackson?' Gregory is snarling through gritted teeth.

'He didn't,' Lara pleads. 'It was in the postbox this morning. Mack found it. It was wrapped in brown paper with a note.'

'A note saying what?'

Lara turns her back to Gregory and paces the floor by the billiard table, one hand on her hip.

'Saying what, mother?'

The fear in her voice is audible. 'It said—'

'It said, "Something I should have done a long time ago",' Jackson cuts in.

Gregory moves back into my field of vision, holding Lara's wedding ring up to the light.

Miranda's footsteps in the corridor startle me.

'The lounge is this way, Scarlett,' she says.

'Oops, so it is. I lost my bearings for a second there.'

In the lounge, I take my glass of champagne back from Sandy. She's returned to her spot on the sofa and is talking to Lawrence.

Pearson. Lara's wedding ring. Another note. He's been here. I feel sick and light-headed. I wash away the feeling with a gulp of champagne. For now.

Jackson, Gregory and Lara return to the room and are followed shortly by an apologetic Williams.

'Argh, sorry we're late, Lara,' he says.

'Amanda!' Her name leaves my mouth a little overzealously as I bound towards her.

'Hey, you!' she says, pulling me into a tight cuddle.

'I didn't know you'd be here.' Then, lowering my voice. 'Does this mean you two are...?'

'Oh Lord, no!'

Williams is staring; he's definitely heard us. We exchange an awkward smile. My fondness of Williams, I realise, never disappeared.

'We were out together last night, that's all.' Motioning to her knee-length, black skirt and Mary Janes, she adds, 'I've only been out of my sloggies for an hour.'

Lara deals with the introductions and Gregory subtly pats a hand onto Williams' shoulder with a laugh.

Lunch is announced and Lara ushers us all towards the dining room.

'Hold on a sec,' I say, gently grabbing Williams by the arm and pulling him back into the lounge. 'I just want to say I'm sorry about the other day. I know you were looking out for your friend and I don't want things to be awkward between us.'

'I'm sorry too.' His voice is gentle and warm. 'None of my business and I shouldn't have said anything. I just didn't want to see you two mess things up. I'm sure you've realised that relationships aren't really Greg's thing, and you're both pretty bullheaded, if you don't mind me saying.'

'It would be too late now if I did.' I nudge him gently and he wraps an arm around me.

Tony's homemade duck pâté is already waiting on each of our place mats. Miranda opens two bottles of wine on an oak side table then wraps a white cloth around one of the bottles.

'Red or white?' she asks as she makes her way around the large, oval table.

'So, Amanda, please enlighten me,' Lawrence says. 'What are sloggies?'

She places her napkin across her lap. 'Sloggy clothes, like leggings and a big jumper or joggers and a tee: lounge clothes.'

'Ahh, I see. These onesies I hear people talk about, they'd be sloggies?'

'Oh no, I think you've got the wrong end of the stick. White for me, please,' she says, sliding her glass towards Miranda. 'You see, the onesie can generally fall into two categories: nightwear, which is entirely acceptable but realistically far too warm to wear in bed and probably best left to the under tens, or cool cats trying too hard. The other type is people who actually wear onesies in public and walk as if one leg is two or three inches shorter than the other. This category is really never acceptable.'

Amanda takes a sip of wine, giving Lawrence a chance to scratch his head, bemused.

Then she quickly chirps up again. 'There's a distinction between the sloggy and nightwear. Sloggies can be worn at any time of the day without feeling like a bum.'

'Feeling like a bum?' Lawrence asks.

'Mmm-hmm, yep. But nightwear can only be worn around

a two to three hour window before or after sleep. Well, unless it's one of few days a year when a person decides to have a duvet day – a normal person, not a try-hard.'

The table falls silent for a second or two until Lara bursts into uproarious laughter.

'Would you look at his face!' She presses a hand to her ribs. 'He's so confused.'

The merriment continues as anecdotes are shared. Camilla regales us with a tale from Lara's bonfire party last year. For some reason, I find myself wondering whether she really did share jokes will Bill Nighy and Sebastian Faulkes. Call it a hunch.

'We'll have to introduce Scarlett around this year, Lara.' Camilla winks at her friend.

I turn to Gregory, who shrugs.

'Oh, yes of course. Scarlett, you'll have so much fun,' Lara offers.

Gregory tries again. 'Mother, we might not—'

'We need to go shopping. I have my dress but we can get you something new, Scarlett.'

'Mother!' Gregory snaps. 'Scarlett knows nothing about the party yet. She might not be ready.'

Lara is visibly wounded but manages to compose herself. 'Of course not, I'm sorry.'

'It's okay,' I say, resting a hand onto Gregory's knee. 'A party might be a good distraction.'

Lara smiles at me and as much as I really don't want to, I tell her, 'I could do with a new dress.'

'Actually, I need a new dress for the party too,' Amanda quickly cuts in. 'Why don't the two of *us* go shopping one night this week since Lara already has her dress and probably has an awful lot to do here?'

'That sounds like a great idea to me,' Gregory adds before Lara can protest.

Camilla moves on to the next topic of conversation and I'm grateful to be relieved from the centre of attention. Tony wheels the infamous honey-glazed ham to the side of the table on a trolley and carves two slices for each person. Miranda serves the ham and vegetables onto our plates. Sandy sits awkwardly in her chair and fiddles with the stem of her glass, which she refused to have filled with wine, I suspect because Jackson isn't drinking either.

I mouth to her, *You okay?* and she nods back to me unconvincingly.

Two men walk past the dining-room window, doing a lap of the house outside. They're almost a mirror image of each other, both in black trousers, knee-length, black, wool coats and black, leather gloves. My body shudders in response. Extra security.

He's still out there.

Gregory puts down his folk and drops a hand to my thigh. 'They're a precaution, that's all.' His warm breath on the bare skin of my neck instantly comforts me. He finishes lunch with his right hand, his left entwined with mine.

After our meal, Charles and Camilla leave to visit her daughter and the rest of us retire to the lounge with coffee. There's a noticeable shift in Lara's attitude once Camilla has gone, as if her pretence is no longer necessary. I much prefer this version of her. Sandy seems to have relaxed too. She's stopped fiddling and is talking happily with Jackson.

I cast my eyes around the room and find Gregory watching me, one hand resting a coffee cup on his crossed leg. We stay locked in that gaze for a moment before my face breaks into a dizzy-in-love smile. He smiles back then leans forwards and places his cup onto the coffee table. 'All right, gents, ready?'

Jackson is first to stand and explains that he's going to check in with Ken and Marshall, who I suspect are the black-clothed *precaution* walking the perimeter of the house. Williams and Lawrence are next up and they, with Gregory, leave the room to talk business.

'I'm glad there's just us, ladies,' Lara says when the men have vacated. 'I wanted to talk to you about an idea I've had.'

Miranda has taken the movement in the room as an opportunity to offer fresh tea and coffee but Lara tells her she should consider herself off duty now and relax with Tony and Mack. She takes an unfinished bottle of champagne from an ice bucket and gives it to Miranda, telling her to finish it if she likes, and that Tony and Mack should help themselves to spare beers in the fridge.

I *much* prefer this Lara.

'Right, my idea,' Lara says, sitting back onto the sofa with her self-poured fresh cup of tea. 'Gregory told me that you've moved in with him, Scarlett.'

'Have you?' Amanda shouts, almost leaping from her chair.

'No, no, not exactly. It's just for a week. I just didn't, couldn't, I didn't really want to stay in the house,' I confess, glancing at Sandy apologetically.

'Well, I was thinking,' Lara continues, 'if you do move in with Gregory, there'll be a lot done for you. I mean shopping, cleaning, that sort of thing. And I don't mean to bring it up and I realise she spent a lot of time caring for your dad, but I know that Sandy did those things for you too.'

Mild irritation murmurs under my tongue.

'To get to the point, Miranda has an awful lot to do around

here and I've been thinking lately that she could perhaps use someone to share her workload.'

Finally, the point is starting to take shape.

'That person could live here, although should she ever want to leave, that would be fine too. She could come during the day, we could arrange something to suit everyone,' Lara adds, smiling at Sandy sincerely. 'Of course, when you spend so much time together, it's important to have someone around who you know you can trust. So I hope you don't mind, Scarlett, but I've spoken to Sandy about whether she might like the position.'

Words, thoughts, actions begin to spin in my mind. *I don't want to lose Sandy.* I know I don't need her any more. Maybe I can't afford to keep her. I don't know if I'll even keep the house. At least if she was with Lara, I could see her and I'd know she's safe. *I don't want to lose her. I don't want to lose her.* Looking to Sandy, Amanda, Lara and back to Sandy, I try to find the right words, the correct response.

Sandy shuffles close and looks at me with her sweet, chocolate eyes. 'I need to work. You're grown-up now. I've done my job. I finished helping you grow up a long time ago. For the last few years, I've kept the house tidy and—'

'Made me pancakes.'

She smiles and tucks my hair behind my ear the way she used to when I was a child. The touch of her fingers makes my eyes glaze.

'But for the most part, I've cared for your dad. You don't need me anymore and to be honest, Scarlett, I don't want to work for you anymore. I've watched you grow into an amazing, clever, beautiful woman. You're not my little princess anymore; you're my best friend.'

I can feel the walls of the dam that's holding back the water from my eyes crack and crumble.

'Are you sure this is what you want? We could sort something, I promise.'

'I think this is a good idea. It's time for me to have my own life instead of being old before my time, like you always tell me. Plus, this way, I'll get to see you more.'

'And Jackson.'

She chuckles, cheeks ablaze.

'So that's settled then?' Lara asks.

Sandy nods with a smile. 'Settled.'

I'm going to break and I can't do it here. 'Okay. I'm just going to get some air.'

'Do you want me to come?' Amanda asks.

'No, you enjoy the tea.'

Following solar lights down a white, gravel path, I arrive at a fence at the end of the garden. Resting my forearms onto the fence, looking into the vast darkness beyond, I wonder where my dad is, where and what his version of life after death could be. The dam finally disintegrates and silent tears spill down my cheeks.

The cold wind carries the sound of footsteps in the gravel moving closer to me. A blazer is hung around my shoulders. I brush away the tears with the backs of my hands as Gregory leans forwards to rest on the fence beside me.

'I know it sounds pathetic, but I just feel like so much is changing and I'm struggling to find a foothold. Yesterday, Dad was healthy and happy; today, he's gone. I've found out your father is a complete iniquitous bastard. Sandy's leaving. And I've met this guy and he has my head in such a spin, I can't think straight but I honestly don't know if that's reciprocated.'

Gregory exhales loudly. 'And here I was thinking I'd never

come across a problem I couldn't fix or at least buy or charm my way out of.'

I shuffle my feet towards him and rest my head on his shoulder. My eyes search the black sky decorated with sparkling crystals.

'It's beautiful,' he says, following my gaze.

'Have you ever thought that the stars only look so beautiful because the sky is so dark?'

His shoulder rises and falls with his breath. 'I guess not.'

'Maybe we're just like one of those stars, Gregory. Maybe all of those bad things that have happened are the reason we're standing here right now.'

He pulls me into his chest and rests his chin gently on my head. 'Jesus, I don't know what you're doing to me, Scarlett Heath.'

My arms wrap tightly around his body and pull him closer to me. 'Thank you for what you did for Sandy. It was sweet of you.'

'I didn't do it for Sandy; I did it for you, to stop you worrying about other people.' He kisses my brow then, leaning back and pulling me towards him by his blazer lapels, he presses his lips to the tip of my nose.

'Take me home,' I whisper.

'Home?'

'Home for this week.'

He takes my hand and leads me back along the gravel path.

* * *

I'm roused in the darkness by the soft tenor notes of a saxophone. Wrapping a silk kimono around me, I follow the sound, pausing at the top of the staircase when I see Gregory in the lounge. Wearing only lounge pants, his perfectly formed torso bare, he stands at the window staring out into the night.

The sound system clicks onto the next John Coltrane track. Gregory continues to watch the city. Lights from high-rise buildings illuminate his body and expose to me for the first time a white scar, healed and aged but permanent, running from close to his spine out to his hip. My perfect Gregory, spoiled.

I want to go to him, to kiss his tarnished skin and tell him he's safe now. I want him to be free of his demons but I can't make that happen. Not tonight. I watch him until one more track clicks over on the sound system and I can't watch my terrorised man any longer. I need to make him forget, the way he can make me leave my mind and thoughts.

He must hear me but he doesn't turn; he keeps his eyes on the darkness. My hands start at his shoulders and move down the length of his arms as my mouth trails kisses across the width of his back. His body rises and falls with his deep breath and exhale.

Something in him snaps. He turns quickly and lifts me from my feet, charging us back towards the sofa. His irises are black. He's hurting, lost behind the darkness. This is real. This is his pain. From the way his eyes trail up and down my body and his fingers dig into my flesh, I know this is going to be hard. He needs me, he needs this and I'll take whatever he needs to lose himself.

He plants me on the floor in front of the sofa and pulls my kimono from my shoulders. His huge erection is ready, hostile, when he yanks down and discards his lounge pants.

He grabs my breasts, too hard, then pulls my nipple with

his teeth, pain attacking the end. Pain that's welcome. Desired. An almost animal growl rumbles from his throat. His hands move to my hips, lifting me and pushing me down to the sofa, then he kneels between my legs. He spreads my knees apart and sucks hard on my clit, causing my hips to thrust back on a medley of bittersweet groans. His fingers drive into me and work roughly, taking me hard and quickly to a clouded mind. I won't come. This is for him. I want to help him the way he helps me. This is our cure.

He withdraws his fingers and flips me by my hips, pulling my knees to the floor, my back to his chest. He doesn't speak but moves his mouth to my neck, biting my skin. Reaching back, I dig my nails hard into his bare thighs, dragging a glutaral yet satisfied groan from him.

He leans me forwards and spreads my legs with his knees. I brace my body with my arms on the sofa and try to relax. Despite his urgency, he strokes a hand between my legs to make sure I'm ready to accept him, then he thrusts himself deep inside me on a bark.

The depth of his relentless, powerful drives has me crying out in a frenzy of spine-curling pain and otherworldly pleasure. He continues his thrusts, maintaining momentum. I'm close and as hard as I'm trying not to, I'm going to tip over the edge if he doesn't end this soon. But my hips are pushing back with my own anger. Anger for the scars on his back and wrists. Anger over his shadows. Rage because his past murdered my dad. This isn't gentle and caring, it's ruthless love, and I'm matching him beat for beat.

He grabs my hair in his fist and pulls my head back then wraps an arm around my stomach and pulls my body against his.

Yanking my hair, he tugs my head towards him and assaults my mouth, more desperate than he's ever been. I push my hips back to meet his thrust and groan into his mouth as we both climax violently, our mouths absorbing our cries.

nibbling my bottom lip as a beat pounds in my core. I could drown in your deep blue that has each time, I pull my lithe body to meet his thrusts before our lips tumble as both of us gasp into your mouth a great big of O es.

31

'Good morning,' he whispers as I open my eyes.

His cool breath smells of mint. He rests on the bed next to me, leaning up on his elbow. He's part dressed for work, his navy suit trousers hugging his svelte hips, his chest bare. I shuffle closer and breathe in his scent – masculine aftershave with a musk that's infinitely more attractive. All him.

'I could get used to waking up like this,' I say, nibbling his enticing nipple.

'Don't. I need to go to the office; I've got a call with China and I already don't want to leave you.'

I run my finger from the waist of his trousers up his side until goose pimples form beneath his skin. He flexes his hips and sighs. I kiss his chest then, wrapped in his white bed sheet, I make my way to the bathroom but not before one last glance across my shoulder. *What has he done to me? Who is this minx who's taken over Scarlett Heath's body?*

'I'll see you later?' I ask.

'Are you going to work today?'

'Mmm-hmm, I feel up to it. Plus, I'm having coffee with a friend this morning. Schmoozing.'

'Schmoozing who?'

'A *friend*, like I said. An old uni friend.'

'She's a client?'

'He and not yet but I'm hoping he'll put some work my way soon.'

'He?'

'Yes, *he*, and relax, Gregory, I'm a lawyer, not a hooker.'

'What does he do?'

'He's in corporate finance.'

'Corporate finance?'

'Yes.'

'What's his name?'

'Why do you need to know?'

'Why won't you tell me?'

Rolling my eyes, I make to leave the room on an obviously disgruntled sigh. 'His name is Luke Davenport.'

'I'll see you at home tonight then,' he says.

'Home for this week,' I say, waving a hand lazily as I exit the room.

With one towel wrapped around my wet hair and another wrapped around my body, I wander to the kitchen and make myself a coffee. Waiting for the machine, I look around the apartment and can't help but think that I could be happy here, with him. But Williams said it – Gregory doesn't *do* relationships. I could be hanging on the precipice of heartbreak. Or I could be special – the one who breaks the mould. He's so guarded, I could be convinced either way.

I watch from the window, my coffee cup warming my hands, as people walk in the streets below and rain streams down the side of the glass building. The first signs of the South

Bank Christmas Market are beginning to show; they're getting ready for the traditional November opening weekend. Wood frames are being erected. For the first year in many, I won't be taking my dad but it dawns on me that the same would've been true with or without Pearson. A chill runs the length of my spine and I find myself snarling.

I take my coffee to the dressing room and search the wardrobe Gregory has given me to hang my things for the week. I select a crimson dress, black, pointed heels and a knee-length, black, wool coat. When my hair is dry, I clip it straight into a French roll to avoid rain-induced frizz later in the day.

The concierge dips his head to me as I pass. Stepping onto the street, I open my dome umbrella as quickly as I can. As I lift it up and above my head, I see Jackson, squinting as rain hits his cheeks, holding the back door of the Mercedes open for me.

Shaking my head, I laugh. 'I give in. Let's go.'

He smiles, closes the door behind me and sits into the driver seat.

I tap the visor that compartmentalises us and Jackson winds it down.

'Where are we headed?' he asks.

'Canary Wharf. One Canada Square, please.'

'Sure thing.'

'I hear you're helping Sandy move today.'

'That's right.'

'I like you, Jackson, I really do.'

'But?'

'But if you *ever* hurt her, I *will* cut off your balls, fry them in sweet chili sauce and feed them to urban foxes. Understand?'

'I think I've got that,' he says, his nearest cheek rising towards his eye. 'I have no intention of hurting her, Scarlett.'

'Well, okay then. But I hear urban foxes *really* like sweet chili. Just saying.'

Turning on my phone for the first time in days, the unread email count in my inbox rises until it shows two hundred and sixteen. A quick check of my calendar tells me Margaret has rearranged almost everything for this week. I quickly fire off an email to warn her that I'll be in the office by ten-thirty.

'I'll get the Tube back to the office when I'm done, Jackson, so you don't need to wait and take me.'

He leans his head to one side in the rear-view mirror as if to say, *Think again.*

I flip an exasperated hand through the air. 'Or do. Whatever.'

When I leave the car, in spite of myself, I can't help but feel sorry for Jackson, always under orders, always having to find somewhere to park in impossible places. I button up my coat and tie the waistband, then walk into a coffee shop as fast as my stilettos will allow. A croissant somehow worms its way into my order with a latte for me and a black Americano for Luke.

'Come here, you,' Luke says, grabbing me around the waist and turning me into a cuddle. He leans back and tucks one loose strand of hair that's fallen from my French roll behind my ear in an overly familiar way. 'You look a million dollars.'

'You always know how to make me feel good. Look at you in your three-piece suit. Very handsome. And when did you start combing your hair to the side like this?'

'It's new for winter.'

I laugh genuinely, sincerely.

'Your latte,' says the plump man in a burgundy apron behind the counter. 'And the Americano must be for you, sir.'

'You always remember how I like things, Scar.'

'I don't forget miniscule but important details like how my

friends take their coffee. There's a little pocket of my brain marked, *Things Luke Likes*.'

'Ah, yes, I forget how similar we are. I too like to hoard meaningless info so I can't fit anything important in.'

With a grin, I let Luke lead us to a table for two in the corner of the café. When we sit, he leans forwards and tears at my croissant, leaving half on my plate and taking half for himself.

'I'm doing it for your hips,' he says as I pout. 'We wouldn't want you to fatten up that ballerina frame now, would we?'

'Not much chance of that with you stealing my food.'

'So listen, Scar, before we start chatting, I don't want to bum you out so I'll say it now. I'm really sorry about your pops. I was at the church.'

'Thanks. Can I be honest and say I really don't want to talk about it?'

'This is me – of course.'

Luke is the only person who has ever called me Scar. Others have tried, Lord knows everyone tried at school, and I've always dismissed it. But Luke calling me Scar always sounded right somehow.

'So before you try to schmooze me into giving you work – don't look at me like that; if you weren't schmoozing, we'd be headed to a club on a Saturday night, not sitting in a coffee shop amongst a load of suits on a Monday morning. So, before you talk business, tell me something new. Anything.'

Something new about me, the woman who works hard, cares for her dad and plays a tiny amount.

'Well, actually.' I play with my coffee cup, rolling my finger around the cardboard rim. 'I'm sort of, kind of—'

Then I stop mid-sentence, distracted by a man ducking his head behind a tabloid. 'Excuse me for a minute, Luke.'

I stomp from our table to where Jackson's sitting and snatch the tabloid from his grip. 'Tell me he hasn't sent you to spy on me.'

'He hasn't sent me to spy on you.'

'He's such a dick.' I growl. 'I'm not going to make a scene in a coffee shop so can you please just leave?'

'I have a coffee.'

'Leave your coffee, or take it with you, I don't care, but don't sit here and watch me from behind your newspaper.'

'Scarlett, you know I can't leave.'

I grind my teeth and breathe heavily out of my flaring nostrils. If I could breathe fire, I would fly to Gregory's office and blow my red-hot flames all over him. But Jackson is just doing his job, taking orders from Mr Irrational Dickhead Bazillionaire CEO.

'Fine.'

'Fine.'

Irritated beyond all imaginable belief, I stride huffily back to Luke.

'You were saying?' He looks like he's suppressing a laugh at my tantrum but he knows better than to tease me.

'Never mind.' I refuse to tell anyone about how truly smitten I am with the annoying, controlling, enigmatic, most mesmerising man I've ever met. Because he's also a dick. 'What's new about you?'

'Erm, single again.'

'You are? Since when?'

'About ten weeks. In fact, not *about* ten weeks, ten weeks and two days as of eleven twenty-two this morning.'

'Gosh, I can't believe it's been so long since we've seen each other. I'm sorry, you guys were great together. What happened?'

'Apparently, it's not me, I have a lot to offer but I just don't look like the dream man.'

'You're kidding!' Of all the reasons Luke might be dumped, being unattractive is just not one of them. When he asked me out to dinner at uni, I couldn't believe it. *What would a guy like him want with a girl like me?* He was shabby then; he had rugged, tousled, brown locks and he used to wear slim-fit jeans and Converse, back when Converse weren't really that cool. His amazing, piercing-blue eyes used to be the topic of every girl's conversation. 'Well, you know, a lot of people are probably counting their lucky stars that you're back on the market.'

He rests his hand on top of mine, leans his head to one side and blows me an air kiss. My smile is short-lived when I remember my stalker watching me from behind his newspaper.

'And how's work?' I coax.

'Okay, okay, we have to go there at some point. Actually, I got promoted.'

I already know that, courtesy of Amanda. 'You did? Congrats.'

'Well thanks and congrats to you too. It means I can manage my own budget for external advisors.'

'So, you could give me work if you like?' I ask with what I hope are twinkling eyes.

'I guess I could.' He chuckles.

We talk about Luke's promotion and his new responsibilities, then some deals he might be financing in the not-too-distant future.

'Well you know where I am if I can help you,' I say, kissing him on the cheek and escaping from his bear hug outside the café.

'I'll be in touch but I'm holding you to that night out too. I'm not waiting three months before I see you again, missy.'

Luke heads back to his office and I turn to scowl at Jackson. He's already out of his chair, key in hand, ready to bundle me back into his car and take me to work.

* * *

'Thank you for the coffee, Margaret,' I call from my office as I take off my coat which, thanks to Jackson, has only a light smattering of raindrops despite the heavy downpour still in full flow outside.

While my computer bounces through stages of set up, I flick through the paper mail that Margaret has already vetted for me. A letter from Companies House has arrived, which states that the new owner of Sea People International is Eclectic Technologies or, put another way, Gregory. I lay the letter out flat on my desk and watch it as I sip my coffee, expecting it to turn black, crawl and attack me. When nothing happens, I cast the letter into my pile of filing for Margaret and open my emails. For the second time this morning, the unread count in my inbox jumps to an impossible number but since I checked in the car on the way here, there's only one new message.

To: Heath, Scarlett
From: Ryans, Gregory
Sent: Monday 3 Nov 2025 10.12
Subject: New Matter

Good morning Scarlett,

As we have recently discussed, I've have been in negotiations with a Chinese company regarding introducing innovative technology to the European market. I should be grateful if we could arrange a suitable time to discuss potential structures for the relationship; one possibility we have considered is a joint venture. Things are moving quickly so I would appreciate your support as soon as possible. Discussions are likely to involve Eclectic Technologies and Shangzen Tek (China). We're about ready to get into the specifics.

> Regards,
> Gregory Ryans
> CEO Eclectic Technologies

As I'm reading, another pops up in the bottom right corner of my screen.

To: Heath, Scarlett
From: Ryans, Gregory
Sent: Monday 3 Nov 2025 10.18
Subject: Re: New Matter

iPhone.

> Regards,
> Gregory Ryans
> CEO Eclectic Technologies

A message waits on my phone screen.

> Please be honest with me and tell me if you're not ready for a deal yet. I won't go anywhere else. I can delay it.

I quickly reply.

> I'm fine. Email...

To: Ryans, Gregory
From: Heath, Scarlett
Sent: Monday 3 Nov 2025 10.22
Subject: Re: New Matter

Good morning Gregory,

Thank you for your email. I would be happy to discuss this further. I can meet with you today. Do you have any available time this afternoon?

Regards,

Scarlett Heath

Director

Saunders, Taylor and Chamberlain LLP

To: Heath, Scarlett
From: Ryans, Gregory
Sent: Monday 3 Nov 2025 10.23
Subject: Re: New Matter

12 p.m.?

Regards,

Gregory Ryans

CEO Eclectic Technologies

To: Ryans, Gregory
From: Heath, Scarlett
Sent: Monday 3 Nov 2025 10:25
Subject: Re: Meeting

12 p.m. is fine. I will see you at your office then.

Regards,

Scarlett Heath

Director

Saunders, Taylor and Chamberlain LLP

Despite the fact I want to breathe dragon flames at his head, butterflies flutter in my stomach at the thought of seeing him so soon. I'm still smiling at my screen when Amanda comes into my office.

'And what do you look so pleased about? No wait, let me guess. I think you're playing the gooey-eyed, lovesick puppy. Am I right?'

'Forget that. What's all this with you and Williams? Are you still, you know?'

'Sleeping together? Actually, no. Well, not that either of us remember. You'd think I'd know, right?'

'You'd hope so,' I laugh. 'Are you still going to Lara's party?'

'Oh, for sure, wouldn't miss it, but I think we're going as friends.'

'Friends? Right, okay.' I shake my head. 'So are we still on for shopping one night this week?'

'Yes, definitely. Oh my gosh, how full-on was Lara yesterday?'

I shrug. 'I guess she was. She was different after that Camilla woman left, though and what she's doing for Sandy is really nice. I probably didn't show it enough but I've been wondering what would happen to Sandy after... my dad, and Lara's fixed that.'

'I assume Gregory had something to do with it?'

When I nod, Amanda smiles and moves to perch on the end of my desk. 'You know, I do think he's really quite miserable and up his own arse but—'

'Oh, there is a but!'

'But, he's kind of growing on me, slowly. Everyone can see

he absolutely adores you. So as long as he doesn't royally fuck it up, I'm going to give him the benefit of the doubt.'

A grin spreads the width of my face, like a child in her first school play who's just located her parents in the audience. 'Well, I'm glad you approve.'

I nudge aside my doubt that he's in this or any relationship for the long haul.

'Of sorts. I'll be keeping a close eye on him,' she adds. 'So, have you googled this party Lara's having? It's crazy, full of celebs; apparently, it's a huge event.'

I *have* actually googled the event and whilst the prospect of celebrities and the press thrill Amanda, I feel an inordinate amount of pressure not to embarrass Gregory and Lara. There's frankly no way that will be possible when the press compare me to last year's guest, Clarissa Fontaine, another Victoria's Secret model. I wasn't snooping exactly; the picture just flashed up on Google images. Naturally, I looked. And I wish I hadn't. They looked stunning together.

'There's only one thing for it,' Amanda says.

'Harrods!' we sing in unison.

'Tomorrow evening?' I suggest.

'Yes, that's fab!'

'Perfect! Now get out of here so I can do some work.'

Turning on her heels and flicking her long hair over her shoulder, Amanda leaves.

I jot down the names of Eclectic Technologies and Shangzen Tek on a Post-it note which I take to Margaret and ask her to run conflict-of-interest checks to make sure there's no reason the firm can't act in any potential deal between Gregory and his Chinese acquaintances.

At eleven-twenty, I head to the ladies' to check that my hair, make-up and dress are in order, as if Gregory hasn't seen me without each of them out of place. I turn in the floor-length mirror to check there are no clicks in my stockings then rub a damp paper towel across the toes of my black, patent, leather shoes. There's a sickly excitement building in my stomach. I'm desperate to see him, even if I'll have to share him with Williams and Lawrence.

A walk will be good for me. It will calm my irrational nerves before I see him. I have to remember to keep things professional.

The rain has stopped when I step onto the street. My excitement immediately dissipates and is replaced by irritation when I see Jackson standing in front of me, holding open the door to the Mercedes. Standing still on the spot, it occurs to me that I could ignore him. What would he really do about it? I take one step right and for a second, I've convinced myself I'll actually walk away but I know it's not Jackson who's trying to strip me of my independence.

'Thank you,' I mumble as I sit into the back seat of the Mercedes.

Jackson inclines his head but I suspect he knows better than to strike up conversation with a woman sporting a scowl like mine. He sits into the driver seat and does not roll down the partition as he pulls out into the continuous stream of traffic.

When we arrive at Gregory's glass tower, I'm out of the car and storming through the glass doors to the building before Jackson has a chance to step out of the driver seat. My toe taps the ground as the lift rises. Irritation has now crystalised into rage.

'I'm here to see Mr Ryans; it's Scarlett Heath,' I unintentionally snap at the blonde on the reception desk. There's no love lost there, in any event. I've seen the way she silently hates on me.

'We're expecting you. I'll take you to his office; follow me.'

'His office?'

'Yes, he ordered lunch for the two of you to his office.'

'Williams, erm, Mr Williams and Mr Lawrence aren't joining us?'

'They weren't on the planner.'

We take the lift up a floor to twenty-eight, where a gleaming, gold sign greets us, stating this is the floor for GJR Enterprises. The blonde leads me along the corridor of floor-to-ceiling windows and knocks quietly, once, twice below the engraving that reads, *Chief Executive Officer*. She opens the door to the oversized office, revealing Gregory, watching the FTSE, Dow Jones and various commodity indexes on numerous flat-screen televisions from behind his chrome and glass desk. A selection of sushi decorates a table flanked by two leather sofas in the unnecessarily large space between his desk and the door.

'Mr Ryans, Miss Heath for you,' the blonde says, standing with one foot outstretched in front of her body the way an A-lister might do on a red carpet.

Watching the flutter of her eyelids and her sickening smile does little to cool my temper. She steps out of the room backwards and closes the office door, all the while undressing her CEO with wild-for-him eyes. Gregory stands from behind his desk with his delectable half-smile pulling on his lips but not even that can contain my fury.

'What the hell gives you the right to think you can restrict my liberty?'

I toss my bag onto a leather chair in front of his desk.

He's visibly taken aback.

'I wanted to get the Tube to Canary Wharf this morning but no, you sent Jackson for me without asking. Then I go for coffee with a potential client and you have the audacity to plant Jackson in the café to spy on me. I can't believe you really don't trust me at all. Then, *then*, I wanted to walk here just now. I *needed* to walk here. Nevertheless, who's waiting to bundle me into the back of a car when I walk out of the office? Yes, that's right, Jackson.'

He lifts one arm across his waist and rubs his chin with his opposite hand.

'I never said I wanted to live in a cage, Gregory. I don't want to fear walking in the streets. I don't want to be watched by Jackson, who, *who*, I currently live with, incidentally, and I certainly don't need to be controlled by you!'

'It's not controlling; it's protecting.'

I pull off my coat and throw it on top of my bag. 'Don't give me shitty sarcasm, Gregory; it really doesn't become you. Why don't you start with something like, "Scarlett, I'm sorry I'm trying to restrain your liberty, I have absolutely no fucking right to do that"?'

'How about I start with this: you left out some details this morning about Luke Davenport.' He loosens his blue, silk tie a notch and takes two steps towards me.

'So now *you're* stalking me as well as Jackson.'

'Social media can be very insightful.'

'Well how's this for insightful: I dated Luke at uni for six months. It was a juvenile relationship and I didn't tell you about him because there's nothing to tell. He's in banking now and I stay in touch with him because he's a good friend and one day, he might put some work my way. Pardon me for not fucking people and ditching them like I don't give a shit. And while we're on the subject, I don't see why I have to share everything with you when you won't tell me anything. I never know what you're thinking or what you're feeling. You're making me dizzy with all your secrets and lies.'

'Damn it, Scarlett, I'm trying. Who do you think you are to storm into my office and start yelling at me like a lunatic?'

I take three strides towards him. 'Lunatic? *Lunatic?* If anyone is driving anyone crazy here, it's *you* driving *me* crazy!'

'I drive you crazy?' He takes another two steps toward me until he's standing so close, I can feel the heat of his anger.

My train of thought has gone. 'Yes. You drive me fucking crazy.'

He takes my head in his hands and kisses me forcefully. I thrust my fingers into his hair and pull. He hoists me around his waist and carries me to the frosted-glass door. Reaching a hand behind me, I turn the lock.

'I think I'm going insane,' I pant.

'That makes two of us.'

He slams my back against the door and rubs a hand up my thigh, moving my dress to my waist. He starts to pull my lace thong down my legs.

'The desk,' I pant.

Casting a lamp and documents to the back of the desk, he sits me onto the edge. With one finger, he unhurriedly draws my thong down my legs to the floor. The feel of lace caressing my charged skin is more than my raging hormones can take. I pull the buckle of his belt loose and unfasten his trousers. He pulls them down to reveal his long, enticing cock.

'You can't keep using sex to get out of the doghouse, Ryans.'

He steps back, breaking our contact. 'No?'

I shake my head. 'No. It's not fair. It's a lethal weapon and I'm defenceless.'

He bends to bite my breast over my dress. 'Then just start doing what I say, baby.'

I gasp as he pulls me from the desk and flips me so I'm bent forwards, my arms and chest face down on the glass top.

'I'm going to spank this beautiful arse, just like you deserve.'

I swallow deeply, strangely turned on by the thought of a spanking. I lick my lips as I watch him over my shoulder raising his big palm and I cry out with lust when the sting lands.

He runs a hand from the top of my back and strokes the pearl of my arse then rams two fingers into me.

'Wet for me.' He slides his fingers through my slickness then uses it to move his fingers like silk across my clit. He draws his fingers back to my rear entrance, applying disastrously good pressure to the place that's *never* been touched. I'm already panting for him, my breathing rising to erratic drags as my temperature rises.

'So fucking beautiful.'

The fact that we're fully clothed, in his office, and his staff are just beyond the frosted-glass wall, adds to my frantic state. We could be caught any moment.

I grip the edges of the desk as he crashes into me.

I know I can't make another sound.

Having to absorb the sensation intensifies the feeling. His breathing comes heavier and faster. He holds my hips and yanks me back onto him, deepening each drive. His hand delivers another spank. I squirm as the heat of my burning flesh resonates in my sex. My hips push back against him, begging for more. He slaps my cheek harder on a low groan.

'Again,' I beg. I can't believe this is me.

Frantic. Sweating. Craving the kind of sex I've only read about.

He thrusts deep and slaps me for a fourth, hardest time. The delicious medley of pain and obscene pleasure taking me to the edge.

'Gregory, I'm going to come.'

He wraps his arm around me and circles my clit as my muscles clamp down on his solid length. 'Come with me.'

Finally, I let go. As quietly as possible, gripping the sides of his desk, I come with him.

He rests inside me until we've both caught our breath, then he helps me up and kisses me gently on the lips.

'Gregory,' I whisper, 'Luke Davenport is gay.'

He kisses me again with tight, upturned lips as he leans around me and takes a handful of tissues from his top drawer then hands them to me as he fastens his trousers.

'I think this is yours,' he says, retrieving my thong from the floor.

'But you would look so good in it,' I tease as I discreetly deposit the used tissues into his bin.

Almost immediately after Gregory unlocks the office door, there's a knock and a lady brings a trolley holding tea and coffee into the room. I don't need a mirror to tell me that my cheeks are the colour of my name.

After lunch, we slip back into our professional personas, taking opposite sofas at the table and discuss options for the structure of Eclectic's new deal with Shangzen Tek. Our little episode has relieved the tension from us both. He talks finance and products and I draw diagrams and discuss tax implications.

It's after four when we finally agree on some options for Gregory to explore in more detail with Mr Cheung and his team.

'Whilst I don't mind arguing with you, or rather I don't mind the making up, it's already dark and Jackson's here anyway so would you please let him drive you home?' Gregory asks.

'You're not coming?'

'I have a few things to do. Jackson can come back for me in a couple hours.'

'You could work from home.'

'Have you seen yourself in that dress? I'll never get anything done.'

I defy any woman to argue with that. Instead, I agree to let Jackson drive me home and plant a kiss on Gregory's brow before I leave.

'Scarlett,' he calls as I'm closing the office door. 'Thanks. You really are a good lawyer.'

'You're welcome, Mr Ryans.'

My mood couldn't be in greater juxtaposition to how I felt when I arrived at the office. Walking past the reception desk, I wonder whether the blonde knows what her precious Mr Ryans got up to at lunchtime.

'Hi, Jackson.'

'Scarlett.'

'I'm sorry for being rude earlier. I wasn't cross with you; he can be incredibly obstinate.'

All Jackson says is, 'I've worked for him for a long time.'

I suspect that's as close to him accepting my apology and agreeing with me as I'll get.

Inside the car, I tap on the partition and Jackson rolls down the screen.

'Is Sandy moved in?'

'Mostly.'

'It'll be strange to see her in a different house.'

A phone rings through the speakers in the car. Leaning forwards, I see the caller is *Boss*.

'Sorry, Scarlett, I need to take this,' Jackson says as the privacy partition slowly draws to the ceiling.

I try not to allow myself to be irritated again.

* * *

'That was Gregory?' I ask, already knowing the answer, when Jackson opens my door.

'Scarlett, I need you to do something for me, okay?'

'It depends what that thing is.'

'I need to you go straight up to the apartment and stay in. I have to head back to the office and I'll bring Gregory home in a couple of hours. Can you do that?'

Rolling my eyes, I head up to the apartment that smells of cleaning products and is as spotless as ever, thanks to Amy. I change out of my dress and into jeans and a jumper. I attempt to switch on the television in the lounge but this damned latest technology is not Scarlett Heath friendly. I make a coffee and sip it at the breakfast bar. As boredom sets in, I start to I feel peckish. The fridge is full of health-conscious snacks but there's nothing to make a meal.

This is ridiculous, I'm a grown woman.

Throwing a tan, leather bag over my shoulder, I resolve to make something tasty for dinner. I have about an hour and a half until Gregory will be home. I can shop and get some good food underway in that time.

I send Sandy a message and she suggests that broccoli and stilton soup is easy enough to make if you have a blender and that it's difficult to go wrong with steak, the worst-case scenario being overcooking it, but at least you can still put a meal on the table.

I fill my basket at the store and pop in a fancy – by my standards, not Gregory's – bottle of red wine.

The concierge is unusually away from his desk when I get back to the Shard. I have a strange feeling, one that I can't describe, like someone or something is watching me, as I wait for the lift. I walk backwards into the lift, looking around the ground floor, but there's nothing to see.

Still, I slam the apartment door behind me and quickly lock it.

After working out how to use Gregory's super-techy sound system, I manage to get the tunes from my phone playing in the kitchen and lounge. My hips swing and my head bobs along to Ed Sheeran. By my reckoning, I have around forty minutes before Gregory's home. Under Sandy's instruction, I boil the broccoli and make a saucy concoction of cream, stilton, corn flour and some less important bits of seasoning. Whilst those things are cooking, I cut some potatoes into chunky chip size and put them into the oven with oil.

'Okay, we're under control,' I tell myself between singing along to Ed.

Gregory should be just minutes away by the time I drain the broccoli and pour it with the sauce into the blender. I'm about to place the lid on the blender when I smell burning.

'Chips!'

I ditch the lid and fling open the oven door to expose a load of hot, smoky air.

'Crap!'

I pull the chips from the oven and rest them on a chopping board in their tray, utterly inedible. I turn back to the blender and just as I flick the switch to *ON*, the smoke alarm starts to sound, then the contents of the blender is swished out of the top where I've forgotten to place the lid. Warm soup is spitting all over me, the smoke alarm is blazing, I'm screaming and I can't find the *OFF* switch. As I pull the plug from the wall, Gregory bursts through the apartment door, closely followed by Jackson, panic evident on their faces. Gregory stops when he sees me and Jackson almost runs into the back of him.

Wiping soup from my face with the back of my hand, I look down to see the cheesy liquid splattered over my body from head to toe. Ed Sheeran stops singing about building a Lego house. The black chips stare at me from the bench. The smoke alarm is still blazing.

Raising my arms up with what I hope is an adorable smile, I say, 'I tried.'

Jackson is first to laugh, then we're all at it, though Gregory's laugh is short-lived. Jackson takes a tea towel from the bench and wafts it under the smoke alarm until it's silent.

'You went out then?' Gregory asks.

'I hate to state the obvious but I've been going outdoors without supervision for about twenty years.'

Jackson quietly takes himself off to his room.

'Things are different right now.'

'What happened?'

He sighs. 'Get yourself cleaned up and we'll talk. Is there anything we can salvage here?'

'A bottle of wine and cheesy-soup-covered steak.'

'I'll order in. And next time, tell me if you want a home-cooked meal. I employ Amy for that.'

By the time I've showered, changed into a fresh pair of jeans and a shirt and blow-dried my hair, two steaks have arrived, not covered in cheesy soup and certainly cooked better than I would have managed. Gregory is pouring the wine, his shirt unbuttoned by three but still tucked into his navy trousers. Too damn sexy.

'Maybe this was a better idea,' I concede.

He slides a glass of wine in my direction and leans forwards, his hands gripping the edge of the kitchen island.

'This can't be good.'

He takes a drawn-out drink from his glass.

'Don't try to sugarcoat it; just tell me.'

'This was hand-delivered to the office today,' he says, unfolding an old-looking document onto the island and sliding it across to me.

I'm looking at the birth certificate of Gregory James Pearson but there's a cross made with pen through his name. Next to the field for Mother, there's also a cross through *Lara Olivia Pearson*. The only name not crossed is that next to Father, *Kevin James Pearson*.

'Your birth certificate?'

'Ryans is my mother's maiden name.'

'Okay. And this was delivered to your office?'

'I spoke to my mother earlier and she said she hasn't had it since South Africa. We just left; there were things she didn't have time to find. If we could buy it or replace it, we left it.'

'So you think Pearson had this and delivered it to your office?'

'This afternoon, when you were there. The notes, the—'

'The wedding ring.'

He shoots me a questioning glare. 'How do you know about that?'

'Is that you confessing that you were keeping things from me again? It doesn't matter how I know. What does it mean? He's coming for us?'

'I think the only question is when and where.'

Goose pimples rise under the hairs on my arms. I gulp from my wine glass.

'What're we going to do?' I try and fail to suppress the tremor in my voice.

'You're going to start listening to Jackson and me. Jackson will be with us and he's got more guys at my mother's house. He's got extra security for the party. But I won't just wait for him, not this time. Jackson's pulled a team together to find him before he finds us. The problem is, he has no base here. He doesn't live in England and he doesn't have a routine.'

I take two deep breaths as subtly as I can. 'Do you...' My voice breaks so I cough to disguise my fear. 'Do you think... How far will he go?'

Gregory refuses to meet my eye. His reaction alone is enough to give me the honest answer but he says, 'We can't know for sure.'

'And you still don't think the police should be involved?'

Gregory doesn't respond. I know exactly why the police can't be involved and it terrifies me. The thought that something might happen to him is unbearable.

We eat in relative silence. In bed, we both lie awake, staring at the ceiling. My mind flits from fear to anger and each time I sneak a glance at Gregory's open eyes, I wish I could tell what mix of emotions he's feeling.

I want this to end. However it happens, I just want him to be free.

32

'Are you ready?' Amanda asks, popping her head around my office door.

'Yep. Just shutting down. Jackson's going to drive us to Harrods, is that okay?'

'Okay? It's great! Some of us *do not* have a problem being chauffeured around.'

Jackson drops us at the Brompton Road entrance to the finest and largest department store in London and two concierges are on hand to welcome us. Concierges at Harrods are somewhat an institution in Britain. They have status. They wind up on postcards, tourists stop to take their photograph, sometimes they even make it to biscuit-tin lids. It's their gentle-manly manner, their cute, knee-length, grey jackets with dazzling, gold buttons and their matching grey top hats. They're part of what makes Harrods *Harrods*.

'Follow me,' Amanda demands.

'Wait, I want to look at the bags first.'

'No, we can do that later, this way.'

She struts towards the lift vestibule where we stare at

bottle-green, marble walls trimmed with gold and wait for the lift. When the doors open on the women's floor, a pristine lady greets us. I'd place in her forties despite her flawless, youthful-looking skin. A pearl necklace hangs over her demure, black blouse, which is tucked into an expensive-looking, black-and-silver-striped pencil skirt. Her brown hair looks as if she's just stepped out of a salon and sits with perfect bounce onto her shoulders. I recognise the scent of expensive perfume as she offers her hand, first to Amanda.

'Good evening, I'm Julia. Scarlett, is it?'

'Oh, no, Amanda. It's nice to meet you. This is Scarlett.'

'I'm sorry. It truly is a pleasure to meet you, Scarlett.'

'Ahh, hi, it's nice to meet you. What is going on?'

Julia titters. 'He's sneaky, isn't he? Come this way. I spend a lot of time styling Mr Ryans, although I think I know what he likes by now so I don't see him as often as I used to.'

'It's so important to have a brand image, I think,' Amanda says, feigning the accent of the Queen, mimicking Julia. I want to laugh but refrain.

Following behind Julia as she strides without fault in her red-soled shoes, Amanda explains, 'Gregory said I could pick whatever I want if I got you here. He said you'd say no if he suggested it to you.'

'I can't afford this,' I try to whisper.

Julia stops in front of a frosted-glass door. Before she opens it for us, she leans in towards my ear and whispers, 'It's all on Mr Ryans' account.'

'But, I—'

'Stop fussing, Scarlett,' Amanda says, wafting a hand past my face and following Julia into the black-walled room. 'He can afford it.' *And you're more than happy to accept it.*

I huffily take out my phone and send Gregory a message.

> You're such a controlling arse...

I get an almost instant reply.

> Enjoy!

In the room, another flawlessly styled woman in a black dress and a man in a three-piece suit with a pink, floral tie are standing to attention and smiling like something out of *The Brady Bunch*. Two embroidered sofas are set back to back in the centre of the room and racks of evening gowns line the walls. A glass table is laden with jewellery and the biggest diamonds I've ever seen. Three white shelves contain a selection of shoes in different colours and styles, highlighted by spotlights above them. Two dressing areas are separated by black velour curtains held back by gold chains.

Turning in the centre of the room, I must look gormless as I take in the spectacular view. *So this is how the other half live.*

'You're the one,' the suited man says, offering me his hand. 'I'm Lucas. This is Genevieve.'

I smile at Lucas and Genevieve as I reciprocate a handshake. 'Scarlett. It's nice to meet you.'

'Champagne?' Lucas asks, turning his hand flamboyantly towards a waiter carrying two glasses of champagne on a tray in one hand and menus for the restaurant in the other.

'I could get used to this,' Amanda says, taking a glass of champagne and sitting on a sofa with the menu.

By the time we've ordered food, Julia and Genevieve have selected the first two dresses for me to try on.

'We'll start with Scarlett,' Lucas says.

Amanda wafts a hand. 'I'm more than happy right here.'

She sips her champagne with her legs lifted, lounging out on the sofa.

Genevieve holds up a satin, floor-length dress in midnight blue. It has a thick halterneck with a triangle of lace inset over the bust and coming to a point at the bottom of the breastbone area. Julia holds up an equally long, black dress with full-length sleeves and a wide, round neck, lower at the back than the front. A slit runs thigh-high on one leg.

'I'll try the blue first, please.'

Lucas clicks his fingers excitedly. 'Shoes!' he sings, as I'm encouraged to move into the dressing room and the velour curtain is drawn around me.

'That bra isn't going to work,' Genevieve says when I've revealed my black lace underwear. 'What size are you? Thirty-two D?'

'Ah, yes, actually.'

'This is my job,' she says, rather pleased with herself. 'Julia, can we get a strapless plunge in a thirty-two D?'

Julia passes through a bra in seconds and, much to my horror, Genevieve doesn't leave the room or even turn as I swap my own bra for the strapless plunge. She helps me into the dress and gestures for me to sit as she places the shoes Lucas has picked out onto my feet.

'Right, let's take a look,' she says.

I have to hand it to them, I look fantastic, for me. The dress gives me a figure I'm sure I've never seen and the lace point reveals enough to make me appear to have a cleavage without being overt. Genevieve draws back the curtain to display me to the room.

Immediately, without taking a breath or giving her heart a chance to beat, Julia says, 'No.'

Followed by Lucas who, with a hand on his hip and the other on his chin, says, 'It's all wrong.'

Amanda laughs, presumably at my bottom lip, which has worked its way out in a childish pout.

'Let's try the black,' Julia says.

After the third unsuccessful dress, my poached salmon and asparagus with a side order of potatoes has arrived with a new glass of champagne. The table has been pulled towards the sofas for us to eat. As I pick up my knife and fork, Lucas swoops in and removes my side plate of potatoes.

'We don't want you to bloat.'

Once again, my pouting lower lip is out and Amanda snorts.

'You too, missy,' Lucas says, taking away her side order as well.

Now it's my turn to laugh.

Lucas is quick to get me back on my feet after dinner. Genevieve and Julia begin searching the racks again.

'Is it all right if I look too?' I ask.

'Of course,' Julia replies.

Searching through a number of black dresses, I pull out one: a satin halterneck fastened with three buttons at the nape and a cut-out back. It's fitted to the waist then A-line in shape, with a short train, an inch or two. Then I see a sheath-cut, black dress, subtly embroidered with small, black crystals. It's strapless with a sweetheart neckline.

'Can I try these?'

Lucas scrutinises the two dresses then says, 'Not bad, not bad. Let's try them.'

This time, Julia helps me dress and Lucas picks the shoes again. First, I put on the black halterneck and step out from behind the changing curtain.

'That's my favourite so far,' Amanda says.

This time, it's Genevieve who disapproves. 'I just don't feel wowed by it.'

I'm beginning to lose the will to live. What started as fun is now laborious and tiresome. I traipse back behind the curtain and Julia helps me slip out of the halterneck and into the crystal-laced dress.

'These will be perfect,' Lucas says, handing Julia a pair of jewelled sandals.

Julia straps me into the sandals and gives me a hand to stand up. The dress feels amazing; it fits my waist perfectly and the silk slip kisses my legs as I walk but I don't bother to look in the mirror. Instead, I step straight out to the lion pack from behind the curtain.

Lucas gasps and puts his hands together, touching the tip of his nose as if in prayer. 'That's it. That's the one!'

'He won't be able to take his eyes off you,' Genevieve adds.

Julia claps excitedly. 'Accessories!'

'This one!' Lucas says, taking a thick, diamond choker from a blue, velvet box and handing it to Julia.

'Hair up, definitely up,' Genevieve says.

Julia places the choker around my neck and turns me to face the mirror. 'Go on, take a look.'

In the mirror, I see Amanda grin and slowly nod her head. It's still the same me, but even I must admit it's a better version of me. I look a million dollars... but that's also the problem.

'There's no way I can let Gregory pay for all this. I'm sorry, I do love it but it must be a fortune.'

'Hunny, do you have any idea how much his clothes cost? Anyway, the necklace would be on loan; people rarely buy these things,' Lucas points out.

'But what about the shoes and dress?'

Julia rests a hand on my shoulder. 'To Mr Ryans? Buttons.'

'You could always soften the blow,' Amanda offers, dangling lace French knickers from one finger.

* * *

By the time we're back in the Mercedes with Jackson, I have a dress, a new pair of shoes and a bag, a diamond necklace on loan and a black, satin corset with matching stockings and suspenders – the 'Mercy Corset,' so I'm told. Amanda has an entirely new outfit as well, minus the underwear, and Julia was more than happy to put it on Gregory's tab and take her commission.

Stepping out into the crisp air has made me realise how much the champagne has gone to my head.

'Sweet dreams,' Amanda calls as she leaves the car.

Jackson and I wait until she's in her apartment block and the door locks behind her.

'Thank you for picking us up.'

'It's never a problem. It's good for Gregory right now too.'

'How is he?'

'About as stressed as I've seen him. Usually, it's just business or even when it's personal, it's only about him. But he's concerned now for Lara, and for you.'

'Has your team had any luck today?'

'Nothing yet but they're good guys; they'll keep trying.'

When we arrive back at the apartment, Gregory is drinking coffee and looking over documents splayed out on the coffee table in the lounge. I gather this is the information the team has pulled together on Pearson so far.

'Did you get a dress?'

I give him a playful scowl. 'Yes, I have a dress but you shouldn't have paid.'

'You could just say thank you.'

I plant a kiss on his lips. 'Thank you.' Then I hand him the smallest of the Harrods bags. 'This is for you.'

He peeks into the bag and moves the black tissue to one side to reveal the Mercy Corset. I take the bag back from him. 'You won't be too late, will you?'

He clears his throat and turns to Jackson. 'I, we, we won't be too much longer, Jackson, will we?'

I hang up my dress then take a shower. It takes some time and skilful manoeuvring but I'm eventually dressed in the corset and stockings. I decide to add the jewelled shoes into the mix and finally, the diamond choker, then I dim the bedroom lights and lie on the chaise longue, waiting for Gregory.

Eventually, the door opens and he stands, observing from the doorway, his arms folded, eyes hooded.

I feel seductive, ridiculous and more feminine than I'd ever have thought possible.

'What are we going to do with you?' His words are low, heavy, promising.

He rolls up the sleeves of his white shirt as he moves towards me. He plants my legs on the floor in my heels, then forces them wide apart in a sudden move that makes me lean back on my hands, the Mercy Corset pushing my breasts upward. Then he kneels before me. Mine. All mine.

Gregory's been pacing the lounge for most of the day. He's become increasingly nervous as the party has drawn closer without the team making strides to find his father. The usual mask of stoicism and confidence has been firmly in place but I'm becoming finely tuned to the man beneath that façade. This morning, he and Jackson drove to Lara's house to brief the team on where they need to be tonight and when. Jackson's team met Lara's hired security for the party. Now the good guys know the good guys and there's a face to match the voices as they communicate through radios later.

'We don't have to go,' I said to him this morning.

I felt sorry for him when his wide, troubled eyes regarded me. 'I can't leave my mother there and I can't leave you here. It'll be safer if we're all in one place.'

Because he's been with Jackson all day, he arranged for a hairdresser to come to the apartment so that I didn't go out alone. After curling and loosely pinning my hair at the nape of my neck, a beautician primed and made up my face.

We have an hour to get to the party in our allocated arrival slot so it's time for me to get dressed. Gregory is in his home office speaking on his phone and in truth, I no longer have a desire to hear those calls. My mind has been racing all day with an almost unbearable mix of excitement, nerves and rage.

My phone beeps to tell me I have a message. The sound shocks me, setting my heart racing. There's no denying I'm on edge.

> I am soooooo excited I can hardly breathe!!!!!!!!!!

Smiling at Amanda's countless exclamation marks, I set my phone to one side and get ready. Somehow, I navigate the dress over my head without catching any crystals in my hair, then, realising it's much easier when someone else does it for you, I put on the new sandals. My stomach begins to churn with anticipation. I hope Gregory likes it. Everything looks in order when I check the floor-length mirror. The last thing I do is gently unhook the diamond choker from its box and delicately place it around my neck, terrified of damaging the extravagant thing.

With a deep inhale, I whisper to myself, 'Ready.'

Jackson and Gregory are already dressed in their finest black tie and waiting in the lounge. Gregory watches the city below with his hands in his pockets. He turns to look at me, takes one hand from his pocket and places it across his chest in that way he does. A smile, so forceful I can't prevent it, draws across my face. His gaze never leaves mine as I move down the staircase. We stand face to face, time frozen, my heart beating against my eardrums. Eventually, he places a hand to the side of my face and strokes my cheek with his thumb.

He kisses me, long and slow.

'This is real,' I whisper to myself. I kiss him again, with the passion that threatens to take over everything I am, my rules, my order, my world as I've always known it. And I'll do anything in my power to make sure I never lose it. Right now, in this moment, the only thing that scares me is how far I'd go to protect what's mine. That awareness is more terrifying that any monster roaming the streets of London.

Jackson clears his throat, reminding me that we're not alone. 'We need to be going.'

Gregory and I walk out the front entrance and Jackson is already there with a black Bentley.

'No Mercedes?'

'Not tonight,' Gregory says.

He opens the rear door then takes my hand and guides me into the back of the car, being careful not to step on the train of my dress.

'Give us five, Jackson,' he says. The partition between the front and back of the car rises.

Gregory takes my chin between his forefinger and thumb. 'You're incredible.'

'I love you,' I whisper. I can't believe I've said it but I mean it.

Briefly, I see his gorgeous half-smile and then he places his lips on mine. I want him so much, I could burst. My abdomen ties itself in knots. I never want to forget this feeling. I love him with every inch of my body and I'll wait and hope for him to feel the same if that's what it takes, but I need him to know that I love everything about him: every mood, every glance. My heart, my soul, my mind, my body – I give it all up to this man.

We're on the gravel driveway of Lara's property before we stop kissing. Faux flame lights line the path to the mansion. Jackson slows the car and crawls behind a chain of other chauffeured cars to the red-carpet entrance. Press line the sides of the red carpet behind a chain fence. My throat is dry with terror. I squeeze Gregory's hand.

'Hey, they aren't here for us. It's just you and me, baby.' He kisses my brow then pecks the tip of my nose. I nod twice, quickly, and take a deep breath to compose myself. My heart starts pounding when the car in front of us, the last car between the red carpet and ours, moves forwards. Jackson gets out and opens the back door. The camera flashes start immediately.

Gregory steps out of the Bentley to shouts of, 'Mr Ryans!' and, 'Gregory!'

'Holy shit!'

Gregory turns and leans into the back of the car to see me taking short, shallow breaths.

'Jesus, Gregory, I can see the headlines now. "CEO Slumming It. From Beauty to the Beast".'

'Or maybe they'll say, "CEO and the Most Captivating Woman at the Gala". Come on, you're with me; I won't let you go.'

He offers his hand and I take it, trembling. 'Let's get it over with.'

As I step out of the car, the flashes come faster and the shouts become, 'Who is she?'

Gregory squeezes my hand tighter and leads me to the middle of the red carpet. 'Smile, you're beautiful,' he whispers into my ear.

I try to remember how I've seen women pose in magazines. Then, completely unexpectedly, Gregory pulls me into him, looks deep into my eyes and kisses me. With his hand holding my hips to him, he leans me back. I open my eyes mid kiss and ask myself if this is the same, private, mysterious CEO I know.

Waiters hold trays aloft, full of champagne flutes, in the

hallway of Lara's home. People looking like members of the aristocracy, covered in fine materials, frosted with diamonds and doused in the scent of money, chatter in small pockets. All eyes watch Gregory as we make our way through the reception, his presence commanding attention. I try to avoid making eye contact with the women who are clearly scrutinising me and whispering their catty findings. At the end of the hallway, an extravagant display of champagne glasses, towering and glowing with the flow of golden bubbles, draws my attention.

'Wow, that's amazing.'

'And incredibly wasteful.' Gregory hands me a glass of champagne and leads us out to the garden.

Flame lights and outdoor heaters are roaring, making the air feel like a summer's night in paradise. Standing at the top of the steps, looking down across the lawn, we see Lara's planning in full view. LED lights are twisted around the stair rails and sparkle in small trees that decorate every third step leading down to the lawn. Hundreds of people fill the grass. The cream pavilion is the focal point and hosts a big swing band. Dressed tables are scattered as far as I can see in the distance.

A lady I'd place in her fifties wearing a purple gown and covered in more black and clear diamonds than I've seen in the whole of Hatton Garden approaches us. 'Gregory, darling, hi!' She kisses him the continental way: one cheek then the other. 'It's wonderful to see you again. Your mother's done a fantastic job, as ever!'

'Claudia. Can I introduce you to Scarlett Heath?'

'You certainly can. It's a pleasure to meet you.'

'The pleasure's all mine,' I say, allowing her to kiss my cheeks.

'Now, Gregory, you must see David; he's around here some-where and he'll be keen to see you.'

'I'll make sure I do.'

The next person we see is Camilla, from lunch. Surprisingly, I'm happy to see her familiar face.

'Oh. My. Good Lord! This is A-mazing!' Amanda screams, running up the steps towards us.

I throw my arms around her. 'This looks even better than it did in Harrods,' I say, gesturing to her from head to toe, her gold, satin gown showing off her figure perfectly.

'You too!' she shouts needlessly loudly.

'Hi, Amanda,' Gregory says, kissing her on the cheek. 'You look great.'

'Well, if you do favours for bazillionaires, good things come of it,' she says, winking at Gregory.

He's amused but typically, not quite enough to laugh. 'I'm going to catch up with Jackson. Will you be okay?'

'Of course she will; she's with me,' Amanda says, snatching my hand and pulling me down the steps. 'I swear I just saw Jude Law.'

I look back over my shoulder and smile at Gregory but he's tense. A look I saw on him at every juncture of the Sea People deal.

My name is being shouted from somewhere on the lawn. Eventually, I match the voice to Lara and she looks astounding. Her deep-purple, crushed-satin dress is fitted to her waist with a subtle fishtail bottom and high, structured collar. Her blue-black, sapphire and diamond, teardrop earrings match a much larger version of the same around her neck.

'Scarlett!' She waves me towards where she stands with two couples.

'Lara, you look fantastic.'

She hugs me and kisses me on both cheeks then turns me to the couples who she introduces as Gordon and Vivienne and

Stella and Jean-Pierre. We exchange pleasantries and I introduce Amanda.

Lara rests a hand on my shoulder and tells the group, 'This is the woman who has tamed the lion's heart.'

My cheeks burn under the four pairs of dissecting eyes. A thousand responses dance around my synapses: gracious, polite, ridiculous.

'I'm not sure he'll ever be tamed,' I say.

'That sounds like the Gregory we know.' Jean Pierre's French accent is smooth. He raises his champagne flute.

'What is it you do, Scarlett?' Gordon asks.

'I'm a lawyer. And you?'

'I design furniture. You might have seen my store in Knightsbridge: Belle Maison.'

'I have, actually. Your furniture is amazing: very chic.'

'That's what we try to achieve.'

'I'm curious,' Stella says with an underlying sharpness to her voice, her lean frame looking down on me by an inch or two. 'How did you meet Gregory?'

Her abruptness catches me off guard. Her plump, red lips pull to a pout and her eyes bore into mine, her fierceness augmented by her severe updo, scraping her bottle-blonde back from her face into a chignon.

'I did some work for him.'

'Uh huh, and what kind of work was that?'

I pause for a second, wondering what's passed between her and Gregory to make her take a tone that I *really* don't care for.

'The confidential kind.'

Vivienne breaks the silence with a high-pitched cackle and the group continues making inane conversation.

'Lara, you don't mind if I just steal Scarlett away, do you? I'm sure I just saw someone I know,' Amanda says.

'Really? No, of course not.'

Amanda drags me away, muttering. 'He's blatantly turned her down before. What a cow!'

'Not just me then?'

'Not. At. All. But forget her, Mr Cover-Me-In-Chocolate-Sauce-And-Lick-Me-Clean is at twelve o'clock!'

'Amanda, that's vulgar. Plus, what's happening with you and—'

'O. M. G. OMG! OMG! That's the guy who plays that guy in *Inception*. Quirky but smokin' hot.'

'Which guy?' I turn to follow the approximate direction of Amanda's stalking eyes. 'Ohhhh, Tom Hardy? Yes, that's Tom Hardy.'

'Holy shit! How can you be so calm?'

'Jesus, Amanda, did someone give you a Viagra? They're just normal people.'

'You're so cerebral.'

'What, have you swallowed a dictionary now?'

She scowls at me as a waiter steps towards us with a tray of full champagne flutes. Amanda takes the last swig from her glass and replaces it with a full one. I deposit my empty glass on the tray.

'You need to be careful,' I say. 'I think Williams likes you and I know you don't really like him but—'

'Really? Do you think so?' She's suddenly bright-eyed and paying attention.

'Of course. Don't you think so?'

'I thought we were just fooling around.'

A moving hand catches my eye. Lawrence is beckoning us over to a pocket of men and women who are closer to our own age than most people we've seen so far – certainly closer than that catty cow, Stella.

'Emily, this is Scarlett, Gregory's girlfriend, and her friend Amanda. Scarlett, Amanda, this is my niece Emily, my nephew-to-be Harry, and their friends Archie and Penelope.'

'Hi, it's so nice to meet you.'

'Lawrence tells me you're a lawyer,' Harry says. 'I work for Bruckheimer.'

'You're almost next door to us then,' I say. 'Amanda and I both work for Saunders.'

'We should have drinks sometime,' Emily says with a genuine smile. 'The four of us meet up with some other friends every Friday at Crux. We've tried to get Gregory there but he's always too busy. Maybe you can persuade him.'

'I'll see what I can do.'

'It's a wonder we've never seen you,' Amanda chips in. 'Scarlett and I go to Crux if we go out straight from work.'

A loud burst of laughter comes from a gathering not far from us. Turning my head to the right, I see Williams telling a story of some sort to the responsive crowd, Gregory relaxed beside him, a rare but handsome sight. When the laughter subsides, Gregory turns his head around the crowd, finally locating me. Fire burns in my body and everything under my ribcage hammers to be let out. I don't think I'll ever tire of watching him. As a waiter offers fresh drinks to the group, Gregory pats Williams on the shoulder as if to say, *You've got this.* Then he replaces his one empty glass with two full flutes.

A silver-haired lady stops him midway but it's a momentary distraction only. He's making a line for me, focused, intent, as if I'm the only person in the vicinity.

'Hi,' he says, handing me a glass of champagne.

'Hi.'

My tongue unwittingly strokes my lips where I'd like to feel his.

'Gregory, we were just saying how we always invite you to Friday drinks and you *never* come,' Emily teases.

'Are you sure I've never been? Not once?'

'You know you've never been,' Emily scolds.

'All right then, maybe I haven't.' Gregory smiles.

After the stress of the week, his good-humoured mood seems both misplaced and incredibly charming.

'I always try to force him, Emily,' Williams says, striding into the group.

Amanda watches him as he chats merrily with Harry. I raise a brow when I catch her eye. She rolls her eyes in response but continues to listen intently to Williams' stories and bumps her shoulder into his when he teases her. Gregory stays by my side through another glass of champagne and maybe thirty, forty or more introductions. I lost count some time ago. Even when I step inside to say hello to Sandy, who's making demands of the agency wait staff, he's with me. Everywhere I go, scowls follow me. Little do those women know that I'm terrified my bubble could burst at any time.

Lara makes a speech around eleven o'clock, dragging an uncomfortable-looking Lawrence to the front of the big swing band's stage to say a few words.

Gregory wraps an arm around my waist as we listen to his mother's speech and I imagine I'm the envy of every female at the party.

At the end of her speech, she announces the final set from the band. 'Before the fireworks take place at midnight and the party continues,' she says, receiving a chorus of cheers.

The swing band strikes up with Michael Buble's 'Everything.'

'I love this song.'

'Would you like to dance?' Gregory asks, holding out a hand expectantly.

I let him lead me to the dance floor. Holding up my right hand, he pulls my waist tightly into him. He winks and the weight falls out of my legs. My breathing quickens in anticipation as I will him to kiss me. Instead, as the chorus kicks in, he turns us around the dance floor, increasing speed until I thrust my head back with laughter.

When the verse returns, he twirls me under his arm then spins me into his body, my back against his chest. He wraps his arms around me and holds us still, his warm breath at my lobe making the hairs rise on the back of my neck, each of my sensitive spots whirring to action. Then he spins me away from him and back, readying us to turn our way through the second chorus. The band picks up pace at the key change and Gregory spins me away and back to him again but this time, he puts his hands beneath my arms and lifts me straight above him, turning me in time to the beat as I gaze into his alluring, brown gems. The music slows and he lowers me down to him. Returning my feet to the floor, he takes my cheek in his hand and rests his brow on mine.

'Kiss me, Gregory Ryans.'

Our mouths meet, slowly, purposefully, full of everything I feel and hope he feels. He swallows my moan as my body moulds to his. My breasts rub against his pecs, my thighs lock onto his, my hips subtly grind his crotch. We're the only two people in our dark, twisted but perfect world.

'Don't do that to me.' His words are heavy and said through gritted teeth.

I open my eyes and look directly into his, starving, craving satisfaction from the only man who can sate my hunger.

'How much do you want to see the fireworks?' he asks.

'Not at all.'

His irises darken and his pupils dilate. Despite all these people, I could make love to him right here and now.

'I'll get Jackson.'

I nod and he leaves to find Jackson while I locate Amanda, who's still quaffing free champagne with Williams, Emily and Harry. By the time Gregory leads me out front to the Bentley, the first firework goes off. I start as it squeals and explodes in a thunderous roar.

* * *

Gregory sits in the back of the car with me but the partition remains down. Our moods have changed – his no doubt following his conversation with Jackson and the team, mine inexplicably. The black leather of the seat is cold and chills my skin through my coat, making me shiver. Tension creeps into my neck and limbs. Gregory places an arm around my waist but for a change, it doesn't remove the uneasiness building inside me.

'You okay?'

'Mmm, sure,' I lie.

The back roads that Jackson takes through the city are pitch black and sinister.

We wait on the declining ramp as the basement door rolls open under the Shard. Florescent lights illuminate the garage and at first, everything seems normal. Jackson starts to reverse the Bentley into a space next to the Mercedes.

The engine's hum falls silent. Gregory moves to get out of the car.

'Wait!' Jackson snaps, already halfway out of his door.

'Stay inside,' Gregory says to me.

Jackson crouches beside the Mercedes and runs a finger along the long, jagged rubber edges of what once was the rear tyre. Anxiety murmurs in my chest.

Gregory looks at the far side of the Mercedes. 'They're all slashed.'

My heart thuds like a jackhammer. My body stiffens. My lungs forget how to breathe.

'The door,' Gregory says, looking at the entrance to the lift vestibule, forced and damaged, ajar.

'Romeo One, come in,' Jackson says into his radio. 'Romeo One, come in.'

There is a crackle on the line then, 'Romeo, this is Romeo One.'

'Send a car. Now!'

Gregory opens the rear passenger door to the Bentley.

'Scarlett, I want you to take the car and leave.'

Panic and adrenalin take over my body.

'What? I... no. I'm staying with you.'

'Scarlett, do as I say.'

'But where would I go? I'm not leaving you.'

'Scarlett—'

'She's right,' Jackson says, sliding into the driver seat and opening the glove box. 'He could be anywhere. We don't know that he's here. She's safer with us.'

That should probably make me feel better. It doesn't. All I can think is that he's out there. Pearson ruined Gregory's life. He murdered my dad. Now he's coming for us.

Gregory grabs my hand and pulls me forcibly from the Bentley. 'Stay by my side. Don't leave my side. Do you hear?'

'Yes,' I croak through my dry throat.

Jackson removes a black, leather box from the glove

compartment and takes what I recognise from movies to be a Glock.

This can't be real.

Jackson leads, holding the gun by his side. Gregory pulls me with them by my hand, his determination the only thing making my hollow legs move. I follow, turning my head left, right, as far back as it will go. At the vestibule door, we line up, our backs against the garage wall. Jackson clicks the safety off the Glock as he slowly moves towards the busted door.

I swallow vomit that rises to my mouth.

He kicks the door open then jumps through, turning left and right, poised to fire. He gestures for Gregory and me to step into the vestibule then radios Romeo One for a time check.

'Ten minutes.'

Then there's a heavy, wet breath on the line. It doesn't speak but its presence is real. Something tells me it's Pearson. If he's jacked into the channel now, he could've been following our moves all night.

He's here.

Instinctively, I grip Gregory's hand.

'Keep breathing, Scarlett,' he says as calmly as the situation will allow.

I nod but I'm beginning to feel light-headed, slipping in and out of reality.

Jackson punches the button for the lift and holds the gun in front of him with two hands, ready for whatever waits behind the metal doors. He ushers us into the lift and takes one more look around the vestibule.

We're silent as we rise to the sixty-fourth floor, the only noise coming from the whir and crank of the suspension cables. The sound of my own breath resonates in my ears. I hold a hand against my chest to keep it from exploding.

The lift pings and I think I could cry. I close my eyes as the doors begin to crawl open. Jackson leaps out and jumps left to face the double apartment doors.

'Wait here,' Gregory says.

'No, I'm coming,' I say.

He doesn't argue but he doesn't hold my hand either. His fists are clenched, his torso rigid. The apartment doors are ajar and the floor sensor lighting is dimly glowing blue. He's in there.

Jackson motions for us to stand behind the left door. He moves to the right and raises his gun with two hands. I jump and maybe scream when he kicks open the door. In a split second, there's a muffled shot, a yell and Jackson's body thuds to the ground. 'He's in! He's in!' Jackson shouts.

Gregory leaps towards Jackson. There's a pool of blood already forming beneath his leg. Gregory pushes both hands against his thigh.

'Leave it! Get him!' Jackson yells through gritted teeth.

Gregory glances at me, then at Jackson. I want to tell him not to go but the words don't leave my mouth. There's a loud bang then the sound of breaking glass from one of the doors off the lounge – the bathroom. Gregory runs towards the sound.

Without thinking, trembling and frantic, I pull my arms from my coat and bend down to tuck it under Jackson's bleeding leg. Using the sleeves, I tie a tourniquet. Jackson winces but doesn't tell me to stop. Another bang sends my body jolting. I shift to look toward the bathroom. Thrashing. More glass shatters. The sound of struggle continues.

Then the gun that shot Jackson slides into the lounge with the power of a kick. Gregory and Pearson burst through another door into the gym, tussling, gasping, brutally fighting for their own lives.

'Scarlett, look at me,' Jackson says.

I look at him and try to breathe. My heart is thudding against the bones of my chest.

'I need you to take my gun, Scarlett. Take the gun.'

I move down the two steps onto the floor of the lounge, as if it's not really Scarlett Heath in my skin, adrenalin coursing through my veins, and retrieve Jackson's gun.

'Look at me. The safety is off. The safety is off and it's ready to fire. Use two hands, Scarlett, and only fire if you need to. Only fire if you have a clear shot.'

My eyes burn. 'I can't.'

There's another crash. Gregory and Pearson burst from the gym into the lounge. There's a thick chain around Gregory's neck and Pearson grips each end tightly from behind, strangling him. Gregory thrusts his elbow back three times into Pearson's ribs. Pearson falls but doesn't let go of the chain.

It's happening so fast. *I need to help him.*

Gregory falls back on top of Pearson and with that leverage, his father pulls tighter. Gregory yanks at the chain, his nails breaking his flesh, and tries to use his legs to bounce out of his father's grip but he's stuck. His face is red. Each sinew and muscle in his neck and face is strained.

'He's killing him!' Jackson shouts.

Gregory flips them both, so he's face down with Pearson on his back. He jabs an elbow into his father's throat, sending him crashing back.

There's blood on the floor and I can't tell who has the wound; they're both smeared with crimson. Gregory pounces, trapping Pearson's arms beneath the weight of his legs. Then he grabs him by the neck and digs his thumbs into his trachea. Pearson kicks but Gregory strikes his face with a punishing fist.

My eyes are wide, shocked and panicked, as I watch Gregory strangle his father with bare hands.

Pearson struggles, his legs kicking and squirming on the ground. His body jerks. Once. Twice.

Then he's still.

Gregory slumps back against the wall, one leg straight, the other bent. He unbuttons his shirt while he catches his breath.

All I can do is watch him, unable to move.

He looks at me, then Jackson, and crawls towards us. 'Can you stand, Jackson?'

'Yes. Help me.'

I'm looking beyond Gregory and Jackson to the evil bastard on the ground.

Pearson's leg flinches. I slowly walk towards him and raise the Glock in front of my eyeline with two hands. My body moving on autopilot.

My arm shakes under the weight of the gun and what I know I'm going to do.

Suddenly, Pearson throws his hand sideways, picks up his own gun and points it at Gregory.

I have no time to think. I pull the trigger.

The bang brings with it an image of the boy from my dreams, holding my dad's hand. They're happy, playing in the rocks by the sea, but the attacker is there too. Then Dad is alone, dead in a hospital bed.

I open my eyes to see blood pooling around the devil's head and splattered on the white walls.

This is it.

This is what it looks like. Revenge.

A father for a father. A father for the life of a son. A father for the man I love.

I drop the Glock to the floor and fall to my knees, turning

my hands in front of my face as though they're someone else's. Then I stare at the dead body, now floating on a red river, a neat hole through one side of his head.

'I killed him,' I say, barely audibly.

I watch the pool of blood continue to expand.

Gregory is on his feet. I'm vaguely aware of two men leading Jackson towards us. Their voices warped and indecipherable.

The sweetest smell of flowers, fully bloomed lilies, fills my nose. I look around me but can't locate a vase. A distorted face moves close to me, so close, it terrifies me. And it's staring right into my eyes. I flop my head to one side to see if I can work out whose face is in front of me but I can't and it's bright, so bright, a mix of bright colours. Those colours are moving, spinning. The movement and the sickly sweet smell of lilies forces me to retch and retch again, a heave so hard, it tears my insides. Vomit projects from my mouth.

I'm cold. My body trembles, then I'm shaking uncontrollably. Until I'm moving through the air, weightless.

The distorted voices become sharper until I can make out some words. The room stops turning and colours separate into distinct lines. I'm on a sofa. Something warm, a hand perhaps, strokes my hair. There's a face in front of me. A man. Slowly, the blurred face comes into focus. I recognise it.

'Gregory.'

Sitting up, I wait as first Gregory then the rest of the room comes back to normal.

'Give her this,' Jackson says, handing Gregory a small glass of liquor.

I take it from him and sip. The brandy burns my sore throat.

'Scarlett, I need you to listen to me,' Gregory says. 'Can you do that? Can you listen to me?'

I nod.

'When we came home, we noticed the tyres of the Mercedes had been slashed. The door from the basement into the building had been broken into. Are you with me?'

'Yes.'

'Jackson put out but it was going to be at least half an hour. We all took the lift to this floor. When we got out of the lift, it was apparent the apartment had been broken into. The door was ajar. Jackson kicked open the door and was immediately shot at. Okay?'

'Okay.'

'Tell me what I just told you.'

I repeat Gregory's explanation verbatim.

'Pearson ran into another room but we knew he had a gun. You tended to Jackson and I ran to get a gun from my safe. It was the only way we could frighten him because he had a gun. Yes?'

'Yes.'

'I went to find him. I found him in the bathroom and he came straight at me with glass. He managed to dig the glass into my side. That's how I have this.'

He moves his hand from a wound just below his ribcage. I wince at the sight of blood, congealed and dark. 'When he attacked me, I dropped my gun. I managed to kick the gun from his hand. We were tussling and ended up in the gym. He threw a chain around my neck. We struggled and I thought he was going to kill me. We were on the floor and that's when I saw the gun. I had no choice. It was self-defence. I picked up the gun and shot him in the head.'

'But—'

'Scarlett!' he shouts, pulling a hand roughly through his hair. 'That's what happened. Say it!'

'But—'

'Scarlett! Say it!'

He's trying to protect you. I stare at the thick, angry burn mark around his neck.

'Scarlett!' he yells, rattling my body with two hands on my shoulders.

Silent tears fall down my cheeks. 'That's what happened,' I croak.

Gregory wipes away my tears with his thumbs. 'Now tell me what happened,' he says.

I tell him three times in his words what happened before the police arrive.

* * *

MORE FROM LAURA CARTER

Another book from Laura Carter, *Twisted Love*, is available to order now here:

https://mybook.to/TwistedLoveBackAd